PRAISE FOR MY BEAUTIFUL IMPERIAL

'Very readable, engrossing. Terrific!'

Karl French, editor, The Literary Consultancy

'The material is fresh – I can't think of anyone writing about these particular historical events in fiction.'

Michael Langan, author of *Shadow is a Colour*

'Powerful and well written. It is a meaty read, one that will satisfy lovers of action stories and historical fiction alike.'

Reader for the Literature Wales Critical Service

'Skillfully blending fact and fiction, drama and tragedy, Rhiannon Lewis has produced an absorbing novel of depth and complexity. The unusual backdrop of the Chilean Civil War adds both colour and adventure as accidental hero Davy finds himself a very long way from his Welsh home. Highly recommended!'

Catherine Hanley, historian and author of the Edwin Weaver medieval mysteries

MY BEAUTIFUL
IMPERIAL

RHIANNON LEWIS

Victorina Press
www.victorinapress.co.uk

Copyright © 2017 by Rhiannon Lewis

First published in Great Britain in 2017
by Victorina Press
Adderley Lodge Farm,
Adderley Road,
Market Drayton, TF9 3ST
England

The right of Rhiannon Lewis to be identified as author of this work has been asserted by her in accordance with the copyright, Designs and Patents Act 1988.

All rights reserved. No part of this book maybe reprinted or reproduced or utilised in any form or by any electronic, mechanical, or other means, now known or here after invented, including photocopying and recording, or in any information storage or retrieval system, without permission in writing from the publisher and/or the author.

Cover art and design: © 2017 Steffan Glynn
Interior design and layout: Jack Williams

British Library Cataloguing in Publication Data
A catalogue record for this book is available from the British Library.

ISBN: 978-0-99575747-2-0 (hardback)
ISBN: 978-0-9957547-3-7 (paperback)

Printed and bound in Great Britain by
Charlesworth Press

For
Steffan, Rebecca, Darcie and Gareth

And in loving memory
of
Owen and Menna, Brynllynan
Dat a Mam

PROLOGUE

April 1914

A bee buzzed. Then stopped. Or maybe flew away. Something small slipped past him in the long grass, touching here and there a drier blade, which rustled and marked out its invisible path. Somewhere close by, near his jacket shoulder, he could smell lemony sorrel and sweet dandelion. The scent of sugary blackthorn was heavy on the breeze. A gorse bush was in full bloom.

His eyes opened, just a little. Light pierced his lashes. So, he was still alive, then? At least, he could hear the wind somewhere in the poplar trees above him. He knew their distinctive sound. Their young leaves clapped like the hands of a discerning audience. Or perhaps this was the sound of Heaven? A host of heavenly poplars.

One thing was certain, he was definitely in a hedge. *El Capitán* in a hedge? If this really was Heaven, surely God would have provided a more auspicious place to reveal his glory? Wherever he was, he should stay here, he thought; lie here in the warmth, and if he was lucky, if he was not already dead of course, things might pass away painlessly. He could merge with the grass, give himself up.

El Capitán in a hedge! How his crew would laugh. *¡Dios mío!* They would laugh until their bellies hurt, until the tears ran down their grubby faces. They would forget their place and shout out for early rations of grog and sing a raucous Chilean song. He tried to move but his limbs felt waterlogged, like a drowned man's body dragged from the waves. The effort of moving brought on a fever. The sun was no longer his friend; he felt sick. His skin burned. He leaned forward, but the hedge had made a cradle around him, a curving grasping bowl. There was nothing to push against and his head fell back. *Oh, Dduw, take me. I surrender.* His crew would laugh to hear him talk of surrender. How many times had they blasted their way through the enemy's blockade or evaded the insurgent ships, slipping away through the dark waters of a moonless night? 'Quietly does it, lads. Not a sound! Not a whisper.' And how they had cheered when their way was clear. Their *salvador*.

The breeze in the poplars was now the sound of waves through the shingle at Viña del Mar. He was not alone. There was a gloved hand on his arm and a face close to his; a sigh at his shoulder. And he was gripped again in the throat. *What is this? Fear? It feels like fear. But I don't understand. Dduw Mawr, how can I be afraid? I'm in a hedge.*

I don't want to be sick. Sick like a dog. Sick like a boy on his first voyage. Those lads never imagined such rough seas when they saw the big mail packets coming into port and quieter waters. They thought, because they were made of steel and rivets, that somehow the sea couldn't toss them around like sleek brigs of wood and cloth. The steamships looked safe and solid. But they would all hate them sooner or later and hope to die soon when they heaved their stomachs overboard, each breath of the coal stench making them retch again.

Now, in the distance, there are footsteps, little clog steps, brisk on the gravelly track. And a girl's voice, half-talking, half-singing.

'*Yr Arglwydd yw fy mugail …*' The Lord is my shepherd.

'I shall not want. He maketh me lie down in …' Hop, skip, 'Pa-stures.' *Gwelltog*. He wants to finish the line. But *El Capitán* needs to merge with the grass and not be seen; not be found here, like this. He lets out a shallow breath, small, like a whisper on Estella's brow.

The steps and the girl's voice are nearer now. 'He leadeth me …' Hop. 'Beside the still … wa-ters.' And now silence. Or, not quite silence, but the soft sound of the world moving through the trees again. His head hurts. He wants to sleep. Sleep forever in the sun's warmth. He wants to be left alone, to be back in Viña del Mar. But this is the irritating thing: even with his eyes shut and merging with the hedge as he is, he can feel the stare. He will stay very, very still and hope she goes away. He stays still. He makes his breath even smaller. She stays still too. Irritating.

Or perhaps he has imagined the sound? Perhaps there is no girl, no clog, no psalm? Cold washes over him. Perhaps it is Elen? His little sister, seven-year-old Elen, perfect again. He wants to be sick, and the fear is back at his throat like a strong man's hands with a cold iron grip. Perhaps, after all, he is dead and Elen is coming to fetch him? She will bend down and ruffle his hair and annoy him and he will swipe at her playfully as if she were a fly. And she will laugh at his bad aim because she knows full well that he loves her most in the world, more than anyone, more than the sea.

He tries opening his eyes again and his lashes release tears. Is it her? He sees the clogs first and the hem of the white apron, hands held primly in front and a little book of psalms. But there is no smile. This little girl stares at him coldly. How ridiculous he must look lying there in the morning sun. He tries to heave himself out of his grassy cradle but his stomach lurches as if he's on a stormy deck. His head falls back. The little girl's gaze is disconcerting. Then, at a loss for something to say, he speaks the next lines: 'he restoreth my soul.' The words come as easily as they did sixty years before, standing in the *côr mawr* of Bethania Chapel. But his voice is hoarse as if his body has cracked. And now, the sudden flurry of heavier feet. Proper shoes this time, rushing; the flash of a grey shawl.

The feet stop abruptly before him and Davy squints upwards to see Margaret Jones, formidable but not quite large enough to block out the sun. She looks displeased. She is always unhappy about something. Today, Davy can imagine, she is late for the early service. And her daughter Annie – for Davy has recognised her now – still hasn't learned her psalm properly despite having two weeks to prepare. The cow has taken too long to give birth this morning, and, instead of rushing on to chapel, the girl is being distracted, as she is so easily distracted by the most irrelevant of spectacles.

Davy looks up at her squirming face. 'Creadur,' it says. *Creature, because you can hardly call him a man.* He sees her glance at the empty beer bottle embedded in the ditch then back to the *chupalla* on his head. *And what kind of hat would you call that? Some dishevelled foreign thing.*

But two can play at this game, Davy thinks. And his lob-sided gaze drifts down to annoy her stockinged ankles.

'A mess and a disgrace…' she says, with disgust. She grabs Annie's hand.

'Come on, Annie *fach*, or else the service will be over by the time we get there.'

Davy turns his throbbing head to watch them hurrying down the road. Annie gives him an awkward backward glance before being propelled forwards again by her mother's shove. He bends with more determination as all the words of the psalm come flooding back to him. *He leadeth me in the paths of righteousness… for his name's sake.*

He heaves himself from the ditch and gains enough momentum to crawl on his hands and knees then rises to his feet like a newborn calf and sways, waiting for power to reach his legs. *Captain to you.* He has known for a while that people have dispensed with the term and that he has, at some point, become *Dafi Pwll-y-brwyn*. Davy who lives in a ditch with reeds. Whether they have forgotten or don't care, he knows not. He corrected the young man at the Mercantile shop the week before, but regretted it as soon as he opened his mouth once he heard the lad giggle and splutter as he left the shop. That woman was still a toddler when he was crossing the oceans and rounding the Horn. What did she know? With her sour face and her starched God.

Davy reached the cottage, put his finger through the worn wooden hole and lifted the latch inside. The door slid inwards and the warm breeze that had encouraged him home gave way to the cold, damp smell of the interior. A black shape skittered across the floor and disappeared under the stairs. Away from the sun's rays the room felt abandoned and desolate. He had not lit a fire for days and whatever had rushed into the shadows had been making ash trails on the hearth in strange meandering patterns. Davy closed the door behind him and frowned as he considered the grate. A wide oak dresser stood against the far wall. It had three shelves for plates and hanging jugs and three shallow drawers above open alcoves for serving plates and dishes.

'You will have to fill it with something, you know,' his sister Jane had commented, eyeing the family heirloom critically when he had first arrived home. 'It looks a bit shipwrecked, all empty like this.'

But the dresser had stayed empty, more or less, apart from the enamel mugs and items of paper propped up in the grooves meant for plates. Davy reached out for the middle drawer and pulled the brass handle until it revealed a bundle wrapped with a woman's printed scarf and tied together with a thin blue ribbon.

He removed the bundle gently and placed it on the table, untying the knot. Turning and unwrapping it with care, he revealed a large photograph album, as solid and substantial as a family Bible. The leather cover was a little worn around the edges but still intact, and its golden-edged pages glowed in the dim room. He put his hand in his jacket pocket and took out a photograph. He knew which page to open. On the right-hand page there was a studio portrait of two young men, both upright and handsome. The younger, neat and dapper in a pale three-piece suit, looked relaxed as he rested his right hand on the scrolled end of a chaise longue. His other arm was proudly around his companion's shoulder. His chin was raised and there was a hint of a smile on his face. The second man, a little older and stockier, looked out of the photograph with dark, serious eyes.

There was an empty frame on the opposite page and Davy slipped the photograph between the two layers of stiff cardboard, adjusting it until it sat properly within its space. *Safe again.* Davy smiled at the woman but her gaze was fixed and serene. She wore a dark dress with a tiny white collar of ruffled silk. Her hair was dressed neatly in three loops at her crown and she wore a single pale orchid behind her right ear. Davy closed the album and, taking the scarf in his right hand, leaned forwards. He folded his arms to cushion his face and fell fast asleep.

PART ONE

LAND

CHAPTER 1

March 1865

'Whoa!' The farmer brought the carthorse to a stop beside them in a flurry of flying straw and jangling chains.

'Where are you two going?' the man asked.

Davy turned to the carthorse and gently stroked the animal's nose while his older brother answered.

'We're off to the beach, Uncle. Davy's learning to swim. We've brought a rope.'

Perched high above them at the front of the cart, Uncle William scratched his chin.

'Up you get, then. I'm going that way. But Griffi, mark my words, if you drown, don't go telling your mother that I helped you get there.'

'Uncle William,' replied Davy as the boys clambered on to the back of the cart, 'if I drown, I won't be saying much of anything.'

William Evans must have thought he was too clever by half, because he cracked the reins so sharply against the horse's rump that it sent the boys lunging backwards almost out of the cart again as the animal pulled away. Gruffudd unloaded the rope just in time to grab Davy's shirt and haul him and his dangling legs back up.

'You won't be minding the sow then, will you?' said the farmer, turning towards them with a wry smile.

The boys hadn't seen their travelling companion nestled in the hessian sacking. It was too late to object now, so they would have to share their journey with the disgruntled creature. It eyed them suspiciously.

'Is the rope good?' shouted William Evans as the horse picked up speed. He didn't say, 'Not rotten through like Bob Morgan's last year. Poor dab.' But the brothers knew what he meant.

'The rope's good, Uncle,' replied Gruffudd. Then they were quiet for a while.

Davy leaned back, assessing the sow and wondering how many hams and slices of bacon could be had from such a creature. Peggy the horse had reached the brow of the hill; the chains and leather sat more easily now and she was in her stride.

'When's your father back?' asked the farmer.

'April sometime,' replied Gruffudd.

Davy looked out over the edge of the cart. The blackthorn was already in blossom. It would soon be April.

'On the *Ellen*?'

'Yes.'

'Ah.'

They were quiet again. It seemed to Davy that the older he became and the more he understood about life, the more he noticed that people like his uncle didn't make idle talk about the sea. William Evans was a farmer but his brother was on the sea, and his uncle before him. Only people who knew nothing said things like 'Oh, she's a fine ship,' or 'He's a good captain,' or 'It's a solid crew'. It mattered little at the end of the day. There were plenty of fine ships and captains at the bottom of the sea. Davy wanted to learn to swim. But it bothered him too. If the ship sank in the middle of the ocean, where would he go? Perhaps it would be best to drown with the ship, to be sucked straight under with the masts and sails rather than to swim around waiting for cold, exhaustion and a slow horrifying death.

Davy shuddered. These dark thoughts were no good. He reached into his pocket and took out a piece of freshly cut willow, then opened the hinge on his penknife. First he surveyed the section of branch, running his fingers over it as he looked for knots or faults. Then he started cutting, first marking out a V shape for the hole then gouging inwards in confident easy movements. He turned the knife around and used the handle to tap the bark gently, moving the wood around between his fingers. The mother-of-pearl handle glinted in the sun. He paused for a second to judge the length of willow then scored the bark all around towards the centre of the piece. Gripping the knife between his teeth for a moment, he held the wood in both hands and twisted the bark firmly on one side. Davy remembered the first time he had seen his grandfather do this. It had seemed like magic when the bark slid off elegantly, as it did now in his own hands, revealing the pure pristine white of the wood inside, the bark still a perfect intact tube. Davy could smell the fresh sap on the breeze. He took his knife and began cutting again, a deeper V and a shallow channel for the air. As he carved, his brown skin grew pale over his taut knuckles. I could make one of these in my sleep, Davy thought.

Before they left the house, Elen had begged, 'Davy, please!'

'But I made you one yesterday!'

'The dog ate it.'

'The dog did not eat the whistle, Elen. Don't be ridiculous. You lost it, just like the one I made you before and the one before that.' And Davy had stomped off in his clogs with no intention of relenting.

When Davy looked up, he found Gruffudd staring at him intently.

'Another whistle for Elen?' Gruffudd asked.

'Maybe.'

Davy watched Gruffudd as he smiled and leant back against the side of the cart. His pretence was a farce, as usual: his brother could see straight through him.

'*Diawl!* It's cold!' Davy slipped off the rocks and into the water, on to a rocky ledge and up to his chest.

'Davy, don't swear!'

'I'm not in chapel now. Christ!'

'Don't swear! Someone might hear.'

Davy had tied the rope around his waist and the other end around a jagged rock, but getting into the sea was proving difficult.

'Davy, don't go down that way, there are too many rocks. Go to the left, the water's deeper.'

'I want to go slowly. Hell's bells! I can't swim yet can I? I don't want to go in the deep bit.' Davy pulled at the rope and slipped on seaweed, this time off the ledge and over his head. Davy tried get a grip on the slimy stone but failed. Gruffudd hauled him up and he appeared again with his dark wavy hair pasted down over his face, cold, shivering and scratched from barnacles.

'Christ, there must be a better way than this.'

'Davy, let's try from the beach, it's safer.'

'Where the hell am I going to tie the rope?'

Gruffudd scanned the beach. 'Don't swear!'

Davy turned his attention to the ridge above them. He could see the outline of the limekiln against the sky. And then, just inside the entrance, something he recognised. 'There! Uncle William's lobster-boat! That'll do. We'll borrow it!'

'We'll never get it down, just the two of us,' said Gruffudd.

'Gravity my boy!' said Davy, imitating the schoolmaster.

'Back up, then – we'll never carry it back up!'

'We'll worry about that later.'

Davy knew that he was testing his brother's patience to the limit. Granted, his schemes were often hare-brained but some of them actually worked. They managed to get the boat on to the grassy slope.

'Easy does it,' said Gruffudd, sounding nervous, 'otherwise she'll run away from us and we'll have a pile of firewood on our hands.'

The boat was much heavier than they'd bargained for, and although there were wheels under her, which made moving her easier, there was a real chance that if she gained momentum they would both be left behind. They heaved and struggled and made slow progress.

'We'll have to make a tack otherwise on this slope she'll run away.'

'Christ, this will take all day,' said Davy.

The water was getting closer but the slope was getting steeper.

'Davy, turn her towards me.'

Davy did as he was told and braced his right shoulder against the vessel. He pushed with all his might and thought of Samson bringing down the temple. The wheels screeched horribly with every push.

'More, Davy, and again.'

But this time the boat was too heavy and on the slope her rusty wheels started to turn properly.

'No, no! Hold her back!' Gruffudd shouted. The wood began to slide and burn through their hands.

To Davy's mind there was a simple answer.

'Get in, Griffi!'

'Christ, no!' Gruffudd looked horrified, 'We'll be smashed to bits!'

Without waiting to see what his brother would do, Davy clambered over the side and into the boat as it was moving. In a second he had reached across, grabbed Gruffudd with both arms and yanked him in too. Now they were flying towards the edge.

'Hold on!'

The ground disappeared – they were moving noiselessly through the air. It seemed as if the seagulls, the waves below, the white clouds were all frozen in time. Only they were moving. Then, an almighty crash. Davy lost his grip on the side and was thrown forwards over the bow. Under the water, Davy was momentarily paralysed by the cold. Something brushed past and instinctively he reached out for it. It was the rope but when he grabbed it, it sank with him.

In the boat, Gruffudd hurled himself forwards, scraping his shins on the cross plank, and catching the end of the rope just in time. Cursing his brother, he wedged himself against the side of the boat and hauled again on the rope which was now wet and even heavier than before.

'Don't you dare drown! I'll kill you!' Gruffudd shouted, hauling as quickly as he could. 'Don't you make me come in after you!' Suddenly, the rope sprang taut and drops of water shot out in the sun like sparks. 'Come on, Davy, kick!' Gruffudd heaved again and, out of the water, Davy exploded in a spluttering mass of hair, spit and scratched arms. Gruffudd grabbed the band around Davy's waist and hauled him roughly into the boat.

'I shouldn't even be here,' said Gruffudd once they'd caught their breath and Davy had stopped coughing. 'You mad bastard.'

Davy was doubled up on the floor of the boat. There was a gash on his shoulder and his arms were covered in scratches and splinters. 'Don't swear, Gruffudd. You know they wouldn't like it at Bethania.'

'I'll tell you,' said Gruffudd, 'you'd better learn to swim today because I'm not bloody doing this again.'

'What in God's name were you thinking of?' she shouted with her back turned, not even looking at her sons. Elinor Davies was moving around the room like a malevolent thunderstorm, clanking the bucket and stabbing the sodden mop into the large slate flagstones. Everything smelled of carbolic. Gruffudd stood limply and apologetically in front of the dresser. Davy, nearer his mother, stepped sideways from time to time to avoid her terrifying path. In the doorway stood Uncle William, with a soft cloth cap in his hand that he was folding and unfolding.

'Elinor, really, as long as they help with the repairs, there's no harm done, I just wanted to ...'

'No harm!' she screeched, grabbing the soap and brush from the table and swinging around in exasperation. 'No harm! Look at them, Will! What am I going to do with them? They'll soon be grown men. The one has some sense but no sense to use it, and the other one is, God help me, just like his father!'

Elinor dropped on to all fours and started scrubbing the floor as if the devil himself had walked across it trailing all the sins of Gomorrah.

Gruffudd turned to his uncle. 'We're truly sorry, Uncle William. We'll be with you tomorrow and bring the timber. We'll call by the yard on the way over. I have some money saved from the harvest last year.'

'Your savings!' screamed Elinor. William Evans and the two boys glanced at each other nervously trying to assess whether now was a good time to make an exit. Just then Elen ran to the door.

'*Mam*, Mrs James has brought a little kitten and says that I can ...'

Davy caught her eye and flashed her a warning glare, but not quickly enough.

'Elen! For Christ's sake go and wash the cow for milking. And where's that slattern Jane got to? Tell her to fetch some potatoes from the barn. And tell her not to bring the seed potatoes like she did last time unless she's trying to be stupid. And not the potatoes meant for Reverend Hughes and his wife, which are in the wooden barrel and obvious to anyone with half a brain!'

Elen rolled her eyes at Davy and turned to go. 'And Elen! Clean your clogs properly before you come in next time, otherwise I swear to God almighty that you will be scrubbing the floor again before your supper.'

Elinor Davies threw the wooden brush into the bucket with an almighty clang and got up from the floor.

'Boys, I'll see you tomorrow morning. Early as you can, then,' said William Evans putting on his flat cap and turning to leave. Davy watched as his uncle tiptoed out of the door, clearly now aware of his filthy boots. When Elinor turned towards them, Davy felt that old familiar dread. The anger was shocking, but the calm was worse. Why was she always so angry? Were they really such bad sons? He had just enough time to see William Evans disappearing down the lane, and to envy him his journey back to a happy home, before his mother came towards them.

'You shouldn't have mentioned the savings,' Davy whispered in the dark.

Both of them had been sent to clean out the cowshed then ordered straight to bed without any supper. That was the worst thing. She had hit them both, of course, but that was nothing unusual; Gruffudd first for being the eldest and the one who should have known better, and then Davy because he was always doing stupid things, and because he was lazy and useless. Gruffudd sighed as if it came all the way from his toes. His sigh said, *Do you think I don't know that? The second I opened my mouth I thought 'here we go'*.

'She can't stand me. She hates me,' said Davy, staring at the ceiling he couldn't see and wondering whether, if he opened his eyes really wide, he would start to make out the shapes of the joists and the planks above them.

'She doesn't hate you. She just thinks you're like Father,' Gruffudd whispered.

'She hates Father.'

'Yes. Sometimes.'

'Well, then.'

Davy opened and shut his eyes, and tried to see whether there was any difference between 'real dark' and 'eyes shut dark'. He realised that he was using the rhythm from his favourite hymn, '*I bob un sydd ffyddlon*'. At least it was a distraction from his stomach and his stinging face.

'Why are you singing?'

'I'm not singing. I'm hungry.'

Gruffudd sighed again in the dark, a long self-conscious sigh of exasperation. Davy sighed too and decided that he was bored with his game. He thought of Lisa Tŷ Hen and how black the end of her plait had looked when he dipped it in the inkwell the week before. If she hadn't flung her head round like a demented horse it wouldn't have made such a mess.

'It's about time your father ... sent you to sea!' Sgwlyn had gasped, in between swipes. 'I'm done with you ... Heaven help me ... the amount of navigation you've learned so far ... you'll be wrecked in a week ...'

Davy thought he had heard him add the words, 'Dull as a brush,' but the pain of the cane had increased to the point where he wasn't sure what he could hear. There had been something unseemly in the whole event, Davy nearly fourteen and almost as big as his teacher, but Sgwlyn had a surprisingly good swipe for a man with one arm.

'I lost it at Waterloo, for your information,' he pronounced one day. Davy had been staring unwittingly at the neatly pinned-back fabric at the schoolteacher's shoulder when he should have been concentrating on his arithmetic. It was only later he'd realised that the man would still have been in his cradle at the time of Waterloo unless he was a hundred and three. *Lying toad*.

He thought again of Lisa Tŷ Hen and the blackened tip of her plaited hair. She was ill now, or so a neighbour had said.

'Do people always die of scarlet fever?' he asked Gruffudd in the dark.

'I don't know. Probably.' Irritated.

Davy felt a pang of guilt and hoped that nothing would ever happen to Lisa. Or Gruffudd, or Jane, or Elen. Or Father.

His limbs were starting to feel heavy and he was about to turn on his side when he saw a misty shape forming between him and the door. It swayed and coalesced into light and shadow, a moving shape with arms outstretched towards him like his grandfather at the end of a working day at the mill, blanched white with flour and hair standing on end.

'Jesus! Griffi!' Davy sprang backwards in his bed, pulling the covers towards him.

'What?' screeched Gruffudd, now exploded upright from his drowsy sleep.

Davy turned and saw his brother's outline clearly and, in the window beyond him, the shadow of the bare-leaved oak tree silhouetted by the moon that had emerged pale and serene from behind the clouds. Davy stared back at the door, his heart still pounding. The outstretched limbs were the shadow branches of the tree; the ghostly face the fabric folds of Davy's own shirt on the back of the door.

'It's nothing.'

Gruffudd scratched his head with both hands as if it were a nest of fleas, then threw himself angrily back down on to the bed and pulled the covers tightly around him. Davy stayed still, staring at the door and the moonlight, waiting for his heart to regain its normal momentum. He thought of his mother's hatred; he thought of the boat with its shards and splinters, the teacher's stump, Gruffudd's linen bag of savings in the old button box under the bed, Lisa's hair. Lisa dying. Lisa not dying.

'Griffi?'

'Jesus.'

'I'm sorry about your savings.'

There was a long silence and another sigh.

'Go to sleep, will you?'

Davy stared at the door for a long while after that and it seemed to him that the figure reappeared to him again as before. It was his dead grandfather's likeness, the miller with the white smiling face and friendly open arms. Then it loomed larger. Now it was Neptune. It held a trident in its bony hands and pointed to an invisible horizon. Come follow me, it said, and we shall have wild adventures.

The tick of the oak longcase clock was the only sound in Tŷ Hagar. Everyone else had finished their chores and gone to bed. Captain Roger Davies, home from the sea for two nights only, was in no hurry to go upstairs. He and Davy had been left, contemplating the last dying flames in the fireplace, when the clock's mechanism whirred suddenly into life and began to chime eleven. *W. Hopkin, Llandeilo*, said the maker's mark on the face, but the scene above it was of some far-away place, of a red-roofed tower near an azure lake edged with tall and impossibly slender trees. *Not Llandeilo*, thought Davy, as the last strike reverberated around the room.

A fire had been lit in the parlour, a rare event usually reserved for special occasions such as Christmas, funerals and hushed visits by the local minister. At first the inglenook had coughed and spluttered, belching retreating plumes of black smoke. But as it warmed, the air had cleared. The whitewashed walls now glowed russet and gold as the faint smell of damp gave way to warming beeswax.

That morning, as she cleared the morning dishes, his mother had said disdainfully, 'We'd better light it – as your *father*'s home.' *Father, dog, vagrant.* She said it loudly enough even though his father was within earshot, engrossed in the newspaper's shipping reports. And so Davy had been ordered to fetch kindling and logs from the outhouse and to mind he used 'the proper cloth to wipe the hearth this time'. His cheek smarted just to hear the words. It was relentless.

And Jane must have sensed his despondency because, passing him on the way to the pig's trough with a pail of swill, she muttered,

'It's no good trying to understand her. You'll drive yourself mad.'

Davy stooped to fill the basket. Was that all he wanted? Merely to understand? He stood with his hands on his knees, like a winded man, wondering how long he could stay in that stance before being shouted at to stop dawdling and get a move on.

He heard Jane return, and this time she stopped beside him.

She sighed and then in a low serious voice said, 'I think some people are born into worlds that don't fit them. They're born to be shoemakers when their talent is for metal or they're gifted soldiers when there are no wars, or they're painters with no money for canvas or poets who never learned to read.' Jane swung the pail absently until the handles squeaked. 'I think Mother is one of those. A captain's wife when she should have been ... oh, I don't know, a seamstress or ... a rich man's courtesan.'

With a gasp of amusement, Davy stretched out his arms and gathered a large armful of kindling, then stood and threw it into the basket. When he looked up at Jane, she had turned her back on the house to hide her guilty smile.

'Can you imagine?' she said, still swinging the empty pail.

Davy brushed the hair back from his forehead then stood squarely with his hands on his hips. 'No, not really!' he laughed.

Just as anticipated, their amusement was interrupted by a long stream of shouting that rose in a deafening crescendo, like thunder gathering for the final lightning crash. Their mother was on the threshold, and the last few words they caught were something to do with them not being too old for a thrashing.

Jane darted off to rinse the pail under the pump and Davy bent down again to gather another armful of kindling.

'I wish she'd spend some time working out what her real talents are,' Davy muttered. 'She's hiding them under some bloody great bushels.'

Now, as Davy gazed into the parlour fireplace, he wondered whether Jane had been right, that the only thing wrong with his mother was an accident of birth. She had been a miller's daughter and a captain's wife when she should have been a governess or a lady's maid. For a moment he tried to imagine her as a contented woman, happy with her lot, then concluded that Jane's first words had been nearer the mark, that there was no use trying to understand, he would only drive himself mad.

By the light of the flames, Davy noticed that his father had taken up the smaller of the two Welsh Bibles and was reading it with the help of the brass-framed magnifying glass. Davy could see his father's lips moving silently as the lens skimmed over the page and wondered which passage he was reading. Perhaps some consoling words for a man trapped between the devil and the deep blue sea.

On his own lap, he had a copy of *Learning to Read, Write and Speak the French Language* by V. Value. Sgwlin must have felt unusually well disposed towards him earlier on that week to lend him the copy, or else his schoolmaster had abandoned all hope of being able to teach Davy anything he considered useful. Davy opened the book and for the next hour or so they both sat in silence, lost to the gods of hope and irregular verbs.

When Davy did eventually take his eyes from the page, he saw that the logs had died down so far that the ash-covered bark was a grey crust over what appeared to be a molten centre. Davy rose from his chair and, gauging that another couple of small logs should do the trick until they went to bed, scraped the fire together with the poker and added them. They had been freshly chopped and they hissed as they met the orange flames. Cherry wood, he thought, smelling their distinctive sweetness.

Davy's father closed the Bible and laid the glass to rest on the cover.

'I have often wondered …' Roger Davies began, then his voice trailed off. '… where God is. You know, at those times when the sea is a churning mass, when it's a valley beneath you one moment and then a mountain above you the next and the whole thing designed to destroy. Or so it seems. When I started out, a lad like you, I would pray …' His father turned away from the flames and looked searchingly at Davy.

'Not pray like they do in the *Gymanfa*, all comfortable in their warm coats and their dry boots, not a gentle, polite prayer. Not asking nicely on a Sunday, "Please God, make our harvest good this year so that we can grind enough corn to feed our children this winter and if we're lucky, perhaps help the neighbours too as they helped us pick last autumn's potatoes." Not that kind of prayer, but a shouting, spitting prayer. "Make me brave, Lord, to uncurl my fingers from this blasted rope and move my foot down to the next rung even though the boat is horizontal and the sea and the wind are all in the wrong place." And all the while the sky is screaming.'

Davy shuddered and thought he could see the tempest his father talked of emerging from the golden flames.

'I often thought that God was there. But rather than watching and waiting and looking out for us, he was the one whipping up the waves, flinging our sails around in the boiling waters and roaring at us, cursing us, laughing at us, perhaps?'

His father reached into his pocket and took out a small silver tin of tobacco. He opened it, placed the lid on one knee and the tin on the other knee, then reached again into his pocket and took out his pipe. Davy had watched him do this many times when he was home from the sea. It made him wonder where Father had been and what countries he had sailed to.

'Don't you believe them,' his father turned to him all of a sudden.

'Who, Father?'

'Any man who tells you that he doesn't fear the sea. Don't take them on as crew for they won't be trusted. A man is either lying or half-baked if he says such a thing and you don't want him on your ship. When you look a man in the face and ask him a question about the sails or the state of the rig, you want to be sure that he's telling you as it is, not some half-cocked story that sounds good in front of his pals.'

Davy looked at the fire again, trying and failing to imagine a day when he, David Davies, would be a captain. Why would anyone in his right mind ever listen to him?

Roger Davies raised his pipe to Davy as if he'd heard his thoughts. 'When you're a captain, you make the decisions. But your crew are your eyes and ears and hands, and if they give you a cock-and-bull story you will end up making cock-and-bull decisions. And don't go thinking you can change a liar. Liars never change. If a man looks as if he isn't scared of the sea, leave him at the dockside.'

'It's like dogs,' his father continued, looking at Davy as if his meaning should be completely clear. He filled his pipe slowly. Davy got up and took a long taper out of the earthenware jar; he dipped it in the fire until it was alight. He passed the taper to his father, who used it to light his pipe. Roger Davies put the pipe in his mouth and drew in the smoke. Then, when he was satisfied that it was properly lit, he blew out the taper and passed it back to his son.

'When I was a little boy, our neighbour had a sheepdog. They used to say, 'Oh don't be worried passing the farm, our dog is a lovely dog. He doesn't bite.' I was only four and I was on my way to fetch eggs when the dog came out. I don't know why, but he was vicious that day and he bit me twice on the arm. I ran home crying and after cleaning the wound under the water pump, my father said, "You must understand that a dog is a dog, and all dogs bite when they want to. Just like a liar is a liar, and sooner or later he lies." '

Davy glanced up at his father. His face was kind and serene but his eyes were far away, back in the sea of fire and the tempest of flames.

'You must learn to read the weather and the waves. But more than that you must learn to read your men. They don't teach you that at the Maritime Board of Trade.'

There was a shout from the room above, his mother's voice. Something about it being late, about keeping her awake, about wasteful pointless nattering, how there were a million important things to be done in the morning. Roger Davies slipped his hand into his waistcoat pocket and took out his watch. He made no response to the time, whatever it was, and slipped it deftly back into his pocket. He moved to the edge of his seat and turning to Davy, whispered, 'You must decide, son, what you want to do. You know that *Datcu* would have liked you to take on the mill. He was very fond of you. A nice safe job. Unless you get your hand stuck in the cogs like Owen Felin Ganol did of course. Or there's the sea.'

Davy shrugged, remembering the words of his schoolteacher and how he would surely be wrecked in a week. He thought of the two short cold voyages he had taken with his father to Birkenhead.

'You need to get to know the ropes, lad, before you try your luck up there!' one of the crew had laughed at him when Davy ventured on to the shrouds. 'Leave it to the experts, boy,' they had muttered, pushing past him on wet ropes, the swing of the mast more pronounced as they rose.

'Take no notice,' his father had said afterwards, and had told him all about the crew. Who was related to whom, back home. Who was foreign. Who could speak Welsh. Who couldn't speak any English.

Davy looked at his father's face. It was tired and worn and his long beard was unkempt and needed a trim. But his eyes were clear.

'It is time to decide. I don't want to lie to you, Davy, it's a hard life on the sea.'

'But you like it? You're a captain.'

There was the sound of bare feet on the upstairs floorboards and Roger leaned in further towards Davy. 'I've seen more of the world than many, that's true. It has its hardships and its compensations.' His father's mouth curled briefly into a smile and for a second Davy thought he saw the young man emerge from the wise and benevolent Neptune. Perhaps his mother was right. Perhaps he was just like his father had been, before his hair turned grey and his face became hidden by an unruly beard. The likes of his father could not have afforded a daguerreotype when he was young. Davy would never know.

Roger Davies moved to the edge of his chair as if he was about to stand up, but he hesitated. 'I don't know what to say to you, Davy.' He scanned the slate flagstones under their feet as if there might be an answer to be found in their pattern. 'I've done what I could. I can't remember whether I had many choices.' He smiled at his own realisation. Then the smile faded into concern. 'It's been hard on your mother.'

His gaze returned to the slates. 'When I was an apprentice on the *Resolution*, I had to help the surgeon. He was about to perform an amputation on a man who'd lost his concentration, only for a moment. The surgeon turned to me, just as he was about to make the first cut. "Here's some good advice for you now, lad. Two things you need to live life to the full. What do you think they are? Wealth? Love? Reputation? Fame? No, none of these. Be present, pay attention; these are the things you need." Those words have helped me in all manner of situations, not just on board ship. They would have helped me in many more too if I had remembered them in good time.' A chair scraped the floorboards in the room above and this time Roger Davies rose to his feet. 'Of course, it took me years to understand his true meaning.'

Davy watched as his father slid the Bible back on to the shelf and ran his fingers lightly along the spines of the other books: an anthology of Welsh poetry, a history book, Gilpin's *Massacre of the Bards*, a book on animal husbandry, *The Ingoldsby Legends*. '*Nos da*, Davy. Mind you turn out the lamp.'

The door closed behind his father and Davy noticed that high in the shadowed corners of the room, a narrow trail of stencilled leaves and daisies wound its path around, under the jutting beams, over the low window and up again over the plastered inglenook. He had never registered them before but they must always have been there. The leaves had darkened with age and the white daisies were dull. But the branches in between had been drawn freehand with a certain flourish and the lightness of touch remained. Davy leant back and followed the trail around and around. The parlour was rarely seen. What kind of person would have considered time decorating it to be well spent? When there were cows to milk, crops to harvest, land to plough and seeds to sow? What kind of person had been here? Davy sank back in the chair and studied the flames. A hopeful person, he thought.

Rhiannon Lewis

CHAPTER 2

Davy walked out of the farmyard, straightening his cap, and started his three-mile walk into town. 'Go to see Neilson,' his father had said, the morning after their discussion. Sam, Davy's friend, had called by last night to tell him that the *Pembroke* was back and that Neilson, a Norwegian sailor who had been a whaler, would teach a group if they were there early.

'No more than ten and first come first served,' Neilson had shouted, 'and no bloody time-wasters!'

As Davy came to the end of the lane and joined the road, the landscape opened out. It was a beautiful spring day. In the distance the Preseli hills were a pale lilac against the blue sky. Below him, every now and again, he would catch glimpses of the shimmering estuary and the River Teifi as it wound its slow lazy way towards the sea. Above the river and dotted against the hillsides were the whitewashed cottages of St Dogmaels, windows glinting here and there in the sun. Over there somewhere, Davy thought, some of his friends would be rushing like him to get to the harbour in time.

The hedges were a riot of colour with dandelions and daisies nearest the roadside and the gorse, honey-smelling and brilliant as the sun, higher up. The blackthorn trees were already giving up their blossom. But Davy noticed none of these things in a conscious way. What he noticed was that his boots were pinching and that the shirt his mother had made him last winter was feeling taut across his back.

'Right then, lads,' said Neilson, hands on his hips and squaring up to them like a bull that was about to charge. Eight boys of different ages, shapes and sizes lined up on the deck. Davy glanced across at the others and felt aggrieved that he appeared to be one of the eldest. One of the lads couldn't be any older than twelve, he thought resentfully, looking across at his puny arms and his ill-fitting trousers. The boy's trousers were half-mast about his ankles and yanked in sharply at the waist with a wide belt. Someone else's trousers, thought Davy. Next to him was a chubby, red-faced lad. I'm looking forward to seeing him get into the crow's nest, thought Davy. There's no way he's going round the futtock shrouds with a girth like that.

Neilson spent ten minutes describing the ship and explaining the purpose of all the ropes. Davy had been on the *Ellen* with his father, but the *Pembroke* was altogether a different story. The first platform here was as high as the topmast on the *Ellen*, or so it seemed. He squinted up into the cloudless sky and wondered how far it was to the top.

'Eighty three feet to the crow's nest,' declared Neilson, as if he had read his mind. 'Now, you may be a lad on the deck, but in the air think of yourselves as spiders – but without the God-given ability to create your own rope. You fall from the crow's nest and you won't be getting up again, mark my words. You have hands and feet to hold on, but once you're on the yards, you'll have to use your knees and elbows too. Your ears if they're big enough!'

The boy in the baggy trousers laughed, but Davy noticed the others were looking pale.

'Who's been up the shrouds before?' Neilson asked, surprising them with a question.

Two of the lads put their hands up. Davy hadn't noticed before but they must have been twins.

'Sir, we've worked on Uncle Wilson's ship. *Sea Sprite*.'

Neilson nodded knowingly and made approving noises.

'Sir,' Davy put up his hand, 'the *Ellen* of Cardigan. But she's smaller than the *Pembroke*.'

'Roger Davies?'

'Yes, Sir. My father.'

Again, Neilson nodded approvingly. None of the other lads put up their hands and Davy felt sorry for them. Neilson stepped backwards and surveyed the masts.

'We'll work in two teams of four. Two either side the mast. A little bit of competition to spur you on.'

Then for the rest of the morning he had them racing up the shrouds against each other, first to reach the platform, first to reach the deck. Up and down with variations in between, how to hold on to the shrouds in a storm, how to help a shipmate tangled in the shrouds, how to stay on the shrouds with both arms free. By noon Davy's hands were raw, red and sore.

'Lads, we'll stop there for half an hour.' Neilson checked his pocket watch and glanced across at the Grosvenor. 'Don't you go disappearing,' he said, as he strolled off. A big man with a surprising spring in his step, thought Davy as he watched Neilson skirting the ruined tower of Cardigan Castle and climbing Grosvenor Hill.

The lads sat down on the nearest barrel or box. All of them seemed to have brought some bread and cheese. Davy hadn't thought about food at all that morning in the rush to leave. And now he was starving hungry. He didn't want to seem like an idiot, or worse still too poor to get a bun from the bakers. Trying not to draw attention to himself, he slid his hand into his trouser pocket, thinking vainly that there might be a forgotten penny in there. Perhaps the lady at the bakers would let him have half a bun? But there was nothing hiding in his pocket apart from bits of straw and string.

He leant forwards again with his elbows on his knees, hoping that no one would notice he wasn't eating. Then into his field of vision came a hand from the right, holding two thick chunks of bread with an equally thick slice of roast beef in between. Davy looked up and saw that the hand belonged to the chubby boy.

'Go on,' the boy motioned without saying a word.

At first Davy shook his head.

'My aunt always makes too much,' he murmured, looking down at the cloth on his lap where several chunks of bread and cheese were laid out. 'I think she's fattening me up for Whitsun market,' he said, without a hint of a smile.

Davy looked at him again. The boy looked as if he had spent too much time indoors with his books and not enough time in a field. Even though they had spent the morning clambering up and down the shrouds, he still looked surprisingly clean, if a little pink.

Davy took the sandwich.

'What's your name?'

'Frederick.'

Davy bit hard into the bread and nodded. 'Your aunt bakes a good loaf, Frederick.'

The boy snorted, scattering crumbs over his lap.

'Oh, my aunt doesn't bake.' He snorted again at the thought of it.

It was the most delicious food Davy had eaten in a long time. The white bread was soft and yeasty, spread thickly with freshly churned salty butter. In between, the slice of beef was pink and tender, with a dark roasted skin that was almost sugary sweet.

Just as Davy was thinking that he could devour ten such meals, there came a sudden burning to his tongue and a foreign taste. Davy froze, thinking that he might have fallen for some trick of poisoning.

'Mustard,' said the boy with a wry smile.

This time it was Davy's turn to laugh and scatter a mouthful of crumbs. As they carried on eating, Davy constructed a whole reality for Frederick. No mother. Must be an orphan. Living with a doting aunt; a well-off doting aunt who feeds him too much.

'Why do you want to go to sea, Frederick?'

The chubby boy passed Davy an apple, and Davy took it without question.

'I love navigation.'

Davy sat upright and took a bite of the apple. Davy's father had taught him something of navigation and Sgwlyn had also tried. Just the basics, but he knew he would have to learn more. Much, much more if he was to become a captain. But the thought that someone might love navigation! What a strange idea. Davy thought that it was something necessary to get from A to B or from Liverpool to New York, but not something to love for its own sake.

The chubby boy told him all about the lady who lived in Llangrannog, the fishing village up the coast. She had been to sea dressed as a man and knew more about navigation than anyone alive in the area. Her real name was Sarah Jane Rees but her pen name was Cranogwen because, unbelievably, she was also something of a poet. Every month she held classes at the town hall and anyone who wanted to become a proper sailor needed to go to them. And if he wanted to be a good captain, he should go too.

Davy stood up and leaned against the rail. He wondered how it would be possible for a woman to conceal her sex. None of the women he knew could be mistaken for a man. And all that coarse language and rough behaviour, she would have to be some woman to deal with that. As he looked out over the river he saw that the tide had come in, and towards the estuary a fine sailing ship was approaching. From where he stood he could see her crew like dark stars on the yardarms furling the sails, their legs braced against the footropes. With a regular rhythm he could see them bend over the mast to reach the sails and their feet rise up so that their bodies were almost horizontal. As they flattened out in mid-air, their bodies hanging over the masts, the star shapes disappeared momentarily. All along the river there was activity of one sort or another, small rowing boats and larger sailing boats, joists and loading cranes jutting out over the water, jetties with cargo being loaded or unloaded. On the town side of the river there was a small forest of vessels at the shipyard where the steady sound of hammering was punctuated by shouts and laughter.

Davy looked back at the *Pembroke Castle* and wondered what it would be like to be her captain. He couldn't imagine anyone listening to him or taking any notice of his orders. Where do you learn the skill of making people obey you, he wondered. Then he thought of all the stories his father had told him of mutinies and revolts, of captains being abandoned on desert islands and being captured by natives.

'I'm going into the Royal Navy,' said Frederick suddenly, cutting across Davy's thoughts. 'My aunt thinks it would be more impressive.'

'Impressive?' Davy sat down next to him again with renewed interest.

'More distinguished.'

Davy was unaccustomed to such long English words. He thought this meant that it was a good thing.

'To fight for Queen Victoria and my country,' continued Frederick.

Davy stared at the wooden deck and considered Frederick's words. He thought how different their backgrounds must be. Making enough money to feed and clothe a family was all his parents had ever talked of. Being honest. Going to chapel. Helping your neighbour. Davy tried to imagine him as a distinguished adult. 'What do you think, Frederick?'

Frederick frowned. 'I don't think I'd like to kill anyone. Face to face, you know.' Then his pink face lit up with a self-effacing smile. 'Either way, I'm going to be seasick, I think!'

Davy laughed in agreement.

Soon afterwards they caught sight of Neilson. He was striding down Grosvenor Hill towards the harbour, and as he came closer Davy could see that his blue eyes were looking slightly bloodshot and his cheeks were much rosier than before.

'Now then, lads! I hope you haven't eaten too much lunch because we're going up and over the futtocks this afternoon.'

He clapped his hands together, grinning mischievously. The boys looked skyward at the masts and wondered how brave they would be.

'Ho! Flower, ho! Lady, turn, turn ... whoa ...!'

Gruffudd pulled the mares to a stop and their reins jangled and glinted in the sun. The air was filled with their musky warmth. It was early April, but it seemed that summer was making a raucous first visit.

Davy had made a quadrant from paper and string and was trying to plot his latitude and longitude with the help of his grandfather's old watch. A textbook was open at his feet and sheets of paper were strewn all around. He paused and glanced up at the field with its wide band of beautifully straight furrows down the centre.

'Not bad! We'll make a farmer of you yet!' Davy laughed.

Gruffudd leaned his head back and wiped the dust and sweat from his forehead. There was a skylark a short distance away, hovering expectantly over the long grass. The team's noisy breathing had quietened and they swished their tails lazily at the season's first flies. During the morning the first straight furrow had widened from the centre outwards as Gruffudd made his steady way backwards and forwards, turning the animals in ever-wider arcs. He adjusted the leather straps around the team and came behind them again. A robin landed on the plough and looked up questioningly. Gruffudd flicked the reins and it flew to a nearby clod.

'Walk on! Flower, ho! C'mon Lady.'

They set off again. Their pace was gentle and serene, yet together they were a powerful team. Gruffudd's stride behind them was sure-footed despite the turned clods under his feet. Davy watched the three of them moving as one, making slow progress across the field. They reached the brow of the hill and made their well-practised turn, their brasses glinting in the sun. In the pause, the skylark returned, suspended high above them against the beautiful blue sky; the two brothers faced each other across the broken ground.

'Ah!' groaned Davy, holding the sheet of paper up to the sun, 'I'll never understand this!'

He picked up his textbook on navigation and read over the entry again while Gruffudd and the mares made their slow turn and their way back towards the bottom of the field. Davy had taken Frederick's advice and joined Sarah Jane Rees' navigation class. The woman was barely into her thirties, and as far as Davy was concerned there was not much doubt about the fact that she was a woman. It was true that she was slim and flat-chested and in that sense could well have passed for a boy, but she had striking dark eyes and lustrous black hair. The other sailors must have been half blind or stupid, thought Davy, not to notice that she was a woman. Either that or she had magical powers of disguise once on board ship. But she certainly knew a thing or two about navigation. There was no doubt about that. Davy raised the sheet of paper to the sun again.

'And you'll have to reverse it all when you're in the southern hemisphere, don't forget!' called Gruffudd over the mares' heads.

'What?' asked Davy, looking over the paper's edge with dismay.

'It stands to reason, doesn't it?'

And then, just as Gruffudd was about to make another turn, two black shapes came swooping across the blue sky to distract them both from their work.

'The swallows are back!'

The birds seemed euphoric, but Davy felt a sudden pang of sadness. His grandfather loved to catch sight of the first swallow. 'Things are looking up,' he would say, and the waterwheel would turn more energetically that day. Davy set his book aside and for a short while the brothers watched the swallows dancing and twisting in the blue sky.

Rhiannon Lewis

CHAPTER 3

They were just finishing their breakfast of bread and tea when they heard quick footsteps crossing the yard followed by impatient knocks at the door. Elinor Davies jumped up to open it and there was Sam Evans with his fist raised, about to knock again. Sam was the same age as Davy, slightly taller but not as broad. He had fair hair the colour of good summer straw and a face like a cherub. Everyone, apart from Davy's mother, loved Sam.

'Davy! Oh, Mrs Davies. I'm sorry,' he whipped off his cap. 'I wanted to talk to Davy.' Seeing Davy at the table and barely able to contain his excitement, he said, 'Llewelyn's back! The *Agenoria*'s in!'

Davy got to his feet so quickly he nearly pushed over the chair as he made for the door.

'Davy, sit down. You can't go. There's too much to do!'

'Mother, you know I need to get to know the captain. Father said so before he left.'

'I'm not just talking about the milking. There are other things. The crops need planting, the coppicing…that's still to be done. It's already April. And fixing the barn door…that's been waiting for months! It's all very well for your father to say, oh, go to see Nielsen! He's never around to do anything useful!'

Davy stood behind his chair but didn't sit. What did she expect him to do? The farm would go to Gruffudd as he was the eldest. In the meantime, was he supposed to stay around like some little helper, never earning enough to support anyone? He thought about saying this out loud, but divulging his true thoughts was never a good policy. Instead he turned to Gruffudd.

'I'll be back in a couple of hours, I promise.' He reached for his jacket, relying on the fact that his mother would not want to say anything more in front of Sam. 'All right Griffi?' Gruffudd looked at Sam shuffling uncomfortably by the door.

'If I'm late I'll do the milking every day for a week, I promise.'

Elinor snorted with disbelief, her face like a great thunder-cloud gathering over Carn Menyn.

'Griffi?' Davy was putting on his jacket. Gruffudd gave in with a nod. 'Thank you. I promise I'll be back in time.'

His temporary victory won, Elen now jumped to her feet.

'I'm coming too,' she said, following him towards the door.

'No, you can't! Elen, it's no place for you. Come back here at once!'

'But Mam!'

'Mother's right, Elen, you're too young. And besides, you're a girl.'

'Mam!' Elen pleaded, 'I want to be a sailor like Father and Davy, I don't want to be a maid or get married or have horrible babies. Davy, please?'

Davy remembered Frederick and his talk of female navigators dressed as men, but this didn't seem like the right time to mention it to Elen.

'You're a girl, Elen – go play with your doll.'

'Oh, for God's sake Davy, just go!' Elinor shouted, grabbing Elen's arm roughly and pulling her back indoors. 'I'm sick of the lot of you!'

And the door to Tŷ Hagar slammed shut. Davy and Sam ran off down the lane, but before they'd rounded the corner he heard the door open and his mother shout after them, 'Stay out of the "Black", Davy!'

'All right, Mother.'

'Even if Llew's paying!'

'Right, Mother.'

The two lads sprinted round the corner, laughing, their jackets flying.

As Davy and Sam reached the main street, the door to the Black Lion sprang open as if the entrance to the bowels of hell itself had been revealed. Nothing happened for a moment, then a young lad was catapulted out of the smoky darkness past them at an odd angle, tripping and sprawling into the road.

'Don't you pull that fast one on me again!' bellowed Tom Bottles, the landlord, appearing in the door with an audience behind him. 'You use proper money to pay for your beer next time, not this cheating foreign trash!' And with a snort of contempt and further Welsh expletives the landlord hurled a handful of coins at the young man, then disappeared quickly back in to the mysterious interior.

'*Desolé, desolé,*' the lad answered, scrabbling around in the dust gathering his coins and looking too remorseful and dazed to be a hardened criminal, in Davy's opinion. He was too busy gathering his money to notice the oncoming horses and the team's driver was too mesmerised by the group of young ladies outside Morris Star's fabric shop to see the body in the road.

'Bloody hell!' Davy grabbed the lad's jacket and yanked him back on to the pavement just in time.

'Look where you're bloody going!' shouted Sam after the carriage, but it drove on, oblivious.

Now that they were back on their feet, Davy looked again at the lad. He couldn't be more than about thirteen, he thought, and all his clothes looked oversized.

'Thank you,' the lad said with a strong accent.

'*Français?*'

'*Oui.*'

'*Tu t'appelles?*'

'Marcel.'

Davy turned to Sam, who was now looking on incredulously. 'Sam,' he said, and then, pointing to himself, 'Davy. *Viens,*' he continued, grabbing the lad's arm and heading towards the door of the 'Black'.

'How come you've been learning French or Italian, or whatever it is you're gabbling?' grumbled Sam, following on behind.

Before they knew it, they had pushed their way to the back of the pub and found Llewelyn, already looking flushed and slightly glassy-eyed. As soon as he saw them Llewelyn stood up, pint in hand, and swayed his way past weathered-looking sailors around the table like a bucket caught on some rigging. Llewelyn was seventeen and had already been a sailor for three years. But this was the first time he had been on a 'proper' voyage, away from familiar shores and down through the Bay of Biscay. It had taken him away for six months and Davy noticed how his build had changed. His shoulders were bulky and solid and his forearms showed the evidence of months hauling ropes and taking his turn at the capstan.

'My old friends!' Llewelyn shouted, looking more drunk with every step, 'Some beer for my friends here!'

'Come on, tell us what you saw! Where did you go?' Davy sat him on a stool and soon the three of them, Davy, Sam and Marcel, were gathered around listening to his sea tales.

'Where are you from, lad?' Llewelyn leant forwards and scrutinised the French boy suspiciously.

'Bordeaux,' he answered.

'Barmouth?' Llewelyn looked confused and picked up his next pint.

'Bordeaux, you idiot. France.' Davy pushed Llewelyn back to vertical against the wall.

'Oh, and there I was thinking you looked like old Captain Parry's son. Well, there you go. There could be a likeness, of course. You could be one of his wild oats flying about in the continental breeze. I suppose there are plenty of them, although I'm not sure about Barmouth. I thought he went further afield myself.'

The French boy looked at Davy, wondering whether or not to be offended.

'Oh, shush you idiot! You don't know what you're talking about,' said Davy.

'*Je m'appelle* Marcel,' said the boy, trying to round his words carefully and clearly.

'Oh, my God, he's speaking French!' Llewelyn blurted with fresh beer froth perched on his lip.

'Christ, Llew, tell us about the Cape!' Davy pushed him again until he was upright.

'Don't let him have any more beer, Davy, otherwise we'll never get any sense out of him,' said Sam seriously.

'Right you are. Give me that, Llew.' And before they knew it, Llewelyn's pint had disappeared smoothly down Davy's gullet.

'Now. Tell us about the Cape and then maybe we'll get you another beer.'

Llewelyn's mouth gaped open in horror as if he was a freshly landed fish. But he soon found a new lease of life and began by telling them about their crossing to Portugal. The weather had been fine. One morning, in the early hours, they had caught whole nets full of writhing squid to supplement their meagre food supplies. Then the night before arriving at Porto a storm had blown up. Two were washed overboard, a Scottish lad and an older sailor from Liverpool who had tried to save him. The rigging was damaged, but they limped into harbour eventually, glad to see land.

In Porto, while they waited for repairs and the captain looked for two replacement crew, Llewelyn had been seduced one evening by a dark-eyed portuguesa who taught him such things as he could not possibly repeat in front of such a young lad as Marcel.

'Look, I'll cover his ears,' said Sam, clamping his palms dramatically on to the boy's head.

'Put your hands down, Sam, let the lad be. Llew, you need to tell us everything if you want that pint. Everything. Understood? Every tiny detail.'

Llewelyn grinned inanely and his head flopped on to his chest.

'He's passed out!' Sam cried.

Davy grabbed Llewelyn's arm and shook him furiously. Llewelyn lifted his face, still grinning but now propped up by Davy's shoulder.

'Lads … I'll tell you.' His voice was quiet so they leant forwards to hear him better. Marcel too, even though he barely understood a word.

'She was wearing, you know …' Llewelyn trailed off bashfully then turned to Marcel as if remembering the English word.

'A corset!'

'*Corsellete? Mai oui!*' Marcel sat up proudly, clapping his hands on his knees. The lads looked across at the French boy and grinned at him with new-found admiration.

'All right, Llew, corsets, you were saying,' urged Davy, turning back to his increasingly spineless friend.

'Well, you know the corsets your mother wears ...'

Davy and Sam exchanged embarrassed glances.

'Yes, I suppose we do,' said Davy, pushing him back to vertical again, 'and your point being?'

'Her corset, Catarina's corset ...'

'Eu!' they chorused in high voices, 'Catarina!!'

'Yes, well, this was not like your mother's corset. This was ...' he paused for a moment then raised his hands and drew the shape of an hourglass, 'and my dear friends, it was red.'

Sam and Davy were mesmerised. Marcel frowned and looked questioningly at Davy.

'Rouge,' Davy answered gravely. Silence descended around the table until Marcel added, full of gravelly respect and a long throaty 'r', '*Rouge* ...'

The friends were subdued and Llewelyn went on to describe the dainty shoes, the stockings which he was very sure were of the best silk, and the lace whatever-it-was-called that she had on over her very perfectly formed ... and here words failed him altogether and he gestured the shape of two beautiful apples, or thereabouts in size. He couldn't quite remember accurately, he said. His eyes glazed over again. He was beginning to resemble some strange, beached jellyfish.

'And then what?' Davy nudged him upright again.

'We were just about to ...' gurgled Llewelyn.

'To what?' urged Davy, smiling at the other two, but to which Llewelyn seemed incapable of responding without grinning and falling over.

'And then guess what?'

Suddenly, Llewelyn was upright as a poker and banging his fist loudly on the table until the glasses jumped. The crowd in the Black Lion went quiet for a moment, thinking that they were in for some excitement.

'It's all right lads, it's all right,' said Davy, turning to smile at them meekly as he placed a protective arm around his friend to calm him down. 'Steady now. What happened?'

'The scoundrel!'

'Who, Catarina?'

'No, her brother, or her uncle or whoever he was, this thug, this big animal the size of the town hall came bounding in, upsetting everything, making her cry and insisting that I hand over my gold chain, the one my mother gave me for good luck before I left!' Llewelyn's hand shot dramatically to his throat. 'She's going to kill me!' he squealed desperately.

'So what about Catarina?' asked Sam, his mind clearly still thinking about the red corset.

'Oh, she was shouting at the man and crying something at me in Portuguese but I had no idea. I can't speak Portuguese! I had to make a run for it though, I can tell you lads.' He gripped his throat again. 'The ugly brute.'

Llewelyn's head lolled and even though Davy propped him up again, there was no more sense to be had from him.

'You will have to learn some Portuguese, my friend,' said Davy at length, 'so that you can go back to reclaim your gold chain.'

'And your woman!' smiled Sam.

Later on, it was difficult to say who was supporting whom when they left the pub. And when they weren't weaving because of the beer, they had to stop and double up because they were laughing so much at Llewelyn's exploits. The four tumbled out of the 'Black' into the path of another carriage, this time a grander affair than the farmer's gig which had nearly run over Marcel. They stood back just in time to see the flash of purple silk and a feathered hat. Sam took off his cap and bowed with a stylish flourish.

'Who was that?' Davy turned to ask him.

'The new Squire of Llangoedmor, Lord Millingchamp. And, I do believe, his very fetching daughter, Miss Winifred.'

Davy turned and sniffed the air then grabbed Sam's arm. 'I can smell roses!'

Marcel ran up to them both, sniffed the air with authority and declared, *'La Belle de Nuit! Ma Cherie!'*

'You're all bloody hallucinating!' shouted Llewelyn as he watched them sprinting up the street after the carriage. 'Bunch of ragamuffins! Who's going to look at you?'

Llewelyn nursed his head and turned towards home.

Long before Sam and Davy reached the outskirts of town, they had lost Marcel. As they passed the Hope and Anchor, French sailors from the *Milford* had spilled out into their path singing a particularly discordant version of the Marseillaise. Marcel had joined them and was probably, by now, sharing more tales of narrow shaves at another of Cardigan's maritime establishments.

At the crossroads Sam and Davy were about to go their separate ways when they heard raised voices in the distance. They stood still and listened again. Nothing.

'I'll see you tomorrow then, Davy.' Sam turned away.

Again, they heard voices shouting, urgent voices, calling across each other.

'They're coming from your place, Davy.'

Davy listened again. Then turned to Sam.

'Come with me?' They ran, and as they turned the corner towards the farm, they could see a dark plume of smoke coming from the farmyard. The farm was surrounded by trees, so at a distance it was hard to see which building was alight.

They turned into the lane, skidding on the loose stones. Davy could see figures running near the barn. The house is all right, he thought, everyone's safe. His pace slackened. He came nearer and saw that the horses were in the yard. That's good, Flower and Lady are safe. He came nearer.

Dark smoke was coming from the roof and flames were lapping around the great wooden doors of the hay barn. And then he saw his mother. Gruffudd had planted himself between her and the barn. She was hitting his chest with her fists and screaming at him. Gruffudd was gentle and wouldn't raise a hand to anyone, but his knuckles were white as he gripped her shoulders. Tears streamed down his face. A long rope was tied to Lady and Mr Watkins, their neighbour, was desperately trying to persuade her to pull down the barn doors but the mare was scared, pulling in the wrong direction and bucking wildly. Davy thought back to that morning's conversation to his mother's talk of planting and coppicing. She had talked of the barn door needing fixing. But it was the lintel. That's what was causing the problem. The lintel was rotten, just like half the timbers of the roof, rotten through with worms. The whole thing needed re-roofing. They all knew that. And now the door was jammed.

Jane ran gasping past Davy with a heavy pail of water. She had filled it to overflowing and there were splashes of water marking her path from the pump to the barn. She ran as close as she dared to the raging flames and threw the contents violently at the door. The door hissed and steamed for a few brief moments then resumed its ominous billowing, throwing off more dark smoke. Davy looked around at the scene; his mother hysterical being held back from the flames, Gruffudd beside himself, elderly Mr Watkins urging the mare as if he was a young man again. And then he saw Mrs

Watkins by the house, her apron raised to her face looking on in horror at the roaring, creaking barn.

'Where's Elen?' Davy shouted, his legs weak. The smoke billowed above the barn. Suddenly, there was a gust of wind and a million tiny sparks escaped through the gaps. There was a roar, and when it subsided they heard the sound of a whistle, small and brief and futile.

Elinor fell in a heap at Gruffudd's feet and Davy felt his whole body tremble as if the ground was about to give way. Davy looked at the solid barn doors. The black smoke around them was giving way to flames and the rope attached was starting to burn. Time was running out. His first steps towards the mare felt as if he was wading through a sea of treacle. He took the reins from Mr Watkins and pulled the animal's head close to his. He felt the bit, warm and dripping with spit, between his fingers. Davy lowered his voice as if in prayer.

'Ho, Lady, quiet now, shhhh.' He needed to calm her down. He needed time but there was no time. She didn't like to be rushed. She liked to take her time. He held Lady's head close and whispered soft, calming words like a trickling stream.

'Easy now. Easy Lady. Good girl. *Dere, di.*'

He closed his eyes and drew in the smell of her skin. *Please do this.* With his right hand he stroked her neck rhythmically. She must not know that I'm scared, he thought, trying to disguise the fact that his heart was jumping with deafening thuds inside his chest. Too soon and he would have to calm her again. Too late and all would be lost.

The mare shuddered as if the fear had left her like a bad spirit and Davy stood back. Gently he pulled the reins taut then began to pull, urging her towards him with calm encouragement. The rope between Lady and the barn door sprang upwards out of the dust and vibrated with new tension. Clouds of fine dust dispersed around it. Mare and boy found a rhythm, he urging, she pulling firmly on the door.

'C'mon Lady, come on girl.' Then when he thought she had regained her confidence, more forcefully. 'Pull!'

Three more neighbours who had seen the fire ran into the yard carrying buckets.

'The rope! Throw water on the rope!' shouted Davy to them and in seconds they had formed themselves into a chain passing the buckets to each other down the line. The air around them was thick with smoke and Davy thought his own hands were on fire, he was pulling so hard on the reins. There was another gust of wind and the building roared again, like an angry dragon breathing out a million tiny sparks. Another faint whistle came from the depths of the barn.

Davy looked across at Gruffudd. He was standing helpless with tears streaming down his dirty face. *No, no no, don't give up on Elen.* He raised his voice,

'Pull! Come on Lady! Pull!' Then, all of a sudden, the animal lurched towards him. The doors had moved. One of them had come off its hinges and was listing.

Davy renewed his urging and Gruffudd, seeing that there was hope, wiped his face with the back of his sleeve and urged Lady on too.

'Come on! Pull!' screamed Davy again.

The doors moved again, but only by inches. The rope was on fire and the flames were so hot that they couldn't throw the water close enough.

'Christ, I'll pull the doors down with my own bloody hands if you don't do better than this.'

He reached down and undid his belt then pulled it through the loops until he was free of it, folded it hastily then gave Lady a sharp slap across her back. The mare lurched towards him again and this time the door moved a foot. They could see the flames inside the roof and the extra air through the door was fanning the inferno. The roar was constant.

'Once more, good girl!' Davy slapped her fiercely and this time the doors came away just as the rope tore. The doors crashed in flames just behind the mare and she reared upwards, terrified. The smoke and flames cleared for a second. Davy ran forwards, and for just a moment he could see Elen, standing small against the back wall, clutching something tightly, flames all around but looking strangely still and serene. She looked right at him.

He ran forwards. It would be a short distance, he thought, even though there were flames. He could be quick. She was small and light, they would be out in seconds. There was a loud crack, and the roar became louder. He would have to run into this dragon's mouth and out again. He moved forward. There was a shout behind him. Elen looked upwards then back at him, frowning. The building groaned: it was moving. He looked up and debris fell on to him and into his eyes. He brushed it away and moved forward again. Through the flames he could see Elen. She fixed him with her gaze and shook her head.

Then something happened to the air around them. For the tiniest part of a second the raging flames became still. There was a dull vacuum and a strange pause. His own breath seemed caught somewhere at the back of his throat. The frantic world around them was suspended. Only Elen moved. She drew the whistle to her mouth. But I'm here, thought Davy, I will help, I will save you. There's no need to call for help. But she did not call. She held the whistle to her mouth in a child's gesture of comfort. There was smallest movement on her lip, a drawing in, a bracing. *Brave Elen.*

Then all that had been suspended in time seemed to collapse inwards. The fire's snarling roar, the mare's neigh, the chains, even the breath in Davy's chest seemed ripped outwards. He felt it before he saw it. The joists, the beams, the splintering slate tiles came raining down. He was engulfed by wood and debris. Flames surrounded him. Something hit his head. He felt heat on his arms and a sensation of being dragged backwards at speed through blunt objects. He heard his mother scream then Jane wail. He was deafened by the fire's roar.

When he opened his eyes he was on his hands and knees. He raised his head, and through the smoke he could see a bonfire where the barn had been. The flames rose forty, fifty, sixty feet in the air. *No! No! No!* He sprang to his feet and aimed for the spot where Elen had been. 'Help me! Help me!' he shouted, running forwards. He grabbed the nearest burning beam but his useless hands recoiled as if they belonged to someone else. He stepped forward but his body wouldn't stay and was beaten back by the heat. His shirt was on fire, but no matter. He could still reach her if only someone would help him move these joists, if only he could wade through the tiles.

Davy heard a scream of frustration. It sounded like his own voice. He forced his limbs forward again into the flames. And then the fire was all around him and he had lost his bearings. Where was she? 'Elen!' he shouted. 'Elen …' His voice broke and he realised that he was sobbing. He wanted to go forward to find her but his body refused again. He was rooted to the spot, lost and useless.

There was another scream. Further away this time. Something crawled through his hair. Flames? There was an unbearable smell. He held his breath.

Suddenly, he felt a rough hand grab the collar of his shirt. He fell backwards against someone's shoulder and was thrown free of the flames. He tried to get up but someone was smothering him with a hessian sack. He could feel the weave on his skin and smell the remains of its musky contents. The hands around him were frantic. Beating him as if they meant to chase the life out of him. Briefly he caught sight of the inferno and heard a voice in his head. *Nothing can survive in that.*

He knew that when the pain came it would not be something that could be quenched with a hessian sack. He closed his eyes again and strained his face and hands against the earth and stones until they tore through his burning skin. Surely, if he willed it enough, he could become one with the dirt and stones. Now, before the full force arrived. Now, he thought as he clawed the ground, forcing the grains under his fingernails.

But it was a different blow that hit him. It caught him squarely on the side of his face. He raised himself on to his elbows and turned just in time to see someone swing at him for a second time with a still-smoking length of timber. His head seemed to vibrate and a strange howling note sang in his ears, deafening him. All feeling had left his legs and he crouched with his hands on his head, fearing another strike. He felt warm blood trickle past his fingertips.

'Where were you?' he heard her scream through the sounds in his head as the words hit him. 'Whoring?' she hit him again, this time on the shoulder, making him roll on to his back. He saw Sam grab the woman's arm and pull her back. It was his mother, but her face was so contorted with rage and hatred he barely recognised her.

'You murderer!' The word hit him in his stomach like an iron bar.

Appalled, Mr Watkins stepped between them and Davy felt someone's gentle touch on his arm.

'*Rhacsyn* ... like your bloody father!' she started to swing, her arms raised in a wide arc, a determined swing, designed to hurt. Both Sam and Gruffudd were now standing behind her, trying to hold her back, but she turned on them like a snarling dog.

'Don't you touch me!' she yanked herself out of their clutches.

'Davy didn't do anything wrong,' said Gruffudd, his face black with smoke and streaked with dusty tears.

'If you had been here ... ' she turned around to face Davy again, the weight of the swinging plank nearly pulling her backwards on to the floor, and she strained to fill her lungs as if the air around her had been turned to lead. 'You could have helped Gruffudd. You could have got the door down. I've begged you to repair it ... you *rhacsyn!*'

Davy rose weakly and saw the scene as an onlooker would. The devastation of fire and a young body somewhere in the flames. A mother, wild with anger and loss, resisting the restraining arms of a son. A kindly neighbour and his wife who had thought to help and had walked instead into some hideous nightmare. An older sister standing back, limp with pain and incomprehension. And a hated son, watching the world dismantle.

The only thing Davy could remember immediately after that was Mrs

Watkins whispering in his ear to *come with us, come away until your mother is calmer, you can't stay here, see how hysterical she is*. After that she had uttered a long stream of words that Davy could not connect or make sense of. He knew the words were kind and soothing like balm, but they all evaporated like froth on the edge of a retreating wave.

'You'll see, she'll come around soon,' said Maggie Watkins, lightly. She had said exactly the same thing at least half a dozen times that day, and at least as many times that Davy could remember in the ten days since it all happened. 'People say the most hurtful things to those around them in times of crisis.'

Maggie Watkins had clamped the loaf tightly to her chest and was cutting thick slices of bread in a sawing motion towards her ample bosom. Davy caught her glance across the table at her husband, Daniel Watkins, who in turn looked back at Davy with concern. Davy had barely said a word since he arrived at the Watkins' farm. He had not been idle, far from it. He had helped them milk the cows, had cleared out the dung, washed the buckets, put down fresh straw, cleaned potatoes, shredded mangels for the pigs to eat. He had been eager to help. Each new task was a refuge, something familiar and mechanical that kept him moving. Inaction was his enemy. Even the briefest pause, to watch blossom being caught by the breeze or a swallow swoop from a rooftop, could catch him unawares. It was like being followed around by a patient assailant whose knife was tight at his back, ready to drive the blade in deep at any moment, once and for all. He had to keep going. Mealtimes were the worst.

Davy knew that Daniel Watkins had gone to Tŷ Hagar the day after the fire to see about the funeral arrangements and to offer his help, only to find Elinor Davies barring the door and screaming hysterically at him that on no account were they to attend the service or the burial. Were they not aware that they were harbouring a murderer? That Davy shouldn't darken the doorstep again as he was no son of hers. And other things he was unable to repeat. Daniel Watkins had returned home, white and shaken. His wife had not asked any questions but had waited for the iron kettle to boil over the open fire and laid a reassuring hand on his arm. The day of the funeral came and went. Daniel Watkins whitewashed the cowshed and Davy helped slake the lime and carry water to and fro.

'You've been a great help to us these last ten days,' said Daniel Watkins, reaching across the table for a slice of bread. Ten days. They've been counting too, thought Davy, as he dipped his head and looked at his steaming bowl of *cawl*. They had no idea. It was they who had been helping.

They had allowed him his endless silences. How different they were from his parents, he thought. Davy wanted to say something in response but the words that formed in his head failed to connect with the rest of him. They, like all the other words, remained unsaid. Davy swallowed and felt the old familiar pressure on his back. His eyes prickled and his breaths were shallow and high in his chest.

'Never mind your babbling, Mr Watkins, you let Davy get on with eating his food before it gets cold. I daresay the lad needs feeding after all your chores. You bear in mind, Mr Watkins, that even the hardest taskmaster has a master above him in Heaven.'

Daniel Watkins puffed on his spoonful of *cawl* and said, 'I have a master much closer than that, I reckon. What do you say, Davy?'

It was all nonsense, of course. The pair were like two peas in a pod.

'And there's some good cheese here,' she added, 'from Mrs Williams. Very kind of her, I daresay. She certainly knows a thing or two about curds and whey.'

Saved again, thought Davy, and they ate their meal in comforting silence.

Once they'd finished, Davy stood and gathered the bowls, placing them in the tin bucket to be washed under the pump. His plan was to clear out the pigsty, but just as he was making for the door Daniel Watkins called him back.

'Davy, the blacksmith in St Dogmaels has been repairing some tools for me.' He hesitated for a moment, then added, 'they've been there for weeks now and I wondered whether you would mind fetching them for me. My feet are not so good at the moment.'

Maggie Watkins looked horrified. 'Oh, Daniel, I'll go! There's no need for Davy …'

'I'll go,' said Davy, 'it's the least I can do.' And before he knew it, he had put on his hat and was out of the door. But he had barely reached the end of the lane before he began wondering what on earth he was doing. He might see any number of familiar people on his way across the river. How would he greet them without starting to blub like a child? They would be full of questions or sympathy or gruesome interest. Yet another terror had emerged. He took off his cap and turned about in circles, filled with a sudden panic. What would he say if someone stopped him? What could he say?

Mot, the black and white collie, had followed him out to the lane entrance. He stood with his head to one side. He wagged his tail a few times then sat, panting expectantly. Davy turned in another circle. But there was nothing for it. He had agreed to go.

'Go back, Mot!' he said, a little too harshly. The dog sprang to his feet and sped back down the lane towards the farmhouse, his tail limp with rejection. Davy flipped the cap back on his head and pulled the peak firmly down over his eyes.

For the entire walk to St Dogmaels, Davy barely took his eyes off the ground. No one approached him or called out. He walked through Cardigan town as if shrouded in mist. On North Road, there were no rowdy lads outside the Farmer's Arms or the Pritchard Arms, no one he recognised outside the Black Horse or the Hope and Anchor. Like an invisible wraith he slipped past the Red Cow and the Salutation, the grocer's, the baker's, the draper's and the market hall. But as he approached the castle and Grosvenor Hill, his resolve nearly left him again. Surely there was no way of crossing the bridge and skirting the harbour without being seen by someone. There he is! Captain Roger Davies' son! The lad responsible for his sister's death!

Just as he was beginning to concoct excuses to present to Mr and Mrs Watkins, he spotted, further down the hill, a cart laden with beer barrels and three bushels of straw which, by the painted sign on the back of the cart, belonged to St Dogmaels' Ferry Inn. 'Headed back?' Davy asked, trying not to draw anyone else's attention. The man on the cart nodded his assent and with a sideways sweep of his head gestured that Davy could climb on the back. Davy leapt on and quickly wedged himself between the bushels of straw so that only his protruding legs could be seen.

'So, how are they keeping?' asked the blacksmith, once Davy arrived and explained his errand. For a moment, Davy panicked, thinking that the man was asking about his own family. 'Mr and Mrs Watkins?' the man asked.

'Oh, they're well, thank you,' he replied, eventually. The man must think him an imbecile. Then his heart sank even further when, as the blacksmith brought out the tools, Davy realised that he had brought no money. Perhaps his mother was right after all. He was useless. Worse still, he could feel tears gathering in his eyes. Over this!

'I'm really sorry, I've forgotten the money.' Davy felt his pockets lamely. As if he was going to magic some out of thin air.

But the man laughed. 'Oh! Danny and I don't deal in money! He kept me in carrots last year. And the year before, it was swedes. Or was it apples and straw? I forget. It was a ham one year when I made him a new gate.' He leant a scythe against the wall and placed a hammer and chisel in a small hessian bag with a long cord. Then he disappeared off into the dark interior and Davy, thinking that the conversation was at an end, grabbed the scythe's shaft and drew the bag's handle over his shoulder. No doubt Mr Watkins' next visit to the blacksmith would involve a discussion about 'that dim-witted lad'.

'Hang about!' the man shouted, emerging from the sooty gloom, 'you can't walk through town like that. You look like the grim reaper himself. Scare the living daylights out of everyone.'

The blacksmith had gone back to fetch some oily rags and an old newspaper. He set about wrapping the blade carefully, oily rag first, then thick layers of paper. Finally he took some string and tied it around so that all was secure. At least the blade was covered now, and safe. Although there was no disguising the fact that it was still a scythe.

'There you go. Tell Danny it should see him out now if he looks after it.' Davy knew there was some kind of irony in the remark but did not have the will to think too deeply. As he left the forge, he could hear the bellows working and the furnace roaring back to life.

On the junction at the end of the smithy's lane, the road led right, back to Cardigan, or left, towards the estuary and the sea. Davy stood for a moment and rested the scythe's wooden shaft on the gritty road. By rights, he shouldn't dawdle but hurry back to his chores. But now that he had made it safely to St Dogmaels and fulfilled his promise, there was something good about being away from the familiar fields and the farm.

He thought of the last time he had been to the dunes. The whole family had joined the Sunday school outing, piling on to various carts, with their canisters of hot tea and baskets of *bara brith*, cheese and apples, and had spent a few hours on the beach. It was a sweltering day and the tide was high. Elen must have been three or four, Davy eleven or twelve. The bigger children had divided themselves into two teams and were busily playing football. Elen was shouting from the sidelines that she wanted to play.

'You're too small, Elen, you might hurt yourself.'

'Well, if I'm that small, give me a piggyback!'

Davy relented, as usual, and before long all the larger children had smaller children on their backs and the new game of piggyback football was invented with Elen shouting directions at the top of her voice until Davy became a little deaf. For a whole afternoon there had been no recriminations or shouting or harsh words. The adults had brought blankets to lie on and each time Davy looked back, they all seemed to be laughing and joking. Even his parents seemed happy. He thought he remembered seeing them walk along the water's edge arm in arm. Did he imagine that or did it really happen?

He would go to the dunes, he thought, and turned left. But then after taking a few steps, it occurred to him that if he was going to take a detour, he might as well leave the scythe with the blacksmith and collect it on the way back. He turned and began to make his way back to the smithy. But after a few steps he decided he couldn't face returning to the man who undoubtedly already thought he was a bit of a fool. He would abandon his idea of going to the beach altogether and return to the Watkins'. So he turned around and went right at the junction.

He hadn't gone ten yards when he stopped again. To be this close and not see the waves seemed wrong. He was going in circles, he thought, like some demented dog chasing its tail. Elen had been with them that day on the beach. Perhaps if he went, something good might come back to him, some memory of things as they had once been. He felt his breaths come shallow to his chest again and cursed himself. How would he determine what to do with his life if he couldn't even make a small decision about left or right? Finally, it was settled; scythe or no scythe he would walk to the dunes.

Davy left the road and entered the dunes. The sand was soft under his feet, and the path between the high ridges was winding and sheltered. He paused to listen to the bumblebees; the gorse that clothed the leeward sides seemed alive with them. It would be as good a place as any to lay down his head, fall asleep and maybe never wake up. He trudged on awkwardly, his heavy boots sinking into the soft dry sand over his ankles. He used the scythe as a walking stick and wound his way as if through an eerie labyrinth. Perhaps the dunes were bewitched? Perhaps he would be lost in them forever, turning right here, left there, never reaching their limits.

But a final turn brought him suddenly on to the expanse of beach as if emerging from a dream. And what a surprise; barely a breeze inland but here on the wide shore there were long breakers reaching from the far horizon. They streamed relentlessly towards him, tumbling and roaring. Remnants of a distant storm at sea, perhaps? His father had talked of such things.

Davy walked towards the water. The place was deserted and the firm sand was spotless apart from the occasional shell, chalk-coloured cockle and dark mussel, razor and barnacled oyster. There were strange frenetic worm casts, thrown up in little coiled mounds by invisible creatures under the sand. Nearer the water, the beach became uneven. The water or the wind had fashioned miniature waves of solid sand; they rose in perfectly formed ripples along the shore, stretching as far as he could see.

He came to a halt and looked out over the breakers. How far had the storm waves travelled, he wondered? From Ireland or the deep Atlantic. America perhaps? *Somewhere on the other side of the world that has no inkling of your existence.* He closed his eyes and tasted the spray, sharp and salty on his face. Then, suddenly, with his eyes still closed, he realised that the pressure on his back had disappeared. His stealthy assailant had left him, bored or dismayed by his victim's lack of visible turmoil. Davy stood and faced the sea, his lungs filling with air in a way they had not done since Elen's death.

He heard the water lap at his feet. *The tide's turned*, he thought, and he had an urge to take off his boots. With his trousers rolled up and his boots tied at the laces and swung over his shoulder, he walked back into the water and flinched at the cold. Turning his back on Cemaes Head, he walked slowly through the white surf, dragging his feet, turning them over as he walked so that the tops of his toes brushed the rippling sand. No part of the water was still and the breakers seemed deafening now. Everything was moving, the sea, the sky, the wheeling gulls, the breeze through the marram grass at the edge of the dunes. It was almost dizzying.

Davy stopped and planted the scythe's shaft into the sand. Another wave broke far out and he watched as its white breaker rushed over the water's surface towards him. An unexpected ray of sunlight caught its edges and the white foam became brilliant and dazzling. Still it rushed towards him and Davy gripped the scythe, bracing himself.

'Look, Davy! Look at your feet!'

Elen's voice.

'Look down!'

Elen's feet, next to his.

'Watch! Davy! If you stay very still, the waves dig around your feet!'

A memory, clear as the light on the crest of the wave.

'See how long before you fall over! I'll hold your hand. See! Here comes another.'

Elen's hand.

'No, don't look at me! Look at your feet! Look at the grains go.' Together they watch the water make deep channels around their heels and toes.

'The sea's stealing the ground back, Davy! It says we can't have it!'

The waves rush in and their retreat sweeps the final columns of sand from beneath their heels. Elen laughs.

'Hold tight!'

Davy loses his balance and with that the memory breaks into a million droplets of foam. He reaches for Elen's hand although he knows she isn't there.

And it must have been that gesture that gave him away. Grief, which had been watching him all along, skulking in the dunes, saw his chance and stepped out of the shadows. Davy walked away from the waves but his legs gave way. Dropping the scythe, he fell to his hands and knees. All this time his grief had been dammed. By guilt, or by his mother's accusations? But it didn't matter which. Elen had gone. Elen had gone and nothing could bring her back. The world would be forever changed. He pressed his head to the sand and his body began to shake. Water lapped around his forehead in eddies. A dozen waves, that's all it would have taken. Davy wept at last and turned his face to look along the shoreline at the constant pulse of advancing waves. Or, a single wave? The smallest part of a single, mile-long wave is all it would have taken.

When Davy returned to the farm, Daniel and Maggie Watkins were sitting outside the barn on wooden stools, sorting potatoes for chitting. They were deep in conversation but as soon as they saw him walking towards them their faces lit up. Mot ran towards him and once Daniel Watkins had taken the scythe and the bag of tools from him, Davy bent down and made a fuss of him. He was relieved to see that he had forgiven him his earlier harshness.

'Here we are,' said Daniel Watkins, 'good as new, I expect!'

Davy ruffled the hair on Mot's neck until he growled playfully. He knelt and Mot nuzzled his wet nose under his chin, forcing his face upwards. He would not have noticed it otherwise. Daniel Watkins, returning to the barn with the tools, stopped momentarily near Maggie. She was so rarely critical but her bowed head, twisted away from Davy at an odd angle, conveyed all the disgust she could muster. Davy heard her whisper, 'Oh, Daniel, not the scythe!'

Daniel Watkins considered her words, then, realising the significance, hunched his shoulders in embarrassment. 'They're tools. I didn't think …'

'No, you didn't. For shame.'

'It's all right, it's all right,' Davy whispered, but they didn't hear him. They had turned towards the house. Mot buried his face in Davy's chest, his head moving in time with Davy's silent sobs.

The following morning, just as they were sitting down to breakfast, there was a swift knock on the door and Davy's father entered. Quiet words of condolence and thank you were exchanged and they turned to look at Davy. His father said something about a ship and a relative and a voyage to Australia.

'We'll collect your things from Tŷ Hagar.'

'Do you think that's wise?' Daniel Watkins turned to the captain.

But Roger Davies ignored the question and turned to leave, thanking them once again for their kindness. The two men stepped outside and Davy could hear Daniel Watkins relating various parts of the story in his quiet tones.

Davy stood up reluctantly and looked at Maggie Watkins properly for the first time.

'Davy, *bach*, I'm so sorry.' She stepped forward and put her arms around him tightly. Davy thought he felt his knees buckle under him for a moment. 'You're a very fine young man …' she pulled away and patted her hand gently on his woollen shirt, '… whatever … you know.'

Davy looked down and, taking both her hands in his, held them firmly, avoiding her gaze. He could have stayed there forever, in their care and out of sight. He could be a faithful son to a couple that had prayed for children. But someone had decided that that wasn't appropriate either. Another change was on the horizon.

Moments later, Daniel and Maggie Watkins stood on the doorstep watching Davy and his father walk down the lane. 'I've a good mind never to utter another civil word to that Elinor Davies as long as I live,' said Maggie Watkins, gathering her skirt about her and turning back in to the cottage.

As they walked, Captain Roger Davies told his son about his cousin, Captain Lewis Davies. He was doing very well for himself and was now commander of the *Royal Dane*, 1,616 tons, 230 feet in length with a forty-four-and-a-half-foot beam, ex *Sierra Nevada*, a splendid sailing ship from the well-known Black Ball Line.

She was leaving Gravesend on 21st April and he would be rated 'boy' or 'able bodied'. Lewis Davies would see to it that he was looked after and it would give him the chance to learn more about charts and navigation. Steam was the up and coming thing, of course, but there would be other opportunities for that. She was a fast ship with a respected captain. Davy would cross the 'line' for the first time. It would not all be work. He would touch at countries on the way and see Australia and its wildlife. He would round the Horn. He talked and talked until Davy stopped hearing. Then they walked on in silence for a while.

'You should say goodbye to your mother.'

It felt like another blow from the still smoking plank.

'I know what she did and what she said,' said Roger, quietly, and they walked on again in silence.

Then you will know that every mile or fathom I can place between her and myself will bring me joy.

When they reached the yard at Tŷ Hagar, it seemed that the place was deserted. Davy tried not to look, but in the corner of his eye he could see that the debris from the fire had been cleared away, leaving the blackened shell of the old granary. They entered the house, and the kitchen felt cold and bare with no fire lit.

His father stood for a second as if gauging the temperature of the house then told him to get his chest from upstairs while he prepared the horse and cart. Although silent and empty, the kitchen seemed to vibrate with the things that had happened. Davy could still feel the shouting and the screaming, the recriminations, the attempts to stand by him, the slamming of doors. He could almost hear the voices and the words. He knew what they said.

The stairs creaked with new accusing groans as he climbed them. When he opened the door, Gruffudd and Jane were sitting on his bed facing him solemnly with their hands in their laps as if they were in Bethania's *côr mawr*, about to deliver their readings to a po-faced congregation.

'You can't go!' whispered Jane, angrily, as if Davy had been part of the conversation all along.

'He doesn't have a choice,' answered Gruffudd.

'Tell her he can't go, Griffi. She'll listen to you.'

Gruffudd looked away. *Her mind's made up*.

Davy came forward and sat on the other bed. The room was so small, there was hardly any space between them, their knees nearly touching. Only the space between two beds, but a gaping world between them now. Jane looked to the corner, where his trunk was still open, and listed all the things they'd put in there: his underclothes and his waterproofs, two new pairs of woollen socks that Jane had knitted by candlelight in bed at night so that their mother wouldn't see.

'I undid an old shawl for the wool.' Jane stiffened and turned her head away like a bird listening for another birdsong.

The three of them sat and listened to the sounds of the house, the breeze around the window joints, the draught through the open door, the faint distant creaking of joists and boards. Then in the far, far distance a voice, like the flow of a stream over pebbles, insistent and unstoppable. Her voice. *She is here then, after all.*

Jane turned back to Gruffudd with a look. *Can't you do something?* Davy strained to hear the exact words but they were impossible to make out. He could only hear his mother's voice. In the occasional brief pauses, he guessed that his father must be saying something but then the flowing stream would return, with greater force each time as if its momentum had been dammed briefly. But in truth there was no need for him to hear the detail. It would be the same litany of hurts and imagined slights, magnified a hundredfold because of Elen's death.

Davy thought of all the mornings of his boyhood when he had woken to hear this shouting. All her life she had been angry. She would still be angry when he was gone; there were plenty of people left to be angry with, his brother, his sister, his father when he was around. Davy remembered the times when he had looked forward so much to his father coming home to tell him of his latest adventures. Roger Davies would barely have reached the door before she started shouting about this and that, the cow that wasn't milking properly, the plough that needed fixing, their old horse that was only fit for the knacker's yard, money. Always money. Never having enough and what they had always going to the wrong place. And sometimes, even before his father had had time to be home long enough to do anything wrong, he had turned tail and crept back to the ship in the early hours of the morning. Back to the *Ellen*, or any other convenient ship that would take him away again, the further the better.

He could see his father reaching the harbour and asking around, 'Skipper to China? Great! Six months? Is that all? Better a year at least. I'll send the best part of my wages home with the mailboats. No need to go back and be an extra mouth to feed. Better by far to stay away and never go home.'

The shouting had stopped. Davy turned to look at the open chest.

'Better get on,' he said, matter-of-factly, and Gruffudd helped him carry the chest by the handles down the stairs, through the kitchen and out to the cart. They lifted up the tailgate and closed the catches. Davy looked for Jane but she hadn't come down and Gruffudd had already retreated to the shadow of the front door. His father appeared around the corner, running the nails of his right hand back through the hair of his scalp. It was his one recognisable gesture of anger and irritation, one that Davy rarely saw. But this time it meant *I have no words for this*; *I have no chart for this eventuality*, and his right hand dropped limply by his side. *She chooses not to say goodbye. You are going to cross the globe and it is acceptable to her that you should go without so much as a 'good luck' or a 'take care'.*

Davy reached in to his pocket and took out his flat cap, flicked it up over his head and pulled the peak down hard over his brows. The two men climbed up on to the cart, his father to his right, taking the reins. Roger Davies gave the leather straps a quick sharp flick and the mares sprang into life. As they made their way up the lane past the orchard, Davy could see his mother with her back turned to them, hanging out the washing on the line. She bent down mechanically and picked up a shirt; she took the pegs from her apron; she raised her hands to the line but she didn't turn.

At the junction, Davy's father paused for a moment. A blackbird, surprised by them, fluttered awkwardly out of the hedge and flew off in a blur of feathers. In the sky far above them, seven geese flew in tight formation; there were patches of blue beyond them. The mares hesitated for lack of guidance. Then with a grunt of disgust and an unusually sharp crack of the reins Roger Davies turned them left, towards the estuary and the shining sea.

Friday 21 April 1865
The Royal Dane
Annwyl Jane,
We will be leaving our moorings off Gravesend early on Sunday morning so this is the last chance to send word from the Royal Dane. The boat will take our letters shortly so I will be brief. They say that we have 598 souls on board, 545 emigrants and passengers and 53 officers and crew. Tell Gruffudd that she is a beautiful ship and Uncle Lewis, or Captain Davies as I must remember to call him, has been very welcoming. His wife, Elizabeth, is a very kind lady who has a good library of books. I heard some of the older crew say that they didn't approve of women on board but I think that is all nonsense. We have already been singing some good Welsh hymns. There are many Catholics on board, but apparently they will be conducting their own services. There is even talk of the ship's own newspaper – the Royal Dane Standard. I hope Gruffudd has finished all the ploughing by now.

I will send word again if we pass a ship homeward-bound.
Your affectionate brother,
David

CHAPTER 4

'You know what? Your face is really bothering me.' Without warning Hoskins had turned on Davy and pinned him against the fo'c'sle wall on the *Royal Dane*. His face was half an inch away from Davy's and bulging with rage, his massive hands around Davy's throat and his knuckles gouging into his jaw.

'Cos everywhere I fucking look it's fucking staring me in the face. And I don't fucking like it.'

Hoskins let go, but only so that he could grab Davy's shirt with both hands and slam his head backwards again with even greater force. His sour breath reeked of grog and the back of Davy's head felt as if it was about to be sieved through the metal grille.

'You may be captain's favourite on deck but we ain't got no favourites down here, see ... '

He spat out the words and Davy could feel droplets of spit running down his cheek. The grille behind his skull felt like a lacework of blades cutting into his skin.

Hoskins was built like one of the American bison Davy had seen pictures of in *The Illustrated News*. His neck seemed to go straight from his cheeks to his chest. Only three days into the voyage and, apart from a brief conversation earlier on that day, Davy barely knew the man. But Hoskins wanted to kill him, he could tell that much.

It was a risky strategy. Davy made a whimpering noise and let his knees go soft. He dropped his head just enough to give the illusion of defeat. Warm blood ran down the back of his shirt. And just as he hoped, Hoskins let go and stepped back, leering like an actor taking centre stage for his final speech. Hoskins strutted and regained his balance; he took a deep breath and pulled up his trousers, half turning to the crowd behind him. For a moment it appeared that his venom had left him and he might walk away. He smiled as if to an adoring audience. But there were no cheers or egging on. All was silent. Davy sensed that most were looking on with barely suppressed horror at what was about to happen. Hopkins squared up and almost sang in his quietest voice, as if he was lulling a baby,

'Let's just do a bit of rearranging, shall we?' And he was released like an immense catapult towards Davy, body first then furious right fist, drawn back and lethally discharged towards his face. Davy timed it perfectly. He flung himself sideways on to the deck and before he hit the floor there came an almighty crack and the most awful scream, not of anger now but of terror, like a pig on slaughter day. Hopkins had drawn his hand back from the grille but there was blood and flesh and bone in a terrifying mass where his hand had been. Hoskins' face was contorted in agony and he fell to his knees. Davy moved slowly to get up, hoping that Hoskins' injury was enough to stop the fight. All was silent again.

Hoskins was hunched forward on the floor, his knees tucked under him, cradling his butchered hand. His shoulders were shaking rhythmically. He's laughing, Davy thought. He's laughing. Davy watched in horror as Hoskins got awkwardly to his feet, still with head bowed, his face hidden. Then Hoskins lifted his face and Davy felt the blood drain to his feet. He was, he realised, utterly out of his depth. Hoskins was not like the thugs who crossed the bridge from St. Dogmaels on a Friday night to pick a fight with the boys from the Netpool and clear off back home again before too much damage was done.

Suddenly there was noise at the top of the stairs. There appeared first the chief officer, Mr Buck, and then the captain, Lewis Davies.

'Make way there,' shouted Buck, 'clear the way!' Someone had alerted the captain and he was marching briskly down the wooden steps.

'What the devil is going on here? Hoskins? Hoskins!'

'Sir,' Hoskins replied straightening himself as best he could and trying to shield his hand as if from a naked flame.

'I pay you to keep order below deck, Hoskins!'

'Sir.'

'I pay you to keep order without resorting – daily – to violence! Is there no way on God's earth that you can keep your fists out of other people's faces?'

Hoskins shuffled on his feet and seemed to reduce in size. He winced.

'Sir.'

Captain Davies looked on at Hoskins with disgust. Then he turned to Davy.

'See me in my cabin this minute.' Then, turning to leave and without looking at Hoskins again, he added, 'Mr Buck, see that Mr Hoskins gets the full attention of the surgeon.'

'Sir,' replied Buck.

'And then lock him in the hold until I indicate otherwise.'

There was stunned silence as the captain left. Davy stretched his hand to the back of his head where the blood was sticky. He kept his head bowed until Buck and Hoskins left.

'Here.' A hand appeared before him, holding a red handkerchief with white spots. Davy looked at the clean cotton square and hesitated.

'Don't worry. It will wash. Cold water. That's the trick. Be good as new. It's about time someone put that monster in his place. And you can't go to the captain's quarters looking like that, can you?'

Davy looked down at his blood-covered hands.

'Thank you.' He took the handkerchief and looked properly at the man's face.

'Tony. Ship's cook.'

Davy smiled and looked at the man's alien features. He wanted to congratulate him on being the first oriental person he had ever seen in his life. Until now, he'd only ever seen cartoons in books and they always made people look silly.

'Thank you, Tony. I'll try to return the favour one day.'

'Oh, don't worry, mate! You've already done that.'

Davy was waiting outside the captain's quarters and it seemed to him that he had descended into a different world. There was a strong smell of furniture polish and hair pomade. The door next to him opened and Chief Officer Buck appeared. He was as tall and pale as a reed, and Davy wondered how he had ever been sturdy enough to spend any time aloft. He looked like the slightest whiff of a breeze would blow him all the way to the Horn.

'Come along, then,' said Buck in a clipped voice as he looked down the length of his chiselled nose at Davy, 'the captain hasn't got all day.'

Despite Buck's formality, they were a comic pair. The sea was getting up and every three or four paces they found themselves colliding with the walls.

At the end of the corridor a door faced them and Buck gave a sharp tap.

'Come in!'

'Davies, sir.'

The door closed behind him and he stood as straight and still as he could. If the captain was still angry, he wasn't showing it.

'Your father and I go back a long way,' he addressed him in Welsh.

'Yes, sir. You're cousins, sir.'

Captain Lewis Davies pondered over Davy's answer. 'Yes, indeed.' Meanwhile Davy felt slightly idiotic. It was a serious situation; he was trying to look like a serious-minded sailor. But every few seconds he had to step to the left or step to the right to steady himself.

'I am indebted to your father for more than I can say.'

'Sir.' Davy noticed that the oil painting behind the captain was sliding gracefully from side to side across the wall.

'Suffice to say, I wanted to help you.'

There was a long pause and Davy felt exposed by what his uncle knew about him. He had assumed that his father would not have said anything about the circumstances of Elen's death and his mother's reaction. But, of course, you didn't get a berth on a ship like the *Royal Dane* for nothing. Not as a wet-behind-the-ears boy who hardly knew a yardarm from his elbow. Davy felt doubly stupid. Perhaps Lewis Davies thought he was a murderer too.

'You know, Davy, the world is changing. Steam is coming. Things are going to be very different by the time you're a captain.'

Davy shuffled awkwardly, wondering why on earth he would think him capable of being a captain given everything he obviously knew about him.

'Come, come! In time you will, with hard work and perseverance. But the ship, sails, square rigged, steam, sloop, galleon, it doesn't matter which ... a ship is only part of it. The heart of a ship is the hands. Do you follow me?'

Davy looked down, ashamed. He had done a good job of smashing one pair of hands.

'Your men. A ship doesn't drive itself, sail or steam. You have to get the men behind you. There is always a Hoskins, or sometimes, God help us, there is more than one.'

There was a gentle knock on the door. Davy looked up to see Elizabeth Davies entering with a dish of tea, which she placed in front of the captain. She was obviously used to the ship's antics because she placed the dish and saucer on the desk without spilling a drop.

'Ah, Davy,' she turned and smiled but realised from his state that this was not a time for chitchat. 'Mind you see the ship's doctor, won't you?' And she turned to leave.

'Yes, Mrs Davies,' answered Davy, looking down at his feet. He felt like a right ruffian, standing here in this pristine room, covered in blood and dirt, wobbling from side to side like a drunk.

Lewis Davies looked up at his wife. 'The doctor is putting Hoskins back together at the moment. It may take a while.'

Before she could check herself, Elizabeth Davies let out a gasp of admiration. 'Oh, Davy!'

Davy smiled and thought immediately that he liked his aunt a lot. She was not as prim as she looked.

'Thank you, my dear,' said Lewis Davies and the door closed gently behind her.

Lewis Davies looked up at Davy again.

'Davy. Let me tell you something about Hoskins. He's a hard man, a very hard man indeed. You were lucky to cross him and not get your neck broken. To my knowledge, he's killed two men, though nothing could be proved against him, of course. He has the devil's own temper. But you know, he's an excellent sailor and in a squall or a gale I could not wish for a better man. I'll do what I can to make sure that he doesn't bother you again. But you need to get on with him, Davy, otherwise it will be the worse for all of us. And it's going to be a long voyage.'

Davy was grateful that the ship stayed on an even keel long enough for him to appear respectably humbled and chastened.

'Davy?' Lewis Davies called after him just as he was going through the door. 'What was it all about?'

Davy wondered whether it was right to say what he knew, then remembered his father's words as they had sat in front of the fire.

'He was bothering one of the passengers, Sir. A young ...' Davy paused thinking of the appropriate word. She was too old to be a girl, too young to be a woman. 'A young lady, sir.'

Lewis Davies grunted with disapproval, whether with Hoskins or with him, Davy could not tell. Davy stepped through the door just as the ship sank violently to port. His shoulder smashed into the corridor and he was reminded that by tomorrow he would be covered in a rainbow of colourful bruises. He heard a wave break over the deck above and a sudden burst of shouts. For the next few hours, he knew that there would be no time to think of anything else apart from doing his work and trying his best not to get washed overboard.

It was Friday, 2nd June 1865 and the *Royal Dane* was becalmed. To pass the time the captain had lowered the jolly boat and had taken some passengers out on to the water. There was no breath of wind. Even so, from time to time a mysterious rolling swell that seemed to have been propelled from the ends of the earth moved under the ship, making her deck dip and rise as if the vessel itself was breathing. A few of the jolly boat's passengers had leapt into the warm waters and their splashing and laughter carried easily across the languid water. Davy had been told to scrub the deck, but rather than throw the filth overboard he was ordered to keep the scrapings in a bucket. There was some logic in it somewhere, he thought, but for the time being he was content to carry out orders without too much thought. Besides, he had other things on his mind, like the dancing on the poop last night.

It had been such a beautiful evening. Someone had a fiddle, someone else a penny whistle. There was an accordion which had been damaged by water, and which sounded a little wheezy and breathless, but which nevertheless kept tune, and a strange drum that he had never seen before which was beaten by what seemed like a double-ended bone. Not that you could hear much of the music over the sound of stomping. Someone had called for a waltz to calm things down a bit, but then there was a debate about which one was the best for dancing. They had finally agreed on the 'Emperor Waltz' although Davy doubted whether it should really have been played with such an energetic 'oompah' in the middle section. A couple of the crew had been brave enough to approach a passenger for a dance but Davy had stood well back. He had never danced in his life and thought how funny it was to see some of the lads, who normally appeared so unrefined as they clambered up the ropes like crabs, doing anything remotely graceful. He stood with some of the other boys feeling very young and inexperienced as they elbowed each other to join in.

He was watching Molly as she danced easily with her friends and relatives, and thinking how she was the prettiest of the girls on board when the Ginger Boy interrupted his thoughts with a jab.

'Go on Twice, give 'er a twirl!' The ginger lad elbowed Davy forward. So now Davy was irritated on two counts, one to be elbowed and one to discover that the silly nickname had stuck. David Davies. 'Twice'. *So clever.*

'Davy to you.'

'You should be glad it's not worse, mate. You should hear what they call me!'

Davy paused for a moment.

'Three Times?' Davy watched the Ginger Boy's face as it went from puzzlement to surprise to new admiration.

'Don't mind if I do!' he laughed.

After that Davy thought that he and Ginger Boy would probably get on all right. And he had been just about to leap forward and join the dancing when everything had come to an abrupt halt. The chief officer, Buck, appeared through the crowd to announce that Neptune would be paying them a visit tomorrow, as they were about to 'cross the line'. It was Neptune's opportunity to welcome new sailors and ensure that they were initiated thoroughly in the ways of the sea. There was a lot of undignified whooping and excitement. Some of the more thoughtful passengers had looked up at the sails and remarked how odd it was that they would be crossing the line tomorrow, because as far as they could tell the sails had been set for three days without a whiff of wind.

'You can still be moving with the currents, see, even if there ain't no wind,' one of the sailors had commented sagely. 'Anyhow, when we do start moving there won't be no time for a dunking then! Not if we know the skipper.'

Davy thought all this as he was scraping the deck on his hands and knees.

'Getting a lot of muck off there now are we, Mr Davies?'

'Yes, sir.'

'Our Ocean Lord will be pleased,' chortled the second mate as he sauntered off down the deck. Davy looked at the contents of the bucket in an ominous new light.

That afternoon, as promised, a red-faced Neptune arrived with his unusually burly, bearded wife and a retinue of rather florid-faced ministers. Their elaborately decorated carriage was being dragged along by two handsome steeds, one of whom looked remarkably like the ship's cook, Tony, cloaked in a brown velvet curtain.

They had all gone to a great deal of trouble with their costumes. The first minister, wearing what looked like a barrister's wig and an old toga, stepped forward to extend his special greetings to those sailors who had never before crossed 'the line'. He announced that Neptune would be expecting a list of the sailors' names from the captain along with a generous measure of the ship's best whisky before the ceremony could begin. The carriage proceeded to the steps of the quarterdeck, where Neptune and his wife disembarked to climb the stairs. Once there, Neptune called for the captain and was greeted warmly by Mr Buck, who was standing in for the skipper.

A very large glass of whisky was produced and Mrs Neptune adjusted her magnificent bosom as she watched her 'husband' gulp it down. Neptune, who had until now been mysteriously grave and silent, smacked his lips noisily and called for a list of his future 'sons'. Buck stepped forward, unfurling a roll of names, and presented them to Neptune. An exchange of ocean wit followed, although Davy noticed that only the older crew members laughed or understood what was being said.

The first minister stepped forward, readjusting his wig, and announced that the ceremony would take place on the main deck. Neptune and Mrs

Neptune led the way, followed by the minister and his sprites. As they crowded around, Davy could see that a temporary stage had been erected, and behind it a water tank cleverly created from sails and spars, a third full of water. Davy's stomach lurched and he wondered why his father hadn't told him more about this tradition. Surely, it must have happened to him? Had the *Ellen* ever sailed this far?

Now that Neptune and his buxom wife were seated at the side of the stage, the first minister stepped forward again and fumbled in the folds of his toga.

'Well, then,' he declared, liberating another scroll from his makeshift pocket, 'on to the list!'

The crowd, which up to this point had seemed like a disparate collection of deckhands and passengers, now came together and made a low bellowing noise of excitement.

'But firstly I would just like to say …' the crowd moaned but the first minister persevered for a few moments, soft-soaping the oceanic gods and declaring how important it was for new recruits to make a good account of themselves in front of their new divine ruler, and that if they did Neptune would be merciful to them when it came to it, the next time they were passing through the Bay of Biscay or round the Horn.

'Oh, get on with it, Bumford!' shouted someone from the back.

'Divine First Minister, if you please,' the man in the wig retorted; he tried to resume his speech in a solemn manner, but the shouts and jeers increased so that he could not be heard. 'Very well,' he bellowed, 'on to the list!' and the crowd gave an almighty cheer and stomped its feet wildly on the wooden deck.

What a peculiar sight this must be from afar, thought Davy. This impotent ship becalmed on an infinite ocean, empty of all other human life as far as the eye could see in every direction. This one tiny point of exultation and hysteria placed on an endless mirrored sea. He looked up at the dazzling sails. They were lifeless, as if the air of the world had been sucked away and was being stored elsewhere in some enormous bellows. What if there is never a wind? What if our water runs out and we're forced to drink the sea? What would happen to five hundred and ninety-eight people crammed together on a tiny wooden world, stranded? Would they eat each other, eventually? Davy's thoughts were interrupted by the first name.

'Mr Lively!' announced the first minister to another raucous cheer.

A lad stepped forward and Davy recognised him immediately as 'Threetimes', the Ginger Boy.

'Well, I never!' Davy turned to his neighbour, a passenger whom he did not know. 'Mr Lively,' he repeated under his breath then cupped his hands around his mouth and shouted, 'Come on, Threetimes!'

'Ho ho! Three times! I think not,' laughed the first minister, 'I do believe once will be quite enough, don't you, Mr Neptune?'

Neptune nodded gravely and stroked his beard. Mrs Neptune hid coyly behind a flowery fan that had been provided for her by one of the female passengers. Ginger Boy looked nervous as he climbed on to the stage and searched the crowd for a familiar face.

The first minister called for Neptune's doctor and explained that before Mr Lively could be admitted into their hallowed ranks, they needed to check his health. He was seated in a chair and examined by the doctor who then announced, with a scowling look, that the patient was not in such good health and that a pill and a draught should be administered. Davy could not see what the pill was made of, something unpleasant from the look of the boy's face, but then, when the draught bucket was brought forward, Davy recognised it as the bucket of deck scrapings that he had been asked to collect earlier on that day.

Davy retched to think of it, and when Ginger Boy saw a mugful of the contents being wielded in front of him, the doctor and the minister had to force the lad to drink. Davy turned away. When he looked back at the scene, Ginger Boy was leaning forward to be sick.

'Ah, this will bring you to your senses!' the doctor shouted, and out of his pocket produced a smelling bottle made from a cork studded with pins. The doctor prodded the cork roughly into the Ginger Boy's nose and distracted him from the contractions of his stomach long enough for the barber to be called.

'A bucket for Mr Lively!' shouted the barber as he leapt on stage and the crowd groaned and cheered in equal measure as the lad emptied his stomach.

The doctor produced the 'smelling bottle' again so that the Ginger Boy shot back in his chair with his nose glowing red and sore.

'A little bit of a clean up and a shave is needed now, I think,' said the barber.

No delicate barber ever had biceps the size of those tree trunks, thought Davy, wondering how awful the next part of the ceremony would be. The barber called for his bucket and made up a vile concoction of shaving 'lather' calling for various celestial ingredients which turned out to be chiefly chicken droppings, bird feathers and tar. Davy looked down at his shirt and wondered whether he should take it off before he was called up. He only had two shirts, and if he got tar on one he would spend the rest of his journey in one dirty wet shirt or no shirt at all. He looked around for Molly and wondered whether she would think him skinny and childish without his shirt. His stomach lurched again, with potential embarrassment now.

The barber, having mixed his lather together, began to apply it gently enough to the lad's face. This part's not too bad, thought Davy.

'So tell me, young Mr Lively, from where do you originate?'

'From Gravesend,' started Ginger Boy, but no sooner had he opened his mouth than the vile sponge loaded with 'lather' was thrust roughly into his mouth. The crowd screamed with laughter although some of the more delicate passengers turned their faces away.

'What did you say lad? Glasgow?' the barber stood poised with another loaded sponge. 'Come on now, lad, you must answer the barber otherwise Neptune will be offended with you,' added the first minister.

Ginger Boy tried to answer without opening his mouth.

'Can you hear him?' the barber shouted at the crowd.

'No!' they all screamed.

'Where do you come from?' he bellowed,

'Gravesend!' he managed the whole word before the sponge was shoved into his mouth. Ginger Boy leaned forward and retched again into the bucket.

'And now bring forward the shaving instruments,' called the first minister. Four of Neptune's Sprites stepped forward, each presenting a different implement including a bread knife and a rusty saw. Neptune was called upon to choose the appropriate instrument according to how docile and accommodating the new recruit had been so far. Neptune chose the rusty saw which was then scraped slowly along the victim's face and chin, leaving it red and scratched.

Ginger Boy was still spitting out lumps and feathers from his mouth when the barber declared that he should be given a good sousing to ensure his proper introduction into the ways of the sea. The sprites moved forward and grabbed the lad by the arms and legs, throwing him bodily into the tank of water. Hopefully that's an end to it, thought Davy, putting a hand on his top button and wondering again whether he should take off his shirt. But the sprites were not done yet. They armed themselves with oars and proceeded to pin the lad under the water for as long as possible. Ginger Boy struggled to get up out of the water, but each time they pushed him back down and kept him under, each time a little longer. The crowd started counting, 'One, two, three,' and started over each time he came up for air. The final time, they reached eighteen before Neptune called a halt and they were allowed to let him up. Ginger Boy looked bruised and scraped with his mop of straight hair pasted to his skull. He clambered out of the water, dazed and half-drowned.

'One down. Fifteen to go!' shouted the first minister. The crowd cheered and the voices ebbed just in time for him to hear the words.

'Next! David Davies!'

It had not gone well for Davy. When it came to it, he had forgotten to take off his shirt. And as he reached the stage, the memory of what he had scraped off the deck earlier on that day had made him retch long before the mug reached his mouth. The crowd had laughed uncontrollably at this, particularly when the minister said something about it being a 'bit of a poor show' and they hadn't even got started yet. He was sure that the barber had asked him a lot more questions although Davy was proud of himself for lying about where he came from. It struck him that Mwnt was much quicker to say than Cardigan and didn't require his mouth to be open for so long. The barber was no idiot, though, and clearly knew his geography.

'And tell us, in what county is that?'

Screams of laughter. Cardiganshire. Mouthful of tar and feathers. Sick in the bucket. His stomach still hurt to think of it. And then when they dunked him in the tank, he thought he had a plan. He could swim and knew how to hold his breath under water. But he hadn't reckoned on such violent jabs from the oars which knocked the air out of him completely and at the bottom of the tank the only thing his lungs could take in, without thinking, was water. He had squealed like a pig when he emerged the final time, gasping for air, spluttering and splashing water everywhere.

Now he rolled over in his bunk. He wanted to pull his knees up to his chest so that he might forget the pain in his stomach and throbbing bruises, but there was no room. He thought of Gruffudd at home in his warm bed. He wouldn't have had tar and muck shoved in his mouth today. No one would have prodded him in the groin with an oar until he couldn't walk straight. Why did they do this to each other, he wondered? Each new generation of sailors would go through it and all of them would hate it. So when did they decide that they would do the same to the next lot? Where was the law written down that said it had to be done? Was it just 'They did it to me so I'll do it to you'? If he discovered who had jabbed him so viciously, would he throw that man a rope as he was about to go over the davits in the next gale? Or would he just not bother and turn away?

In Tŷ Hagar the house would be quiet, the moon would be watching over his family with her sad face. His father might be home, sitting in front of the fire with his Bible and his pipe. Jane, restless, wondering whether James Glanllynan really did like her after all or was he just pretending. The orchard, quietest of all, being surveyed by a silent, stealthy fox. He wanted to be home. Not home as it was when he was there last, but the home of his imagination. Where Gruffudd and Elen and Jane were bringing in the hay on a fine day, his father was home from the sea and his mother was happy. He wanted to be there instead of in a smelly fo'c'sle listening to the snores and farts of people he barely knew. In that strange, imaginary world he would go to see his grandfather at the mill. Davy would put his arm around the man's dusty shoulders and tell him that he missed him.

No sooner had Davy fallen asleep than he was being woken up again by a crewman's sharp elbow.

'Come on, slacker, all hands!'

Davy tumbled out of his hammock and every part of him hurt. The previous day's jabs and wallops were mapped out on him in intricate, burning detail. Thoughts of the slop bucket crowded in on him again and he barely reached the deck in time to be sick several times over the side.

'Ah, Jesus! Who's fucking sick to the windward side?' came an Irish voice as Davy realised that most of his stomach's contents had been blown back on board.

'Fucking Taffy,' came another voice, but before he could turn to look who they were Buck shouted and waved him over. He was to stay at the helm in case of accidents. The man already there seemed older than most of the crew.

'Here lad, stand close, and do as I do.'

Davy's first thought was that surely there must be someone more experienced than him who could help. Why would they want to endanger the ship in the hands of a boy and a useless one at that?

The sailor told Davy how to hold the wheel then added, 'Don't you be letting go unexpectedly now, otherwise she'll take my hands off, d'ya hear?'

It was a terrifying thought, but Davy felt strangely comforted by his voice. For the first time since he had boarded the ship someone seemed to have some faith in him.

Davy placed his hands on the wheel. He had not seen in the semi-darkness but the wheel was vibrating violently, and when he touched it the whole vessel seemed transformed to him. He was no longer holding on to a configuration of wood and brass, but a living creature with sinews and bones and a heartbeat. Davy looked up at the sailor in wonderment and laughed with surprise.

The man laughed back at Davy and seemed pleased with his reaction.

'She's a fine ship and no mistake. She'll see us through. Won't you, lass?'

The skies darkened still further and the last of the daylight disappeared. Lamps had been lit but they cast little useful light. Between them they held the *Royal Dane* steady on her course, keeping her as close to the wind as they could, aiming her bow obliquely at the oncoming waves. When a wave came crashing over the side the man at Davy's side lost his footing momentarily, but Davy took the strain. When he recovered and returned to the helm the sailor said nothing, but Davy knew that his alertness had been noted.

As the ship lay increasingly on her side, the man's face became stern. The wheel seemed to be straining more and more under their hands, and Davy looked across at him a few times, wondering how it was that the ship could survive such force. The very sky itself seemed to be screeching. Davy had never heard a sound like it. The deck was awash and water rushed past them up to their knees. Suddenly, in a swift practised movement before Davy was barely aware, the captain had stepped forward and taken his side of the helm away from him. Davy watched as the men exchanged quick shouts. With a flick of his head the captain motioned Davy forward again.

Within seconds there were shouts around him to shorten the sails, to strike the topgallant then the gallant, and to reef the mainsail. Despite the storm and the darkness Davy could just make out the shapes of men making their steady way up the shrouds towards the top of the mainsail. There were shouts mingled with the screams of the wind, and steadily the sailors hauled on the sail together until half its area was gathered upwards and tied at the mast. Davy had seen pictures of trapeze artists and acrobats, but their antics seemed child's play compared to this. The cloud parted momentarily and the moon cast unexpected light on the grim scene. Another massive wave washed over the deck. The moon hid itself again.

Just when Davy was asking himself whether it could get much worse, it began to rain. It came in solid sheets filling the air so densely that it was almost impossible to breathe. Davy tried to shake the water from his face, but it enveloped him from all directions. He gasped, wondering whether in reality the ship was already underwater and he should swim for his life.

The man next to him shouted encouragement although Davy could not make out his exact words. An enormous wave broke over them both and the ship lurched. Davy lost his footing completely and found himself gulping water in a panic. He was face down watching the water draining through the scuppers, so he scrambled to his feet on the slimy deck. His companion was gone and the wheel was turning wildly at speed. Davy remembered his words about how the wheel could take off your hands and he waited until it paused for a moment. He judged his moment well and fought to bring the wheel around in the right direction.

'C'mon, old girl. Show us what you're made of,' muttered Davy to himself.

He felt the strain on his arms reduce as his companion returned, gasping, at his side. The storm seemed to continue like that for hours, until Davy could barely feel his hands at all and the muscles across his back burned as if he had taken a dozen lashes. Eventually the storm began to subside and they were relieved at the wheel by another sailor, a short man with impressively square shoulders.

'Out of the way, old timer. And you, boy,' said the newcomer, pushing between them.

'Take no notice of Malone,' shouted the older man deliberately, 'he's Irish. He can't help being dull.'

Malone waved them aside and planted himself at the helm as if every muscle and sinew in his body had been designed for the work.

As Davy made his way below deck he thought of how he had survived his first real storm. It had been terrifying, but also exhilarating in a way he had not expected. He peeled off his soaking trousers and hung them from a nail, knowing full well that by the next watch they would still be wet. He thought of all the fuss his grandmother used to make if they were caught playing in wet clothes as children. If only she could see me now, he thought, and as soon as his head touched the hammock he was fast asleep.

It was not Davy's watch and by rights he should have been catching up on his sleep. But the captain's wife had lent him a copy of the ship's newspaper, *The Royal Dane Standard*, which was being printed on board. And so Davy had tucked himself into a corner away from the prevailing wind where he might stand a chance of reading it through without interruption. The print was frustratingly fine, and his calloused hands had trouble turning the delicate pages without the whole thing catching the wind like a kite and blowing away. The first thing to draw his eye was an insert presented in a bolder, fussier typeface under the heading, *Wise Saws and Modern Instances*. 'On a voyage take with you a good conscience, a sound heart, a good courage, good resolutions, honest self-reliance, persevering industry and the good wishes of your friends.' Not much chance of that, he thought, and nearly dismissed the idea of reading further. But despite himself he read on, turning away from the wind and the fine spray. 'Take care not to leave your head behind you, nor your keys, nor a bad name; no debts, aching hearts or any enemies. Live so as to be missed.' *A total, unmitigated, dead loss, then.*

Davy was about to shove the paper into his pocket when he noticed Hoskins loitering around the corner. The two of them had successfully avoided close contact since their first disastrous encounter and Davy was in no hurry to alter the situation. He buried his head in the paper and read on.

The diary of the ship's voyage catalogued each event and spell of bad weather experienced by the *Royal Dane*. Davy could remember them all in vivid detail and wondered why anyone else would need to be reminded. Since crossing the line they had seen flying fish and nautilus, sharks and yet more stormy weather. The captain had shot several birds, although to what purpose other than to practise his aim Davy wasn't sure, as none of the birds could be retrieved and eaten. Rounding the Cape of Good Hope had been comparatively uneventful, although, when Davy mentioned this to one of the ship's officers, he had laughed back at him,

'Oh, there's plenty of time to see wild work yet.'

And sure enough, before the week was out, disorder reigned supreme. Furniture, hardware, pots and pans careered madly around the slippery cabins. Freshly served soup and tea became treacherous, scalding missiles, while on deck, pigs, fowl and ducks slid about in wild confusion, disappearing comically every now and then down the fore hatchway. But time and time again, even the most treacherous winds had blown them in the right direction.

On Sunday 25th June they had passed the Crozet Islands and Davy shuddered to think of his father's stories about how the crew of the *Princess of Wales* had been wrecked there in 1821 and marooned for two whole years; one of the most isolated places on the face of the earth. In early July they had sailed fourteen consecutive days, averaging a distance of 268 miles a day. Later that month they had travelled 1382 nautical miles in less than a week. The crew had been ecstatic. Where would that have got him, he wondered, if he had travelled the same distance overland from Cardigan: Paris, Milan, the middle of the Swiss Alps?

Davy glanced up to see whether Hoskins was still there. He could not see him, but someone standing around the corner was casting an ominous shadow on the deck, so Davy read on. On 9th July they had seen a sight not often seen at sea, that of a moonbow or lunar rainbow. Apart from the crew, few people were there to see it appear, as it did, two hours before sunrise in the darkest part of the sky, directly opposite the moon. Davy had just emerged from below deck for the morning watch and was grateful that Buck had allowed them to be idle for a few moments so that they could gaze at its eerie beauty.

The newspaper diary continued. On 10th July a sailor had died of an unspecified illness, and later that week a love-struck passenger had taken laudanum to end his life. Davy had often noticed the young man taking a turn about the deck. He was well dressed and strikingly handsome, with elegant manners and an easy way. What could possibly be so bad about his life, wondered Davy, remembering how the surgeon superintendent, Mr Hodgkinson, had walked the young man around and around the deck for hours trying to keep him awake. After pumping his stomach, of course. Davy squirmed and made a mental note that if he ever decided to kill himself, he would try something a little more decisive than an opiate.

Then Davy noticed that the wind must have changed direction, because fresh salty spray came across his face from an unexpected angle. He glanced up and the shadow on the deck had gone. Beyond the ship, the ocean seemed colder than ever. The sky was darkening and black thunderous clouds were closing in.

The storm lasted three whole days and just as it subsided, the *Royal Dane* was hit by a measles epidemic. The youngest passengers were the most vulnerable, and the sight of tiny bodies sewn up in spare sheets being thrown overboard became all too familiar.

That morning, as the crew for the forenoon watch emerged from below deck, grumbling and wiping the sleep from their eyes, the captain had shouted at them to keep their voices down; a couple were about to bury the third and last of their small children.

Mr Hodgkinson said a few words and then quoted from Ecclesiastes:

'The wind blows to the south and goes around to the north; around and around goes the wind, and on its circuits the wind returns. All streams run to the sea, but the sea is not full; to the place where the streams flow, there they flow again.'

From his perch on the ratlines Davy watched as the woman sobbed quietly on her husband's shoulder and thought how oddly inappropriate the words were if they were meant to bring her comfort. He watched the woman's shoulders shake, and thought how she must feel that the sea was full to the brim with her own children.

The matron, Mrs Edwards, brought a small white bundle to the side and then in a swift, almost irreverent, movement, threw it overboard. The mourning mother sprang forward instinctively to the rail and watched as the little bundle floated playfully for a second or two then yielded to the green waves.

'Another poor bugger,' said one of the crew, as he came up behind Davy and shoved him onwards and upwards along the ratlines now that the service was over.

When Davy reached his spot on the crosstrees he glanced downwards again. The small gathering had dispersed and only the mother and father were left standing at the rail watching the green waves. Davy thought of Elen's funeral and how he had not been allowed to attend. How had his mother been at the graveside, he wondered. Had she leant against his father's shoulder or stood aloof from him? Had she wept? He heard Elen's laugh as if caught by the ship's white sails. His throat tightened and the scene around him blurred with his own tears.

'You'll be next, mate, if you're not careful,' cautioned another sailor, adding that it was wise to keep his eyes ahead of him and not 'dilly-dally' on the ropes.

Shortly after that the lookout had seen the first sight of land. The sombre mood had been replaced with shouts of excitement and a different gathering of people on deck.

'Do you see it? That's Cape Otway!' the sailor shouted, pointing at the broken horizon and explaining how they would soon see the light station there. Then they would skirt around the coast past King's Island, Melbourne and Port Philip. They would see Rodondo and Curtis Islands, the Sugar Loaf and the Devil's Tower. 'All the way around until Sydney and Keppel Bay, mate. You'll be able to call yourself a proper sailor then, eh?'

Davy wiped his eyes and leaned back, loosening his grip on the ropes a little. The skies were clearing over Victoria and the sun was breaking through. The captain and his crew had brought the passengers safely to a new continent. From high above the deck Davy could see the sleek bow of the beautiful *Royal Dane* slicing gracefully through the waves. He found himself remembering his mother's revulsion and his father's faith. The rope ran through his burning hands until it had no tension; only his own equilibrium held him there, and he was poised as if on the arms of a balancing scale. He weighed his losses, and for a brief moment it seemed that they would overwhelm him. But there was something else too; something that might become a compensation of sorts. Perhaps the sea was in his blood after all; it had been in his father's blood and his father's before him. As he grasped the twists of rope and halted their escape, Davy thought again of the surgeon's words,

'To the place where the streams flow, there they flow again.'

PART TWO

SEA

CHAPTER 5

1888, the South Pacific

The South American Steam Ship Company's *Benalla* had scarcely left the harbour at La Serena when Captain Colin MacDougal Stewart and David Davies, his chief officer, spotted Mrs Wilkinson approaching them along the deck.

Stewart turned to Davy and muttered under his breath, 'God save us – that infernal woman. I'm going below.'

Mrs Wilkinson, whose little grey husband trailed some way behind her, had laced herself so tightly into her high-necked maroon taffeta gown that her chest seemed to protrude from right under her chin.

'Captain Stewart!' she exclaimed, cutting short his escape. 'How wonderful to see you again!' She stretched out her long gloved hand towards the captain.

Stewart made a very acceptable attempt at being courteous and bowed down elegantly to kiss her hand. He then turned to Mr Wilkinson, who was mostly overshadowed by his wife's dramatic hat. The hat was perched miraculously on top of an impressively constructed mountain of hair. Davy marvelled at the unseen maid's engineering skills.

'My husband!' exclaimed Mrs Wilkinson, almost as an afterthought, and Davy caught the grey man's discreet grimace of embarrassment. As Wilkinson stepped forward to shake the captain's hand, billows of pink gauze flew into his face. Stewart turned to introduce his chief officer, but the woman had more important things on her mind and carried blithely on.

'Captain Stewart, imagine my excitement when I read your passenger card and realised that we are to be joined by Mr Robert McKeig who, a little bird has told me, is in fact your cousin! How lucky we are!'

The little grey man behind her looked skyward as if surveying the heavens for some rare albatross. The captain gazed bashfully down at the deck, a picture of modesty.

'Yes, I must say,' she continued to coo, 'your cousin has done very well for himself. I feel we should be introduced as we turn in similar circles, as it were.'

Stewart nodded vaguely and also looked upwards, searching for the same rare and mysterious albatross.

'And I am sure your cousin would find Mr Wilkinson's connections incredibly useful.' There was an awkward pause, but Mrs Wilkinson was undaunted. 'Do you remember, dear?' She half turned to her husband who seemed to be shrinking in stature before Davy's eyes. 'When we sailed on the *Aconcagua* and Captain Wade introduced us to one of the Rothschilds.'

'Oh, I don't think they were actually …' Mr Wilkinson started to say, but a well-timed puff of wind blew the gauze across his face again and cut short his unsolicited comment.

'Captain Wade was such a gentleman,' Mrs Wilkinson continued, 'and what a fine ship!'

Sure enough, the implied comparison with Wade's ship was the gauntlet required and Stewart rose predictably to the challenge.

'Mrs Wilkinson, I would be delighted to welcome you both to dine with myself and my cousin this evening.'

Mrs Wilkinson was triumphant, and after exchanging the usual pleasantries she strutted off with her sharp chin in the air, her little grey husband trailing dutifully behind.

'Dear God,' groaned Stewart as they watched the pair disappearing below deck. But where Stewart had appeared to be a picture of calm a few seconds before, now he was like a thing possessed and the directions came in a quick torrent.

'Tell the steward I want to see the table plan myself. As soon as possible! And send a message to McKeig to see me in my cabin before dinner. Forearmed is forewarned. He won't take kindly to this. Make sure the Islay is out. And …' he began to walk off, adding, 'get Webb to take your watch. I want you there to stay my hand when I'm about to commit a heinous crime.'

Stewart marched off, muttering colourful Glaswegian profanities that Davy only vaguely understood.

Once Davy had delegated his responsibilities, he returned to his cabin to prepare for that evening's dinner. The thought of spending an entire evening trying to make idle chatter with the likes of Mrs Wilkinson filled him with dread and his stomach lurched much as it would have done in the worst kind of gale.

'What you have to understand,' Stewart had said to him not long after he was appointed chief officer, 'is that it's all part of the job. We've reached a point where it's not about the engines and the navigation any more. Our passengers have already made the assumption that we can get them safely from A to B. Now they concern themselves with the quality of the cut glass goblets or their allocation of fancy writing paper. The fact that they entrust their lives to us is neither here nor there. We are to entertain them too!' Stewart had snorted and waved his arm like a disgruntled emperor.

Davy closed the cabin door behind him and took off his jacket and shirt. There was still fresh water in the enamel jug and he poured some in to the washstand bowl. He took up the soap and damp flannel and washed his face, neck and torso. He couldn't remember the last time he'd had a bath of warm water, even though the *Benalla* was by far the most sophisticated ship he'd ever sailed on. Even on the hottest day, the waters off the coast of Chile came all the way from Antartica so they were never very warm. It was a desperate man who took a swim just to get clean in these seas, he thought, even if he was prepared to brave the risk of sharks.

Now he needed his smarter suit, reserved for functions and dinners, and a clean shirt. He opened the closet door and there was the suit just as expected, perhaps needing a bit of a brush across the shoulders. But the shirt? There was no sign of it. He rifled through the hanging items one by one: the oilskin, the off-duty clothes, his cold weather jumpers, spare trousers, long coat. But there were no shirts. There were a couple of shallow drawers under his bunk, but there was no sign of them there either. The metal trunk; perhaps there was a shirt in there? It seemed unlikely. The old trunk, the one he'd left home with, followed him around from ship to ship but he hadn't opened it in years. It was almost an embarrassment, now that he was a chief officer. He dragged it out from under the bunk, its high curved lid barely scraping its way from underneath the bed frame. Looking at its battered surface he knew full well that no serviceable clothing could possibly be hiding inside, but all the same he swept his hands across the rusty top and an unexpected surge of excitement shot through him as his hands eased the lid upwards.

The interior, protected from the salty air and dampness, was almost pristine. There was no rust or flaking paint. Inside the trunk, time had stood still. Even the air released seemed to have come from a different time. There were no shirts. Nothing resembling a shirt. No clothes at all, in fact. An odd assortment of things: books, papers, a small model boat. He rummaged through them, aware that he was being distracted from his more urgent task. He delved deeper; his certificates, edged by bamboo frames, not that they'd ever been hung on a wall, photographs, unwritten postcards which he couldn't remember buying … and letters, bundles and bundles of letters. There was Jane's hand, and Gruffudd's hand, even a few from his father in his unsteady, formal script. Written on a wallowing ship, no doubt. No letters from his mother of course. But there was another hand; a hand that Davy had almost forgotten.

There was a knock on the door and one of the cabin boys appeared with three newly washed and ironed shirts on wooden hangers.

'Sir, the captain says to remind you that dinner is at seven sharp. And I'm to give you these, sir, captain's orders.'

The lad dithered on the threshold, taken aback, it seemed, to find his chief officer sitting half naked on the floor, delving into an ancient chest. He hung the shirts quickly on the back of the door and made a quick exit, but not before adding, 'Captain says to tell you that it's a quarter to seven, sir.'

Davy nodded and would normally have thought of a clever response. But his mind was elsewhere. He was transfixed by the bundle in his hand, and the elegant curls of his initials on fine writing paper. I will come back to them, he thought, returning them to the chest and closing the lid. He pushed the chest under the bunk and prepared for dinner.

The first course had just been cleared away and the stewards were preparing to bring out the main course tureens. The saloon on the *Benalla* was among the finest on the mailboat ships, and when all was laid out Davy felt proud to be her chief officer. It wasn't usual practice for him to sit at the captain's table. On previous occasions Davy had been asked to attend so that he could 'see how things are done'. But this time he knew that he would be required to contribute to the conversation and steer things in a particular direction.

The meal was passing relatively painlessly despite the slightly steely veneer on Stewart's face. His smile disappeared too quickly or it froze in one place, giving the impression of a man who was bravely anticipating some awful disaster.

Mrs Wilkinson was cooing again. 'Don't you feel, Mr McKeig, that the main challenge of running a business is keeping a tight rein on your staff?'

According to Stewart, Robert McKeig was a quiet, thoughtful man not much given to small talk. He had built a successful business by working hard, but also by dealing honestly with those around him. Apparently, he had an enviable reputation; his employees were thoroughly loyal and could not be induced to say a bad word against him. He kept his own counsel and did not spend time with anyone he didn't like, even if they could further his own interests.

McKeig took a sip of wine and considered the question carefully. 'I find, in all honesty, Mrs Wilkinson, that a horse runs better with a loose rein, as long as it knows you're there.'

Mrs Wilkinson's face was a picture of fawning confusion. She smiled and ran her fingers self-consciously through her ostentatious amber beads.

'But when staff need to be reprimanded, when a horse has misbehaved, as it were, surely you have to show it who is master?'

McKeig smiled and stroked his beard. Davy also detected the shadow of a curling smile on the face of the little grey man as he examined his napkin discreetly. The whole table was hanging on McKeig's every word. Everyone could tell by the effortless cut of his suit and the quality of the fabric that this was an extremely wealthy man. Mrs Wilkinson's appearance, however, was anything but effortless. She had chosen a pale, flesh-coloured creation that would have looked delectable on someone half her age. The tiny beads on the bodice were beautifully worked, but they failed to soften her austere bearing. And consequently she looked older and more haggard than her years. She leaned forward eagerly to hear what McKeig had to say.

'I don't like to manage my people in an adversarial way,' began Mc Keig again, 'I find it inefficient in terms of time and energy.'

The little grey man coughed convulsively into his napkin. Everyone, apart from Mrs Wilkinson, looked around to check that their fellow guest was not choking to death.

'I see,' smiled Mrs Wilkinson, eager to prolong the conversation, 'how enlightened.'

A few of the guests exchanged uncomfortable glances and a gentleman at the end of the table drew breath as if about to change the topic, but Mrs Wilkinson wasn't done yet.

'And tell me, how many properties do you own by now?'

There was a gasp of incredulity, but McKeig didn't flinch.

'My wife and I live in Houghton Villa, a very modest affair ... don't we, dear?' He glanced fondly at the serene young woman who sat further along the table. 'And we have some other small properties around.'

'Oh! How delightful!' exclaimed Mrs Wilkinson, turning her full attention to the young woman whom she had evidently assumed all along was a daughter or young cousin of the same name. Davy was amused to see her making a full assessment of the price of the dress, how expensive the fabric, whether Paris or London, how elaborate the cut, whether they were Gulf pearls or not, and how skilled – and therefore expensive – her maid was at arranging her hair. In Mrs Wilkinson's mind there was being constructed a detailed logbook of expenditure, adding up accurately to Mr McKeig's level of esteem and devotion. On closer scrutiny it was undeniably high, although somewhat surprising as the woman had seemed at first so plainly and unremarkably dressed. Davy watched as Mrs Wilkinson squirmed, completely wrong-footed by the entire understated ensemble. And to top it all, there was a suspiciously expensive gem on the woman's left hand. Mrs Wilkinson's poker-straight back and jutting chin perfectly conveyed her resentful conclusion. Clearly, the young woman had done very well for herself.

'Forgive me, Mrs McKeig,' she exclaimed at last, 'I didn't realise. I assumed you were …'

'May I propose a toast!' interrupted Stewart abruptly and rather too loudly, springing to his feet, 'to our dear friends, Robert KcKeig and his most beautiful wife, Amelia!'

The whole table sighed visibly with relief. The McKeigs exchanged discreet glances, and the only person around the table who remained unaware of the ill-bred *faux pas* was Mrs Wilkinson herself who was already concocting new and more ingenious ways of ingratiating herself with Mr McKeig.

The stewards, who had not been expecting a toast at that stage of the meal, were caught off-guard and hurried forward *en masse* to fill the glasses with champagne.

'Oh, let's do!' exclaimed Mrs Wilkinson, eyes glistening with delight and glass raised high.

The meal ended just before midnight; immediately afterwards, Davy took the middle watch, relieving the second officer until four in the morning. He felt utterly exhausted, but descending the steps from the bridge to the officers' quarters, he remembered the chest. Half a bottle of wine was waiting for him too, the remains of a pilfered bottle at the end of the evening. He was fairly sure he had done the guests a huge service by taking it, given the drunken state of some of them by the end.

Davy dragged out the chest and opened the lid. Before kneeling beside it, he poured himself a large glass of wine. He took out the topmost bundle of letters and laid it to one side. There were other things he wanted to see first. Out they came, one by one: *A Practical Seaman's Handbook*, dated 1871 with his name written inside and the ship, the Guion Line's *Nebraska*. He remembered buying the book in a tiny bookshop in Liverpool. 'For your examinations?' the man behind the counter had asked, and Davy had felt bashful and shy of his own ambition. A postcard of an opera singer in New York. The woman had, according to a fellow sailor, 'a stupendous décolletage'. Davy had joked ungraciously, and much to his friend's consternation, that she looked more like one of the heifers on his uncle's farm. He remembered now, the card had been bought as a memento for his friend but it had been mislaid and then forgotten. Where was the lad now, he wondered? The last he'd heard he was sailing the China seas. No longer a lad.

His marble-patterned logbook, the one his father had given him when he left home. 'You must keep a count of all your service,' his father had warned him, and handed him the smart new notebook with a marbled ink cover in gaudy reds and blues. 'There you are, lad, keep it in there, because although you think you'll remember, you won't. You'll need it for all your certificates.' Davy looked back and thought how important those words had been to him. The words that were said, and the words unsaid. *There will be ships, and more than one certificate. It is to be expected because you are capable.*

The book was worn at the corners by now, but he had taken good care of it, and when necessary he had wrapped it in oilskin so that it wouldn't get wet amongst his things when water gushed over the decks and swilled around under their bunks. Davy flicked open the pages: ship's name, port of registry, rank, date of commencement, date of termination, time in each ship in years, months and days, remarks. His first ship: the *Ellen* of Cardigan. *Part-owned by my father, captained by my father, built in Cardigan, square rigged brig, 11 feet in the hold, no figurehead, steadfast in a storm.* Seven months and twenty-four days.

The list went on, *Royal Dane, Kilvey, Recompense, Sunlight, Merrington, Holland, Alexandrina* ... they were more than names. It was like looking at the firmament, each ship had been its own constellation to which the captain and crew were bound. And their circuits had taken him around the globe: British North America, Greenland, Iceland, Honolulu, Australia. The list of ships went on, *Helvetia, Illimani, Truxillo* then ... oh, the *Missouri*. His heart nearly broke again when he saw the name and in the blink of an eye he was back on her deck.

The end of February, 1886. Davy, now a certified captain, was third officer of his largest ship yet, the majestic *Missouri*. The ship had left Boston, bound for Liverpool with 395 head of cattle and a large general cargo. They'd had an uneventful voyage and, having made Fastnet rock on the Irish coast, they shaped a course north through St George's Channel, towards Holyhead. But at eleven o'clock in the evening the wind picked up, and it began to snow: a suffocating, obliterating blizzard.

The captain gave the order to reduce speed and they used the lead to feel their way. But the wind had pushed them off course and by the time dawn broke and the storm had abated, the mass of land that loomed above them was far too close. The engines were put hard astern, but it was too late. The *Missouri* struck rocks at Porth Dafarch. The coastguard rigged up the breeches buoy and in a slow and painstaking process, most of the sixty-odd crew, the doctor, some cattle and three stowaways were brought ashore. Seeing that the ship would capsize as the tide ebbed, the captain and officers drove as many of the cattle as they could release into the sea so they could swim ashore, but only half of them made it. Finally, as the ship listed still further, the captain and his remaining officers rushed to the last boat, abandoning their ship and her trapped cargo to the waves. Davy's metal chest and contents had been safe at his lodgings in Boston but many of the others had not been so lucky. Some of the men had stood on the cliff weeping as they watched everything they had ever worked for disappearing under the waves. And all on the morning of the first of March, St David's Day.

But that was not the end of it. At the Board of Trade inquiry a few weeks later, the captain, Reuben Poland, was found negligent. Though the crew could find no fault with him, the inquiry insisted that he had continued at too high a speed, and that the lead had not been used often enough. They conceded that the lighthouse beams and foghorn could have been muffled by the storm but, still, they suspended his certificate for six months. The last Davy heard of him, he was a resident of Walton workhouse. Others managed to profit from the wreck. It was found that some of the surviving cattle had found their way, quite independently it seemed, to the bustling butcher's shops of Penllyn.

Davy poured the remaining wine into his glass and came, at last, to the bundle of letters. He had tied them with a piece of hessian string and hadn't looked at them since, a good ten years. Looking at the small pile of identical-sized envelopes, he wondered why he had kept them at all. Guilt? He flicked through them. The addressee was the same on all of them, David Davies. But the addresses themselves varied, ships, lodging houses, the Well Street Sailor's home in London.

Maud Downey. She and her parents were first-generation Irish emigrants who were trading the jewel-green poverty of Wexford for the grey tenements of New York. Davy was an able bodied seaman on their outward-bound ship and once he caught sight of her light auburn hair on that first afternoon, he wasted no time in making dark eyes at her green ones, striking a delicate balance between friendly approachability and trying, as far as he could, to exude an air of professional preoccupation. The lads would laugh and compare their successes at the end of each watch. Mostly, it was a harmless distraction from the punishing ropes, the relentless wet and cold.

But Maud smiled back. And eventually talked. She would linger on deck and he would steal moments between tasks. She embroidered a handkerchief for him, he sewed her an apron from scraps of sail. Below deck the lads pulled his leg, then they stopped. And Davy knew, the second they stopped, that some change had occurred. Somehow or other, Maud had become 'his' girl. When Maud's father laid his accepting hand on Davy's shoulder, a serious hand with the entire weight of an ancient peat field behind it, he knew that he had miscalculated. Yet even so, he still played the fool, scouring the pawnshops of Liverpool looking for a respectable ring: three miserable amethysts on a band of gold. What on earth had he been thinking?

Then the letters started. At first they were endearing and gently cajoling. Would he send word of his next voyage? How would she know when he had arrived? Was he eating well? Was there scarlet fever on board? Davy spaced his replies yet always there were more letters than he could respond to. He began to dread his arrivals in New York and to resent the published shipping reports. Then one day, the death knell rang for good with a sentence that began, 'My father says …'

And that was it. Davy gave up the voyages to New York and found other berths, first to Scandinavia, and then to South America. Her letters dwindled, he never replied. She behaved like a lady. He behaved like a child. Now Davy looked down at the neat bundle, the paper she could ill afford, and felt ashamed. And doubly ashamed because it was the first time he'd felt it. He knew for certain that when he tossed the bundle into the trunk all those years before, he had not given them another thought until now. He weighed the letters in his hands but decided that he would leave them as they were, still tied, unopened, un-divulged. A feeble, late-found mark of respect.

Davy took out his silver watch and made a quick calculation. Three hours' sleep if he was lucky. He downed the last of his wine, closed the lid and in one swift, bad-tempered move, pushed the trunk back under the bed.

At eight the next morning Davy was called to the captain's office. As he entered the room the steward, Sepulveda, was just leaving. Captain MacDougal Stewart was sitting at this desk, his head in his left hand and his right hand nursing a steaming mug of treacle-thick coffee.

'Shut the door, Davies. Do you know … how many bottles of wine we got through last night?' he groaned and brought the mug to his lips. Davy opened his mouth to speak but Stewart put down his mug before taking a sip.

'Twelve! That young Italian fellow has just told me. Four of the people around the table were teetotal, Mrs McKeig only drinks the merest dash of Angostura bitters … in fact hardly any … which leaves twelve bottles of wine between five people. Over two bottles of wine each! No wonder my head is pounding. And all because of that infernal woman!'

Stewart raised the mug again then remembered. 'Did she actually suggest to Mrs McKeig that she should send her boys to a better school where they wouldn't pick up a Scottish accent?'

'I'm afraid so,' replied Davy cheerily. Stewart growled and took a noisy slurp of the black liquid. The memories of the previous night's meal were clearly flooding back with a lurid vengeance.

'She didn't suggest improvements to Robert's business did she?'

'She did, sir.'

'Please tell me she didn't call Mrs McKeig's outfit … what was the word she used … "Bohemian"?'

'Oh, yes.'

'God preserve us! What's to become of the world, Davies, when there are no boundaries any more? There's no breeding! No sense of propriety! For God's sake, before we know it, we'll all be like the bloody Americans!'

The truth was, the evening could have been much worse. Davy knew that one of the other passengers was a literary man, a subject he guessed Mrs Wilkinson would know very little about. So the conversation was steered in a safe direction and one in which all the other guests could be engaged. Mrs McKeig spoke of her love of poetry; there was a lively discussion about women writers and the novels of the Brontë sisters; Mr McKeig spoke of the writings of the explorers and how their findings had helped him develop a good philosophy for life; even Mr Wilkinson managed a half-decent observation on the writings of Dickens, which he had read in various instalments but had never had the time to read in succession. All the while Mrs Wilkinson smiled on in mute admiration, hanging on Mr McKeig's every word.

Luckily she fared no better when the topic turned to art. Although she did interrupt an evaluation of Turner's work with a comment on how some woman she once met had shared a carriage with Turner on his first train journey and had thought he was a complete lunatic.

'Surely,' she laughed, 'Mr McKeig, you don't have time to be thinking about such things as art and literature when you have such a successful business to run?'

The table had become very quiet, but still McKeig was unperturbed and answered calmly as if he had been constructing his reply for some time.

'Have you ever visited the British Museum, Mrs Wilkinson?' to which she made some muttering response of *oh yes, once, but a long time ago.*

'Have you noticed what is left, at the end of the day, as it were, after all these ancient civilizations have been and gone, disappeared into the mists of time?'

Mrs Wilkinson smiled vacantly as she held her wine glass to her lips.

'I'll tell you,' he said smiling disarmingly, 'the beautiful things that people have made, and occasionally, if they are lucky, the things that they have said. That is all that remains. Not fame, nor fortune or notoriety: these things pass. All that remain are the words and objects of mostly invisible, nameless people. We may think we are powerful and important, but even the most powerful and important will pass into dust. I take a huge pride in my business, Mrs Wilkinson, indeed I do, but at the end of the day I am only a businessman. I make money, yes, but that is not a virtue in itself. If I do good with my money, then that could be considered a virtue. I believe that we should strive, but not so that others should fail. And above all, we should not pretend to be something we are not. I am a simple man, Mrs Wilkinson, and I wish to lead a simple and honourable life. And …' he continued, turning to his wife, 'we take very seriously the gift of art and literature, as these are the things that will be left after all our empires are gone.'

'Hear, hear!' someone said from the other end of the table. Mrs McKeig had gazed at her husband with such admiration that it was clear to Davy that a gem the size of a marble was not what bound these two together. It had been a decisive put-down. Mrs Wilkinson still smiled but her eyes had grown cold.

'Oh, I couldn't agree more,' she replied, eventually, with a slight drawl over the rim of her swilling wine glass. And that was the end of that, more or less. Until one of the young men at the table happened to mention that he had been to Eton and his father was Lord something-or-other, at which point she turned her attention to him, poor lad, flirting outrageously until her husband started snoring at the table and they were forced to excuse themselves.

Davy thought of all these things while Stewart stared ahead of him with large haunted eyes, growling intermittently with each awful recurring memory.

CHAPTER 6

The *Benalla* steamed in to Valparaiso harbour at half speed, then quarter speed, then under the tugboat's power alone. Valparaiso was a wide natural harbour, and on a late summer afternoon like this it was a beautiful blue-green bowl. The peaks that ringed the bay were arranged so closely together that they looked like an army of hills that had uprooted themselves from Chile's interior, marching until they came to a sudden halt at the water's edge, each one piling abruptly into the next.

Davy watched as the tug nudged them towards their berth on the pier. Soon there would be commotion and noise and activity on board as the passengers were disembarked and the mail taken to the *Intendencia*. There was cargo to be unloaded – today it was mostly fabric and olive oil, relatively clean goods. If all went well perhaps there would be time enough to walk to the top of Cerro Concepción to take in the view. Every month, it seemed, some new villa or beautiful Italianate mansion was built there for the latest successful businessman, usually English or Scottish or German.

Even the dirty windows of the dockside buildings glittered in the sunshine, and the harbour water, which so often looked filthy with the detritus of heavy shipping, looked azure and cool. There was a hush of expectation on board. Davy wondered what was waiting for the other crew. What kind of families and friends did they have, how warm would their welcome be? Did they have a home to return to or merely dusty lodgings and bad food?

And then he thought of himself. What was waiting for him? Mrs Ebrington would be hovering near the lodging door when he arrived, fussing over him and making sure that all was as it should be in his room. Her grand house, built in the Gothic style with the fruits of a successful, long-running hardware business, had been Albert Ebrington's pride and joy. Careful and thoughtful in death as he had been in life, his wife Agnes had been left comfortably off. There was no financial need for her to take in lodgers, but she did so for the company and so that the house would not feel so empty.

They reached the dockside and the ship burst into hyperactivity. Davy joined Captain Stewart at the portside to see off the passengers, shaking hands and wishing them an excellent forward journey. Mrs Wilkinson disembarked quickly, having latched on to another unsuspecting passenger. As she descended along the gangway, Davy could hear her quizzing her new companion as to the nature and size of his business interests. Mr Wilkinson, who trailed a long way behind, appeared to have become almost transparent and shook the captain's hand with a grimace.

'Good luck to you, sir!' said Stewart, with rather more enthusiasm than was appropriate, thought Davy.

Mr and Mrs McKeig lingered over their departure; partly, it seemed, to keep a respectable distance from the Wilkinsons. The businessman approached Stewart with his arm outstretched.

'Colin, my good man!' Robert McKeig shook the captain's hand firmly and they embraced. Davy saw that the two men were on much closer terms than he had realised.

'I'm afraid we haven't taken care of you so well this time,' muttered Stewart under his breath.

'Nonsense,' said McKeig, still holding on to Stewart's hand and giving him a hefty affectionate swipe on his upper arm, 'Amelia and I come across that kind of thing all the time, I'm afraid. People make so many assumptions. Imagine how colourless the world would be without people's constant urge to pontificate on matters they really know nothing about.'

Davy watched as the couple walked down the gangway arm in arm, their cases and luggage already being loaded on to a carriage just ahead of them.

'Where the devil are the rest of them?' Stewart grumbled. 'I'm invited to a dinner this evening at the British Club. I'm damned if I'll be late!'

Davy turned to Sepulveda and motioned him to round up the stray passengers. Captain Stewart was normally a patient man, apart from when his meals were interrupted.

'Damned nuisance,' he muttered again.

Just then Miss Hetherington appeared through the door, closely followed by her maid and an overloaded baggage handler. She had donned her largest pale pink ostrich-feather hat, and for a moment Davy thought she might get caught by the breeze and float to shore without any need for a gangway.

'Miss Hetherington!' exclaimed Stewart, jovially, walking towards her and taking her outstretched hand. 'A vision indeed! We will be most sad to see you leaving us.'

She offered her sincere thanks to the captain and wished him to pass on her gratitude to the crew for such a serene and peaceful trip. She wafted past Davy, trailing a good deal of expensive crimson brocade behind her. Then, just as Davy thought he was going to be spared her attentions, she turned to him, 'Would you mind?' she asked Davy, peering out from under her cloud of pink feathers.

'My pleasure.' Davy took her hand and guided her down the gangway.

As they reached the harbourside, she tipped her head towards him and said, 'I will be practising my bridge skills before I meet you next, Mr Davies.' She leant in towards him as if she was sharing a secret. 'So that I can wreak my revenge.'

Davy bowed gallantly, conveniently hiding his expression. 'The pleasure will be all mine, Miss Hetherington.'

The answer pleased her. She released his hand with a flourish and continued down the gangway, closely followed by the maid, who threw him a look of mild disgust, and the baggage handler who merely rolled his eyes. Davy watched the pink feathers and substantial shapely bustle disappear into the crowd. A few other straggling passengers went past him as he walked back up to gangway, and he shook hands and wished them all well as they passed.

'You old dog, Davies,' muttered Stewart, as he watched Miss Hetherington's bustle moving across the harbour.

Davy sighed. 'Merely being polite, sir.'

Stewart snorted with amusement, clearly not believing a word. Davy felt irritated. He felt irritated that Stewart believed he could see right through him. Irritated by the fact that he, Davy, could be so transparent. Irritated with himself that, yes, he could at times behave in ways that were not completely honourable. The truth was that – for some inexplicable reason – certain women found him irresistible. He hated himself for thinking it, but there were times when relations needed very little effort on his part. Women would fall into his lap, sometimes literally.

He thought back to the time when he had been second officer on board the *Truxillo*. The chief officer had taken a fancy to an American woman, Miss Allen, bound for La Serena. She was reportedly joining her fiancé there and planning to get married in the following weeks. Her elderly chaperone was miserably seasick, despite a relatively unchallenging voyage, and completely incapable of carrying out her duty of keeping an eye on her charge.

Unfortunately, the object of the woman's affections was not the fiancé nor the chief officer, a tall, lanky and rather earnest young man, but Davy. Some of the passengers, including the American woman, had been invited to dinner in the saloon that evening, despite the heavy seas. Everything that wasn't attached or screwed down slid around the table, and the scene resembled a finely choreographed ballet dance with a series of swinging and sliding objects being caught just in time by practised hands. Miss Allen rose from the table on some pretext of returning to her room briefly when a sudden wave hit the ship sideways. Her timing was perfect; she slid gracefully and squarely into Davy's lap. All Davy could remember was being presented with a décolletage that was so abundantly close that his eyes could barely focus. He looked up to see the chief officer, ashen-faced and more than a little agitated, grasping a platter of fruit to his chest and glaring at Davy through the spiky leaves of a pineapple.

Later on that evening Davy was made better acquainted with the depths of the chief officer's infatuation. He also discovered that, although the man's expensive education had given him all the right stances and verbal bravado for a decent fight, he was in fact shaping up to be pretty ineffectual.

'You're being ridiculous,' Davy pleaded in bewilderment, as he watched the first officer dancing around with his fists in the air. He reminded Davy of the hares on Rhos Common. Davy stood with his hands on his hips, still in his officer's jacket and making no move to engage with his challenger.

'You, sir! I am challenging you, sir, and unless you are a damned coward I expect you to defend your honour!'

Davy's hands slid to his side. He really did not want to fight this man. It would be such an unfair conflict. His adversary obviously assumed that, because Davy was shorter than him and loath to respond, he would be easy to defeat. Davy watched him bouncing back and forward, wasting all his pent-up energy. He was already pink with exertion and he hadn't even thrown a single punch.

Reluctantly, Davy took off his jacket, and as he did so a small, black hand appeared at his side. Davy looked down to see one of the young African stokers grinning up at him and waiting to hold his jacket.

'Jimmy, you shouldn't be here.'

'No, sir,' said the boy, taking the jacket neatly in his arms but not budging an inch.

Davy sighed again and rolled up his sleeves, then adjusted his belt. No use rushing. By the looks of the man opposite him, if he waited a little longer his opponent would collapse of exhaustion.

'I insist you defend yourself, sir!' the hare exclaimed, bouncing around.

It was all over in a second. Davy took two languid steps forward without even raising his fists. The officer leapt forward and punched towards Davy's face, but Davy had already ducked to the side so there was nothing to hit. The officer's own weight propelled him into the rail. And as soon as he turned around, Davy's right fist connected perfectly with his jaw. And he was down.

Davy turned to Jimmy and took back his jacket. 'Get him a bucket of water will you, Jimmy?' and then, turning to the small crowd, 'Now clear off, everyone, back to your stations.'

The atmosphere in the officers' quarters hadn't been good after that. Added to which the American woman had got wind of the fight and had assumed it was over her. And better still that the object of her affections had won. Even now, Davy groaned inwardly to think of it. Perhaps the chief officer had been right. He had been a cad; was still a cad. He hoped that the American woman had got married quickly after that. There was a good chance that the newly married couple's firstborn would bear a strange resemblance to a swarthy Welsh merchant sailor.

'Well, Davies,' interrupted Stewart, bringing Davy and his thoughts back to the quayside in Valparaiso, 'I must leave for my dinner. I'll meet you at the *Compañía* office tomorrow morning, all being well.'

One of the crew appeared with the captain's trunk and within moments two harbour boys came scrabbling up the gangway and carried it away in the direction of the town, the captain shouting Spanish expletives after them and reminding them to be careful with the contents.

'Oh, I nearly forgot,' Stewart turned and shouted back at Davy, 'I may have some news for you tomorrow, so don't be late!'

Davy laughed and raised his hand to show that he had heard. He laughed because Stewart was always up to something, some extra cargo here and there for somebody-or-other followed by the mysterious appearance of some unmarked wooden cases. He also laughed because Stewart knew full well that Davy had never been late for anything in his life. Davy watched them weave their way through the crowds and piles of cargo until they disappeared into the narrow streets beyond.

I feel tired, he thought. Then, as he gazed at the teeming crowds on the dockside, smiled to think what the captain would say. 'You dog, Davies, no wonder you're shattered, burning the candle at both ends.' But there was more to it than that. Perhaps the world of steam was too easy. Were the dangers at sea fewer? The ships safer? Perhaps he was weary of routine? La Serena on a Monday, Pisagua on a Wednesday, Viña del Mar on Friday with an occasional extended trip to Liverpool. Then back again. Normally he would be eager to get to the English Club, or maybe a concert at the hall, but not this evening. He turned and faced the open sea. The sun was sinking gently in a cloudless sky. There would be a beautiful sunset, just like the sunset over Cardigan Bay.

He felt his stomach twist and, for the first time in a long while, he wondered whether he actually missed the place he still called home. For so long he had forced himself not to think of it, in case the possibility of jumping ship at some cross-channel port should seem too easy. Over time, thoughts of home had become less frequent and less troublesome. *Hiraeth*. It was not something he had found a word for in English, or Spanish for that matter. Was that what troubled him, unexpectedly, after all these years?

He shook himself back to the present. The crowds on the harbourside were beginning to disperse. Everywhere he looked there were people on the move, carrying parcels or pushing trolleys with trunks. Women with beautiful hats climbed into carriages, children in rags begged for something to carry so that they could earn a few *centavos*.

He was about to turn back to his cabin when he caught the flash of bright blue silk moving swiftly through the crowd. The colour of cornflowers, thought Davy, and then immediately, as if he was sat on his shoulder, Captain Stewart's voice in his ear, 'At it again, Davies?' The glimmer of blue disappeared and then appeared again as it wove its way towards the harbour, vanishing once more behind two stacks of cargo covered in tarpaulin. This time, it didn't re-appear immediately. Two skinny Chilean children, a girl and a boy, ran up towards the stack and stopped abruptly as if they were talking to someone. They seemed pleased and happy, and the girl appeared to have a basket in her hands. They turned and started to make their way along the harbour towards the Almendral, the poor part of town where many of the unskilled dock workers and sailors lived. Suddenly, the children stopped again and turned back to the person who had given them the basket as if they had been called. They smiled and waved excitedly then turned again, making their way through the crowd. As they ran towards the far side of the harbour, through the carts and the crowds, the blue silk stepped forward from behind the stack of cargo and Davy saw her clearly.

Nothing about her was remarkable. Her build was slim. She was of average height with dark hair. Apart from the vibrant blue of her skirt, her clothes were plain and unadorned with no feathers or glittering gemstones anywhere in sight. She wore a close-fitting, plain black hat. She was not a young woman, nor an old woman, neither beautiful nor unattractive. She stood motionless, gazing after the two children walking away into the distance. Davy watched her. All the sounds and movements of the harbour faded away. She was so perfectly still, Davy thought, that she could be posing for a portrait, waiting for an unseen photographer to tell her that her image had finally been preserved for ever on his camera's glass plate.

While Davy watched the woman, a hunched man drove past with a cart full of noisy chickens in wire boxes. Three Chilean stevedores, bare to the waist, pushed a squeaking trolley piled high with sacks of flour. Two young lads rolling barrels of vinegar made their way towards a waiting cart. A woman selling apples passed. Two young women with hard faces sauntered along arm in arm, scanning the harbour. They stopped to look at Davy and spoke to each other as if sharing a secret. The taller one threw back her hair self-consciously and brought her hand to her hip as if in a challenge, thrusting out her ample chest.

But Davy took no notice. On other occasions he might have looked at the girls, might even have tipped his cap at them if no one was watching. Just to be gentlemanly. But other than that he would have thought that they were too young and desperate for money, and that somewhere further down the harbour they were sure to find someone more appropriate who would take them up on their offer. The taller girl's countenance changed. Frustrated by his disinterest, she sneered at him and pulled her companion away with her and along the harbour.

The woman in the blue skirt had watched the children weave their way through the crowds all the way to the Almendral where they disappeared into its narrow streets. Davy watched her as she dipped her head, and he thought he saw her sigh. Then, as if she had sensed his eyes on her, she turned in one movement and looked directly at him. Instinctively Davy stepped back into the shadow of the upper deck, feeling suddenly embarrassed. She turned and moved off along the harbour, her back turned towards him now, making her way towards the narrow streets of the town just as Captain Stewart had done earlier.

Davy felt strangely wrong-footed. He felt as if he had intruded on something but without knowing quite what. He wanted to run after the woman and explain. *Explain what?* You're more than weary, he told himself. You need a good bottle of wine, perhaps two. He watched the flash of blue as it weaved its way through the crowd until it finally disappeared.

CHAPTER 7

Mrs Agnes Ebrington was as ebullient as ever. Everything was larger, noisier and more colourful in Mrs Ebrington's world.

'Oh, Captain Davies, home at last from those vicious seas! Come, let me take your coat. Miriam! Come and help Captain Davies with his things.' Davy already felt a little deafened by her enthusiasm. 'Oh, it's so good to have you back, dear Captain Davies. You don't mind me calling you 'captain' do you, Captain? I know you're not actually a captain yet even though you have your colours, as it were, but it's only a matter of time. And what I mean is, you've passed as a captain, which is the main thing isn't it? Miriam!'

Miriam appeared sheepishly from the scullery.

'Miriam, I didn't save you from that awful orphanage just so that you could stand around looking decorative. Please take Captain Davies' coat. And where's Peter, to help carry the trunk? Peter!'

Miriam seemed totally unperturbed by the woman's shouting and smiled shyly as she took Davy's coat.

'Mrs Ebrington, really, I must insist, I'm perfectly capable,' said Davy.

'Nonsense. Peter! Where is that boy? Miriam, go and fetch Peter! Why is it that when guests arrive everyone seems to disappear? You know, Captain Davies, between you and me, I have half a mind to turn them both back out on to the streets. They really have no idea how lucky they are. Please have some tea – it's already prepared in the parlour and I've made some fruitcake especially.'

Davy found himself wishing he was rated boy once more, back on the *Royal Dane*, battling with the mainsail in a howling gale. He mustered all his charm and put a gentle hand on her elbow, drawing her close.

'Please, wonderful Mrs Ebrington,' he lowered his face close to hers and blinked his dark eyelashes at her earnestly. 'You must excuse me. We sailed through an appalling storm last night and I must just put my head down for a few moments. I shall be with you directly.'

Davy could tell that Mrs Ebrington was making a hundred and one small calculations in her head. *Wonderful. I'm wonderful. That's excellent. Storm? How odd. We've had no bad weather. Fruitcake will dry out while he's having a nap. Lord, he has such nice eyes. But where's Peter? And why is Miriam just standing there?*

Davy made it safely to his room. He took off his shoes and lay carefully on the bed. Almost immediately he could feel himself drifting off to sleep. He was on the topsail yards, his hands freezing cold, struggling to reef the sail. Mrs Ebrington was telling him to hurry up otherwise they would all drown. Now the sails were made of silk, blue silk, billowing around him. He was falling, falling, about to hit the deck and he jolted awake briefly.

He was so tired. And there was something more. He realised that the room was moving. The ceiling was moving. In fact everything was moving independently of everything else. He didn't feel well.

'I'm afraid Mr Davies won't be going anywhere for some time.'

Davy realised that the elderly man's voice was talking about him. He was aware of a shocked response to this statement and then came Mrs Ebrington's distressed reply. 'Oh, Doctor Edwards, is it ...?'

'Marsh fever, or malaria as people like to call it these days. Mr Davies has been bitten by one of the buggers.'

Mrs Ebrington gasped in alarm.

'Forgive me. By a mosquito. One of the *Culicidae*. Fascinating insects. They carry the infection, it seems. Not proven yet, of course. Amazing proboscis if you'd ever like to take a look at one under my microscope some time.'

Mrs Ebrington gasped again.

'No, of course not,' said the doctor. 'Probably bitten in Panama. Nasty place. Rest and quinine! Have Peter collect it from my house, if you would? Mr Davies has a strong constitution. He's sure to get better. These sailors are never completely cured, of course.'

Davy heard the metal clasp of the doctor's bag snap shut and tried opening his eyes to respond.

'There, there, Captain Davies, you rest now,' said Mrs Ebrington, patting his shoulder as if he was an ailing dog. 'We'll get you better in no time.'

The following day, Agnes Ebrington was allowing herself five minutes' peace and quiet in her private sitting room just behind the parlour when Miriam rushed in.

'Captain Davies is shouting, ma'am. You must come quickly!'

Mrs Ebrington glanced longingly at the fruitcake and the freshly poured tea, but made her way up the stairs, lifting her black woollen skirts well clear of her feet. When she entered the room, she was shocked to find Davy naked and out of bed, spinning aimlessly around the room, frantically looking for clothes.

'Where's my uniform?' he wailed, half crying, his shoulders rounding forward with exhaustion. 'I need my uniform. I haven't told the skipper where I am. I need to go!' he cried again, leaning his hands on his knees. 'They'll leave without me, I have to send a message!'

Mrs Ebrington felt ill-equipped to deal with the situation. She was no nurse and wasn't sure how to respond. She looked at Davy. He was a strong man, with broad shoulders and every ounce of him seemed to be made of muscle. He could swipe her away like a fly if he chose. Not a bit like Mr Ebrington had been. In fact, without his clothes on Captain Davies looked much more like one of those Greek statues she had seen in London's British Museum than any of the men she had ever known.

'Oh, my dear, we've already sent word to Captain Stewart. The ship is perfectly fine. You must rest and get some...'

'No! No, No! You don't understand. There's a fire. I have to get the horses. They're not listening to anyone else. They only listen to me! I must get back. Please get me my clothes!' he turned to her, half-snarling this time, and she stepped back in alarm. Davy fell to his knees on the floor. 'Please, I'm so sorry, Mrs Ebrington, but I need to go with the ship. It's all my fault.' He put his head on the floor and wept.

Mrs Ebrington stepped back on to the landing and called down the stairs without taking her eyes off Davy. 'Miriam! Run for the doctor this instant. Tell him Captain Davies is very ill indeed. He must come back at once!'

She moved forward again, and without drawing attention to herself, reached around for the key. She took it out and then replaced it on her side of the door. She closed it quietly and locked it, hoping that Davy hadn't heard. Out of the landing window she could see that it was another beautiful day with not a cloud in sight. There were no fires and no storms, and no anxious horses anywhere to be seen. He was certainly delirious, that much was sure.

When Mrs Ebrington opened the front door, she found it hard to hide her frustration.

'I was expecting Doctor Edwards.'

'Doctor Edwards is attending to casualties at a railroad accident. He asked me to come instead.'

The woman looked at Mrs Ebrington with a serious and determined expression. She seemed to be suggesting that this was as much explanation as the landlady needed. But Mrs Ebrington didn't like strangers in the house, and was about to insist that she would only allow Dr Edwards to look at her patient when the woman added, almost apologetically, 'I'm Estella, his daughter.' When Mrs Ebrington still didn't move aside she added, 'I am training to be a doctor.'

Mrs Ebrington eventually stepped back into the shadow of the hallway and made way for the woman. Rather than lead her up the stairs Mrs Ebrington motioned for her to go first so that she could have a good look at her. She was somewhere in her thirties, slim, agile and rather proud. Her clothes were plain but of suspiciously good quality. Doctor Edwards indulges his daughter, thought Agnes, noting the trademark tailoring of Monsieur Charbonneau. Her clothes certainly did not look like those of a nurse. Under the black bonnet, her dark hair was tied in a simple knot at her nape.

Just as the women reached the landing there came a terrible shout, 'There's no more water!' followed by quiet sobs.

Mrs Ebrington went to unlock the door but before doing so turned back to Estella. 'He is a strong man, Miss Edwards, take care.'

'Mrs Taylor.' Estella corrected her with emphasis. 'Mrs Estella Ignarra Taylor.' Clearly, now was not the time to talk about family ties and relationships, and before Mrs Ebrington could make any comment Estella had closed the door behind her.

She had a vague recollection that Dr Edwards' wife had been a Spanish woman so the baptismal names were not a surprise. But Taylor? What kind of man lets his wife become a doctor? He can't be much of a husband, thought Agnes Ebrington as she descended the stairs. *Albert would never have allowed it, what with all these strange foreign ailments about the place.*

Inside, the room was hot and stuffy. Estella went straight to the bay windows and opened the sash panes on all sides as far as they would go. Then she closed the curtains to keep out the sunlight. Although the other side of the room was facing away from the sun, she did the same there too, opening the windows to let in what breeze there was. The room felt immediately cooler.

Davies was still crouched on the floor over his knees, his forehead on the rug, sobbing quietly. She took off her short cape and sat on the corner of the bed wondering how best to approach him. His breathing had calmed, and she wondered whether in fact he had fallen asleep. Then, very slowly, he turned his head sideways, laying his cheek on the floor.

'Blue skirt,' he whispered.

Estella looked down. It had been a very long day, and she had not given a moment's thought to the colour of her skirt.

'Yes, blue skirt,' she replied. He closed his eyes.

'Please come back to bed,' she ventured, 'so that you can get better.'

'Blue skirt in the harbour,' he whispered again, and then his shoulders shook. She couldn't tell whether he was laughing or crying. 'Blue skirt with a basket.'

This time it dawned on her that she had seen him before, the previous afternoon. He was the officer with the lady in the pink hat. She had seen him lead the woman down the gangway with a look of easy triumph. And she had also seen the look on the woman's face as she sauntered towards her on the harbour followed by her minions. Her bustled swagger told its own story. And then later Estella had noticed him staring at her from the ship's rail, probably wondering how Mother Nature could have produced such different female forms, such extremes of plainness and beauty.

Thinking of these things, Estella resented being at Mrs Ebrington's fussy house when she could be helping any number of other deserving cases. *Where is your pink-hatted woman now? Too grand to mop your brow?* Irritated, she undid the ribbon of her bonnet. 'Come, Mr Davies, I don't have all day.'

For the fourth day in a row Estella had called to check on her patient. The fever had subsided and returned several times. On the second day she had thought he was dying. He had sweated and shivered in such quick succession that she wondered how his body could tolerate such physical tempests. One moment he seemed completely lucid, then the next he would talk of strange people and events that could not possibly be true. Flying boats, dolls in fires, horses that spoke strange Celtic languages. He had talked of someone called Elen, and every time he said the name his body would be convulsed with grief.

'I'm a murderer!' he had gasped, grabbing her hands.

And each time Estella prised his fingers away and gently mopped his brow.

'It's the fever talking.'

On the third day he had climbed out of bed and swore that he would return to the ship no matter what. There was no need to restrain him. By the time he found a shirt in the wardrobe and put on his socks and shoes he was bathed in sweat.

She had looked at him with a mixture of sympathy and mirth before commenting 'The ladies along the Grand Avenue might take exception to your rather informal attire.'

Davy looked down to see shirt, calico drawers, socks and shoes but no trousers. He sighed and sat back heavily on the bed.

'You're right. I'm not fit to go anywhere.'

Today when she arrived he was fast asleep. This was a small indication that he might be getting better, and by rights she should have been content to leave him sleeping and walk on to see her next patient. But few people knew she was here. She had brought two completely different books with her, *The Sixteen Principal Homeopathic Medicines* and the *Ingoldsby Legends*. The quiet room offered a serenity and escape that was hard to find elsewhere.

The evening was beginning to close in, and with the curtains drawn both sides of the room it was getting more difficult to see the words. She looked at him. The brow which had been furrowed with pain and distress was smooth now, the skin less translucent. The linen sheets she had pulled firmly across his chest were still unruffled.

Gently she placed the ribbon across the open page then closed the book, placing it on the mahogany chest to her side. Gathering her skirt towards her so that she wouldn't make a noise, she tiptoed slowly across the room. A beautiful cool breeze came through the window, a breeze that perhaps had skimmed the ocean waves all the way from Australia or New Zealand. She held the curtain aside and felt it caress her face, the fragrance of orange blossom close by mixing with the distant salty sea. She breathed in deeply and gazed out over the rooftops of Valparaiso. In the distance the Pacific glistened like a bed of jewels. It struck her how different was the landscape of her mind, not still and serene with distinct and exquisite pinnacles of inspiration like the horizon, but rather a noisy and crowded place like the lightning-damaged tree on the slopes of the Intendencia, its branches black with giant petrels.

'Oh, don't be so silly, Estella,' she heard her mother's cold and haughty voice in her head again after all these years. 'You're always so dramatic.'

And with that piercing memory, the dazzling sea, which had seemed briefly so magical, was once again just a sea, the rooftops and chimneys just houses, and the blossom just a common plant. She closed her eyes and breathed as deeply and quietly as she could. Even now, ten years after her death, her mother still had the ability to reduce the joy and wonder of the world to mere mechanics and mathematics. The absolute need to be sensible.

Estella had been motionless for a while when his voice broke across her thoughts.

'You've been very kind,' she heard him say, his voice surprisingly steady.

She was startled and half-turned to face him, until she realised that tears had been streaming down her face. Turning quickly back to the window, she wiped her cheeks roughly with the back of her hand and fussed with the edges of the curtain.

'I didn't want to wake you, Mr Davies. I …' And needing a reason to stay there a little longer, she leaned in to the window and tried to push the sash pane further up. 'Perhaps we should have some more fresh air?'

The jammed window, after some pushing and tugging, sprang upwards at speed with an awful screech and the curtains were now billowing around her. With dismay, she realised that she would now have to close the window, but the lower edge had flown totally out of reach. She stood on the tips of her toes. Oh, this is so idiotic, she thought. Why do I have to make such a spectacle? With a hop she managed to catch on to the frame briefly and pull it down to an acceptable height.

'That's better,' she said, stepping back, hoping that she hadn't caused too much hilarity, and pulled the curtain which had billowed around the dressing table back in its place. Then came the unexpected sound of sliding followed by an awful crash and water everywhere. The washbasin. She had forgotten all about the washbasin, and now it was in tiny jagged pieces all over the floor. The pieces looked expensive. She groaned. A family treasure no doubt.

There was a loud knock on the door and Mrs Ebrington burst in.

'My goodness, what is going on? Are you all right, Mrs Taylor?'

'Yes, yes,' Estella apologised crouching down on her hands and knees between the puddles and broken crockery.

Mrs Ebrington turned pale. 'Oh, the *Meissen,*' she exclaimed flatly and then tried to make light of it. 'It's really nothing – just an old wedding present. From an ageing aunt. Quite wealthy. But really not fashionable any more … the washbasin, I mean to say, not the aunt. The aunt is dead, of course. Bless her soul. Please don't upset yourself. Really. Miriam!' she screeched at the top of her voice and then remembered about the invalid close by. 'Oh, Captain Davies, I'm terribly sorry. How thoughtless. But you're looking better, I see.'

Miriam arrived with eyes like saucers, then went away again under orders to get the bucket and mop. Then after some more shouting Peter arrived carrying the ash bucket to take away the broken crockery. And every time Mrs Ebrington said, 'Don't upset yourself, dear,' the tears came brimming to Estella's eyes again. What she really wanted to say was, 'I'm not upset about the washbasin. It's my life that upsets me!'

'There, now!' Mrs Ebrington stood still for a moment and stopped swirling around. 'Everything is ship shape. Oh, Captain Davies! Ship shape!

Do you see? How wonderful! What a wealth of poetry the sea has taught us. Let me make you both some tea. A cup of tea will solve most things.'

Mrs Ebrington could be heard shooing Peter and Miriam down the stairs in front of her and once again the room was still.

'That was quite eventful,' said Davy, smiling.

Estella turned back to the window again and pulled the curtains here and there in an attempt to make everything neat. But really she was wishing that the fresh tears, which were perched precariously on her lower lids, would retreat to where they had come from. If only she could have another moment to compose herself.

'I'd like to sit up. Would you mind?' she heard him say.

'Of course,' Estella walked towards his bed and, trying not to look him in the face, rearranged the sheets and covers around him. She propped the pillows behind him then hesitated. The skin on his back was smooth and surprisingly olive coloured, but stretching from his right shoulder diagonally across his back was a collection of deep red scars, as orderly as a series of train tracks. How could she not have noticed them before?

'My old war wounds,' he turned to her, sensing her gaze.

'Oh, I'm sorry, forgive me.'

'I was quite young. Probably deserved them in hindsight,' he smiled and pulled the sheet to his chest. Even the effort of sitting up had exhausted him and he leaned his head back on the pillows closing his eyes. Estella sat down in her chair again; now that he was awake, it seemed a little too close to the side of his bed. He had incredibly dark hair and eyebrows for an Englishman, she thought, with only a very few grey hairs here and there. Under normal circumstances she would say he was swarthy, almost Spanish-looking. But there was little natural colour in his cheeks, and where he had caught the sun he looked strangely yellow and waxy. Tiny beads of perspiration glistened on his forehead.

He opened his eyes and smiled at her again.

'I fell asleep on the watch. That was a cardinal sin, of course. Especially on the *Kilvey*. The captain was a sadist from Bethesda. He came from this big chapel-going family who thought they were all saints. We hated him.'

Estella was about to tell him that he should stop talking and get some rest when, without opening his eyes this time, he said,

'I think my mother had that book, years ago.'

Estella realised that he must have noticed her copy of the *Legends*.

'Oh, my mother wouldn't approve of me reading this,' she replied, moving her chair back a little while his eyes were still closed.

'Do you care what your mother thinks?' he smiled.

'How are you feeling?' she looked at him intently, changing the subject.

He opened his eyes and returned her gaze with a weak smile.

'Fabulous.'

The door burst open and Miriam arrived with a tray of tea, which she placed nervously on the little black lacquer table.

'Oh, Miriam, for goodness' sake, not there!' said Mrs Ebrington, following Miriam with a plate of cake. As deftly as an expert magician, she produced a folding table from the corner and placed it between the bed and Estella. 'There, that's better, otherwise we will have rings and patches and goodness knows what on our furniture.' She turned to leave but then stopped. 'Ah, I nearly forgot. Mrs Taylor, a telegram for you.'

Mrs Ebrington handed over the slip of paper and waited for a moment. But Estella put the telegram straight in her pocket and began pouring the tea.

'Thank you, Mrs Ebrington. That's very kind.'

Mrs Ebrington paused for a moment as if preparing to say something, but reconsidered and left the room.

Then came the questions:

'How long have I been ill?'

'Have you been here all the time?'

'Where is the ship now?'

'Why did you stay?'

'Have I been a good patient?'

'No!' She burst out laughing, 'you've been a hopeless patient! All these questions!'

Davy set his cup down a little quickly and there was a clash of china. No more broken ceramics, please, thought Estella.

'Really? I'm so sorry. Please forgive me. I hope I didn't offend … my language …'

'You were delirious. I learned some new words.'

He cringed and bowed his head.

'And some new songs …' added Estella.

'Not the one about the about the … you know?'

She smiled in agreement.

He groaned and sank further into the bed.

'I'm teasing,' she added.

'No. I think you're telling the truth but you're too polite to say otherwise. I will get the full story out of Mrs E in due course, one way or another. Bribery. Promises of oak matured port, snippets of naval gossip.'

Davy took a sip of tea and returned the cup to its saucer, but with difficulty, Estella noticed. His hand shook. Looking at him lying there, cradled by the white pillows, holding his teacup tenderly with both hands as if it were a holy relic, two visions came back to her: a pink hat and a telegram. Oddly deflated by these thoughts she set down her own teacup and saucer especially gently.

'I'm afraid I have to go, Mr Davies.'

'You've hardly drunk your tea. Please call me David by the way. Do you always put telegrams in your pocket without looking at them?'

'Yes.'

'Bad news?'

She wasn't sure and failed to reply.

'Will you be back tomorrow?'

'No. I think you are on the sure road to recovery, in my professional opinion. Mrs Ebrington is very capable. Besides, she is very fond of you. She won't neglect you. I might call in to see you in a week or so to see how you are getting on.'

'A week!' gasped Davy, then added quickly, 'I can't be ill for another week!'

Davy groaned as he placed his cup and saucer back on the tray and watched her as she gathered her shawl and book. She opened the door to leave.

'Estella?' he said, and it stopped her in her tracks. It was a long time since anyone but her father had called her by her first name. And she realised that he had the faintest trace of an accent, something she hadn't noticed before.

'You mustn't worry about the bowl. It was quite ghastly. Really. I will get Mrs E a fine replacement. Something oriental, perhaps?'

Estella smiled and closed the door behind her.

Mrs Ebrington was sitting in the parlour as Estella descended into the hall but rather than call for Miriam, she rushed out to open the door for Estella herself.

'Where is he from? Originally? Mr Davies?' asked Estella as she put on her lace gloves.

'Oh, from England, or rather Wales I should say. Somewhere on the coast I think I've heard him say.' But before Mrs Ebrington could ask Estella a million questions about how long he would need to stay in bed, or what he should eat or how warm he should be kept, Estella had escaped through the front door and made her way down the street.

Estella decided not to go home. Instead, she turned left on the Cerro Alegre and carried on up the hill towards Plaza Victoria. By the time she reached the Neptune fountain the sun was setting peacefully over the sea. The streets were empty although here and there, as she passed the tall houses, she heard snippets of conversation or gentle laughter. Now that it was getting late she could feel the sandstone around the fountain releasing the day's warmth, and she chose a place that was free of spills and splashes to sit down. She smoothed the folds of her skirt and thought that she would have to reach into her pocket at some point to read the telegram. Not that she needed to read it to know who had sent it or what it would say. Her stomach lurched and twisted inside her but when two Chilean women passed her, a mother and a daughter arm in arm, she smiled sweetly. *A married woman who has no need of a chaperone*, they would have thought as the dark lace of their headgear fell over their eyes once more.

Estella closed her eyes and listened to the sound of the trickling water, hypnotic as it fell like notes of music into a singing pool. Somewhere on the breeze there was the smell of jasmine. Slowly she reached into her pocket and took out the telegram. She slid her thumb under the closed fold and loosened it until it opened before her.

Returning on Tuesday p.m. S.S. Aconcagua Stop Will stay 1 week Stop Want to see Tyler Williams-Edwards at the Club Stop Please arrange Stop Your darling husband Laurence.

Your darling husband. She refolded the telegram and looked across the jagged rooftop skyline towards the sea. Here and there tall palms caught the gentlest of breezes and shone like glass shards. She looked at it all as if it was a gallery painting. She was a spectator. *All this light and it stops just here.* She raised her hand and stretched it in front of her. *This is how far it comes and no further. I am a watcher in a dark gallery.*

She looked at her outstretched hand with its single gold band. Her hand quivered. In a doorway ahead of her, a young boy appeared. He gazed at her with suspicious eyes. She smiled and rose to her feet and made her way home. *A week to prepare and a week to endure.* She would need to air the rooms, arrange his appointments, cancel her appointments, engage the occasional staff, draw up menus, arrange deliveries. The proper chores of a dutiful wife.

The following day Estella had just left the tailor's shop when she heard footsteps running up the street. She turned to see Peter, red faced and wheezing. The boy seemed to have run halfway around Valparaiso; he was bathed in sweat and his shirt was mottled with dark patches.

'Oh, *Señora* … I went to your house … and then to your father's house but you weren't there either and nobody knew where you were …'

'For goodness' sake, what is it?' asked Estella, as the boy doubled over to catch his breath.

'It's the *Capitán*. *Señora* Ebrington says please come at once … she says he is dying.'

Dying? Estella looked at her basket of purchases. She could tell Peter to find the German doctor in Cerro Alegre or the nurse high on the hill in Higueras. There was too much to do for her to tend to a sick man today.

Peter stood upright again and grabbed her arm.

'Please, Doctor Taylor,' the boy pleaded, tugging at her to follow him. Estella looked at the boy's face, and for the first time it occurred to her that he was insisting, not only out of duty to Mrs Ebrington, but out of fondness for the sick man. She took the basket from her arm and passed it to Peter.

'Very well. Take the basket to my house. Walk. Don't run. Leave it there and then go to my father's house, Dr Edwards's house, and ask for quinine. Say I have asked and that it is for Mr Davies. And bring it to Mrs Ebrington's house.'

Peter took the basket eagerly and ran off towards her house.

'Peter, walk!' she shouted after him, and when he turned she added more gently, 'we don't want you to be ill too. Besides, you did well to find me.'

The boy smiled, but he looked terrified, as if some horrible event was about to turn him to stone.

'Go now and I'll see you at the house. I am sure everything will be fine.'

Estella walked at first. Then, when Peter was out of sight, she began to run. Some people she knew were out for a promenade.

'Estella, what's up?' they shouted after her, but she didn't stop. She had never run so far in her life.

When she reached Myrtle Villa, Estella realised that her hands and legs were shaking uncontrollably. Miriam opened the door, and as she walked into the hall she could see Mrs Ebrington sitting at the parlour table with her face in her hands. Agnes Ebrington was in tears and couldn't speak, but just motioned for Estella to go upstairs with a vague wave. Miriam ran ahead of her and opened the bedroom door. Estella's heart sank. Davy's body seemed convulsed with pain. The sheets and blankets were in disarray, tangled around his twisted body. He was turned towards the wall but his body was completely still.

He is already dead.

But when she came closer she saw the sweat glistening on his scarred back.

'Mr Davies? David?' she touched him on the shoulder and he moaned quietly.

He turned towards her and there was a brief smile of recognition.

Then, 'I'm going to be sick.'

She had time to grab a bowl from the chest of drawers, and think *oh, not another Meissen* when he was violently ill. She held his forehead while his body folded into itself with pain.

Miriam brought a clean bowl but only as far as the door.

'Bring it here, there's a good girl. Haven't you seen someone being sick before? Now put the cloth over this and take it away.' The girl grimaced and left the room gingerly.

'I'm so sorry,' he groaned in a lucid moment, 'I'm a bad patient.'

'That's true,' she smiled and wiped his face and neck with a damp cloth.

He was the colour of ash.

'Am I going to die?'

'I don't think so.'

'Oh. That's not very inspiring.'

He was sick again and grasped her arm as he was thrown forward into the bowl. She held his forehead firmly and thought, *in truth, I have no idea.*

Davy was delirious again. He was on a ship and the ship was in a barn. Sea, waves and straw were all around. The waves crashed in on him and the captain, who was not familiar, was shouting at the top of his voice through the storm, 'Where's north?'

'I don't know!' Davy wailed and picked up a sodden copy of his navigation book from the water.

'You must find north!'

Davy looked up, searching for the patterns in the stars. At first he thought they were hidden behind thick blankets of cloud, but the shapes came together to make the beams of a barn, grey and tightly knitted. There were only tiny chinks of sky.

'Where's your compass, you stupid boy!'

He looked down at the compass hands turning wildly. A wave came crashing over him and the brass dial slipped from his hands and into the green water.

'Oh, that's it! It's all up now,' came another voice, 'All up lad, unless you can find North Star. Or South Star? Or any fixed, bloody star!'

Davy woke, but only briefly. Estella was sitting at the foot of the bed, reading. Turned a little away from him, she was concentrating intently. He stayed very still so that she would not guess he was awake. Her long dark hair was pulled back and pinned high on her head in three neat loops, a fashion he had seen amongst some Chilean women. A simple tortoiseshell comb held the fine hair at the back of her head but some had escaped. Her plain navy dress had a high collar edged with a tiny white ruffle. Every now and again she frowned with concentration, and as her hands moved noiselessly over the pages the tiny red ruby on the end of her earring quivered.

'There she is!' he gasped out loud, so that Estella was startled and looked up from her work.

Embarrassed by his own delirium, he closed his eyes and in the infinitesimal space between wakefulness and fitful sleep he felt the utterly foreign sensation of being happy.

CHAPTER 8

Agnes Ebrington's garden was a small corner of Heaven. At least, this is what she liked to think. Her husband had adored all manner of plants, particularly roses, and Agnes often had to reprimand him on his latest shipment of new varieties.

'My dear Albert? Where on earth are you going to plant them? There's no more room!'

They were usually shipped from Liverpool and had the most bizarre names: *Prince Camille de Rohan*, *Triomphe de L'Exposition* and *Rose du Roi à Fleurs Pourpres*. She had taken little more interest than that when Albert was alive, but after his death she had started reading his gardening books and learned all about the mysteries of pruning.

'Albert, what shall we do about this black spot? I really don't think this *Pompom Blanc Parfait* is happy against a north wall. Perhaps I'll ask Peter to move it? I know you like the pale pink against the acacia tree, but what do you think? And perhaps *William Lobb* needs a bit of a chop? He's always getting a bit big for his boots.'

The *snip, snip* of deadheading would accompany her questions, and Miriam and Peter had learned not to interrupt *La Señora* when she was talking to her plants.

'Perhaps she's going a bit funny in the head,' whispered Peter one day as he and Miriam hid behind the palm near the conservatory door.

'Not so funny that it's affecting my ears, young man,' said Agnes without so much as turning to look. 'Which means, I suppose, that you've finished your chores?'

Peter and Miriam grinned at each other and disappeared back into the house.

On that particular day Agnes Ebrington had just finished cutting out the old wood from an ageing sulphur-coloured yellow rose when Peter appeared with Davy leaning on his arm.

'Incredible, Mrs Ebrington! You are a horticultural genius! On top of all the other things we already knew you were. It's a perfect Eden.'

Agnes stood back momentarily and admired the tumbling roses, the neat beds, the paving edged with lavender and herbs, but she was much more excited to see Davy. She crossed the garden and helped him into a chair, arranging a tartan blanket over his knees.

'Dear Captain Davies! I can't tell you how glad we are that you're feeling better. I don't mind telling you, we were distraught. That day Peter went to fetch Mrs Taylor, I really thought you were dying. Particularly as you had been getting a little better. Fetch another cushion from the parlour, Peter dear,' said Mrs Ebrington. Then she sat down close to Davy and whispered quietly, 'Poor Peter was so upset. I can tell you. He went racing all over Valparaiso to find Mrs Taylor and couldn't find her anywhere. He went to her house, to her father's house, to the shops. When he got back here with the medication he was as white as the Rio Blanco, and you know that's not normal, with his colouring, as it were …'

Peter rushed back in with the cushion and placed it carefully behind Davy's back.

'Thank you, my dear,' said Mrs Ebrington, 'and Mrs Taylor wasn't much better herself when she arrived. She was a heap of nerves. It really isn't good for a woman to run that far in this climate. I thought I would need to fetch the smelling salts! She was shaking all over. Can you imagine! Trying to revive the doctor so that she can tend to the patient! I'm really not sure it's a profession for women. Not at all! But there we are. This is the modern world we live in.'

Agnes Ebrington paused and looked at Peter.

'My dear, go and ask Miriam to boil the kettle. I think Captain Davies is still looking rather pale, I must say. Let's make you a nice cup of tea.'

Peter went back into the house.

'I don't mind telling you, Captain Davies, Peter is very fond of you.'

With eyes a little brighter than usual, she stroked Davy's arm protectively and sighed.

Later that afternoon Mrs Ebrington went to visit friends and left Davy dozing in the dappled shade of the acacia tree. The sun as it crept across the sky was now warming his shoulder. He could smell the musky clove and lemon scent of the roses blending with the freshness of lavender. He could be dead, he thought. If he had caught malaria on the *Royal Dane* or the *Kilvey*, he would surely have died a miserable death in his lonely bunk without anyone's hand to hold.

In the distance he heard a loud knock on the door. Then, a few moments later, voices, Miriam's and that of a man. He was aware of someone's presence in the garden, and as he opened his eyes he heard a familiar voice.

'Dammit. We've woken him.' It was Stewart and he was armed with various items. 'There we are, young lady. We'll have some recuperative champagne to celebrate Mr Davies' return.'

Davy laughed.

'I didn't know I'd been anywhere.'

'You've been a long way away, from what I hear.'

Stewart fell into the chair next to him and looked at him very seriously.

'You've lost weight.'

'Quite probably.'

'And you're a very funny colour.'

'Thank you.'

'Apart from that, you look in excellent health.'

There was a very loud pop and a squeal from the kitchen. Miriam appeared with a tray laden with a two glasses of champagne and an open bottle.

'I'm afraid some of it escaped, Captain Stewart. I'm very sorry.'

Stewart picked up the bottle and assessed the remainder.

'Dear me,' he tutted playfully, 'The ability to open a bottle of champagne is one of life's most essential skills. I must have a word with Mrs Ebrington about the deficiencies of your upbringing.' Miriam rolled her eyes and made a quick exit.

Stewart passed a glass to Davy and leant forward excitedly.

'Now then! I have two pieces of very good news. I have found us a new second officer. I can't believe my luck. He's an excellent seaman. He has every qualification going, including a master's certificate. He's been with PSNC for a few years and we've poached him from them. But listen to this. Not only is he well qualified, but intelligent too! He reads! Not just any old rubbish, but the classics, Shakespeare, Milton ... you name it. He knows the works of artists. He can tell you the difference between a Rembrandt and a Titian ... I'm damned if I can ... music, architecture ... every subject you care to name. He is going to be a wonderful asset during those interminably long dinners. And all of these things wrapped up in the most amiable and easy character you could ever wish to meet!'

'What on earth is he doing in the *Compañia?*'

'Well, it gets better. He was born here, apparently, though he didn't say much about his family. They are clearly decent people. Business people, I would imagine. It matters not. Speaks fluent Spanish, obviously. And the best bit of all is that Wade on the *Aconcagua* is perfectly livid that I got to him first!'

'How did you find him?'

Stewart held a forefinger up to his nose. 'Never you mind, laddie. Never you mind.' The Scot in Stewart would always escape when he was excited. 'And it doesn't end there.'

'By God, I'll have to be ill more often.'

'We have an entirely new ship!'

This time, Davy really was amazed.

'Triple expansion engine, 2,700 tonnes, propeller propulsion, top speed 15 knots, soon to be on her way from Laird in Birkenhead with her very own team of crack English engineers. She will be the finest mailboat anywhere in South America.'

Davy knew that the fastest sailing ships in the world, the China tea clippers, could reach a top speed of 16 knots. But they were ocean-going racehorses and not passenger ships. They could not offer the comfort and elegance of a fast mailboat fitted out with comfortable cabins, saloons and promenades.

'Look here,' said Stewart, opening an envelope and taking out two photographs, one of the ship's exterior and the other showing a very grand saloon. He reached across and clinked his glass against Davy's. 'Cheers, my good man! To your continued good health and our glittering careers!'

Davy examined the photographs carefully. It was no small thing that Stewart had achieved; to be the captain of such a fine steamship which itself was part of a renowned company, one of the most successful shipping lines in the world.

'She will be yours Davy, when I retire. I'll see to it. It's high time you had a ship of your own and stopped playing second fiddle. There's only one small problem,' said Stewart, reaching for the bottle so that he could replenish their glasses, 'Walker isn't happy.'

'Wasn't it Walker's decision?'

'Not on this occasion.'

'How is that?'

Stewart emptied a second glass then sat forward and peered uncomfortably into the empty vessel. 'Well, on this occasion I had a little help from some of the Board members.'

Davy had heard many stories about Walker, about his petty vindictiveness and straightforward unpleasantness. It was said that he had been a sailor in his youth, but that his personal dalliance with the sea had been brief and undistinguished. Searching for another route to power, he had elbowed his way through the bustling subsidiary offices of Liverpool, until finally being appointed general manager at Valparaiso. A stunning promotion but, according to Stewart, the devil himself could not have been given a better testimonial; they were so keen to be rid of him.

'Will he cause problems?' Davy asked.

'Not immediately,' Stewart reached again for the champagne bottle. 'But he wants to see you.'

'Me?' Davy said, surprised, 'what could he possibly want with me?'

'When you're better of course.'

Davy looked again at the photographs. There was no mistaking that the *Imperial* was a fine ship, from her glinting brass candelabra to her pirouetting dining chairs. What would his father think if he saw her?

'It's a long way from the *Ellen* of Cardigan!' laughed Davy.

'Keep them,' said Stewart, getting to his feet and patting him firmly on the shoulder as he turned to leave. 'And what do you know? The chief engineer is Welsh too, so they tell me!'

After Stewart left, Davy felt stunned but exhilarated. A few weeks ago, he had been standing on the harbour in Valparaiso wondering why life had become so dull and easy, asking himself whether he should look for new challenges, perhaps even return to sail. Now he was about to become chief officer of a newer, larger, more powerful ship built by Laird Brothers of Birkenhead, a renowned company with a long and not altogether uncontroversial history. Laird had built the blockade-runners that ensured the cotton mills of England had not ground to a halt for want of American raw materials during the Civil War, a fact that the abolitionists conveniently forgot when they donned their crisp new shirts and pantaloons. Laird had even built two Confederacy warships, a fact that even fewer British people, particularly industrialists and politicians, liked to discuss in public.

Even as he looked at the photographs again and read the ship's name out loud, his thoughts wandered back over the previous weeks. A little more rest and he would be back to work. Whether he liked it or not, he was being propelled into the future. The world was constantly changing and evolving and he was lucky enough to play a part. Miriam came in to the garden and was about to take away Stewart's glass.

'Have you seen Mrs Taylor at all?' asked Davy, trying to sound as casual as possible.

'No, Mr Davies,' she answered, looking alarmed, 'are you feeling worse?'

A vague recollection of Miriam carrying covered bowls came back to him and he smiled apologetically.

'Oh, no. I'm feeling much better. I just wondered whether she had called?'

'Mrs Ebrington told me that Mr and Mrs Taylor are hosting an important dinner this evening. I think she is very busy. Some of the government ministers will be there. There is a rumour, maybe even the president himself.'

Davy thought Miriam had misunderstood his question and was talking of someone else.

'No, Mrs Taylor, the lady who looked after me when I was ill?'

Miriam blushed.

'Yes, she is the same. We only know one Mrs Taylor and she is Dr Edwards's daughter. She is training to be a doctor too. She is Mr Laurence Taylor's wife.'

Davy looked up at Miriam, wondering why that name should have any significance for him.

'Of Taylor Copper Mines,' Miriam added, disappearing back in to the house.

Suddenly, Mrs Ebrington's garden was transformed. Instead of roses and lavender, Davy could see thousands of workers with pickaxes and shovels, trainloads of copper ore being transported over barren plains, molten smelting ovens and pits of fire and smoke, Captain Stewart poring over his copy of *El Mercurio* and commenting on the progress of his 'Taylor Shares'.

CHAPTER 9

Davy looked down at the proposed itinerary for the *Imperial*'s first voyage. It was smartly printed with coloured inks on expensive paper. The company is doing well, he thought.

Itinerary. Steamer Imperial:

Day 1	Depart Cristobal, Peru.
	Arrive Balboa, Paita, Peru
Day 5	Eten
Day 6	Pacasmayo
Day 7	Salaverry, Callao
Day 8	Depart Callao
Day 9	Arrive Mollendo
Day 11	Arrive Arica, Chile
Day 12	Arrive Iquique
Day 13	Depart Iquique
Day 14	Arrive Antofagasta
Day 15	Arrive Coquimbo
Day 16	Arrive Valparaiso
Day 18	Depart Valparaiso
Day 20	Arrive Tomé
Day 20	Arrive Talcahuano
Day 21	Arrive Lota

Now that he was well again, Davy had been summoned to see Walker, the company manager. It was rare for staff of the *Compañia* to be called in front of him, even first officers. Walker usually only dealt with the captains and would channel all directives through them.

Davy arrived at the building and presented himself to a middle-aged man who was sitting in a tiny office near the entrance. The office was barely bigger than a broom cupboard, and although the man sidled out from behind his desk and came into the corridor, he merely pointed in the direction of the office and did not accompany Davy.

'Go as far as you can and it's on the right. Mahogany door. Make sure you knock first.'

Davy thanked the man, who was so pale and dusty that Davy wondered whether he had ever seen the light of day. In fact, he wondered whether he was actually a living person or some strange cupboard spirit.

Davy reached the mahogany door and knocked firmly. There was no reply, so he knocked again. There was an immediate bad-tempered response, although Davy could not hear the exact words. Davy turned the brass handle and an unexpectedly grand office opened out in front of him. Showy velvet curtains hung either side of the windows and an ostentatious desk had been placed at the very centre of the room. But Davy was struck by how little else there was. There were no pictures, no books; the desk was entirely absent of paperwork or any evidence of work in progress. A leather holder supporting sheets of blotting paper seemed to be totally free of marks or ink.

Davy had expected to move forward quickly to greet Walker and shake him by the hand, but the man was leaning back in his leather chair with both feet up on the desk, his legs crossed at the ankle, and holding a long cigar to his mouth. Davy paused, thinking that perhaps he had entered the room too soon or that he had misheard the directive to enter.

Wrong-footed, he mumbled an apology and turned towards the door.

'Mr Davies,' exclaimed Walker in a flat tone of voice devoid of any warmth. He had the high-pitched voice of a Liverpool boy, not that there was much of the boy left in him. He must have been at least sixty but he still had a full head of wiry hair. It was a strange shade and Davy guessed that from the nature of his skin and the amount of brown freckles on his face and neck he must once have been a vibrant redhead. Everything about him seemed to be the colour of a sharp and rusty nail.

'Mr Walker,' Davy replied.

'Close the door, sir,' said Walker, still with his feet on the desk.

Davy did as he was asked, wondering how he should react. When he turned back to Walker he noticed that he was leaning so far back in his chair that Davy could see the red hairs inside his nostrils. The feet stayed on the desk.

'It appears that Captain MacDougal Stewart,' Walker began, then stopped to smile at some private joke or other before carrying on, 'has arranged for you to join him as chief officer of the new *Imperial*.'

'Yes, sir,' replied Davy cautiously. Walker turned his head in surprise, like a chicken eyeing up some seed before giving it a good peck.

'Oh, so you are aware of this?' He smiled at Davy, but his eyes were cold and unfriendly.

'He may have mentioned it in passing … that he was going to make a request.'

'Ah, yes, that's it. A request. I had almost forgotten the word.' Walker brought the cigar back to his mouth and nodded, inhaling deeply. There was a long silence and clouds of smoke gathered around the man's head.

'The fine *Imperial*, the new crowning glory of the entire *Compañía* fleet, arrives next month.'

'Yes, sir. So I believe.'

'So you believe or so you know, Mr Davies?'

'So I've been told.'

Walker's mouth twisted into something halfway between a wince and a sneer. 'So you've been told.' Walker mulled over his words, then very slowly he took his feet off the desk and leaned forward to reach for the ashtray.

'Let me tell you something. Let me explain to you, Mr Davies, how this company works, under – how shall we say – *normal* conditions.' Walker spoke very slowly, as if explaining something to a child. 'The owners of the *Compañía* employ me to manage the company. Because of my experience, they delegate authority to me to make all decisions regarding the day-to-day running of this company. They permit me to use my own judgement as to who should be promoted ... or demoted. They require me to shield them from the petty details of daily business. Then they expect me to make the decisions. I listen to ... requests, as you call them. And I make my decisions.'

He brought the cigar to his mouth again and Davy noticed that his hand was shaking. But despite that, Walker looked down and smiled at another private joke.

'I am well aware of Captain Stewart's ...' he enunciated the words slowly and deliberately, 'connections.' Walker leaned forward and tapped his cigar until every loose flake of ash had fallen into the ashtray. 'And as it seems that, on this occasion, there has been no need for my involvement, I thought I would see for myself what kind of people we have in our employment.'

Davy felt deeply uncomfortable. Walker was examining him as if he was a new museum acquisition that had just been put on display in a glass case.

'I will be very happy to answer any questions you might have, Mr Walker,' said Davy, more to fill the uncomfortable silence than out of any genuine desire to help.

Walker looked down at the ashtray again and smiled to himself. 'Do you know how many years the *Compañía* has seen fit to employ me in this position, Mr Davies?'

A good long while by the look of you, thought Davy, and smiled inwardly at how Walker made his 'position' sound as if he had been elevated to the status of a Greek god.

'Your position as *Compañía* manager, sir?' asked Davy, suspecting that Walker's actual title probably sounded much more important and contained many more superlatives underlining his godly significance.

Walker's eyes narrowed. 'This company would not be where it is now without me, Mr Davies. Do you think the shareholders get up to anything useful with their time? They are all …' Walker paused and lowered his voice, '… imbeciles. They care about their profits and their reputations, nothing more. They don't care about your timetables or your crew or your wage packet.' Walker twisted his neck from side to side, as if his collar was too tight, and continued. 'They may,' he said, pausing to draw on his cigar, 'interfere when the fancy takes them, but they usually see sense. Eventually.'

Walker looked up and fixed Davy with a cold accusatory stare. Davy was sure that it was better for him not to make any kind of response at all so he waited, still on his feet, and tried to ensure that his face was as expressionless as possible.

An excruciating silence descended on the room. The conversation was clearly not going the way Walker had intended. He pushed the ashtray away from him and leaned back again in his chair. He brought his feet back up on to the desk, a little more agitated now.

'Are you a chapel man, Mr Davies?' asked Walker, with his head tilted strangely on one side. 'What I mean is … are you a Christian man?' Walker blew a huge puff of smoke into the air and waited for it to disperse a little.

Davy was about to ask Walker whether this was why he had brought him all the way to the offices, just to ask him this question. But as Davy opened his mouth, Walker broke across him.

'There is a growing laxity of standards, do you not think, amongst our employees these days? It seems to me a disgrace that so many of our captains and officers spend so much of their time whoring and drinking in the 'True Blue Saloon' or any of Valparaiso's other more dubious establishments. Do you not agree?' Walker turned his head again, the papery skin around his neck folding as he twisted his sour face towards Davy. 'Licentiousness, fornication, filth and degradation everywhere I turn. It sickens me to the very core; it disgusts me. There are no standards any more; there are no role models. Our captains are all as devious and depraved as each other. Liars and fornicators all!'

Davy wasn't sure whether this lecture required a response from him and, in any case, the last time he had opened his mouth to answer a question, he had been interrupted. Walker blew another cloud of smoke above his head then turned his icy attention back to Davy. The uneasy silence returned, but not for long.

'Well, I would expect some kind of response from a senior officer who is about to take on the role of chief officer on one of our most prestigious ships. Or have you turned into a fucking mute?'

The swearing was totally unexpected, and Davy was shocked into the sudden awareness that this was a genuinely nasty and vindictive man.

'Forgive my reticence, sir, but I have no idea what you're talking about. And furthermore, I'm not familiar with conducting conversations over the soles of people's shoes,' Davy answered.

Walker tossed his cigar into the ashtray in front of him but didn't raise his voice. 'You'll respond to me over whatever I choose, Mr Davies.'

My dead body was the first thought that came to Davy's head, and somehow the thought must have imprinted itself on to his face, because Walker shot to his feet and came around the desk towards him.

'For your insubordination, I'm cancelling all shore leave for the *Benalla's* crew until further orders.'

Davy couldn't help laughing at the archaic term, and wondered perhaps whether he had travelled back in time and was actually one of Horatio Nelson's crew.

'With all due respect, Mr Walker, shouldn't you be telling Captain Stewart this?' Davy knew he should add a formal 'sir', but couldn't quite bring himself to say the word. He looked across at the purple-faced man and was relieved to realise that, in a real fight, this man would not be standing for long. Unfortunately, this was a different kind of fight and not one that Davy was properly armed for.

'With all due respect, Mr Davies,' Walker spat in Davy's face, 'it appears that Captain Stewart is far too important to take directions from anyone any more.'

'I've always found him to be an excellent captain – decent, hardworking, and a perfect example to his crew.'

Walker could not contain himself any longer.

'Get out, you fucking filth. Clear out! You might have got yourself a new ship but I swear to God I'll get rid of you. You and your conniving, whoring captain and poxy crew! Get out!'

Davy said nothing, but left the room. He nearly closed the door behind him then it occurred to him that leaving the door ajar would irritate him further. Davy let go of the brass handle and walked briskly down the corridor. By the time he reached the far door he could hear Walker shouting,

'Shut the fucking door!'

The pale and dusty spirit emerged from his broom cupboard and gave Davy a wry smile.

'Problems?' the man asked.

Davy would have thought this a little impertinent coming from anyone else, but he felt a good deal of sympathy for this man who spent his days in a windowless cell.

'Yes. It seems that Mr Walker is not the omnipotent being he thought he was. He is a cog in the wheel after all, just like the rest of us. I don't think he likes it.'

The dusty man's face twisted into a smile. 'Oh dear,' he said, looking rather pleased, 'what a dreadful blow.'

More shouting could be heard from the room at the end of the corridor, including a man's name, which Davy took to be that of the cupboard spirit. The man shook Davy's hand warmly and retreated into his room, making a vague gesture around his ear. 'Been having terrible trouble with my hearing lately, yes, sir. Good day to you now.'

By the time Davy came out on to the street outside the company offices he was shaking. He was emerging from some hideous nightmare. A snivelling playground bully had been allowed to ascend through the ranks of an organisation and no one had seen fit to put him in his place. Ever. Or if they had tried, they had not succeeded. How was it possible? And what about the other man? What series of poor decisions or tricks of fate had led him to that miserable prison? No air, no light, no broad horizons? Dealing with the daily whims of a whingeing, petty tyrant. Davy had never felt happier to be returning to the harbour. Even the prospect of telling the lads about their cancelled shore leave could not dent his elation.

July 1890, Valparaiso harbour

Long before the *Imperial*'s arrival at Valparaiso, Davy had heard several reports of the ship's launch earlier that year. The weather in Birkenhead had apparently been unseasonably fine and a substantial crowd had gathered to witness the christening. The entire Laird family, including wives and children, had turned out for the event and Liverpool's most prominent newspapers had listed the attendance of an endless array of influential dignitaries.

That morning, from the deck of the *Benalla*, Davy looked across the harbour at a similar scene. Hundreds of people of all ages had turned out to inspect the *Compañía*'s brand new ship, a fine addition to their ever-expanding fleet. Davy's first sight of her had been the previous evening. Despite problems with the winches, all the *Benalla*'s cargo had finally been unloaded. But it had gone midnight and was much too late to return to Mrs Ebrington's, so Davy decided to stay on board. Just as he was about to turn in, he had heard, in the far distance, the deep hum of an unusually powerful engine coming in to port.

A mist was coming in from the sea, and for a long time Davy waited alone on deck, straining to see her outline in the darkness. As she came closer he could hear her speed reducing by degrees. She emerged from the mist, twinkling mast lights first then her clipper stem and bow. Davy could make out two decks, two slender funnels sloping backwards and three masts. She had arrived quietly, to very little fanfare and with the grace and elegance of a grand old sailing ship drawing in her canvas for the night. Davy was mesmerised.

Now, in daylight, as he looked across at her, he felt almost sorry. The *Compañía* had dressed her up in garish ribbons and flags as if she was about to enter a shire-horse contest. Hundreds of people milled around her decks and a band played enthusiastically at the harbourside.

'Come and meet the new lady,' said Stewart, emerging from below deck. They were both expected to attend the inauguration, and although Davy was looking forward to seeing the ship he was dreading the whole public ballyhoo. 'Wouldn't do to be late.'

Stewart and Davy made their way across the harbour, weaving their way through the crowds until they reached the *Imperial*'s gangway.

'Make way for the captain!' someone shouted above the commotion, and they were quickly ushered up a set of steps from the shade deck on to what Davy assumed must be the first-class passenger deck above.

'This way, sir,' said a smartly dressed steward, and before they knew it they had stepped through a door into a lavishly decorated first-class saloon. The room was full of carefully selected guests, including many of the company's major shareholders. There was an awkward hushed silence as if someone in the room had already begun speaking.

'Good morning, gentlemen! Or should I say afternoon?'

Davy looked to the front of the room and his heart sank – it was Walker. He was standing behind a lectern and had clearly begun addressing the room before they arrived.

'Ladies and gentlemen,' Walker continued, 'let me introduce you to Captain Colin MacDougal Stewart and his chief officer, Mr David Davies, soon to be in charge of this fine vessel.' Walker coughed and took a sip of water. 'As you can see,' he continued, 'the *Compañía* prides itself on its excellent time-keeping.' Walker coughed again and without looking up at the new guests continued with his address.

'I thought it was supposed to start at midday?' whispered Davy, as they took their seats at the back of the room.

'It was,' replied Stewart, taking an embossed invitation from his pocket and placing it discreetly in front of him on the table. Stewart whispered something to a neighbouring guest, who also extracted an invitation from his pocket. The man set it down on the table next to Stewart's and grimaced. The times printed on the invitations were clearly different, Stewart's a full half-hour later than that indicated on the other guest's card.

'How childish,' muttered Stewart, looking up at Walker.

'So, ladies and gentlemen, I would now like to pass you across to Mr Thomas Dewsbury, the *Compañía*'s agent at Birkenhead and our consulting engineer. He will no doubt illuminate us as to the ship's fascinating technical details.'

The man who stood up at the front of the room did not look in any way as if he relished the prospect of public speaking. Carefully, he took Walker's place at the lectern and thanked him for the introduction. Despite his apparent reluctance, however, the man spoke with a quiet authority and succeeded in making even the most obscure facts sound interesting.

He began by saying that the *Imperial* was very similar to, but of larger dimensions and more powerful than, the *Cachapoal* and the *Mapocho*, also constructed by Messrs Laird some years earlier. Both ships had built a name for themselves along the coast. He explained to the crowd that the *Imperial* was relatively unusual in that she had an elliptic stern, noting that in most respects this was superior to a square or round stern, unless the ship was exposed to a combat situation.

'Good job we're not going to war, then!' interjected Walker.

Mr Dewsbury smiled politely and continued.

'The *Imperial* is fitted with water ballast and has both steam windlass and steam steering gear, including six steam winches. She has a complete electric lighting installation and all the latest most approved appliances as a first-class passenger steamer.' Someone at the front of the room made some comment of approval, someone else agreed and there was a brief flurry of applause. 'To facilitate effective communications with the shore, particularly in emergencies, one of the boats carried on board will be a steam launch. The *Imperial* is propelled by a set of triple expansion engines supplied with steam at 150lbs pressure by two double-ended steel boilers with six of Fox's corrugated furnaces in each.'

Thomas Dewsbury looked up and a brief smile crossed his face. 'The engines are calculated to provide about 3,000 horsepower,' he added, speaking over another round of applause, which had broken out spontaneously at the front of the room, 'and will drive the vessel at a very high speed, fourteen or possibly fifteen knots.'

The audience could contain itself no longer and the entire room erupted into cheers and applause.

'One of the finest ships in the whole of South America,' said Stewart, nudging Davy with his elbow.

Dewsbury continued. 'As you can see, this saloon is perfectly capable of accommodating over 160 first-class passengers in the most sumptuous comfort. Later, on your tour around the ship, you will see that on the deck above we have provided a social hall, including music room, card room and smoking room lit by a beautifully designed cupola skylight. Like the saloon, these rooms are panelled in the best quality hardwoods and artistically decorated with paintings and other ornamental work.'

Mutterings of approval rippled through the crowd.

'The whole of the accommodation for the first-class passengers and the officers is provided in spacious deck houses under cover of the shade deck, which itself will afford a magnificent promenade the whole length and width of the ship and be protected by canvas awnings.'

Thomas Dewsbury went on to provide a brief summary of the sea trial results at Birkenhead, and concluded by adding that the *Imperial* was a significant addition to what was already an impressive fleet.

'Finally, may I add,' said Dewsbury, looking down at his papers for the first time during his address, 'how fortunate we are at the *Compañía* to have such skilled and experienced officers. Our company would be nothing without the dedication and professionalism of our men. It is one thing for us engineers to build modern ships in the safety of our drawing studios and our dry docks: it is another thing entirely to sail them. Ladies and gentlemen, the sea has not modernised itself. It remains as challenging and wilful as it ever was. Captain Stewart has a long and distinguished career as a merchant mariner and the ship could not be in safer hands. I congratulate you on your appointment, sir, and commend you to the *Imperial*.'

There followed a very warm round of applause and cheering as Stewart grudgingly took to his feet and raised a hand in thanks. The guests who had turned and frowned at their late arrival had clearly forgotten all about it.

Thomas Dewsbury took to his seat, and it would have been appropriate at that point for Walker to thank him for his contribution, but he stayed resolutely in his chair. It was left to the steward to announce that a three-course luncheon would be served in the saloon directly after the tour of the ship and that guests should proceed outside in their own time.

It was much later that afternoon, when all the guests had left, that Davy had his first opportunity to inspect the ship unhindered. He had already been to the heart of the ship, the boiler room and the engine room, and was now walking along the spar deck opening the deck house doors here and there, consistently surprised by the ship builders' workmanship and technical skill. All he could hear in his head was his father's amazed response as if he was there beside him, 'Well, well! Good on you, lad!'

There were footsteps along the wooden deck, and Davy turned to see Thomas Dewsbury approaching. He stepped forward to shake the design engineer's hand.

'What do you think of her, Mr Davies?'

Davy drew breath. He was not sure where to begin.

'She's magnificent, really, quite remarkable.'

Dewsbury looked pleased. 'Yes, the men at Lairds have done us proud, yet again.'

Davy glanced down and noticed Dewsbury's notebook; it was covered in intricate notes, drawings and mysterious equations.

'Oh, the work of an engineer is never done,' said Dewsbury, almost apologetically. 'We are always looking for ways to improve things, searching for greater efficiencies.'

Davy had the distinct impression that this was ordinarily a man of very few words and that today's address must have been a secret nightmare for him. Here on the deck with his notebook in hand he looked far more at ease.

'There are bigger, faster ships, of course,' Dewsbury continued, still sounding apologetic, 'Harland and Wolff's *Majestic*, for example. A fine ship. But what you gain in speed and bulk you lose in manoeuvrability. It's like comparing a whale with a trout. Soon they will be building ships that are so colossal they can't possibly negotiate unexpected obstacles, particularly at top speeds.'

Dewsbury looked genuinely concerned so Davy tried to lighten his mood. 'I hear your daughter christened the ship?'

'Oh, yes. Dear Florence. She's only twelve, you know. She was very nervous.' Dewsbury smiled the bashful smile of a proud father. Then his smile waned. 'She lost her mother several years ago. I think Laird's wanted to do something, you know … they've been very good. She wants to be an engineer!'

Dewsbury laughed apologetically, but Davy thought of Elen all grown up. How formidable she would have been, studying to be a captain. He thought of his mother too, struggling with heavy buckets, wishing that her life had led her elsewhere. He could see, as clear as day, Sarah Jane Rees glowering at a man in the front of her class who'd muttered something careless about 'unsuitable feminine skills'.

'With an attitude like that, Johnny Jones, the only navigational skill you're going to need in a hurry is the one that will get you to the front door. Look sharp!' And she'd wasted no time in boxing him around the ears with a reference book and propelling him out of the village hall on to the street. 'And thank your lucky stars we're not aboard ship, otherwise I'd shove you in a barrel and drop you over the side!'

Davy looked at this unassuming, slender man with his fine nose and desperately hollow cheeks, and thought he could probably benefit from a large glass of wine after the day he'd had.

'Stranger things have happened, Mr Dewsbury. Stranger things, indeed! Let me buy you a glass of something at the English Club. I would be honoured if you would allow me.'

Thomas Dewsbury was not a big drinker, Davy could tell that much by the man's response. Nevertheless, the sailor and the engineer set off for the English Club and a very pleasant evening was had by both of them, discussing ballast tanks and awnings, stanchions and propeller shafts.

CHAPTER 10

Derby Day, Valparaiso

William, Davy's new second officer, who had until now appeared to be a calm and collected sort of character, had been rushing around like a dervish all morning making sure that the skeleton crew would have everything under control in their absence.

'Davy, come on! We're going to be late! Do you hear me? You can do your paperwork tomorrow.' William was clearing things away from Davy's desk, even from under his very nose.

'I promised Stewart I'd finish this letter to the consul before we went,' said Davy, defending sheets of paper from William's grasp.

'Why aren't you wearing your best suit?' interrupted William, looking at Davy with horror.

'I don't know … the steward has it … I think … somewhere.'

'Oh, for God's sake!' William paced to the door and shouted 'Sep!' at the top of his clear tenor voice.

'Why all the fuss? You're just like my mother. Actually, not like my mother. My mother didn't really care much what I looked like unless I was in danger of embarrassing her … but anyway, somebody's mother. You'll make somebody a fine mother one day.'

William rifled through the clothes in the hanging space amid intermittent snorts of disgust.

'And in any case, I don't think this is an appropriate way to speak to your superior, even in private.'

'You don't appear to have one single, decent, clean suit. Do you actually want to be a captain one day?'

Davy was considering William's question, dabbing the finished letter with blotting paper when Sepulveda arrived at the door.

'Where on earth is Officer Davies' suit? We're expected at the races at two o' clock and we are going to be … incredibly late!'

'It's being repaired sir, there was a hole in the …'

'Just get it! There's no time!'

'But sir …'

'This instant!'

Sepulveda ran off down the corridor, muttering Italian expletives under his breath. Davy stood up and looked properly at William. He was wearing a new beige suit with a very fine check, the new style of white shirt with a collar that laid flat at the front and a dark blue neck tie. He looked incredibly clean and tidy.

'Why, William, I have to admit, you're looking very dashing indeed! If I was a nice young lady I would certainly be asking for your calling card.'

William gave him a withering look and handed him a pile of clean undergarments.

'You have three minutes. I'm calling a cab.' Sepulveda was at the door as William went past him.

'Please help Mr Davies to get dressed,' William shouted, leaving Sepulveda open mouthed, and Davy eyeing his Italian steward with deep suspicion.

By the time Davy reached the gangway, William was already sitting in the cab with the door wide open. The horses were glistening in the midday sun and eager to be moving away from the dusty harbour. William gave the driver instructions and they set out at a brisk pace for Viña del Mar. Luckily the harbour was fairly quiet and the gig and horses did not have to slow to avoid many people or obstacles.

'Strange. It's unusually quiet,' said Davy.

'It's quiet because everyone of any consequence has already left,' said William, speaking each word slowly, carefully and with saintly restraint.

Before long, the horses were climbing the hills above the city. It was a truly glorious day and Valparaiso was living up to its reputation as the Jewel of the Pacific. Despite his earlier reluctance, Davy was glad to be away from the ship. He looked across at William, who was still looking mightily annoyed, and thought back to the day Captain Stewart had introduced them to each other.

'Officer Davies, I want you to meet Mr William Keen Whiteway, our new second officer. I've asked William to take a particular interest in navigation, with your permission. Mr Davies has an excellent head for navigation. You will learn much more from him than you would from any book. What he may not tell you is that he was taught by a woman! Sarah Jane Rees, wasn't it, Davies? Most incredible! I forget the details now, but I'm sure Mr Davies can tell you all about it later. It's strange to think that when I started off as a boy we used to call the second officer the 'sailor's waiter'. What do you think of that, William? In those days it was a right dog's berth, running around after everyone's beck and call. "He is one to whom little is given and of whom much is required." That's what they used to say. Luckily for you, things have come a long way since then.'

William and Davy had exchanged amused glances. Even though it was 1890 Davy suspected that William would still be required to do a lot of running around, and by the looks of it William knew that too.

The journey to the racecourse took a little over an hour. Once they arrived and opened the carriage doors the sight that greeted them was a glorious one. Thousands of people had gathered to see the Derby Day races. From where they stood at the entrance to the field they could see the entire course, a beautiful, elegant oval shape laid out on a flat plain with snow-capped mountains in the distance. White canvas tents had been erected all around, and even from a distance Davy could see endless strings of bunting fluttering in the breeze. William paid the driver and they made their way on foot down the hill towards the course. A band was playing in the bandstand and a man in long black tails was singing an incongruously jolly rendition of 'Three Fishers Went Sailing'. They stopped for a moment to listen to the refrain, 'For men must work and women must weep.'

'Don't they all drown in the end?' asked William. But before Davy could answer they were distracted by a waiter carrying a tray of glasses, full to their brims with champagne.

'*¿Señores?*' said the waiter, presenting the tray.

'Excellent idea!' replied Davy, extending his arm and thinking that a glass of champagne would certainly lighten William's mood.

'Actually, no. Thank you,' interrupted William, leading Davy away. 'I'm sure my uncle will have laid on a feast for us.'

The bubbles rose enticingly in the glasses, but William's tone of voice suggested that it would be impolite to turn up at their allotted tent already holding a glass. *I'll be damned if I've just turned down a glass of champagne in return for a cup of weak tea*, thought Davy, now starting to feel quite bad tempered himself.

But despite his efforts, Davy could not stay irritable for long. Everyone was dressed in their finest clothes, jewel-coloured day dresses, shawls and frills, hats and parasols. Even the men were colourful with their patterned cravats, handkerchiefs and colourful waistcoats.

'There it is!' exclaimed William, sounding cheerful for the first time that morning, and he strode forward ahead of Davy.

There were perhaps fifteen people already in the striped marquee, the back and front of which had been rolled upwards so that it was possible to see the racetrack through it. Chairs had been placed around and several tables overflowed with food and drinks.

'Ah, there you are!' a tall, very smartly dressed middle-aged man vaguely resembling William stepped forward. He placed both hands on

William's shoulders and then embraced him warmly.

'This,' he said turning to face the guests behind him, 'is my very favourite nephew!' William looked bashful and glanced around apologetically at the other people in the tent.

'Ha! They all know you're my favourite, William. No use in hiding it.'

'Uncle Howard, I would like to introduce Mr Davies, chief officer of the new *Imperial.*'

Although Davy had never met the man before, he knew exactly who he was. He was a major shareholder in Chile's largest silver mine.

'Mr David Davies? It's an honour to meet you at last. You've transported much of our cargo over the years in various ships, very efficiently and reliably, if I may say. I'm indebted to you. I think we shall have an excellent afternoon. My horse is racing. Did William tell you? And I have a good feeling in my bones. Young man!' he shouted at the waiter, 'Bring these fine fellows some champagne at the double.'

The waiter was slowly filling champagne saucers with what looked suspiciously like *Laurent-Perrier*. Everything around them had been perfectly arranged, from the lace tablecloths to the decorative palms that adorned the marquee. William's uncle excused himself to welcome some other guests and Davy turned to William with fresh admiration. 'I've very pleased I came.'

'I knew you would be,' retorted William with a wry smile.

Apart from the Day of Independence, Derby Day was the biggest day of the year in Chile and the races had been arranged in such a way that each one, more prestigious than the last, led up to the grand finale. At the Whiteway tent Davy was introduced to many members of William's family, people he had not met before and some familiar faces too. He had always known that William's father had been a sea captain and that he had helped establish many of the natural history collections for the museum in Liverpool, bringing back hundreds of specimens from his journeys around the world. Not long after they met, William had told him all about the strange human-faced monkey that his father had brought back from the Congo. But Davy knew nothing of this side of the family.

'You're a dark horse yourself, and no mistake,' Davy had muttered to William, moments after they were introduced to yet another family member who was prominent in Chilean affairs.

Each time the starting pistol went off the guests would move forward to the railings, the women seated towards the front and the men cheering behind them. William's uncle seemed to have horses running in many of the races. One called 'Turn to the Light' came cantering back down the racecourse after coming second in the Crystal Bowl.

William's uncle ducked under the railings and rushed forward to congratulate the jockey. Davy had seen racehorses before, of course, but not at such close quarters. This creature bore little resemblance to Flower and Lady he had known on the farm, great lumbering beasts that were designed to pull practical loads. This skittish animal would have buckled under the smallest plough with legs so spindly they barely looked strong enough to support its own weight. The jockey dismounted to cheers and shouts of congratulations from the guests and a boisterous series of embraces and friendly punches from his sponsor.

'William! Come here! Your cousin wants to speak to you.'

William walked forward and ducked under the railings. But there were shouts along the track, and it became clear that the organisers were not impressed with this little impromptu party taking place on the course. The jockey quickly mounted and galloped across the finishing line again just as the horses for the next race were gathering.

The straying guests came back under the railings and to their seats. There was one more race and then a lull in proceedings.

'Let's take a turn about the field,' said William.

'I've heard that there are some acrobats and fire-eaters further on down.'

Since they had arrived that morning the crowds had increased again. What little breeze there had been had dropped away and hundreds of pretty parasols could be seen amongst the crowds. An enormous hot air balloon carrying an advertisement for *Mackenzie's Scottish Shortbread Biscuits* was preparing for take-off.

Davy and William looked on in awe.

'Just look at that, William, no part of the universe will be safe from us soon. Just imagine, if we could combine flight with steam, what kind of machine that would be?'

Just then three young men in the crowd caught sight of William and ran up to him excitedly.

'Let me introduce Chief Officer Davies,' said William, carefully, hinting that perhaps the three of them should calm down a little and behave in a respectful manner and not get quite so carried away.

'These are three old chums from school.' William gave their names along with brief derogatory descriptions of their school-day attributes, but Davy forgot the details almost immediately in the midst of their noise and chatter. Davy excused himself and carried on walking around the oval course. As he walked through the crowds, thinking how prosperous everyone looked, he thought how far away his hometown felt; the farm above the Teifi estuary, the Preseli mountains in the distance. That landscape, as lovely and dramatic as it seemed to him as a boy, would be nothing to the mountains of Chile. The scale of things was completely different here. The mountains were higher, the sea was wider, the colours more intense. Even the people themselves were more vibrant and passionate. It seemed to Davy that whatever thin grey veil existed over the rest of the world had been lifted here, revealing the earth's true colours.

He was lost in thoughts of Wales and Chile when he sensed someone looking at him through the crowd. There was a familiar face but the sun dazzled his eyes and he looked away momentarily. When he raised his eyes again, he saw Estella walking purposefully towards him, with an older man by her side.

'Captain Davies, I thought it was you. I didn't recognise you at once under your hat. This is my father, Dr Edwards. You won't remember him, I fear, as you were so unwell.'

Davy looked at the kindly face and shook his hand warmly.

'Yes, I do remember you, as a matter of fact, but I'm afraid you did not see me at my best.'

'No matter, we have seen it all and worse, haven't we, my dear?'

The doctor was full of questions, and when it transpired that the Whiteways were well known to the doctor it was agreed that they should both accompany Davy back to the tent to meet Howard Whiteway. Estella took her father's arm and walked between the two men.

'Describe it to me, where you were brought up.' Estella leant forward eagerly to hear his answer. They had both found a corner to sit while the doctor, who seemed to know half of Valparaiso and was creating quite a stir in the tent, made his way through the crowd, greeting and shaking hands as he went.

'Your father is admired,' Davy remarked as he watched an elderly lady receiving an elegant kiss to the back of her hand. For a brief moment it seemed she was transformed into a dizzy young woman of eighteen again.

'Oh, yes. He has great charm,' Estella smiled and watched as her father made some remark that made the old lady step back with delight. 'But you know, there's no falsehood at all. He loves people. All people. They sense it and that is why they love him. It is a rare thing. But you haven't answered my question!' she turned back impatiently, 'what is it like?'

Davy looked down for a moment as he thought.

'It's colder. Wetter. Greener. Beautiful, but very different. The sun sets over the sea.'

'Like it does here!' she smiled in mock surprise.

'Yes. Yes!' and Davy laughed, realising how odd it sounded.

'But you know, when I was a young lad I thought, stupidly, that the sun set over the sea for everyone. As I became older I knew that this wasn't the case, but still in my heart …' he faltered and looked around, slightly embarrassed to be talking like this, 'I thought that everyone saw the same beautiful sunset. It was only when I began to sail the world that I realised that for some people even the most beautiful sun sets over wastelands, or mines or mountains that obscure all light after mid-afternoon. It seems like such an obvious thing to me now.'

'You're so lucky to have seen so many places. I've only ever seen the sun in Valparaiso. Oh, and Santiago, of course, and some other small places here. But they don't really count. So what else?'

Davy was finding it difficult to think of any time before that day; everything around him seemed so bright and colourful and real to him.

'Oh, I don't know … there are fields, green fields and a big sky, farms everywhere around … the Preseli hills which look black or lilac depending on the weather …'

'Like the Cordilleras …'

'Yes, but much smaller, much less dramatic …'

'But no less beautiful?'

'No, no less beautiful. And then the river: a fine river, full of salmon, wide at the estuary, winding its way to the sea. And at dusk the sound of the curlew; a haunting sound.'

'We don't have them in Chile?'

'No, at least not here in Valparaiso.'

'What kind of song is it?'

Davy thought hard how he could describe it. For a moment he was back on the heath with Gruffudd, trudging home through the long grass and heather with half a dozen rabbits strung over their shoulders, laughing and joking at the end of a long day. Then in a sudden explosion of feathers and wings, the startled cries of two curlews disturbed from their rest, rising into the air. Later, at a distance, when the sun was lower and melting like candle wax, they could hear them again, their long diminishing cries as they flew back towards the coast.

'I don't think I can …' began Davy, then as he looked upwards and read her smile, realised that she did not expect him to reproduce the sound.

'You are playing …'

'No, no!' she reached out and placed her hand briefly on his arm.

'I want to hear more. Please. I'm only happy that you are well and I have the chance to ask you all these questions. You asked your fair share of questions, do you remember?'

'Yes, I do. I did not get answers to all of them.'

It was Estella's turn to look away, and Davy wished he could take the words back. They seemed more accusing than he had meant them to be.

'Tell me about your family. When did you see them last?' she asked and Davy was relieved. *Ask me a hundred questions and I'll answer them all.*

'Was your father a sea captain?'

'Yes, and still is, I'm pleased to say. He still takes the brigs along the coast.'

'Is he like you?'

'I'm not sure. What am I like?' Davy laughed. No one had ever asked him such a question before.

'Proud, stubborn, opinionated …'

Davy was flabbergasted. 'Mrs Taylor, you save my life only to insult me to my very core!'

'Oh, you're not insulted. Besides, you are also a gifted officer, an inspired leader of men, trustworthy, honest and kind.'

'Oh, you've been talking to Mrs Ebrington!' Davy laughed. 'I wouldn't believe too much of what she says.'

'There's a great deal of hilarity going on here,' interrupted William's uncle, 'and look here! Neither of you appear to have any champagne in your glasses at all!' He waved at the Chilean waiter. 'Young man, what am I paying you for if you won't look after my guests properly?'

Estella and Davy chorused that there was no need to worry at all; they had been deep in conversation and oblivious to all forms of food and drink.

'Nonsense. This is Derby Day. On Derby Day we do things properly.'

The races had come to an end and William had disappeared, so Davy gladly accepted the offer to travel back to Valparaiso with Estella and her father. Over the noise of the carriage and the horses' hooves it was difficult to sustain a conversation, and in any case after a while, Dr Edwards had nodded off to sleep, and rather than wake him Davy and Estella had shared amused glances as he snored. Only once did the carriage stop briefly and the noise inside subside.

'You did not mention your mother,' Estella whispered. 'Is she still alive?'

Davy looked out of the window and remembered the day a letter had arrived for him at the Custom House in Trieste. The letter appeared to have been stamped in most of Europe's major cities and his first thought on seeing his sister's handwriting had been 'someone's died'. Sure enough it was to say that his mother, had 'passed away quietly' after a long and debilitating illness. Something to do with the lungs. *Quietly*. It would be the first thing she had done quietly in her entire life, thought Davy. Twenty-four years had passed since Elen's death and he could still feel the blows from the smoking beam. In all that time he had not returned home. There had been no words of forgiveness or reconciliation.

'Were you very fond of her?' asked Estella.

Davy could not bring himself to lie, even though he was sure she would find his answer disturbing. 'I don't know,' he replied, looking out of the carriage at the peaks of the Cordilleras capped with snow. 'Is that shocking?' he asked, turning back to her again, fearing her reaction.

Davy watched her trace the outline of his hair and face and shoulders with her eyes, and a brief smile of recognition passed across her face.

'No, it's not shocking.'

The carriage jolted and they were on their way again. On opposite sides of the carriage, Davy and Estella looked out of the windows, admiring the landscape as they travelled along the road from Viña del Mar to Valparaiso, catching each other's glances now and then.

The carriage set Davy down on the Grand Avenue. On his way to the harbour he stopped at the True Blue Saloon and chatted briefly with the American sailors there. He did not join them at their table as he might have done any other evening, but sat at the bar and drank a quick whisky before carrying on his journey towards the harbour.

'Not stopping with us this evening, *Capitán?*' said the man behind the bar.

Davy fished around in his pocket for some coins then spread them out on his palm before choosing the Chilean ones.

'No. Time waits for no man, particularly the man from the *Compañía.*'

The bar man swept the coins from the counter without checking, and threw them nonchalantly into the ornate brass cash register as it sprang open with a loud ring.

'Adios then, *Capitán*. Till next time.'

A couple of the Americans tipped their caps to him as he passed and he realised that he had reached that age when, even without his officer uniform, he had acquired a certain salty gravitas. What did other sailors see? He wondered. *A survivor.*

But as he stepped through the narrow streets, down through the old part of town, past the tall houses perched on impossibly steep hillsides, his mind was not really on any of these things, not on the merits of good whisky or uniforms or loading cargo. He was thinking of something else. The races had seemed to him like a blur, a dizzying collage of feathers and horses, leaping, cheering crowds and clinking wine glasses. And, in the middle of it all, a conversation. It seemed to him that he could remember every word. He replayed it in parts, over and over. He had talked of the farm and his family; his first ship; the trips around the Horn. Chapel. Navigation. It seemed that he had talked of things that he had never consciously considered. He cringed to think that he might have been like a burst dam, spilling his strange internal world on a bored and mystified listener. But he reminded himself that she had talked too, of a devoted father, an urge to travel, to study and train as a doctor. There were things that she talked of only obliquely – a logical marriage, an absent partner.

Davy followed the steps down and down, through the streets of Valparaiso. Where the path widened out, rough lads hung about on corners. They registered him but did not bother him. He knew they would pose no problem if they fancied their chances, or tried to knock him to the ground to rifle through his pockets in search of a gold watch or silver tobacco box. He nodded at them, but did not break his stride as he descended between the high terraces and coloured plaster walls towards the harbour.

CHAPTER 11

New Year's Eve, 1890, Valparaiso

It was not often that Davy was able to celebrate New Year's Eve on dry land. He thought back over the evening. From the outset, the normally reserved and elegant Colin MacDougal Stewart had been well disposed to a night of serious celebration. Davy had never really understood the Scottish ability to celebrate New Year's Eve with such wild abandon and with such impossible quantities of whisky. Davy always felt maudlin at the thought of another year gone by and no real way of knowing what would happen in the next. Usually, towards the end of the evening, he would withdraw to a corner and harbour unreasonably dark thoughts when everyone else was on their fourth rendition of *Auld Lang Syne*.

But that evening they had been joined by the crew of an American warship. They had started proceedings at the True Blue Saloon then wandered in a good-natured and relatively sober crowd along Cochrane Street, stopping at some of the other bars there. From there some of them had climbed the hill in the direction of the Municipal Theatre. A new production had arrived from New York, and the leading lady was apparently quite a beauty and destined for great things. Davy hadn't been in the mood for theatre and headed instead for the new Hotel Victoria on Via Sotomayor where he knew he could get a decent steak.

The atmosphere had been lively, and just before midnight the owner had encouraged them all on to the terrace to watch the fireworks over the harbour. The brilliant stars over Valparaiso competed with the gaudy exhibition, and as the warm breeze wafted the sulphurous smoke away after the frenetic finale they shone out still, serene and undisturbed above the commotion. Everyone on the terrace seemed to be hugging and cheering, and Davy received a few sharp congratulatory slaps on his shoulders from guests he vaguely knew but who seemed to know him well. When he returned to the lounge at the English Club, Stewart was sprawled on one of the velvet sofas looking uncharacteristically relaxed.

'Davies! Where have you been? You missed the best display ever!'

Stewart stood up and with a flourish turned to the others, who were seated opposite.

'Friends. This is my chief officer, David Davies. The most excellent mariner I have ever had the pleasure of sailing with.'

The young officers stood eagerly and shook hands, and more introductions were made. They were British sailors from the Royal Navy.

'Mr Davies started on the Black Ball line, you know? Damned baptism of fire, if you ask me. Before some of you were born, I dare say.'

Davy mumbled something about not being that old and Stewart sat down. Next to him was a tall, half-empty bottle of expensive-looking whisky. The waiter brought another glass and Stewart sloshed a good measure into it.

'Come on, Davies, get some golden nectar down you. It's 1891 and I'm going to get you a ship this year if it kills me. Walker or no Walker, the rabid dog.'

The conversation began light-heartedly enough, but soon someone mentioned President Balmaceda and everyone had an opinion.

'Power has gone to his head. He's become a dictator,' said one.

'But he has Chile's interests at heart, don't you see? Look at the money he's invested in the railways and in municipal buildings,' said another.

'The country's money when people are starving?'

'Look at the way he's stood up to Colonel North.'

'Chile would be nothing without North's investment.'

'North's monopoly of the nitrate industry has been built on the backs of Chilean workers. *The Nitrate King!* To hell with him. All the profit goes back to England!'

'Quite possibly. But think of this – he invests in coal mines like the Navigation in Maesteg which employs six thousand miners. If Balmaceda gets his way, they will all be out of work. Did you think of that? No.'

And on and on until there was an awkward silence. Davy looked up and saw that the lamp above the fireplace was spluttering gently, causing the light to flicker. Stewart seemed to be in a world of his own, holding up his drink, examining the refracted light through the amber liquid and cut glass.

'What's your opinion, Captain Stewart?' asked one of the sailors.

Stewart swilled his glass and considered its contents carefully.

'I think it would be as well for us all to keep our noses out of other nations' affairs.'

No one responded immediately, and a relieved Davy was about to turn the conversation in another direction, to the races at Viña del Mar, or to the new *ascensor* that was being built at Cerro Artillera, when one of them added, 'But surely, we can't pretend not to be involved? Countries like Chile need foreign investment. They need English engineers. American railroads. Even the *Compañía*'s ships, they all come from Glasgow don't they?'

'Birkenhead.'

The young sailor laughed. 'We can't just go home and leave them all to it!'

The other sailors laughed too, as if they had never heard anything so ridiculous. Stewart smiled patiently, still examining his whisky, and waited for their mirth to subside.

'Oh, no. I'm sure we'll send for our missionaries and do-gooders to clear up the mess when we've finished.'

There was another awkward silence. The sailor was looking flushed, and Davy thought that he looked like a lot of young men he had known, who did not like to be seen to be losing an argument in front of his friends.

'You are involved whether you like it or not, Captain Stewart,' he persisted, irritated, 'you carry the government mail.'

'Gentlemen,' Stewart announced, finishing off his whisky in one swift gulp, 'Mr Davies and I will be taking our leave. I may take a turn about the Neptune Fountain on such a pleasant evening. A Happy New Year to you all, whatever your political leanings.'

And he rose to his feet with the same steadiness and sobriety as a man who had been drinking English breakfast tea all evening. As Davy followed him outside, he was thinking of two things: why it was that they were both leaving so soon, and where on earth it was that Stewart was putting all that whisky.

'I can't abide all that political talk late at night,' Stewart muttered, buttoning his jacket and straightening his hat. 'They're barely out of nappies and they think they can solve all the world's ills. If they'd watched those lads coming back from the Crimea in shreds they wouldn't be so keen to pontificate about war.'

And so they had gone their separate ways, Stewart grumbling his way to his 'fountain' and Davy, whose head was already throbbing from an unusually random concoction of alcohol, towards Mrs Ebrington's house.

When he reached the gate at Myrtle Villa he was surprised to find all the lamps ablaze and the sound of piano music and laughter coming from the parlour. He tiptoed into the hall and had nearly reached the bottom of the stairs undetected when Mrs Ebrington burst through the parlour door. She was delighted that he had returned so that she could introduce him to some of her guests. Davy was about to be led unwillingly towards the gathering when a smartly dressed, fair-haired man came to the parlour door. He looked as disappointed as Davy felt to be detained.

'Ah, Mr Taylor, this is Captain Davies I spoke of, who owes so much to your wife's medical skills.'

The man's look of impatience gave way to something else. Davy stepped forward to shake his hand and found himself being examined closely by a pair of dazzling pale blue eyes, the colour of a clear wintry sky. From his shoes to his shirt to the cut of his jacket, Davy was carefully surveyed. Laurence Taylor's hand was smooth as a girl's and cold despite the warm evening.

'Indeed,' the man said, savouring the word, 'I wish I could say that I have heard a great deal about you, Captain Davies, but I'm afraid my wife shares very few of her interests with me.' The man smiled fleetingly as if the words were meant to be light-hearted.

There was a pause in the conversation where another kind of man would have asked about the illness, and how long it had taken him to get better, how well was he now, how proud he was of his wife for being so able and clever. But obviously he was not that kind of man. Davy caught the faint smell of sandalwood cologne wafting expensively towards him.

'But surely, you're not leaving already, Mr Taylor?' said Agnes Ebrington.

The man muttered something about having a prior engagement that he could not avoid, much as he would have liked to. And then, when Mrs Ebrington called for Miriam to get his hat and coat, it appeared that he already had them to hand.

'I didn't want to interrupt proceedings, you see, so I kept them close.'

Davy watched as Taylor turned to thank Mrs Ebrington for a truly fascinating evening. Then, as if he had remembered something, he turned to look again at Davy, tapping the brass of his cane against his hat absently as he made a mental note of his face.

'A Happy New Year to you all.'

Laurence Taylor disappeared and Davy felt as if he had just been caressed by icicles. Mrs Ebrington closed the door and looked confused, like a woman wondering whether she should feel affronted by the man's behaviour. Davy saw his chance to make a renewed attempt to escape, but Mrs Ebrington was shocked and amazed that he did not want to meet everyone, and grabbed his arm. After all, it wasn't New Year's Eve every day. He couldn't retire before saying hello.

Mrs Ebrington eased Davy through the parlour door like a foot being persuaded into an uncomfortable shoe. He had never seen so many people squeezed into one room: there must have been approaching a hundred in all. Every window was wide open and the fine lace curtains swayed in the breeze. The noise and chatter gave way momentarily to brief necessary introductions, then thankfully someone called for a music hall song and the crowd's attention focused elsewhere in the room. There was an empty seat and, making his way towards it, he realised to his surprise that Estella was sitting next to it, oblivious to all around her, deep in her own thoughts. He faltered, thinking that he might be intruding, but she had already seen him and gave him the warmest of smiles.

'Was Mr Taylor called away?' he asked discreetly as he sat down next to her.

'In a manner of speaking,' she replied. Davy looked at her but she had turned away. What kind of reply was that? *In a manner of speaking.* Davy had taken an instant dislike to the man. What kind of man left his wife to make her own way home at the end of an evening? Davy raised his right hand and ran his nails backward from his hairline to his crown then realised with dismay that this was the very gesture his father made when something annoyed him.

'He's gone to the English Club,' Estella said, turning towards him. 'I can send for a carriage. But you know, it's perfectly safe on a night like this with so many people around.'

Davy looked down at his hands and shook his head in disbelief.

'What's the matter?' asked Estella. 'Are you trying to send me home?'

'No. I'm laughing at myself. I'm becoming my father.'

Davy knew that his meaning would be lost on Estella but any further explanation was put aside as a pair of ruddy-faced men took their positions at the piano. They declared their intention to sing something from *The Pirates of Penzance*, and there were roars of laughter as various items of flamboyant piratical costume were relayed through the crowd to adorn the two singers. Mrs Ebrington seemed to have a costume or prop for every character imaginable ranging from tram conductors' hats to lightning bolts for evil Greek gods. She was upending like an enormous duck delving determinedly into the 'theatrical' trunk.

By half past two in the morning the gathering had exhausted its knowledge of all the best Gilbert and Sullivan pieces. There had also been a few risqué renditions of some of Marie Lloyd's songs, including 'The Boy I Love is Up in the Gallery', which involved one of the ruddy-faced men donning a wig and wielding a defective parasol which wouldn't open.

'I haven't had it up for ages!' squealed the man in a high-pitched voice that made all the other men in the room roar with laughter. Mrs Ebrington and the female guests looked askance and pretended they either hadn't heard or didn't understand. Thankfully the singers couldn't remember all the words, or if they did, left off the more dubious sections out of respect for their hostess. Eventually the crowd began to leave in twos and fours with lively shouts of Happy New Year.

'Mrs Taylor, as you saved my life, the least I can do is make sure you get home safely.'

Davy stood up and offered his arm to Estella. He half-expected a good-natured debate about calling a carriage or making her way home with another group, but without hesitation she placed her hand on his arm as if it was the most natural thing in the world.

The entrance hallway was full of people and Estella took her gloves and shawl from Miriam. They turned to look for Mrs Ebrington who, at that moment, was being embraced affectionately by a very portly man with an enormous white beard. There were peals of laughter all around and the portly man didn't look as if he was keen to leave very soon.

'Please say thank you to Mrs Ebrington,' Estella smiled sympathetically at Miriam.

Outside the still evening air was thick with the smell of firework smoke and fragrant blossoms. Rather than taking the dark narrow lanes, which were quicker by day, they walked to the Grand Avenue where the sky opened out above them and made their way up the hill from there. Every now and again they stopped and turned to look behind them at the bay and its sinuous curve.

'There's no moon!' Estella exclaimed.

Davy looked up and examined the stars, their position in the sky and made a mental calculation.

'She's hiding behind that peak,' Davy gestured above the city and away from the sea. 'You'll see her soon,' he said confidently and they carried on walking.

Davy could have told her how he knew where the moon should be at that time of year. It was a matter of certainty. A matter of necessity when circumstances called for it, that the moon should be in the right place. Not just anywhere in the sky. Just like the North Star or the Southern Cross could only be in one place at any given time. And Orion's belt could only tilt one way. Once you knew what to look for the sky was not vague or indiscriminate. Not like the sea, which could shift and change, or even the earth that could be moved and built upon, its horizons changed over time, churches which were used as landmarks demolished or destroyed in earthquakes, harbours rebuilt, spires erected. At a certain time on a certain day the moon could only be in one place. Unless the world was coming to an end and someone had forgotten to tell them. He could have told her this. But he was thinking of something else. He had been thinking of something else all evening, even as he was laughing at the awful jokes and singing along to the tunes he knew. He was thinking of two skinny children, and a blue dress.

'That day,' he paused, 'on the harbour, the day before I was taken ill, who were the children?'

For a moment, Estella made no reaction. Then, when she did move, she slowly took her hand from his arm but did not move away. She turned her face aside and in the lamplight he could see her trying to remember the events of that afternoon.

She reached out for his arm again and they walked on a little further. He wondered whether she had chosen to ignore his question; pretending, perhaps, that it had never been asked. But then she began, very quietly, almost in a whisper.

'They are my husband's children.'

They walked on a few paces in unison while Davy absorbed the words. When he stopped and turned to look into her face she urged him on.

'He isn't aware that I know about them. They live in the Almendral with their mother.' The Almendral! Davy knew what that was like. It was where the poorer crew ended up on a drunken evening when they had nowhere else to go. When they were too drunk to worry about which disease they might catch or who might beat them up if they didn't pay up and leave quickly enough. Not somewhere for a captain; certainly not somewhere for a respectable businessman like Estella's husband.

Estella's walk was steady and determined, 'When he says he is going to the English Club, that's where he goes. As far as I am aware, no one else knows. But I have known for a long time.' She paced on again for a while, then stopped abruptly to look up at the stars. 'She's actually quite beautiful. Despite ... well, you know. You're a sailor. You would know about these things.'

How could she be so calm?

'But why do you help them? Why don't you confront him? How can you bear him ...?' Davy swung around in disbelief.

'There's no need to be angry with me,' she whispered.

Her words struck him like a frozen sail swinging around on a sudden tack and hitting him in the face.

'I'm not angry with you,' he whispered, as a smartly dressed couple strode past in the lamplight, walking boldly downhill. 'I want to kill him!'

Estella laughed and stepped forward, taking his arm again and urging him on up the hill.

'How can you laugh?'

'What can I do but laugh? Believe me, I have tried alternatives. It is not just about me. My father depends on Laurence's generosity; his practice is based in Laurence's buildings. My father's best patients, the ones that can afford to pay, are Laurence's friends. The children think I am some mysterious benefactor. They have no idea. If I confront him, they will suffer the most. Then there will be no help for them at all. He treats her badly. That's strange, don't you think? Because I really believe he loves her.'

'So you would put everyone before yourself. And what about you? Does he treat you badly?' Davy tried to stop again but she pulled him onwards.

'Beyond deceit and dishonesty? No, he lets me be. To tell you the truth, I think he's a little scared of me.'

Estella's pace had quickened and Davy was out of breath, but not because of the hill. He had walked this hill a thousand times. He could run the length of it easily if he wanted to. It would be nothing to running up and down the shrouds of the *Royal Dane* in a gale. He eased his arm away from hers and turned to look down over the chimney pots and roofs towards the harbour.

'He's right to be scared of you,' Davy scanned the horizon, the observer in him thinking that there was a lightness about the sky and that soon it would be dawn. Somewhere in the distance they could hear a door opening followed by shouts of laughter and exclamations of '¡*Un feliz año nuevo a ti!*' then distant footsteps, a door closing, then stillness again.

'You think less of me,' she said calmly.

And when Davy turned back to her she looked as cool and enigmatic as the moon. There he stood, outwardly calm. Only he could feel the tips of his fingers trembling and see the water funnel of confusion stretching up and around him as if to suffocate him. He wanted to run down the hill, all along the harbour and into the dingy backstreets of the Almendral, to grab the man by the scruff of the neck and kick him along the cobblestones until his teeth clattered and his expensive suit smelt of dog shit and rotten fish.

He began before he knew what he was saying, 'You know what kind of man I am ...' and as he said it, he knew that he had started the sentence all in the wrong place and he knew that this was not really the point of what he wanted to say. He heard Captain Lewis' voice in his head, *For God's sake boy, say what you mean!*

'I wasn't asking for help,' she said, quietly, and began to walk on.

It seemed that he needed every ounce of strength to shout after her, to beg her to wait, and when it came, it was barely more than a whisper. *Wait.* Davy stood and watched as Estella strode on more purposefully.

'Oh, I know what kind of man you are. You're the kind of man who makes women waft their feathers at you and distract you with their enormous bustles as they pass,' she wiggled deliberately for a few steps and nearly tripped. 'You don't deny it?' she recovered and walked on with Davy following at a distance.

'No. I don't deny it.'

'Mrs Ebrington says you have lots of lady friends.'

'Oh, Mrs Ebrington …'

'And that you entertain them …'

'I have done …'

'That you break their hearts …'

'I doubt it …'

'Discard them and move on to the next.'

In a few sudden exasperated steps he overtook her and stood in her path. 'Estella! Your husband is down in the harbour with some woman, with some whore, rutting away and probably fathering more unwanted offspring as we speak, you have every reason in the world to be angry with him! You should be beating on his chest and screaming at him … for God's sake, why are you angry with me?'

Davy walked backwards in disbelief, his arms outstretched either side of him. Above them in the silent street a figure leaned from a window, paused a moment then closed the shutters gently. Then it came to Davy that for the first time he didn't care whether he was the first to the mizzen mast or strongest in a fight or the fastest swimmer, or the one who had survived the most wrecks or captained the fastest ship, as long as he was first in this woman's eyes.

'Estella. You're married …' She sighed visibly and began to walk away from him. '… to a fool. If I was,' he faltered, 'If I was your …' *Say what you mean!* '… husband, I wouldn't want to be anywhere else. Not in some whorehouse, or saloon or English Club or anywhere else on this earth.'

And then Davy thought that the strangest thing happened. Although Estella stopped walking, the space between them seemed to become as wide and empty as the blue Pacific and she seemed so small and far away that crossing the space seemed impossible. And as the seconds passed in silence, even when she turned, the emptiness seemed to take on a life of its own, to become a third person that eyed them critically, so that when he went to her side and she took his arm again they walked on more carefully than before as if the whole avenue had turned to a path of glass.

The inscrutable moon rose over the hills of Valparaiso and cast her blue light where the lamplight failed to reach. She lit the dark corners where poor children slept in rags, and the curtained windowpanes of the grand houses on the hill. She lit the empty hallway where Mrs Ebrington was turning out the shiny brass lamps. She lit the grubby damp sheets of a crumpled bed, where a deceitful man lay fast asleep in a woman's arms. She lit the woman's face and her stray tears.

The moon watched this other man and woman as they walked on through the glass city. She watched them pause at the fountain to look at its crystal waters dance in the pool and search for visions in its ripples, some reality they could not yet see. She watched as they listened to its babbling, straining to decipher clues in its strange fountain language. They walked on.

And when they reached the closed gates of Villa D'Este on Avenue Lautaro Rosas, the woman lifted the catch quietly and slipped inside. She raised her gloved hands to the railings, and for the first time since he had said those words she looked at him properly and he looked back at her. He raised his hands and rested them on hers, softly at first, feeling her warmth though the soft white satin. The woman watched him as he closed his eyes and laid his head to rest on the warm iron.

The moon saw all of this. And when the couple pulled apart she lit the space between them. She lit the patterns in the acid-etched door as it swung open briefly then closed. She lit the man's steps as he walked down the hill. She lit his pale, distracted face.

PART THREE

WAR

CHAPTER 12

1 January 1891, the National Congress, Santiago

José Manuel Emiliano Balmaceda Fernández, the Chilean president, had arrived early at the National Congress that morning. His faithful secretary Vásquez had made him coffee and Balmaceda had taken it in to the Chamber itself. It would be frowned upon if anyone could see, he thought. And then as he drank his first mouthful he also thought, *They will have other things to think about by the end of the day.*

He wanted to read his speech through one more time. He had a reputation for being a fine speaker, and consequently people thought that it came easily to him, which to an extent it did. But he would also spend invisible hours refining and rewriting what he wanted to say and then rehearsing his delivery. In reality, it never came as naturally to him as it seemed. He would ask his wife Emilia to listen, which she did happily despite complaining that she often ended up knowing his speeches better than he did himself. She was a good critic. She would interrupt and ask, 'What exactly are you trying to say?' Invariably he would go back to the writing, delete, simplify or sometimes expound in places where he had assumed too much knowledge. Even his children listened to his rehearsals. They wouldn't all understand the subject, but the smallest one would say things like, 'Father, you sound a bit frightening. I don't think I would like to disagree with you.'

Today Balmaceda would deliver the most important speech of his life. It would be short and to the point. Its effects would be, he anticipated, wide-ranging and immediate. Not because it was full of ambitious new proposals or audacious plans that would transform the economy, the kind of speech he wished he was in a position to make. No. Today he would propose the unthinkable: to maintain the status quo. His longed-for new budget would be shelved. Congress had frustrated him at every turn. The members had behaved like wilful children who were tired of their toys. So he would, instead, propose maintaining the previous year's budget, despite no agreement.

'You are committing political suicide if you do this!' his friends had warned him. His friends, who numbered fewer by the day.

He entered the Chamber, as members of Congress would later on that day, through the main doors. He walked slowly up the centre aisle, looking at the empty chairs either side of him. They were arranged in lines six rows deep, as dark as ebony and sombre against the creamy walls of the Chamber. The lower sections of the walls all around were plain and unadorned up to a height of perhaps twenty feet. From there upwards the Chamber's columns and gilding became gradually more opulent until its high vaulted ceiling curved over his head, sixty or seventy feet above him. With all its members in attendance the Chamber could hold nearly two hundred and fifty people. The red carpet gave way to steps at the front of the podium where five chairs sat facing outwards towards the room. He walked around and stood where he would be standing in a few hours' time.

It would be his manifesto to the nation. But in reality it would be his final diplomatic attempt to stamp authority on an increasingly intransigent Congress. They had refused to pass the Appropriations Bill, and slowly each side had backed itself into a corner. Today he needed to convince them that his motives for doing this were, as ever, honourable and that Chile was his first concern. He needed to show them, yet again, that Chile's natural resources were being pillaged, and as soon as there was a downturn in the country's fortunes the Scots, the Irish, the Germans would all be turning their steamers into other ports. He had been accused of being anti-English. But that was not true. He was no more anti-English than he was anti-American. As far as he could see, they were all at each other's throats fighting for the deepest mines and the biggest reserves. Chile's bird shit had made millions for silver-tongued crooks from all over the globe, while the children of Chile still lived in hovels, without education or aspiration.

He thought back to his early successes, to the exhilaration of his work for the *Club de la Reforma*, then his eventual inauguration and overwhelming support. At that time it had seemed to him that he could do no wrong. Congress had allowed him to institute the reforms he wanted so badly. He had built long-promised schools and colleges so that Chile's young people could stand shoulder to shoulder with educated foreigners. He had strengthened the navy, providing modern equipment and commissioning new cruisers and torpedo ships so that Chile's navy was the envy of the world. The railways had been extended so that it was possible to travel from one end of the country to the other, without risking life and limb on the back of a donkey trudging over some high precipice on a godforsaken mountain.

He had wanted Chile to be proud. Not a country to be pillaged at will by whoever happened to be passing her shores in a tin boat. And he had done these things for his country, not for the benefit of his own pockets. 'Corruption!' some had shouted when contracts were handed out. But those who cried loudest were usually the ones whose own companies were losing out because their proposals were flawed or their finances were vague and incomprehensible. If there was corruption, no monies had flowed into his pockets. He had not been the one handing out unmarked packages under tables in darkened smoking rooms.

And so the early dizzying ascent had gradually fallen away, and like Icarus he was tumbling now with his wings in flames. Grumbling and unhappy faces stared back at him wherever he went. Worse. A few weeks previously, on his return to Santiago from Talcahuano, where he had inaugurated the new dry dock, he had been greeted with such loud whistling and jeering insults that armed officers had to lead him to safety through the crowd. The shock of it had drained all his strength. He barely made it inside the building. A kindly guard had placed a supporting hand under his elbow until he could lean safely against a wall and collect himself. And all the while, increasingly, his real enemies were hidden from him. He had thought naively that power resided with government, that if he could persuade Congress then all would fall into place. But his adversaries were not now in plain sight. There were other forces at work, unexplained allegiances that formed and re-formed, the spectre of foreign commerce on Chilean soil. And behind it all money, money, money, flowing away from Chile and into foreign chests.

He would say these things again in his manifesto just as he had said them before. And like before they would fall on deaf ears. In truth, he knew that his speech was a mere formality. Something to be got through. A mere clarification of intentions. A one-way trip. He looked out over the empty Chamber and wondered where it had all begun to unravel. Which month, which day, which remark? When was it? That exact moment when they had begun to turn?

In his head he began to read through the first words of his document, *Neither as a Chilean, nor as a Head of State, nor as a man of principle can I accept the political role the Parliamentary Coalition seeks to impose on me* ...

7 January, the *Imperial*, Valparaiso
'Launch coming up on the port side, Captain, sir.'

Between them and the mole they could see a launch approaching quickly through the choppy water towards the *Imperial*.

'Who is it, Webb?' asked Captain Stewart.

There was a pause. Webb strained to see through the telescope. 'Sir, I can see ... the harbourmaster, sir, and, blow me – sorry sir – Mr Walker, sir.'

'Are you sure? About Mr Walker?'

'Quite sure, sir. I can see his barnet from here, sir.'

'Webb! That's quite enough! Davies, Whiteway, follow me!'

'Sir, there are two other men in the boat ...' began Webb, but Stewart didn't even look around. He was making straight for his quarters.

The previous day Captain Stewart had received an abrupt and enigmatic note from Walker instructing the *Imperial* and its crew to remain in Valparaiso harbour. They were not to embark passengers or cargo. They were not to communicate with anyone on shore apart from himself until further orders. Nevertheless, under cover of darkness, Stewart had sent ashore three of his most trusted crew; one to get news of the latest events, one to procure a copy of *El Mercurio* and one to guard the boat in case someone commandeered it. The three descended into the shadowy launch armed with rifles stowed in the bottom of the boat and pistols inside their jackets.

'I'll be damned if we're going to sit here like bloody ducks in a shooting gallery,' Stewart had muttered to Davy as the men rowed away silently towards the lights of Valparaiso harbour. Then he had ordered the officers to get some sleep.

That was the night before. Now Stewart was leading Davy and William to his quarters, presumably to tell them what he already knew.

'If I am not mistaken,' said Stewart, sitting down at his desk, 'the men in the boat with Walker are Moraga and his second-in-command, Fuentes. Their intention is to seize the ship. They will take the ship for the government because the government has lost the navy.'

'Lost the navy!' William gasped in disbelief.

Stewart leaned into one of the desk drawers and pulled out a folded copy of *El Mercurio*. He unfolded it and flicked it on to the desk so that the front page was facing them. The headlines spoke of the *Junta de Gobierno* and an Act of Deposition.

'Captain Jorge Montt has set himself up as the leader of the insurgents. Along with a couple of others – Waldo Silva and Ramón Barros.'

Davy and William leaned over, scanning the Chilean paper for information.

'But surely, the *Compañía* won't allow it?' asked Davy.

'I doubt they can stop it. They have no choice,' replied Stewart.

William laughed, 'But sir, it's not much good having a ship without sailors!'

Stewart slumped back in his chair and looked at the two men. Davy thought he had the countenance of a benign father who despaired at his own ability to teach his sons anything useful. Davy groaned inwardly with realisation.

'They mean to ask us, don't they?' Davy said, and then turned to

William, 'That's why they've brought Walker.'

It all made sense. Davy leant back against the door. The three men contemplated the approaching boat and the possible scenarios. Then, with a resigned sigh, Stewart reached for his captain's hat and stood up. He lowered his voice.

'It is not my intention to go to war.'

'Sir?'

'Not against anyone. I don't intend to kill one Chilean to benefit another Chilean. Or worse still, kill Chileans to benefit some businessman the other side of the world. I'm afraid you must look to your conscience as I will look to mine. They may ...' and he paused, collecting himself, 'they may not accept a refusal, of course.'

'But sir ...' William began.

'William, listen. Walker is with them. That can only mean one thing. He has agreed. He has agreed to let them requisition the *Imperial*. He is coming to ask ... no, to *tell* us that we need to service the ship. He needs us to stay, otherwise – as you rightly say – the ship is of no use to them. And even if they could get some of the navy to return to the government's side, no one knows this ship like we do.'

'A fine war this will be!' Davy laughed. 'Balmaceda has all the army and the insurgents have all the ships – they will never even meet, let alone kill each other!'

'Balmaceda has made too many enemies amongst the wealthy, particularly the British, I fear. He talks of more independence for Chile. Industrialists like Colonel North will never endure it; they have all invested too much,' said Stewart.

They heard the sound of a whistle followed by a series of quick orders. The launch was approaching.

'We'd better go and put on a good show.' Stewart put on his cap, pulling it down firmly until it was just so over his eyes. 'You must consider what you will do, lads,' Stewart whispered as they made their way to the deck.

Davy's head was spinning. It had never occurred to him that he might have to sail on a man-of-war, and for a foreign country at that. They reached the deck and Stewart stepped up to the rail, ready to greet the visitors. The weather was deteriorating and the visitors disembarked with difficulty from the launch. Davy watched with particular enjoyment as Walker almost lost his step completely between the two vessels and got a good soaking. He was saved by Moraga's quick action, grabbing him by the scruff of the neck and drawing him back into the launch before he disappeared entirely under the foam. It was not the most graceful of manoeuvres. Walker looked ungainly and out of his element, and as he eventually emerged over the side of the ship he resembled a narrow-eyed water rat, the hair on his forehead pasted to his skin. One of the stewards rushed forward with a towel so that he could dry himself, which he did impatiently while trying to make light of the incident. When Walker had finished, he threw the damp towel back at the steward, barely looking at him and without so much as a 'thank you'.

Ignoring Davy completely, Walker made all the necessary introductions then asked that they be taken to the saloon, which would be more spacious and comfortable for a meeting than the captain's quarters. Moraga was accompanied by three of his officers, who were also clearly not used to a life at sea. One looked particularly pale.

'Should we follow?' Davy whispered. Stewart nodded his assent.

Once in the saloon, Walker went straight to the head of the table. Before sitting down, he pulled up the waistband of his trousers so that it seemed almost halfway up his chest, in a gesture of 'right, let's get down to business'. Moraga sat to his right, Stewart to his left. The soldiers and crew remained standing, taking up their respective 'sides' of the table.

'Gentlemen,' began Walker, 'as you know, war has broken out. The insurgents have declared against Balmaceda. The navy has defected, in its entirety, leaving the president with no naval capability whatsoever, barring a couple of transports. The *Lynch* and the *Condell* remain true to the government, but they are currently making their way back from Laird Brothers in Birkenhead. We're told they have reached Punta Arenas. The president is confident that it is only a matter of time before sections of the navy return to the fold. But until such time President Balmaceda has requested that the *Compañía* place the *Imperial* on loan to the government. The *Compañía* has agreed to this request. As of today, you will command this ship under Colonel Moraga's instructions.'

There was a long silence, then Moraga spoke.

'I know that you will be concerned for the safety of your men, gentlemen, but I can assure you that our intention is merely to use the ship to transport troops and supplies to various points along the coast. The crew will be considered entirely neutral and will not be placed in any unnecessary danger.'

Stewart, who had been listening intently but looking out of the porthole windows gauging the increasing spray, turned to look at the colonel.

'And are we to assume, then, Colonel Moraga, that we will receive those same assurances from your enemies?'

The question had been directed towards Moraga, but it was Walker who answered. 'The country is at war, Captain Stewart, no one can guarantee anyone's safety.' He spoke patronisingly, as if he had recently acquired some vast expertise in naval warfare.

'In that case, Mr Walker, I do not wish to prolong my employment. My officers and my crew must decide for themselves,' replied Stewart calmly.

Moraga and his soldiers stared in disbelief at Stewart. But rather than being angry as Davy expected, Walker began to smile slyly.

'I'm afraid, Captain Stewart, you are all bound by your contract, which states that any member of staff wishing to terminate his employment with the company must provide at least three months' notice unless a suitable replacement can be found sooner. I think you will agree that under the present circumstances, "suitable replacements" will be rather difficult to find.'

All the dining chairs of the saloon were fixed to the floor so Walker could not lean back and place his feet on the table. Instead, he swivelled menacingly, elbows planted either side on the carved armrests.

Stewart's eyes narrowed. 'My crew would have enlisted with the Royal Navy if they wanted to spend their days blowing people's brains out. We are contracted to ship passengers, cargo and mail. That is all. Not troops and arms under enemy fire.'

Walker smiled and continued to swivel slowly from side to side. He reminded Davy of the poker players in Marseille who just couldn't hide the fact that they held all the cards.

'I'm afraid, Captain Stewart, you have no choice,' smirked Walker, his voice high pitched with satisfaction as if he had just presented all his aces. *Go on, you little shit*, thought Davy, *put your feet on the table so that I can beat some manners into you.* Moraga looked uncomfortably from Walker to Stewart. Davy could tell that Moraga did not think much of Walker's negotiation skills and would have preferred to deal with the matter himself. Neither Moraga nor Walker could have anticipated Stewart's reply.

'That's where you are mistaken, Mr Walker. It appears that I know the contents of my contract better than you do, sir. I have a choice, right enough. I don't intend to remain on this ship for one second if it is to be a man-of-war. I know that the minute I step off this vessel two things will happen: my wages for the last three months will be forfeit and I will never find employment with the *Compañia* again. As to the latter, I have no concerns for my career. Half a dozen companies will employ me tomorrow, and I have no desire to work for a company who cannot look after its own men. Men who, I may add, are responsible for making this one of the most profitable shipping lines in the world. As to forfeiting three months' wages, which, incidentally, you have not yet paid me, I would rather be penniless for a few months than accept the proceeds of war. I take it you will be amply rewarded for your pains, Mr Walker?'

It was not Walker's purple face that Davy noticed first but rather Moraga's. He had the look of a man who knew that all wars are won by small battles. If all the battles in this war were going to be fought by people like Walker, then they had already lost. Davy could see that Moraga regretted the involvement of this man, who, rather than moving things forward as he had naively hoped, thinking that Walker would know his own men better than anyone else, had now set them back, irredeemably backwards because of his big stick and his ignorance. How did such men find success in commerce? On a battlefield someone would have put a convenient bullet in his back a long time ago. Moraga rose to his feet, and although the three soldiers behind him made no real move to engage their weapons, they appeared intensely alert to what was going on around them. Walker was about to add something, but Moraga cut across him in time.

'Captain Stewart. I must respect your opinion. I am truly sorry that we have not been able to persuade you of the validity of our cause. I had heard good reports of your abilities. We need people like you on our side, but not, of course, under duress.'

Moraga extended his hand towards Stewart and Stewart reciprocated amiably enough. Still seated, Walker turned aside in disgust and sniffed loudly as the two men shook hands. Davy and William followed Stewart from the room, and as they did so Davy glanced back to see Walker seething in his surprisingly stationary chair. Events had overtaken them, and for the time being Davy was not thinking any further than showing solidarity with his captain.

In the space of a few days the entire political landscape of Chile had changed. Davy had hoped, naively, that it would be possible to remain disentangled. But they were being thrust headlong into a fight that was not theirs. Now they had to make their own choice.

'The whole thing is ridiculous,' muttered Stewart as they walked back to their quarters. 'Haven't we learned anything at all in the last few thousand years? People rise up against one so-called dictator only to replace him with someone who is even worse. There's all this fine talk of freedom and justice, and all the while the sons and daughters of Chile will be slaughtered mercilessly when the people who really hold the power are sitting in their plush hotels in Buenos Aires, London, Paris or New York. Stick them all on a bloody ship, I say! They'd get on soon enough!'

Stewart returned to his cabin, and through the walls Davy could hear him cursing as he threw objects and books into his trunk.

'What are you going to do, Davy?' asked William at the door. 'Are you going with Stewart?'

Davy sat on the edge of his bunk with his head in his hands, then sat up and looked around the cabin. He had no desire at all to pack anything or leave the ship.

'I don't know. Don't you think that it is all a storm in a teacup, and before we know it Balmaceda will have relented and everyone will be happy again?'

William looked doubtful and leaned back against the door. 'Congress has been unhappy for a long time. It's a case of "Thus far you shall come, but no farther", perhaps?'

'Yes. "And here shall your proud waves be stayed."'

Davy thought of all the newspaper reports he had skimmed over recently. He wished that he had taken more notice of what was going on in *El Mercurio*. But although his Spanish was pretty fluent by now, it wasn't the sophisticated Spanish needed to understand the subtle nuances of a political situation. He could converse perfectly confidently with his Chilean stevedores, he could crack a joke, even sing in Spanish, but now he felt at a loss. He knew a little about the navy's warships, but not enough to prepare him for conflict. He needed to know their exact capabilities, their speed and manoeuvrability, where their weaknesses lay, how many crew, what guns? He was the chief officer of a merchant ship, not a trained officer on a man-of-war. What if things became protracted? Earlier that week he had heard some of the crew talking about Gatling and Hotchkiss guns and the latest torpedoes.

Davy's heart sank with a new awareness: many of the men could not afford to forfeit their wages or risk being without work. Someone had to think of them too. And what if Moraga was putting on a show? Stewart might be right, after all. Perhaps they didn't really have a choice?

There was a knock on the door and William stood aside to open it. Moraga seemed to fill the entire frame. He smiled at both of them and asked if he could speak with Davy. William excused himself and left them to talk.

Davy had not met Moraga before that day. He was surprised at his smartness and elegance despite the fact that he had a reputation for being a fearless soldier. When relaxed, his face was kindly too.

'Mr Davies,' began Moraga, pulling a wooden chair across the door and sitting down in a gesture that could have been threatening if it wasn't for his general friendly demeanour.

'We need to take provisions and ammunitions up the coast so that we can support the troops in Tarapaca. At the moment we have a ship, but no crew. I understand Captain Stewart's misgivings about the dangers: I would feel the same in his position, I can assure you. But let me paint a positive picture: we are confident that the war will not last long. The *Opositores* are badly organised, they have no weapons on land and no troops to speak of. Their soldiers, such as they are, come from the country. They are farmers and labourers more used to carrying scythes than guns. The *Imperial* is fast. Apart from the *Esmeralda*, not one of the opposition ships can match her speed. And if necessary we can place a certain number of guns on deck …'

Davy frowned at the thought.

'But there are other reasons a man may wish to dally with the risks of war, are there not, Captain? It would be your first commission?' Davy got the distinct impression that this was a man who did not ask questions unless he already knew the answer.

'I gather you gained your Master's certificate in '76. Fifteen years is a long time to wait for your own ship? Is it not? Even when the shipping line is a renowned one.'

Davy was disconcerted to think that Moraga knew so much about him and confused by the thought that he would have learned most of it through Walker. Moraga considered Davy for a moment then reached into his soldier's coat pocket. Davy's heart quickened; for a moment he thought Moraga might be pulling out a gun, that perhaps he was tired of slow persuasion. Moraga stood up from his chair and walked towards Davy. He was carrying a cloth bag.

'Open it,' said Moraga, smiling. 'President Balmaceda has allowed me to negotiate directly with you. He is prepared to offer you additional remuneration for …' Moraga could not find the right words to end the sentence and stopped short.

Davy looked in the bag. There were several hundreds of pounds' worth of gold coins, more than several years' wages.

'I can't accept this, unless my crew are looked after too. Those who wish to stay, that is.' Davy heard the words as if they came from someone else. Without hesitation Moraga replied, 'If you tell me what they are earning, I will double it.'

'Up front,' said Davy, firmly, again inwardly surprised at his own confidence.

'You have my word,' replied Moraga, stretching out his hand to shake on the agreement.

'Very well! And if the war is not over in three months, I reserve the right to leave, and for my crew to leave safely with no recriminations.'

It was a vain hope in wartime, Davy thought, but still he felt he should lay down the principle. Moraga lowered his face and frowned, but nodded his assent and shook Davy's hand. The colonel left Davy gazing down in disbelief at the overflowing bag of gold coins on his desk.

Davy closed the cabin door behind him. He looked around at his own captain's quarters for the first time. Sepulveda had made up the bunk with clean stiff sheets. All was neat and polished. His best suit hung on a hook, with his chest nearby. For years he had envisaged this moment. He had thought he would be dancing with glee.

'Yes, yes, yes! Father! Wherever you are ... see me now, a captain at last! Are you not proud? Your crazy unreliable son made good at last. Captain of the *Imperial*, not just any old steamer! Not just any old barnacle-encrusted *Cardigan Girl* dawdling around the Welsh coast with a load of dusty old coal. But a beautiful, sophisticated steamship, built by the world's best engineers.'

He wanted to be overjoyed. He wanted to revel in his achievement, in his small victory. If indeed it was a victory. The truth was that he had been appointed captain by default. Perhaps Walker knew that no one else would be fool enough to take the commission? Stewart's words came back to him over and over again: *the proceeds of war*.

When Stewart came to say goodbye after the meeting with Moraga and Walker, Davy had felt like Judas. Stewart had not talked of politics but only of the ship. He had given Davy some advice on handling the crew that remained.

'You need to keep an eye on Moretti. Don't give him the watch. He's not reliable any more. Too much grog. Although where the devil he's getting it from beats me. Silva has just lost his wife and child to cholera. Go easy on him. He's a bit distracted. I'm leaving you a case of *Islay*. You'll be needing it. Ask Sep. He knows where it is.'

Then he had placed his right hand on Davy's shoulder and looked at him sadly. 'I wanted to get you a ship, by God, but not like this. They're all bloody fools.

We must do as our own conscience dictates, Davy. I'm too old for this nonsense. But for you, who knows? Some good may come of it. You may get a chance to distinguish yourself. And you never know, if we're lucky, perhaps Walker will be obliterated by some friendly torpedo.'

Stewart had shaken Davy's shoulder and then embraced him warmly. Davy had been transported back over twenty-five years to the quayside in Cardigan, his father trying his hardest to find a way to say goodbye. That day, for whatever reason, his father had merely extended his hand, perhaps to underline that, although Davy was not yet sixteen, he was now a man in the eyes of the world, making his way to Gravesend to join the *Royal Dane* and a long voyage to Australia. His father's arm had held him firmly at a distance that day.

Stewart had turned to leave then added, with sudden gravity, 'If they try to put you in a Chilean uniform, it's time to quit. You know what I mean? The first chance you get, eh?'

Davy had nodded and watched the door close. And then had listened to the sound of Stewart's footsteps receding along the corridor. He had waited a while before appearing on deck so that the crew could say goodbye to their old captain properly. It had not seemed appropriate for him there at that moment.

After Stewart had gone, Davy made his way to the deck as captain. The change in people's response to him was immediate. He was now the skipper. All decisions and outcomes, both good and bad, rested with him. In the hierarchy of power on board ship, there was God, then there was the captain. Like a parent, he would learn to take pride in his crew's achievements and find his own way of dealing with their weaknesses and failures. And from now on all his own inadequacies as a man and a sailor would be like an open book. The cargo, the passengers, the crew, every rivet and ounce of coal would be his responsibility. This is what he had wanted all his life, to be captain of his own ship. To be called a captain. And he had been a sailor long enough to know that when an officer became a captain, there was no knowing what this new creature would be like. Some quietly efficient officers became vindictive tyrants. Some grey-faced invisible officers displayed unexpected strengths and reigned with the lightest of touches, gaining vast reservoirs of respect. He knew when all eyes turned towards him on deck that his men would be asking themselves the same question. How will he be, this new creature, Captain David Davies?

He caught sight of himself in Stewart's old full-length mirror. He had never thought of Stewart as a vain man, but there was no doubt that he had taken care of his appearance. Now Davy examined himself in the same mirror. Sepulveda had hurried to sew on his new badges and stripes, but his suit, although not exactly threadbare, could look better, Davy thought.

The man staring back at me has dark serious eyes and the weathered skin of a person who has spent his life outdoors. He has the strong broad shoulders of one who has been accustomed to ropes and weights and wheels. He has the bearing of one you would not wilfully antagonise. His hands are not those of a musician.

8 January, National Congress, Santiago

President Balmaceda scanned the long list of people that his secretary, Vásquez, had placed in front of him. The secretary had waited briefly in the room, no doubt expecting further orders, until Balmaceda had waved him out impatiently. In truth, Balmaceda did not know how he would react to this new information and wanted to be alone. He already knew who the main culprits were, of course: Jorge Montt, Ramón Barros Luco and Adolfo Holley, who had left Valparaiso on board the Chilean fleet. The entire fleet! He shook with anger at the thought of their duplicity.

He scanned the list pausing every now and again to take in the significance of every unexpected name. *Emil Körner*. He paused as if his heart was running a race and looked out of the elegant windows of his office at the National Congress building in Santiago. *Waldo Silva. If Silva has gone, then so have others. Every one a Brutus.* It was worse than he expected. Much worse. As if it was the scene of some awful carnage his eyes were drawn back to the atrocious list. And then he saw it. Written in blood, or so it seemed. *Errázuriz. No!* His body let out a wail as if an invisible hand had twisted and turned his intestines. *Federico Errázuriz Echaurren. No.* He would not believe it! He rose to his feet and paced around the table to the window as if movement might obliterate what his eyes had already taken in. *No, it's not possible. It's a lie!*

But each name was accompanied by a signature. Balmaceda turned the papers around frantically.

The Act of Deposition
We the undersigned blah, blah, blah …

Balmaceda screwed up the paper in his hand and growled at his own weakness. Errázuriz had less to be angry about than anyone. Balmaceda had indulged him at every turn. Only the previous August he had named him Minister of War and Navy. He had not complained then! He had been happy enough then to support the work of the Conciliation Cabinet. Strutting around in his fine suits, parading his importance. *The importance I gave him!*

Balmaceda unscrewed the paper and drank in the rest of the names as if they were a final draught of bitter poison. *What?* He held the papers out in front of him in disbelief. *What are they thinking? That this rubbish is constitutional? For all their talk of tyranny, do they think this is any more lawful that what I have had to do?* He paced around again with the papers in his clenched fist, not seeing anything real any more, just their faces, lined up in the corridors of Congress, smiling their sly smiles of betrayal.

The cold realisation that he had been shouting aloud washed over him. Calmly, he returned to his desk where he placed the list and began to flatten it slowly with the palms of his hands. *Ah, mis amigos queridos you think you have beaten me. But you have been like slugs hiding under dark stones. And the storm has brought you out.*

He stared coldly at the list, remembering each favour, each advantage bestowed, every word in the right corner that had benefitted each and every one of them at various times.

I have been blind. But I see you all now.

10 January, the *Imperial*, Valparaiso

The *Imperial* was moored at Valparaiso harbour, being fitted out as an armed transport. Although Chile was now officially at war with itself, very little had happened in the first three days. The town seemed peaceful enough but Davy was uneasy. He paced the decks keeping a watchful eye on Moraga's engineers. On his circuit, approaching the stern, Davy came across William, deep in conversation with one of the lookouts. Both had their spyglasses trained on the bay.

'What is it, Mr Whiteway?' asked Davy.

William looked puzzled. 'We're not quite sure, sir. It appears that the rebel navy is trying to pick a fight with the coastal forts. They've been steaming backward and forward all morning trying to draw attention to themselves. It's rather comical. We can make out four ships, the *Blanco Encalada, Esmeralda, O'Higgins* and *Magallanes*.'

Davy shuddered. William might as well have said, 'The Four Horsemen of the Apocalypse' for all the damage they could inflict on their ship if they chose to approach. It would be catastrophic.

'And the forts?' Davy added.

'Taking absolutely no notice whatsoever.'

William passed the spyglass to Davy and he found the ships easily, looming large just short of the horizon and circling as if on innocent manoeuvres. Far enough away to be out of the fort guns' range but still close enough to be threatening.

'Let's hope they stay where they are,' said Davy, handing the spyglass back to William and thinking that he would take another turn about the deck to get rid of some more nervous energy. He might walk for miles at this rate. Davy left the men and was about to climb the iron steps to the upper deck when he was called back.

'Captain Davies,' the lookout shouted, 'there's a launch!'

Davy returned to the lookout's side and the man passed his spyglass. The casing was not as smart as William's, the brass was tarnished and scratched and there was no ebony inlay, but when Davy brought it up to his right eye, the lens was good. The man was right. Emerging from between the larger ships was a steam launch puffing her way through the choppy waves, heading straight for the harbour. Davy strained to see how many people were on board. From this distance it was impossible to say. If the fort guns ever woke up, the launch would find it difficult to defend itself. Whatever it was they wanted, it was worth risking lives for.

'Fetch the colonel,' said Davy, handing the spyglass back to the lookout then turning to William. 'They may be coming for us.'

William laughed. 'How big is that launch? There are twenty, maybe thirty sailors in there, at the most. Moraga's lot will make short work of them if they come anywhere near us.'

'But the rebels may not know. Moraga has kept it quiet, for very good reason. They may only expect to find the *Compañía*'s crew.'

William was silent for a moment, pondering Davy's suggestion. Then, reaching into his pocket, and without taking his eye off the horizon, he removed a folded sheet of newspaper and handed it to Davy.

'I don't think they need us,' said William. 'They already have most of the ships in Chile.'

Davy opened out the paper. 'How on earth did you get this?' he asked, amazed. It was that morning's copy of *El Mercurio*. None of his crew would have been allowed on shore for fear of rebel snipers or spies. Davy scanned the sheet and found the section he wanted.

Compañía ships seized by the congressional fleet.

Beneath the heading, the list included the *Amazonas*, the *Cachapoal*, the *Limari*, the *Copiapó* and the *Itata*, all to be used as transports.

'And the *Aconcagua*' Davy gasped. She was the *Imperial*'s sister ship, also built by Lairds of Birkenhead, older, not as fast as the *Imperial* but still a fine ship. Davy knew all the captains and many of the crew on these other ships, and wondered whether it was a sheer coincidence that they were now the only *Compañía* ship in government hands. 'Under duress? Or has Walker done a deal with both sides?' asked Davy, knowing that William would not know the answer any more than he did.

Even to the naked eye, the launch was clear to see. The fort guns were eerily quiet and just as Davy was beginning to wonder whether the government had already surrendered before the war had hardly begun, Moraga appeared, striding towards them in his shirtsleeves with one of his soldiers following on behind.

'What do we have here?' he asked, accepting William's offer of the spyglass and holding it up to his eye.

Davy expected a robust response from Moraga but the man merely smiled.

'We have been expecting this all morning,' he said, looking entirely unperturbed and handing the glass back to William. 'They're certainly taking their time.'

Davy was aghast. 'But we're completely defenceless!' he said, wondering why on earth Moraga hadn't warned them that the ship was likely to be stormed. Images of hand-to-hand combat and a bloodbath on deck flashed across Davy's mind. They had been at war for mere days, not even made it out of harbour and now they were all going to be massacred where they stood.

'Our friends are heading for the *Huáscar*,' said Moraga, pointing across the harbour with a very self-satisfied laugh. 'So our intelligence tells us.'

Davy was struggling to keep up with Moraga's logic.

'*Señores*, the *Huáscar* was decommissioned before the war. It will make it out to sea but not much further than that. It will soon have, how shall we say, unexpected mechanical problems.' Moraga raised an amused eyebrow. 'However, its current value as a decoy is immeasurable. As you see, I, myself, am a decoy, gentlemen.'

Davy realised that the soldier behind Moraga had also removed his jacket and cap, as had the few soldiers gathering further down the deck.

'And what if your intelligence is faulty?'

Moraga sighed. 'Do you see those stacks of cargo?' He pointed. 'And that disused carriage there?' He went on to explain that over a hundred men had been stationed secretly, armed with enough weaponry to blow ten launches and their crews out of the bay. 'All incognito, of course.'

Davy had been keeping a watchful eye all morning, or so he thought.

He had not seen anything out of the ordinary. He had much to learn about war.

Moraga turned back towards the bow then added, 'Forgive my reticence, *Capitán*, but I am sure you can understand the need for secrecy. They will not come anywhere near your ship, I can promise you.'

For the rest of that afternoon the crew of the *Imperial* went about their usual business, only occasionally casting surreptitious glances across the harbour to where the *Huáscar* was churning out smoke and making her laborious way out to sea. Without drawing too much attention to themselves the engineers carried on with the work of fitting out the ship just as efficiently as before, but with a little more urgency.

'So, did the papers say which ships have been left to the government?' Davy asked William later that evening as they watched the last of the *Huáscar*'s smoke disappearing into the sunset's final glow.

William brought the spyglass down from his eye and folded it back in to itself.

'The small corvette *Abtao*, which is somewhere in the Mediterranean, the gunboat *Pilcomayo*, which is in the Straits of Magellan and two new torpedo-boat catchers, the *Almirante Lynch* and the *Almirante Condell* that have only just been fitted out and are still en route from England.'

No wonder the president needs the *Imperial*, thought Davy.

'Oh, and don't forget,' added William, 'the *Maipo* and the *Louis de Cousiño*.'

As both men crossed the stern, Davy laughed at the thought of the *Maipo*, not much bigger than a tug, and the creaking *Cousiño*. He leaned forward and placed his elbows on the rail. 'So Balmaceda has forty thousand troops, but only the *Condell*, the *Lynch* and the *Imperial* to move them around?'

'Yes,' William answered, 'and the *Condell* and the *Lynch* haven't arrived yet.'

Davy let his head drop forward. *Only the Imperial.* When he turned to face his chief officer, he half expected to see some expression of defeat or hopelessness on his face. But there was no such thing. William had his eyes fixed on Valparaiso, looking as confident and secure as a man who was about to embark on a week's mundane coastal mail deliveries.

'And you consider yourself to be a lucky man, William?'

William did not answer immediately, then laughed with bemusement at his own response. 'Yes!'

Over the sea, the sky was losing its burnished glow, and one by one the lights of Valparaiso began to twinkle above the harbour's crowded mastheads and funnels.

'Any other news we should know about?'

'It's snowing in England, and Madame Patti has received £30,000 for twenty operatic performances in Rio de Janeiro.'

'We're in the wrong bloody job!' Davy laughed.

They leant on the rail side by side. It was a sultry evening and the doors of San Francisco Church on Barón Hill must have been thrown wide open because over the tiled rooftops and through the narrow alleys, skimming the scrubbed decks and the rising tide soared the exquisite rising notes of the late sung mass.

'Tallis,' said William as if his meaning should be clear.

The choir, which seemed to have begun with only a single voice, now seemed to have swelled in numbers. There were ten, perhaps twenty …

'Forty voices,' said William, reading Davy's mind. Was no subject a closed book to this man, wondered Davy? How deficient his education seemed in comparison. He realised once again how much he envied William's effortless knowledge. Yet he always used his learning so lightly.

They listened. The song seemed to move between voices like a baton being passed through a crowd, now here, now there, rising and falling. Voices joined, then fell silent, then caught up the melody further along where it soared. It had an arc, thought Davy, like the arc of a life. A single voice starts then is joined by others. Sometimes one's own voice is drowned out. Or sometimes the melody is taken up by another which makes it stronger. Now the song seemed to pass back and forward in a series of questions and answers. Each question more complex, each answer more elaborate than the last. Still new voices joined and others fell silent.

Or like the arc of a war. Davy thought of the voices that had entered his life in the preceding weeks. Moraga, Balmaceda, the unseen voices of journalists, telegraph writers and distant politicians. Even familiar voices had taken on a different resonance, William's, Stewart's, Walker's. His own voice, which he had fought for so long to make the only voice of the deck, had to share its space now. He would have to find his way through all these others, here leading, there following. But from now on the story of his life could not be told in isolation. His fate was bound to theirs.

The voices of the mass diminished and for a moment, Davy thought they would fall off one by one until only one remained. But the voices rallied and although each one took a different pathway, the destiny was a single triumphant note, held long. The song ended, the sound cut as if by a sudden slice, though it echoed and echoed all around.

Estella looked down at the poached haddock which had been set before her and wondered, for a brief second, what on earth it was.

'*Señora,*' said the serving girl kindly, perhaps sensing her unease.

It was early morning at Villa D'Este and Estella was sitting opposite her husband at the long dining table. It was Laurence's particular wish that they should always breakfast together when he was home, although Estella was often bemused as to why. Most mornings he would eat his breakfast shrouded by the voluminous rustling pages of *El Mercurio*, oblivious to anyone. Every now and then he would splutter with agitation or mutter comments such as 'Enterprising businessmen will all be driven away at this rate!'

None of these utterings required a measured response from Estella and she would usually manage to ignore them, often having her own distraction of a medical journal. But since her walk back from Myrtle Villa that evening she could not concentrate on anything. She felt like an explorer on the verge of a momentous discovery. The conversation with Davy played over and over in her mind. She tried to dismiss it out of hand as the ramblings of two people who had drunk too much on New Years' Eve. They had both said too much. By now, no doubt, Davy would be sailing north as fast as his ship could carry him, propelled by embarrassment.

Estella prodded the fish with her fork, her eyes drawn to the pattern on the porcelain. It was the King pattern from the now 'Royal Crown' Derby. When Laurence read that the company was to be 'Manufacturer of porcelain to Her Majesty' he had insisted on buying an enormous dinner service complete with tureens and bizarre shell-shaped dishes. At first she had thought it attractive but this morning the blues and reds seemed almost tawdry, the pattern too frenetic. The food seemed to swim in front of her eyes.

The rustling newspaper had become silent. *Things must be serious*, Estella thought, still pushing a perfectly cooked flake across the glaze so that it lined up exactly on one of the gaudy leaves. But something had changed in the room and when she looked up she was alarmed to find her husband staring at her with interest.

'Unwell, my dear?'

Estella had never met anyone who could make a seemingly caring enquiry sound like some sort of rebuke.

'No. I was thinking about the coup,' said Estella, turning her attention back to the fish. She did not feel in the least bit hungry. She heard the paper rustle and Laurence ask for more tea. She pushed the fish flake between a red bloom and a gilt leaf.

'It's worrying,' he said, interrupting her thoughts. 'The rebel blockades will certainly make it difficult for shipping.' Estella heard him remove the silver lid from the sugar bowl, followed by the slow clinking of a cube against the porcelain as he stirred it around. 'And the work on the medical college will no doubt have to wait.'

Of course it will, realised Estella, and her heart sank. One of Balmaceda's most important projects had been the construction of new buildings at Santiago University. They were to house a dedicated medical school with some of the most advanced facilities in the world. There was even talk that women students would be admitted. Estella had broached the subject with Laurence some months before. She was surprised he had remembered.

Estella looked up and realised that her husband had folded his paper and his pale wintry eyes were concentrating intently on her. An image of Laurence came to her, the day they met.

It had been a perfectly normal day. She and her mother were carrying out errands and their final task was to pay for some parcels at Cumming's store.

'I would have them delivered to you today, ladies, but my boy is ill,' said Richard Cumming. 'Will tomorrow do?'

There was an ominous pause and Estella knew that her mother was working herself up to make a huge fuss.

'How many parcels are there, Mr Cumming, if I may be so bold as to intervene?' came a voice from behind them. And Estella turned to see a strikingly elegant man with such pale blue eyes they appeared to be almost transparent. After that, Estella barely got a word in edgeways. Before she realised what was happening, her mother had taken up the stranger's offer of arranging conveyance for the parcels, although for some inexplicable reason this stranger, Laurence Taylor, had insisted on carrying one of the parcels himself and walking them both home. Along the way, Estella had listened to animated talk of afternoon teas, picnics at the races and boxes at the opera.

'That was Laurence Taylor!' her mother had squirmed with delight as soon as the door was shut behind him. 'Of Taylor Copper Mines!'

'Really, Mother. You know I can't bear opera.'

'He's a very wealthy man!'

Estella sighed, untying her bonnet roughly and handing it to the maid. 'At least you could show a little gratitude.'

Estella wasn't sure what her mother meant. Was the gratitude supposed to be shown to Laurence Taylor for carrying some boxes, which could so easily have waited for delivery the following day? Or should she be grateful for her mother's attempts to embarrass her?

'He's obviously taken a liking to you.'

'He knows nothing about me.' *And neither do you*, thought Estella.

Yet over the following weeks and months, somewhere between afternoon tea at the Hotel Franc and the opening night of Verdi's *Otello*, Laurence Taylor's icy aloofness had somehow become attractive. For a brief period, which extended for the months of their engagement to a few months after their marriage, Estella had concocted a reality in which Laurence Taylor's reserved exterior was just a protective veneer, which, given a little time, would melt away to reveal a more complicated warmth, a more inquiring frailty.

These things had been revealed, as it turned out, but not to her. They had been laid bare to a woman in the Almendral, a dark, sensuous woman with a sharper wit and more forgiving curves. Conveniently for Estella's mother, death had turned up unannounced just before the whole disagreeable truth was discovered, denying Estella what might have been an exquisite *denouement*. Estella smiled absently to think of it then realised that she was still in the dining room, Laurence still concentrating on her.

'Something amuses you?'

'No, Laurence.'

For a moment, the urge to tell him what she knew was almost overwhelming. Would it not be better for everyone if they all lived honest lives? Laurence could install his mistress at the Villa D'Este, Estella could study medicine at Santiago. Everyone could be happy.

'No, Laurence. Nothing amuses me.'

Even as she said it, a vision flashed across the room, the twinkling lights of Valparaiso bay laid out below her and the smell of spent fireworks in the air.

Laurence took the napkin from his lap and Estella thought she saw him sigh.

'I am meeting a German diplomat this evening,' he said, getting to his feet slowly. 'So I shall be late.'

Estella couldn't resist. 'At the English Club?'

Laurence paused, then, placing the napkin carefully on his plate, said, 'No. I have grown rather tired of the club of late.'

And then he did something extraordinary.

'Would you see me to the door?' he asked.

Estella had not accompanied him to the door since the first days of their marriage.

'Of course,' she said, rising to her feet.

Laurence walked ahead of her. The lad at the door brought Laurence's coat and helped him put it on. 'That's all,' said Laurence. He took his hat and waved the lad away. Estella followed and they both stood on the doorstep, like awkward strangers not quite knowing how to bring their encounter to a close.

'This war won't last too long,' said Laurence, looking down at his hat. Before Estella could think of a reply, he leant across and kissed her on the cheek. It was the briefest of kisses and it felt, to Estella, like a kiss of regret, or of a final parting, or possibly both.

She watched as her husband walked down the path towards the iron gate. His shoulders were less angular than she remembered and his gait, which had always been upright and brisk, seemed to lean ever so slightly to one side, giving the briefest impression of a limp. Estella struggled to recollect some recent injury or damage but the truth was, she realised, Laurence was getting older. He passed through the gate without looking back and carried on down the avenue, soon passing out of sight.

CHAPTER 13

20 January, 1891, National Congress, Santiago

It was impossible to know what to do. All morning Balmaceda's ministers – those that were left to him – had been briefing him on the latest developments. Reports came in by the minute, it seemed, and everyone walking the corridors of the Chilean Congress appeared to be waving some ominous piece of paper, each more serious than the last. But the ministers' opinions on the best course of action differed. Even the facts differed depending on whom he believed. The telegraph stations were all still under his control but messages contradicted each other. Someone, somewhere, was lying.

The coast was being blockaded by rebel ships. This much he knew because he had seen it with his own eyes the previous day at Valparaiso, where the *Blanco Encalada* prowled the extremities of the bay.

'Why on earth is the *Imperial* still in Valparaiso?' he had shouted at two of Moraga's men earlier that morning.

They had made feeble excuses about the engineers waiting for suitable fittings for the guns, ammunition not arriving because of the blockade and other technical details that Balmaceda did not understand.

'She's not a warship, sir,' added one of the men; patronisingly, or so Balmaceda thought.

'I know what she is, you fool! I'm telling you that unless we get troops to Tarapacá before the rebels do, we might as well surrender right now. We need to keep our hands on the revenue. Get that ship out of harbour and past that bloody blockade! Or do I have to do it myself?'

Balmaceda turned away in disgust. The province of Tarapacá was at the heart of the nitrate industry, Chile's main source of income. He thought this was obvious to anyone. Why, at this crucial moment in his presidency, was he surrounded by imbeciles?

Vásquez entered the room at that moment and, seeing the look on the soldiers' faces, hastily urged them out.

'Sir. We're getting reports that the garrison at Pisagua has revolted.'

Balmaceda turned to his secretary and scanned the telegrams. 'How many?'

'Over three hundred.'

Balmaceda paused over a section of information. 'They've been offered money?' He looked at Vásquez in disbelief.

'It seems so. We need confirmation. We need your permission to question Rivero.'

They both knew what this meant. The last time Balmaceda had spoken privately to Rivero it had been a week or so before the outbreak of war. They had talked of their children and their education, their temperaments, how they thought things would go for them in the world.

Balmaceda sat down at his desk and put his face in his hands. This was the real meaning of war. Not the necessity of firing at some faceless army across a barren wasteland with guns so destructive that you never had to look at your opponent's face, but the cold detachment required to turn on a friend who had walked the same corridors as you. Balmaceda uncovered his face and leaned forward for his pen. He knew the contents of the document. He had helped to write it. He had hoped never to use it.

'Not those Alvarez thugs. Get someone else,' said Balmaceda, staring at the gaping space at the bottom of the document.

Reluctantly, he scrawled his signature in the gap followed by the date. Instantly, the page was whisked away. Vásquez hurried out of the room, and for a moment Balmaceda thought of the document's journey through the busy corridors, past the Chamber and by messenger to the gaol where Rivero was already being held. He seemed for a moment to stand at the very door of the cell itself, and when Rivero turned to him with surprise, Balmaceda looked down at a man who was already broken, beaten and bruised. Sorrow overwhelmed him. He shook himself back to his desk at the National Congress to find bitter tears of anger and loss streaming down his face.

11pm, 27 January, the *Imperial*, Valparaiso
Davy couldn't believe they were still in Valparaiso. Every day was going to be their last. But each morning, one of the government engineers would pipe up that they needed more time for some essential last-minute adaptations. *They're in cahoots with the rebels! They must be!*

Davy was making a vague attempt to organise his desk, throwing reference books and charts on to the shelf behind him and slamming drawers. But in truth, it was more to relieve his general impatience with their circumstances than with any real desire to sort out his paperwork. 'I'm telling you, William, we might as well paint a massive bull's eye target on the side of our ship if we stay here any longer.'

William said nothing. He crossed the room and rearranged the items that Davy had just placed on the shelf which were now precariously balanced.

'When we agreed to stay on the ship, we agreed to sail her, not just sit on her, in harbour, for nearly a month!'

'Twenty days.'

'We're sailors. We're meant to be on the water! In boats!'

To make matters worse, Moraga had informed them half an hour earlier that the *Imperial* would most likely remain in harbour at least another week. Davy was furious, and vocal with it. With Moraga's back turned, William had rolled his eyes in Davy's direction just soon enough for them all to avoid a major confrontation. Davy had left the room with an utterly pointless Parthian shot, exclaiming that Moraga should really read up on the exploits of the Confederate raiders to learn how proper blockade runners did it.

'You're never going to win a war sitting in the dock tarting up the ship for an entire month! Doesn't the president need troops in Tarapacá?' At which point Davy had found himself being bundled out of the door by William's magnetic glare. This recollection brought Davy abruptly back to the cabin and to the fact that William was delving quite deliberately through his desk drawers.

'What are you doing in there?'

William smiled innocently and extracted a brand new pack of cards. 'This will do the trick!'

William was right, of course. He really did need a distraction. Action was most definitely the best antidote for frustration, and there were only so many times one could check the stowing of the hold or the contents of one's logbook.

Less than an hour later, Davy, William, Evans the engineer and Tony the cook were settling in to a game of whist in a corner of the games room. It was dark outside and the atmosphere on board the *Imperial* was subdued. Evans had just won a second trick and was about to deal again with his old miner's hands when there was an unusual vibration through the ship. The men around the table froze and looked up at Davy. Around the saloon, conversations stopped abruptly. Then in the distance, through one of the open windows, came a shrill scream, 'Torpedo!'

The men abandoned their cards and ran to the deck. Moraga was already there, and armed soldiers were gathering around him looking towards a steam launch, which was speeding away from the *Imperial* towards the eastern part of the harbour.

'¡*Ah, Canalla!*' Moraga shouted above the commotion. 'You missed!

You scoundrels! Come back here and try that again, you cowards!'

The ship was already out of the Gatling guns' range but nevertheless the gunners sent a round in its direction. A loud raucous cheer rose from the troops.

The second officer rushed up to Davy and explained how the crew had spotted the unmarked launch approaching the harbour. Within seconds, the unmistakable wake of a self-propelled warhead was seen tracing its way towards them in the moonlight, but at the last moment it had veered off course towards the harbour. Not only had it narrowly missed the *Imperial* but also the Pacific Steam Navigation Company's *Britannia*, which was moored right next to them. However, nothing had exploded, and the officer could offer no explanation for what had taken place.

'Ha! They won't come back now, Captain, with all these guns pointing at them!' shouted the officer over the din of the Gatling guns' continuous firing.

Then, as if the launch had heard the officer's taunt, it turned unexpectedly in a graceful, deadly arc and began making its way back towards the *Imperial*. For a moment, the gunners and the soldiers were stunned into silence. Indignant, and like a badly rehearsed chorus in a pantomime show, they were whipped up into a comical frenzy. Every weapon that could be turned towards the oncoming boat was fired at will.

Nothing will stop them, thought Davy. We are sitting ducks. They watched, powerless, as the launch advanced on its audacious and seemingly suicidal mission. At the very least the ship would sink, but if the torpedo came anywhere close to their stocks of ammunition, they would all be blown to kingdom come. The launch kept coming. The soldiers stood firm but the crew began to scatter. Once the launch came within range, sparks and flames erupted around it as the gunners hit their mark.

'Now we have you! *¡Bastardos!*' shouted Moraga through the noise and smoke.

When the launch began to turn away from them a second time, the gunners and soldiers were so surprised that for a moment they gawped, open-mouthed, at the inexplicable manoeuvre.

'Ha! Changed your minds have you?'

As the launch retreated to the other side of the harbour, the soldiers opened fire again, resentful now that they had been denied a decent fight. They looked away to the east and saw the guns at Fort Andes opening fire on another vessel in the far distance. Davy strained to see the ship's outline, the telltale number of masts and funnels that would show him which of the rebel's ships this was. Each time the guns were fired he counted: two tall masts, one shorter mast at the end, a central funnel (squat, not tall) armoured (he could see the orange lights reflecting on her cladding in the darkness): it was the *Blanco Encalada*. The famous *El Blanco* that had captured the Peruvian monitor *Huáscar* during the War of the Pacific; built by Earls of Hull, two compound engines, six boilers, twin screw and, most importantly, only 12 knots to the *Imperial*'s 15.

Now that the guns at Fort Andes had woken up, they would be enough to ensure the defence of the *Imperial*. But the troops on board were still excitable and not about to leave their guns in a hurry. They broke into one of their rousing Nationalist songs.

Davy turned to William and muttered under his breath, 'I think everyone knows which side we're on now, don't you? Let's get back to our cards. I've just remembered Stewart's bequest of Islay. I think we deserve a few glasses after that performance.'

William laughed, but in truth they had been in a perilous position. The ship was loaded to the gunnels with ammunition and high explosives.

'Aye, Captain, that could have been curtains for all of us, no mistake,' Evans came up to both of them. 'It's a good job he was chicken.'

Davy followed Evans and William back to the games room, leaving the president's troops cheering and singing to the sound of the guns at Fort Andes echoing around Valparaiso bay.

The men resumed their game, and had only been playing for a few minutes when Sepulveda, the steward, came striding into the room.

'¡*Capitán!* We have a problem.'

The men looked up and drew their cards to their chests instinctively.

'The *dottori*, he has jumped ship. The lookouts have just seen him running away from the harbour. Shall I send men after him, sir?'

'Christ. We only took him on before Christmas!' said Evans, throwing his cards down in disgust. 'I knew he was a bad 'un the second I clapped eyes on him.'

Davy thought for a moment. 'No, don't send anyone. Let him go. He was free to choose. It just took him longer than most to make up his mind.'

Sepulveda nodded and left the room.

'What are we going to do without a doctor?' asked William.

It wouldn't be easy to find a replacement. A commandeered mail ship, desperately outnumbered by enemy troops, was not an attractive prospect for any man. Davy lowered his hands and considered his cards. Not the best hand he had ever seen, but he could do something with them.

'I'm sure Moraga will find us a replacement,' said Davy, 'and in the meantime, well, Tony, you're a dab hand with a hacksaw aren't you, now?'

Tony grinned, which was a rare thing because no one could remember ever having seen Tony's teeth before. They were small and yellow like rows of corn and looked particularly menacing.

28 January, Valparaiso
Word travelled quickly the next morning. The Whitehead torpedo had been disabled and placed on display outside the *Intendencia* so that the crowds could see what manner of evil machinery had been hurled at the government's army during the night. People looked on, amazed at its terrible beauty, as if one of them had just dragged a real live witch-mermaid from the depths of the sea. One or two brave onlookers approached it gingerly to stroke its sleek metal skin.

'It's perfectly safe!' declared a man in a top hat and red cravat, who seemed to have appointed himself guardian. A photographer and his assistant appeared, and soon queues of people were lining up to have their photographs taken alongside the torpedo.

'Ladies and gentlemen. Let me present the Whitehead torpedo: eleven and a half feet long with a diameter of fourteen inches and packed with a forty-pound deadly warhead.'

The crowd gasped and shrank back.

'It wasn't very dangerous at all was it, *Señor*? It didn't explode!' shouted a boy in the crowd.

'Not on this occasion, no. And a good thing, too,' shouted the man in the top hat, scouring the crowd for the faceless heckler, 'otherwise the *Imperial* and the PSNC's *Britannia* would be sitting at the bottom of the harbour as we speak!'

The man turned his attention once more to the alarming missile.

'Ladies and gentlemen, look carefully at this wonder of engineering, this testament to British invention and ingenuity. This is the way of the future in the world of modern warfare!'

All day there had been a constant stream of onlookers, but eventually the crowds thinned and Davy watched from the bridge as the last few stragglers headed for home. The events of the previous evening had played on his mind. He had slept fitfully, dreaming of duplicitous engineers concocting dastardly plots to scupper the *Imperial*'s engines. This evening he had posted double the number of lookouts, and with the guns at Fort Andes providing a comforting defence Davy was looking forward to a solid night's sleep. He turned to leave, bidding goodnight to the officers on watch, and made his way down the flights of metal stairs towards his cabin. Deep in his own thoughts, he almost walked headlong into Moraga.

'Captain Davies,' Moraga began, 'you will be delighted to hear that we are leaving tonight. I have my orders from the president himself. Following last night's little escapade we thought it only wise.'

'This evening?' replied Davy, making no attempt to conceal his surprise and irritation. Davy's bunk now seemed like an enticing, dissipating hallucination. 'But where are the troops?'

'Gathered in warehouses on the outskirts of town, awaiting my orders, eight hundred of them.'

Davy did a quick mental calculation.

'And provisions,' Moraga added.

Davy calculated again. Unless they were careful, it would be getting light by the time they were ready to leave.

'We must get as many troops as possible to Tarapacá, Captain Davies. We must take Iquique from the rebels as soon as we can.'

Davy took off his cap, scraped his nails back through his hair in one slow sweep. After three weeks' deliberation, it seemed they were finally going to war. Many evenings would have been perfect for sailing out of Valparaiso under cover of darkness, but this was not one of them. The tides were contrary. The crew were worn out after the previous night's encounter with the torpedo launch. He himself was feeling tired and irritable.

And Moraga, who was usually in the habit of barking orders at his men and then walking off in the confident knowledge that his exact instructions would be carried out to the letter, was still standing there, facing Davy. The colonel had the look of a man who was waiting patiently for an answer, but Davy wasn't sure what the question had been and his heart leapt momentarily.

'Are you with us, Captain Davies?'

It had all the appearance of a question, but there was a trick in it. This was a question to which there could only be one answer, and the answer itself was not enough. Davy raised the cap to his head and pulled it on firmly.

'Yes, Colonel,' Davy replied, hoping that Moraga had not heard the crack in his voice or noticed the tiny part of a second that passed in hesitation. Moraga lingered. 'All hands it is, Colonel.'

Moraga nodded, apparently satisfied, and made his way along the deck towards his gathering officers.

Davy turned towards the bridge.

I will go before thee, and make the crooked places straight: I will break in pieces the gates of brass, and cut in sunder the bars of iron.

Davy heard his father's voice and steadied himself against the handrail. He was a young child at the kitchen table, he and Gruffudd begging their father, yet again, to read the story of Cyrus being called by his God. The images of omnipotent destruction had appealed to the boys much more than the wishy-washy lambs and angels favoured by their sisters.

'I will make the crooked places straight!' Davy had bellowed later, wielding a makeshift wooden sword while tumbling through stacks of hay.

'And I will break in pieces the gates of brass!' returned Gruffudd, his willow bow twanging with the release of a pointy stick.

Davy thought about his family for the first time in months. His retired father, now eighty-three and still going strong. Gruffudd, married to an ambitious woman with no humility and even less sense of humour. Jane, contented with her childhood sweetheart. Six children and counting. They had been reduced to people in photographs and letters. Davy strained to remember the smell of his father's pipe or the damp wool of Gruffudd's working jacket.

Davy climbed the steps to the bridge and, without further explanation, gave the order for all hands on deck. The officers, who like him had grown accustomed to waiting, looked around in surprise. The last watch had only just gone to their bunks. They would not be pleased. But the order was carried out and soon the deck was crowded with irritable crew and clumsy soldiers.

'And enough ammunition to catapult us all to the planet Mars,' said William, joining Davy on the bridge.

Davy thought of the eight hundred soldiers trying to get into the two remaining lifeboats which had been left to them after all the engineers' adaptations. If it came to it, an explosion would probably be a blessing.

On that first voyage the *Imperial* steamed north out of Valparaiso under cover of darkness, staying well away from the coast for fear of spies. All was quiet on board. Eagle-eyed lookouts were ordered to scour the horizon in every direction for signs of the enemy.

'Don't you remember, Captain?'

Davy had asked Evans to join him and William in a quiet corner of the saloon to discuss blockade-running tactics. Evans was recounting tales of the American Civil War and the daring escapades of the Confederate ships.

'The *R.E. Lee* ran the blockade twenty-one times in ten months, she did. *Duw*, they were cunning! Master sailors, mark my words.' Evans set his whisky glass down decisively as if he had just pronounced a benediction.

'We're just as fast,' said William.

'Oh, yes, that's true. Speed is our ally. But we'll need something more than that.' Evans leaned in towards Davy. 'You need to throw out your timetable, Captain.'

Davy wasn't sure what Evans was getting at. It was a while since another sailor had told him how to run a ship. But Evans pressed on.

'Captain, in all your time with the *Compañía*, you've had to be at a certain place at a certain time, haven't you? The shareholders wouldn't like it if they thought passengers were waiting for you at Pisagua when you were still dawdling at Callao, would they? It's always had to work like clockwork. Never mind the weather and the tides. You've always had to be where you say you're going to be, when you say you're going to be there.' Evans reached for the bottle and topped up his glass. 'But not any more. Get rid of it, Captain. You've got to start thinking like a rodent! That weather you thought was your enemy can now be your friend. You can disappear in the squall and the fog. Those coves you know so well, which you've always avoided, they'll be your hidey-holes. You will conspire to be where they least expect you to be, and the moment their back is turned …' Evans made a whistling sound, and for a brief second Davy could swear that his chief engineer had turned himself into a mouse and darted out of the door. Davy noticed William's smile and knew exactly what he was thinking. With all his dramatics, Evans really should have been on the stage. 'Think of it this way, Captain, the blockaders have all the disadvantages. They have to sit around in their tubs all day, twiddling their thumbs, hardly touching land for weeks on end waiting for that one fatal moment when you slip past them in the dark, and unless they're sharp it's all over in seconds!'

Davy was about to admit that this was a good point and to agree that being a blockade runner was a much more exciting prospect than being a blockader when Evans downed the last of his whisky and turned to them in horror.

'Why haven't we painted out the funnels?'

The three of them looked blankly from one to the other.

'Hell's bells!' said Evans, setting his glass down with a thud and getting to his feet, 'Red funnels with black tips, we might as well announce our arrival with trumpets! We're a fine set of musketeers. Camouflage, gentlemen! Camouflage! We're not being nearly devious enough.'

And with that Evans left the saloon, muttering something about mixing cans of grey paint the exact same colour as fog.

Less than an hour later, when Davy was just drifting off to sleep in his bunk, he was woken by one of the junior officers. The lights of an approaching vessel had been spotted in the darkness.

Davy reached for his trousers and clambered in to them, losing his balance momentarily, his shoulder colliding painfully with the panelled wall.

Days earlier, before they set sail, Davy had agreed with crew that at night they would sail in virtual darkness with the least number of lights as possible betraying their whereabouts. When Davy came out on deck, he saw that most of those lights, even the ones which until then had been deemed essential, were now switched off.

Davy scanned the horizon and there it was, the unmistakable dazzle and reflected glow of a warship. At this distance, in the dark, there was no way of telling which one it was. She could be a neutral American or British warship. She could be an enemy torpedo ship. Few of them would be as fast as the *Imperial*. Only the *Esmeralda* was capable of overtaking them with ease.

But, whatever she was, she was heading straight for them, more or less, on the starboard side. Davy watched her approach. His natural instinct was to steer the *Imperial* away. But to do so would mean turning her starboard on to the approaching vessel, making her even more vulnerable.

Davy fumbled his way to the bridge and gave the order to reduce speed but to hold their course. Almost immediately, Moraga appeared.

'Captain Davies, I have no intention of engaging with that ship, we must head straight for Iquique,' he said, very loudly. Davy winced. On a still night such as this, it was possible to hear even the quietest voice over water.

'Colonel,' Davy replied calmly and quietly, 'you have requested that I keep the soldiers out of harm's way.'

'Indeed I have! So why are we sailing straight towards that ship!'

Davy explained to the colonel that with their bow facing the approaching vessel and with their lights dimmed, they were virtually invisible.

'That's if the moon stays hidden and no one waves his shiny bayonet around in a matchlight,' he whispered. 'Or makes a noise, Colonel. The men must be silent. Not a sound. Not a whisper.'

There was a long pause and Davy could only guess at Moraga's expression.

'Very well, Captain,' replied Moraga, quieter this time. 'I will see to it.' And he left.

The *Imperial* slowed until her engines were barely turning. Even the glint of reflected light on a bow-wave could give her away. On deck, Moraga gave instructions that the men should lie low, hide their faces and not utter a word unless they wanted to be court-martialled the following day and shot by himself, personally.

As the ship made her final approach, Davy gazed in wide-eyed amazement. It was the *Huáscar*, the very ship which had been commandeered by the enemy from under their noses only a few days before. She came so close that Davy was able to see soldiers walking about on the deck and hear them singing.

Slinking by in the darkness, Moraga's men were desperate to open fire from the *Imperial's* decks, but the colonel calmed them down.

'We must choose our battles carefully, men. Our priority is to take Iquique. The *Huáscar* must wait if we are to win the war.' The troops fell silent again and watched regretfully as the enemy vessel's lights faded into the night.

The following morning they were disembarking troops at a small deserted harbour when a ship was spotted on the horizon approaching directly from the west.

'Colonel, we must get the ship out of harbour now!' shouted Davy. 'We don't have time to land them all!'

Moraga was incensed. '¡*Loco!* That would be suicide! I can't leave half my men stranded here with no ammunition and no food.'

'Then we must bring them all back on board! The ship must leave now if we are to stand a chance.'

'You crazy English! You know nothing of warfare!' Moraga had shouted in between orders to carry on disembarking the troops.

In reality Davy had no choice but to concede. Hundreds of troops ran down the gangway. Ammunition, animals, guns and provisions were offloaded in record time. Men carried boxes between them rather than wait for the hoists, and anything round was rolled. A crate of rifles, roughly handled, split open and tipped its contents into the churning waters.

'You idiot!' a soldier shouted and someone else pulled a pistol. There was a scuffle and a shot rang out, but within seconds Moraga was at the scene.

'Bind their hands! Both of them! And get them on the carts. ¡*Santo Dios!*'

Davy watched Moraga as he shouted orders. He was an effortless and gifted leader of men, thought Davy, and a frantic situation, which could have descended into utter chaos, was deftly managed.

'There, *Capitán*, we are done,' said Moraga as Davy watched the distant ship through his telescope.

'Our friends in the west have reconsidered their course, it seems, and are heading south after all, Colonel.'

Moraga sighed with relief or frustration, Davy could not tell which.

'Let's hope it's the last we've seen of them. Now we must return to Valparaiso to collect reinforcements while these men make their way to Iquique.'

'We won't be going anywhere until nightfall, I can promise you,' remarked Davy, still watching the ship, 'not with so many enemies prowling the coast. We've had another narrow escape I would say, and I can only assume that they mistook us for one of their own, the *Aconcagua*, most likely. An easy mistake to make at a distance.'

Davy thought of the *Imperial*'s distinctive funnels. There had been no time to carry out Evans' plan of camouflaging the ship, and on this occasion it had worked to their advantage. But the chance that their enemy would make the same mistake twice was slim. Misty grey paint was not a bad idea at all, and he decided that, on balance, complete invisibility was infinitely preferable to a lucky case of mistaken identity.

CHAPTER 14

30 January, London

The Right Honourable Sir James Fergusson, Undersecretary of State for Foreign Affairs, Member of Parliament for Manchester North East and sixth Baronet, left his London residence in Curzon Street and began his brisk walk towards the Houses of Parliament. The sky was a dirty white and heavy with the threat of January snow. The new footman had asked him whether he wanted the carriage brought around 'on account of the weather', but Fergusson had answered him sharply that come hell or high water he would always walk to work and that it benefited his constitution to do so, and what's more it was his time to think about the day ahead. He regretted his tetchiness now, and resolved to be friendlier when he saw him next. He knew little about the personal details of his staff, and even nine years after Olive's death he took little interest in the workings of his own house. Staff came and went. He learned some of their names.

But he thought about Olive every day. And lately he had also found himself thinking about his first wife, Lady Edith. Was it disloyal, he wondered, to miss both his dead wives? Pulling his woollen coat tighter, he strode along the street with his head down. He thought about the previous evening's reception at the Royal Geographic Society and of his meeting with Isabella Twysden. His son, Richard, would like her, he thought, brushing away the first flecks of dry snow from his eyes and nostrils with his gloved hand. She had a gentle face and an elegant bearing.

A tramp crouched down in a doorway looked up at him and called out, 'Look out Guv'nor, there's a blizzard coming.' Fergusson strode past, ignoring his words and only vaguely registering his subsequent mumblings for spare change. As he approached the Houses of Parliament, the bitter wind whipped around the great building and tiny flakes of white billowed in the sky. The Commons porter, white as a sheet, smiled grimly as he passed through the doors and into the entrance corridor.

Fergusson watched as James Archibald Duncan, the portly, unmarried Member for Barrow-in-Furness, rose to his feet in the Chamber. Duncan's father, also a James, had been in business with Balfour. Fergusson disliked him intensely and wondered how many queries the long-winded Duncan would be able to fit into one question this time.

'I beg to ask the Undersecretary of State for Foreign Affairs,' Duncan began, waving his papers in front of him but not referring to them at all.

Well rehearsed, then, thought Fergusson. *Centre stage now.*

'Whether Her Majesty's government is in telegraphic communication with the British Minister at Santiago, and the Commander of the British Squadron on the coast of Chile …'

Not really a question, unless you're insinuating that I am not doing my job properly?

'Whether he will state what the latest information is which has been received by the government with regard to the course of the revolution in Chile …'

Why would I not tell you, if I knew?

'And whether there is any truth in the report recently published that the British and other Foreign Ministers at Santiago have threatened to withdraw from the country.'

Fergusson knew full well that another question was on its way, but began to stand up.

'And,' resumed Duncan pointedly at which point Fergusson sat down again with a thump, catching the amused glances of the Members opposite. Everything about Duncan was amusing, thought Fergusson.

'And, if that report be true, and the threat be carried into execution, what protection would be available to British subjects in Chile in the absence of the British Minister?'

Fergusson would have liked to answer that he knew Duncan's father had business interests in Valparaiso, some of them more 'fly by night' than others, it had to be said, and that despite all his high-sounding ideals he was merely looking after his own and his father's pockets.

Fergusson looked down at his papers and took his time before getting to his feet. *Stand tall. Chin up. Deep breath! For Heaven's sake, try to look as if you know what you're talking about, Fergusson.* He could hear his debating master at Eton shouting even now after all these years.

He delivered his answer to the entire floor in a deliberately leisurely fashion without so much as glancing at Duncan, and the murmuring and fidgeting fell away.

'The latest telegram from the admiral in command of the squadron was received from Callao via Lima on the twenty-third of January. He was about to start for Coquimbo. He reported that telegraphic communication from thence with Chile was interrupted, but he would, of course, have means of sending back messages to Callao, where he has left a vessel to bring messages from home if necessary. HMS *Champion* had brought news that Valparaiso and Iquique were blockaded, and that there had been firing between the ships and the shore on the eighteenth of January.

'The latest telegrams from Her Majesty's Minister at Santiago were received on the eighteenth and nineteenth of January. At that time he did not apprehend bombardments nor serious injury,' Fergusson paused and placed his emphasis carefully, 'to general commerce.'

A Member next to Fergusson coughed the kind of cough you make when you want to draw attention to something rather than one that is a physical necessity. Fergusson went on.

'No report whatever has been received of any threat on his part or that of the other foreign representatives to withdraw. Inquiries will be made of Her Majesty's Minister. We have no reason to believe that either the government or the insurrectionists have any hostility to Englishmen or other foreigners.'

Or to tradespeople. Fergusson sat down and dug his elbow discreetly into his coughing colleague's ribs. Even though the topic was of minor concern to most of the Members, someone on the benches opposite felt compelled to make a derogatory comment about the government's foreign policy, and a ripple of belly laughter spread outwards, gaining momentum as it went. By the time the joke, whatever it was, reached the back of the Chamber, those Members on the furthest benches guffawed as if they had just heard the funniest comment in their entire life. Fergusson was pretty sure none of them had any idea what was going on.

Around him, Fergusson's colleagues were now making reciprocal bellowing sounds.

'Order!' shouted the Speaker.

Fergusson raised his face to the gallery, scanning it dispassionately for any familiar faces. He recognised no one, so he looked upwards again towards the high wooden panelling and the fading daylight coming through the stained-glass windows. He let his head relax backwards as far as it would go, and surveyed the dark geometry of the ceiling directly above him. If the room had been silent, his colleagues would have heard him let out a prolonged groan of disgust and frustration. As it was, no one heard him because, by that point, the Chamber had descended into predictable chaos.

'Order!' bellowed the Speaker, rising to his feet.

When Fergusson eventually emerged from the House, London was swaddled in a thick white blanket. The bitter wind had eased and dry flakes of snow spiralled gracefully downwards all around. He often emerged from the Chamber dazed by the machinations and wondering what real difference any of it made, all the stuff and smoke. Duncan had been like a puffed-up pigeon, thought Fergusson, remembering how he had watched him in the panelled corridors afterwards, sidling up to the Speaker, finding things too funny, laughing too loudly. *These strutting people are full of self-interest.* He cringed at the memory of Duncan boasting publicly that it was 'who you know and not what you know' that really mattered in the modern world. *Heaven help us. They have no grace.* 'We all know he's a revolting toad,' the Speaker had whispered later, leading him away by the elbow. 'Come on now, Fergusson, humour him, there's a good man. Don't get so agitated.' The Speaker was right, of course. *God save us.*

The bleached white of the morning sky was changing and what daylight had been was fading into an eerie blue dusk. Here and there he could see the golden glow of gas streetlamps being lit by swift shadowy figures. The world seemed close by: all sounds dampened. He wound his way through the familiar streets and thought of the people who had approached him in the Commons lounge afterwards. They had professed an interest in the welfare of British sailors, but Fergusson knew that a considerable amount of British wealth was invested there. His friends on the benches had a multitude of fingers in numberless pies. It seemed to him that, as long as business interests were unaffected, many people did not really care whether Balmaceda or the insurgents won through in the end. They haven't realised yet how much of a Nationalist he is, thought Fergusson. *Things will be different when it dawns on them.*

Then, as he turned the corner into Berkeley Square, he decided that for once he would put aside thoughts of parliament. He conjured a picture of Isabella and wondered whether he might write her a note. Perhaps she would enjoy a visit to the British Museum on Sunday? Take tea at the Dorchester afterwards? He thought of his sad-eyed twelve-year-old son, Richard, and tried to remember exactly when and where he had seen him last. Three months? Four? Prize Day at Eton? And then he wondered whether it was time to get married again.

Saturday 7 March, Valparaiso
Davy watched as members of the regiment filed quietly up the gangway one by one in the near darkness. Very little else was moving in Valparaiso. The orange street lamps were still alight higher up the slopes where the more expensive houses stood. Dawn was only just visible as a lilac glow behind the dark mountains. The troops made him think of children attending their first day at school. The rifles and bayonets seemed oddly incongruous. Their uniforms were clean and their faces, as they passed by the lanterns, appeared

eager and shiny.

By his own reckoning, the *Imperial* had transported well over 5,000 troops since the outbreak of war. She was a presidential success, lauded by the press. And yet military successes had been slow to follow. Although the troops they had taken to Caleta Camarones went on to reclaim Iquique, Pisagua was bombarded and virtually burned to the ground before it eventually surrendered to the rebels. Government troops were defeated at Quillota and Coquimbo, and after terrible losses and hard fighting on both sides, Dolores also fell. The troops that had reclaimed Iquique held on to the town for a matter of weeks, and then it too surrendered for a second time under intense bombardment. Yet the government recruits kept coming.

All of a sudden, Davy recognised one of the faces.

'Peter!' he called, trying not to draw too much attention.

'Captain Davies!' Peter pushed towards him through the crowd. 'They said you were now the captain! It's a beautiful ship. I've never been on a big ship before. Does everyone get seasick the first time?'

Davy looked at Peter, desperately trying to reconcile the boy he knew with this fresh-faced soldier in a baggy uniform.

'Peter, surely you're not old enough to be here?' Davy lowered his voice.

Peter looked around before answering. 'You only have to be fourteen and I'm only a few months younger. My friends call me Pedro now, by the way.'

'Does Mrs Ebrington know that you're here?'

A dark shadow of guilt passed over Peter's face.

'You know she will be worried about you. Peter, you must send word where you are.'

'But then she will be even more worried.' Peter looked at his rifle sadly.

'Have they shown you how to use that properly?' asked Davy.

'They say we'll have rifle practice on board.'

Davy turned away in disgust.

'Please, Captain Davies. Please don't say anything. My friends are all here. I wanted to fight for Chile too. Balmaceda has promised to build a new college. You know how much I want to be an engineer. Mrs Ebrington would be proud of me then, wouldn't she?'

'I'm sure she's proud of you now, Peter.' Davy looked at the boy's guileless face with its olive brown skin, and the sleek black hair that lay thickly on his head and long over his eyes.

The young lad turned and followed the others to stern.

'Well then, Captain, do we have our orders?' asked William by Davy's side.

'Not yet. It's all very mysterious.'

'Wasn't that Peter? Isn't he too young to be here?'

Davy looked beyond William's shoulder at the others coming up the gangway. Most of them looked too young. Or too old. Or too scared. Surely, Balmaceda couldn't be running out of trained soldiers already?

'William, do you think you could find someone to take a message to Mrs Ebrington?'

William scanned the harbour. During a normal day there would be plenty of youngsters hanging around waiting to run messages here or there for money. But it was still dark. No one in their right mind would be looking for errand work this early in the morning. In the middle of a war.

'One of the galley boys might do it. He's a good runner. He'll have to make it there and back, though.'

'Tell him I'll pay him double. I'll delay things a bit.'

William disappeared and Davy watched the remaining regiment file on board. He had been told that there would be four hundred of them or thereabouts but there were always more.

'Half of these should be at school,' Davy muttered to himself, unimpressed.

William descended briskly into the depths of the *Imperial* towards the ship's kitchens. There was the usual cacophony of clanking pots and equipment overlaid by the high, taut-as-elastic voice of the ship's Chinese cook.

'Anthony here! Anthony there! I'm like fucking Figaro. My kitchen is designed to make food for high-class passengers, not hundreds of soldiers, just like they're going to be eating the same food for Christ's sake … just like soldiers are going to want flambé king prawns when what they really want is mutton stew … and what am I going to do with a storeroom full of ingredients for fucking choux pastry? For Christ's sake! Tony'll sort it out! Tony always does! 'Cos Tony's a fucking genius!'

Despite the blaspheming, Tony had learned perfect English. The more colourful parts of the cook's vocabulary could not have been in his teacher's repertoire, because his swear words were the only ones he pronounced with a strong London accent. William appeared at the galley doors just as Tony threw an enormous quantity of pastry on to a floured board, creating clouds of white dust all around him.

'What do you want?' asked Tony.

'I need to borrow one of your lads to take a message.'

'What? It's like the Twelve Tribes of Israel on deck! Why don't you ask one of them? I can't imagine they're doing anything useful with their time, parading around like Christmas turkeys!' Tony pummelled the pastry as if it was a mortal enemy about to leap up at him and strangle him at any moment.

'It's for the captain.'

'Well, why didn't you bloody say so? Gabriel! Get your arse over here.'

Tony and Davy went back a long way, although none of the crew had never been able to fathom out the details. For some reason, Tony needed no encouragement to publicly belittle anyone on board, apart from the captain and the lads that worked with him in the kitchen. These two groups were sacrosanct even though Tony screamed and shouted at the latter with impunity.

A young lad with a shock of surprising white-blonde hair, an apron and a small chef's hat emerged from the stores carrying a bucket of potatoes.

'Gabriel. Put that down and go see the captain. Now!' The boy set the bucket down and began to follow William down the corridor towards the deck.

'Take off your apron, you idiot!' The boy ran back and deposited his apron then left again. Tony pummelled the pastry.

'And your hat!' screamed Tony, slowly subduing the glutinous creature.

The boy ran back in for a second time, grinning with excitement, looking for all the world like someone who was going to go on an important mission for the captain, through the dark streets of Valparaiso, dodging rebels here and there, with some crucial secret message which would turn the tide of the war effort and eventually, after many escapades, make him a famous war hero.

'Fool,' muttered Tony as the hat flew across the room.

Colonel Moraga and Captain David Davies stood together watching the last of the troops and cargo being embarked.

'When this awful business is over, Captain Davies, I hope we can enjoy a pleasant evening at the Hotel Franc.' Moraga laughed heartily, but the smile waned and a shadow of seriousness fell across it. He twirled the end of his moustache thoughtfully.

'Our orders are to proceed to Caleta Camarones, north of Pisagua,' Moraga spoke quietly. 'Do you know the harbour there?'

'I do,' replied Davy.

'We are to land the troops and artillery. It should be straightforward. Our troops are still in control of that area, and we have no intelligence to suggest that the *Esmeralda* or any of the *Opositores*' warships are cruising that part of the coast.'

Davy wondered how he could be so sure, what with many of the telegraph wires in shreds and no easy overland means of getting messages conveyed.

The colonel twirled the ends of his moustache then said decisively, 'We sail north, immediately.'

Just then William appeared, and without exchanging words Davy took out a small white envelope from his pocket and handed it to him. Davy watched William make his way to the gangway where a young lad waited. There was a discreet exchange then William turned and came back towards Davy. The blonde boy made his way down the gangway, squeezing past soldiers and stevedores.

'Oh, and Captain,' added Moraga, 'I would like to leave as silently as possible. I wish to draw as little attention as possible to our departure.'

Davy felt his stomach tighten. He turned to William who was pale, deadpan and apparently determined not to respond to Davy at all.

Davy coughed sharply, 'We shall do our best, Colonel.'

'Silently!' Evans, the chief engineer, was shovelling best Welsh anthracite coal into the furnace. He stood upright, dwarfing Davy, and wiped the soot off his face with the back of his hand. 'What the fuck does 'e think we're on, a bloody hot air balloon!'

Davy had thought it best to take the somewhat unusual request to Evans in person. He had anticipated the lively response and it was always best to try to keep your chief engineer happy if possible. In Evans' case this was not always easy. Under normal circumstances, Evans as chief engineer would not be expected to get involved in the dirty work of hauling coal and stoking engines. But half the engineers had jumped ship at Valparaiso and the Chilean lads left to him were young and inexperienced.

Evans turned to the lad standing next to him and gave him the shovel.

'That's the way you do it. You don't chuck it in any old bleedin' how. It's got to be even, see? Flat as a virgin's bed.'

The lad, who had yet to develop Evan's towering physique or his worldly knowledge, took over, but struggled to wield the shovel piled high with glinting coal.

'*Iesu mawr,*' Evans muttered, rolling his eyes.

'Evans, you know you can do it. We crept past those corvettes in Iquique. They never heard a thing.'

Evans snorted dismissively. 'Entirely different situation altogether, Captain. Momentum was on our side that day.' Evans, bent down to pick up the tiniest bit of coal he could find and flipped it delicately into the furnace with all the grace of a ballet dancer. 'We'll chuck it in bit by bit then, shall we, sir?'

Davy groaned. There was no way on God's earth that he would tolerate this behaviour from anyone else, but Evans was the finest engineer he'd ever worked with, and the price of genius seemed to be the occasional turning of a blind eye to his considerable dramatics. Davy turned to leave.

'Evans, you should be on the stage. Do what you can, will you? We don't want Valparaiso's sleeping gorgon woken up just yet.'

Evans must have known that he'd reached the outer limits of the captain's good favour because he returned to his struggling apprentice, muttering under his breath.

The Custom House, Valparaiso

Benito Rafael Herrera had reached the office of the Custom House on Valparaiso's waterfront while it was still dark. Some days before, he had sneaked out of the office with the Custom House keys and persuaded his friend at the key cutters to make a copy. The master keys had been placed back on the hook and no one was any the wiser.

He was only the messenger at the Custom House but he was not stupid. Benito had been watching the Morse code operator for months now. He had also acquired a book from a drunken American sailor that listed all the letters of the code. Benito had spent weeks practising which unique sequence of dots and dashes represented each letter. Each dash had to be three times the length of each dot. Every letter in a word had to be separated by a space equal to three dots. Each word had to be separated by a space equal to seven dots. At home in the crowded house he had improvised two pieces of wood with a spring between to simulate the machine. Benito hated Balmaceda and wanted to play his small part in getting rid of the dictator once and for all.

His mission was simple. 'Report on the *Imperial*, movements and whereabouts.' Benito had sidled through the oak doors of the Custom House just moments before the long lines of soldiers had marched past the building towards the waterfront. At first he had strained to see their movements through a narrow gap in the shutters. He lit a small candle and took his seat next to the machine. He was nervous and began signalling slowly.

FIVE HUNDRED TROOPS BOARDING IMPERIAL

Benito did not recognise the colonel or the name of the regiment, so he was at a loss. He thought for a moment.

ARMED WITH RIFLES AND BAYONETS

That was pointless, he thought, and got up from the desk again to look at their movements. The operator at the other end signalled briefly that they had received the message. And then there was silence.

Benito leaned against the window watching the long lines of soldiers trudging forward slowly, only barely visible in the lamplight. At this rate I'll have to wait a long time, he thought. He took out a piece of bread from his pocket and ate it in a couple of mouthfuls. He had an apple in his other pocket, but he fingered its smooth surface and left it where it was, thinking he would save it for later. These days he could never be sure of his next meal, and he liked to think that he had something kept back for an emergency. And the length of time between 'emergencies' had become longer and longer, he realised.

As he watched the shadows on the harbour and the occasional glint of lamplight on shining rifles or artillery casings, he wondered what the person on the other side of the Morse code machine looked like. Whether he hated Balmaceda as much as he did.

Then, he thought he saw a swifter movement near the ship. He strained his eyes through the darkness and prised the slats of the blinds apart with his fingers to see better. It disappeared, and just when he thought he had imagined it, the shadow moved again. Something glistened briefly in the darkness. It had a rhythm. Now he could see it clearly; a young boy, running towards the Custom House. Running very quickly.

Benito's heart lurched in his chest and he ran to the desk to blow out the candle. Standing behind the door, two things occurred to him: no one had thought to provide him with a gun in case he was discovered or attacked and no one in the world, apart from some mysterious messenger, knew that he was here. His adversary could throw him in the sea and his friends would never find out what had happened to him, that he was killed defending his country from a dictator's grip.

Benito listened out for the footsteps. He must be wearing canvas shoes with string soles, he thought. His heart was thudding louder than any other sound he could hear. Benito put his ear to the door but could hear nothing. Then, the swift steps passed close by the door and faded as they ran up the hill. Satisfied that he was out of danger, Benito returned to the window and began another long wait.

After a while the sky began to turn slowly from jet black to an inky sapphire blue. He thought his view of the ship would be improved by daylight when great black clouds of smoke began to rise silently from the ship's funnels. There was very little wind to disperse the smoke, and Benito found to his frustration that the ship had now almost completely disappeared again under a billowing cloak.

Suddenly there was a long *daaah* sound. The operator on the other side was obviously getting bored. In the small dark office the sound of the *di dit dah* seemed unreasonably loud. Benito sprang back to the desk and wrote down the code in pencil as fast as he could.

He felt flustered. It was much harder than he had expected. With all his practice, he wasn't sure where the message began or ended.

Course? What course? They wanted to know the direction. North or south?

He wrote down his reply and then converted it to code. Slowly and paintstakingly he replied, trying to make sure that the length of his *dits* and *dahs* were precise and properly spaced.

AWAITING DEPARTURE

He got up from his chair and peered through the shutters again. He was puzzled. The smoke cleared briefly but they were still stationary. What were they waiting for? Everything seemed to be on board. He laughed inwardly. Perhaps their engines had broken down, and any minute now the *Esmeralda* would emerge from the half-light and blow the lot of them to smithereens.

This time, when the message came in again, Benito recognised it as a repetition. Hold your horses, he thought. I can't make them leave. Benito stayed at the window, peering through the wooden slats.

All was quiet. Then, without warning, there were footsteps at the door. Benito leant back against the window, thinking that it all ended here, pinned to the wall at the *Intendencia*. And he hadn't even achieved his goal. His heart was in his throat again, but the footsteps passed quickly and seconds later he turned and saw the running shadow's familiar shape returning to the ship.

'I'll be damned,' Benito murmured, seeing the distinctive crop of white-blonde hair disappearing through the crowds on the deck.

'Ricardo Garcia. *Mi querido amigo*. Now we know where your allegiances lie.' He sneered to think that Ricardo was his brother's friend. That he had even been in his family's house.

But the person on the other end of the line was getting impatient.

Benito ignored the insistent sound and watched the ship carefully. The gangway was taken up hastily and the *Imperial* seemed to be making way. He sat at the desk and signalled that the ship was leaving. That'll keep them happy for a moment, he thought. But no sooner was he back at the window than the message came again,

NORTH OR SOUTH?

The operator seemed to be suggesting that the ship would not go in any direction other than north or south. But with the smoke clearing and more daylight, Benito could tell that the *Imperial* was not going in either direction. West. They were sailing west.

Benito returned to the desk and drafted the reply. His hands were shaking but he took the brass key between his fingers.

SAILING WEST STOP

Then a long silence. Should he send it again? Perhaps they had missed it or hadn't understood. He returned to the window again to check that he was telling the truth. A trail of white foam was following the *Imperial*. If it had been drawn with a wooden ruler it could not have been straighter.

NORTH OR SOUTH came the reply. Benito was irritated. Did they think that he didn't understand the compass? What were they playing at? He drafted again then laid down the pencil and took up the brass key.

REPEAT WEST STOP

Silence. He waited and waited but no more messages came. Benito thought it would be wise for him to finish and lock up before there was any chance of someone arriving early. His boss, the harbourmaster, was not an early riser, but nevertheless he did not want to be seen. He made sure that everything was back in its place and he folded the paper neatly and placed it in his pocket. He had at least contributed something to the war. Tomorrow he could come again if necessary, and every day after that if they wanted him to.

He walked to the window to check one final time that there was no deviation in the *Imperial*'s route. But no, she was headed out to open sea, just as he had said. The troops were far enough away now, he thought, and he opened the glass window carefully and released the shutters a little just to get a better view. He watched her steaming out to sea and prayed that the *Esmeralda* was waiting for her somewhere around the headland ready to fill her full of torpedo holes. He prayed they would all drown.

The breeze felt cool against his face. He closed the shutters and then the window, checked the desk and left, locking the oak door behind him.

Davy had delayed things for as long as he could to the point where the crew were beginning to get suspicious.

'Check it again,' Davy had said for the fourth time, even though the crew had assured him that the ammunition was stowed safely. Despite the sailor's puzzled look, Davy had given nothing away.

'I said, check it again.'

Then just when he thought he would have to give orders to raise the gangway or risk Moraga's wrath, out of the morning's half-light appeared the boy's blonde head racing towards the *Imperial* as fast as a gleaming dart from the direction of the Custom House.

Within seconds the boy reached the deck, the gangway was raised and the ship began to make way.

Davy beckoned the boy towards him. 'What did Mrs Ebrington say? Did you wait?'

'Yes, sir. She was frightened at first, because it's so early. Then happy the note was from you, Sir. Then,' Gabriel squirmed as if he was remembering something unpleasant, 'Then she burst into tears, sir.'

Davy turned away from the boy and towards Valparaiso city. He had thought it would be better for Mrs Ebrington to know where Peter was, but now he was not so sure.

'She gave me twenty centavos, sir.'

Davy looked back at the boy's beaming face.

'Good lad. It's Gabriel, isn't it?'

'Yes sir. That's what Cook calls me. My real name's Ricardo Garcia.'

The *Imperial* steamed slowly out of sleepy Valparaiso and, as far as Davy could tell, their departure had attracted no special attention. But as he looked back at the bowl of mountains around the town, and the rows of streets and houses hugging its contours, he felt sure that there must be dozens of eyes, watching their movements from behind the wooden shutters and the twitching Spanish lace curtains.

'William, take us due west,' said Davy.

'But the colonel …'

'Yes, but as we know he's no seaman. Take us straight out to sea, far enough to lose land and then bring us back in to the coast at Caleta Camarones. We'll stand out as long as we can. No clues.'

As they steamed directly out of Valparaiso harbour and into open water, they increased speed and the billows of smoke that had clung about them were swept away by the fresh sea air. The first rays of morning sun glinted over the ridges of the Cordilleras, and as they moved from the shallower harbour waters out into open sea the sound of the ship changed as if from tenor to bass. Darker, colder water parted over the glinting steel of the bow. Nothing could catch them now apart from the *Esmeralda*, thought Davy. If their paths crossed, well, it would be touch and go: he would need to be devious. They had not heard anything of her these past few weeks; she had been lying low. Hopefully not in some hidden inlet having her bottom scraped, thought Davy. That would be very bad news. He took his spyglass from his pocket and scanned the harbour and its buildings. There was movement but nothing unusual: the first fishermen getting their boats ready for the day ahead.

    Just as he was about to look away, he caught the glint of a window opening in the sun. He looked again. A window in the Custom House. The manager is early, he thought, adjusting the brass lens. *Not like him.* The eyes and ears of Valparaiso were alert after all. And then he wondered, *friend or foe?*

CHAPTER 15

8 March, Mendoza, Argentina

Although Maurice Hervey would later write of 'the wild delight of that glorious ride', his emotions at that very moment were decidedly mixed. A group of English engineers had persuaded him that the best way for a *Times* special correspondent to get a good view of the Cordilleras would be by perching alongside them on the train's cow-catcher as it steamed its way up the new stretch of railroad from Mendoza to Uspallata. Until then, Hervey had believed that the sole purpose of the metal structure, which fanned out from the front of the train, was to clear away unexpected debris that had fallen on the tracks. The engineers had painted such an exhilarating picture. Only a coward would have turned down their kind invitation. However, the shouts of one to 'keep your head cool going round the curves and through the tunnels' had already filled him with early misgiving, and this had quickly turned to alarm as he realised that the only way of 'holding on' was by wedging his feet against the protruding bars in front of him, while simultaneously trying to hold his back away from the engine's red-hot furnace behind him. They reached the first bridge, and suddenly the whole mountain seemed to give way beneath them as the engine flew through the air, suspended by a flimsy configuration of steel and sticks.

'Oh … my … God,' groaned Hervey as thin air enveloped them and the river Mendosa appeared far beneath them but with alarming clarity. He pressed his back against the furnace in a completely involuntary movement of terror, then immediately jerked forward again as the searing heat penetrated his jacket.

'Sit still, sir!' warned his nearest neighbour, 'it's not safe to throw yourself about on this perch until you're a bit used to it!'

Used to it! Screamed Hervey inwardly, and he felt a fool for his early bravado. He wondered yet again whether the regular *Times* reader had even the remotest inkling of the stress and danger encountered by 'special' correspondents in the process of gathering foreign intelligence – all so that readers could keep up to date with world events from the safety and comfort of their breakfast tables.

Maurice Hervey's orders had been twofold. Get to Buenos Aires as quickly as possible to report on the vexed question of Argentine finance, then proceed to Chile to discover more about the outbreak of civil war. *Report on what you see to the best of your judgement.* As instructed, he had proceeded to Paris, and from there to Bordeaux by night mail to catch

Messageries Maritimes' steamer *Portugal*. As the special correspondent *du grand journal Anglais*, he had been shown the most marked courtesy by the captain and his officers; he had been provided with a very comfortable cabin, all to himself, and a seat of honour at table. The food on board had been excellent, lighter and daintier than that on board an English steamer, but nevertheless quite sufficient for most stomachs at sea. English steamers were superior in only one aspect, he thought, as they hurtled into the air over another unfeasibly narrow bridge. Hervey jammed the soles of his shoes with increased determination against the iron bar. English regulations called for one distinct advantage: the separation of the second-class from the first-class passengers. The *Portugal* had the misfortune of carrying a troupe of theatrical artistes bound for Rio de Janeiro, and some members of the band had been distinct nuisances. Some of the noisiest, most indecorous young women even had to be relegated to their cabins!

Hervey contemplated how, if he were the director of the *Messageries Maritimes*, he would certainly try to rectify this serious defect. How else would they secure the patronage of English travellers? After all, he thought, *les Anglais* did not believe in liberty, fraternity or equality, least of all on board ship.

The chugging and labouring of the steam engine was intensified as the length of the metal creature was funnelled in to the mountainside through a freshly cut ravine. The engine driver clearly had a questionable sense of humour, as mid-way through the narrow channel he tugged on the whistle and let out a deafening 'WAAAAA!' Rather pointless, thought Hervey, wondering whether he would ever be able to hear again, as there's no room either side of the track; whatever gets in the way will be blasted to a pulp.

'Messy business if we come across a stray cow!' laughed his neighbour jovially.

At that moment Hervey decided that if he ever reached Uspallata with all his limbs intact his first mission would be to wring his neighbour's neck. He really did not want to consider the implications of a bovine collision, and so tried to ignore the man and his precarious position by casting his mind back to the journey he had made to Chile.

Four days after leaving Bordeaux the *Portugal*, a fine boat of 4,500 tons, had anchored briefly at Lisbon. Hervey had gone ashore for a quick meeting with the local agent of *The Times* over an excellent breakfast at the Braganza Hotel. Another four days from Lisbon and the steamer had arrived at Dakar. What a place! How was it possible for the men to be so remarkably lean and agile and the women so exceptionally obese and abominably ugly? No wonder French troops regarded garrison life there with such disfavour.

Hervey caught a brief glimpse of the high snow-topped Cordilleras as they hurtled around another bend in the track. All my exertions have come to this, he thought. *It is our sad responsibility to report the tragic death of our special correspondent Maurice Hervey, thrown from an engine's cow-catcher during his latest daring mission to the Argentine/Chilean border. His body is still to be recovered.*

Alors, he thought. They had dropped anchor off Rio de Janeiro then five days later at Montevideo where he had stayed one night on shore. The prettiest town in South America situated on the northern bank of the River Plate.

Then on to the Argentine capital of Buenos Aires, where he had arrived on the last day of February. Barings had made some risky investments in Argentina, and only the hasty support of the Bank of England and the Rothschilds had averted a total collapse of the London banking system. The papers, including *The Times*, had been full of condemnation for Edward Baring's excessive risk-taking. So now Argentina continued to suffer the most awful recession. Trade was at a standstill and most of the shops were closed. Hervey had thought the place looked decidedly out at the elbows. At least a catastrophe in London had been averted.

But no sooner had he arrived in Argentina than a telegram arrived, instructing him to 'Go on to Chile.' Hervey knew very well that 'Go' from a grand journal to its special correspondent meant 'Go at once'. So, 'go at once' he did, or rather, was doing.

Then it seems to Hervey that a miracle took place. He realised all at once that he had stopped thinking about his journey to Chile and that his head was crowded full of superlatives. His terror had subsided entirely, and in its place he found himself struggling to find words to describe what he could see. The awe-inspiring precipitous descents, the towering Cordilleras, the exquisite hues of the mountains, more wondrous than any painter's palette, the narrow tracks over death-defying bridges.

'It's incredible!' he gasped, and the other men turned and laughed with him in admiration. Like a conjurer, one of the men pulled a couple of bottles of Bass's red triangle beer from his pockets, and before they knew it they were sharing the beer around, drinking to the health of the Queen, *The Times*, Messrs Clark of the railway company, and even the Chilean cows for staying away from the tracks.

There was not a drop of beer left by the time they reached Uspallata, the end of the line. Hervey could barely feel his legs as he clambered down from the cow-catcher. The railroad company's plan was to extend the line eventually right across the Andes from Mendoza in Argentina to Santa Rosa de Los Andes in Chile. But this was as far as it went for now. In the next day or so they would start on the remaining hundred miles of the journey by mule, over the Andes, reaching a height of 13,000 feet before descending over the border into Chile.

10 March, the *Imperial*, South Pacific, en route to Caleta Camarones
Once the sight of land had sunk below the horizon in their wake, the *Imperial* turned to the north. For two days they posted lookouts to scour the ocean, checking every cloud and wisp of mist for any evidence of the predatory warship. Once they spotted a steamer coming south, and being unsure of her identity Davy determined to put plenty of sea between them. The sea itself was benign and playful and dolphins could often be seen swimming alongside. They saw shoals of flying fish. Some of the more enterprising soldiers caught a few and fried them up. There were some jealous glances. And everywhere Davy turned there seemed to be soldiers, perched on railings, leaning against doorways, sitting on the iron steps. William and the steward had found blankets for many of them and those without huddled together in corners. To pass the time, many of the youngsters sang patriotic Spanish songs of death and honour. Davy shared their sense of excitement, the thrill of cat and mouse, and although he was not fully in charge of the ship, the lives of all these soldiers depended on him, his skill as a captain and his ability to evade these new dangers.

On the third day, late in the afternoon, the *Imperial* turned inland and made for Caleta Camarones. Approaching with caution, as areas of the harbour were not visible from open water, they reduced their speed; half speed, quarter speed. Davy had given the order for absolute silence on deck, and when one of the cabin boys inadvertently shouted out to another lad almost everyone on deck turned to him with silent grimaces. It must be serious, thought the crew, because for once 'Smokey' Evans was quietly compliant and the captain hadn't needed to use his velvet-voiced tones of persuasion.

Davy was on the bridge, scouring the harbour with his eyeglass. As the ship came around the headland he realised how much of the harbour was hidden. He had never needed to approach from this angle before. Even at quarter speed they seemed to be approaching far too quickly. The harbour opened up like the jaws of a great leviathan and they were much too close.

'Cut the engines,' said Davy to William, who was now standing at his shoulder.

William relayed the message, and within seconds the beating heart of the steamship stopped. The ship still had momentum and the only sound to be heard was that of silky water slipping over the steel bow. They slowed but the harbour kept widening out. Sailing ships, fishing boats, harbour buildings and tugs came into view but no enemy carrier or stealthy warship. They came around the final rocky outcrop, and there was a cry from the bow.

'Corvette!' and almost immediately there were other identical cries from the lookouts and Davy saw her, skulking like a grey crocodile. She was beautifully placed, side on to any incoming ships. They were directly in her line of fire and she had seen them.

The corvette's missiles were already whistling over their heads. It would not take them long to adjust their trajectory and hit them. Moraga was quick to respond, and within seconds Davy heard the shout to fire. But they were at least 3,000 metres from the corvette and they needed to be within 1,000 metres to be sure of hitting her accurately. The *Imperial*'s missiles fell miserably short, but the enemy fire screamed perilously close to their heads.

'We're out of range, Commander,' shouted one of the soldiers, but Moraga was not about to be denied the chance to fire at the enemy.

'Dammit man, it will give them something to think about!'

While Moraga shouted instructions to the artillery, Davy concentrated on getting the ship away to a safe distance. Once again, speed and manoeuvrability were their assets. The air filled with smoke, and the harbour water around them churned and foamed as the ship struggled to increase speed.

There was shouting all around, and the whole ship vibrated so violently that the palms of Davy's hands and the soles of his feet seemed charged with electricity. Just then, the air around them seemed sucked away, even from their lungs. There was an almighty thud followed by a violent wall of displaced water that threw Davy off his feet. A missile had hit the water just short of the ship. *They have adjusted their aim but not taken into account our increasing speed*, thought Davy as he clambered to his feet again. They were too long, now they're too short. You won't catch us that easily.

'Fire!' Moraga screamed.

Davy heard a cry and turned to see William sprawled on the floor, a blood-soaked hand raised to his head. He had a deep gash where he had hit his head on a reel of wire and there was a lot of blood.

'Get him below!' Davy shouted to the crew who came to help. When Davy turned back to the corvette, the second officer, Webb, was already there at his shoulder.

'Fire!' Moraga shouted again, and almost simultaneously another missile landed horribly close. *You're learning*, thought Davy. Yet another missile careered into the water near them and the wave sent them slipping and sliding on the deck. Davy wiped his face with his jacket sleeve. The corvette turned slowly – not to catch up with them, but to bring her portside guns to bear on them. She had lost her original advantage, but if she could manoeuvre quickly she would surely sink them before they could get away.

'C'mon Mr Evans, do your worst,' muttered Davy.

Suddenly, there was a new momentum and the ship gathered pace. The smoke lifted up and away from them and the next missile fell further away.

'We're getting away, sir,' Davy heard the second officer say, almost squealing with delight.

Again and again missiles hit the water, but only fine spray reached them now. A cheer gathered amongst the troops and rose to a crescendo. '¡Viva Balmaceda! ¡Viva Chile! ¡Viva El Imperial!' they choroused, and as the distance between them increased there were crazy whoops of laughter followed by singing.

Davy turned to Webb, who was grinning from ear to ear and standing too close. Davy could not help himself, but he was overwhelmed by a sudden and intense dislike for the man. 'For Christ's sake,' said Davy, turning to face him, 'what do you think this is? Some kind of game? Check on Mr Whiteway and find out who left that bloody coil of wire there!' Webb stood frozen for a moment, blanched pale as if someone had just slapped him. Then colour returned vividly to his cheeks.

'Yes, sir,' he replied as he turned swiftly away.

Davy could tell that he had offended him. Webb had been enjoying a brief moment of elation. God knows, in war there would be few enough of them, thought Davy, critical of himself for being so easily riled.

All around the deck there was cheering and celebration. The *Imperial*'s speed was still increasing and she was steaming away from the harbour at Caleta Camarones. Moraga was in the midst of his men now. '¡Viva Moraga! ¡Viva Balmaceda!' shouted the soldiers as the plumes of displaced water fell further and further away.

Some time later, Davy descended to the main deck and leaned on the rail. Every sinew in his body felt rigid with anticipation, and even the sound of the cheering soldiers and the ship's frantic engine could not mask the feeling of his heart thudding urgently in his chest. *The last time I felt like this I was a boy, heading for the Horn in a screeching gale.* He watched the struggling corvette puffing smoke and missiles from every orifice. *That was before I decided that I had nothing to lose and that fear was a wasted emotion.* The *Imperial* had been within seconds of disaster. But what had he seen in all the smoke and spray? Not the efforts of two warships to annihilate each other, but rather Estella's face. And so the prospect of loss had brought back his old friend, Fear. *After all these years.*

'Bit of a close shave, Skipper, eh?' laughed one of the crew as he sauntered past with a crate. Davy smiled in agreement but as he stood at the rail watching the corvette receding into the distance Fear stood with him. And together they watched the green waves, hoping that it was true what they said, that aside from the *Esmeralda*, no other ship could catch them on the high seas.

CHAPTER 16

Tuesday, 10 March, Valparaiso

All morning, Agnes Ebrington had been wandering around the house in a daze. She had pinched herself several times, hoping that she was in the throes of an awful nightmare, but each time the very real pain confirmed the stupidity of it all.

Why had she not taken more notice of his friends? How could Peter have picked up these ridiculous ideas of death and glory without her knowing? From under her nose! Two days earlier, when the blonde lad appeared at her door, half asleep as she was, and unusually early as it was, she had thought for a brief moment that he was an angel, sent to collect her to join Albert.

Then the true horror of Captain Davies' letter had sunk in. The boy wouldn't wait for her to check Peter's room. The ship was about to sail, he said, and there was no reason to doubt the message. So she had closed the door behind him and rushed to the attic to find Miriam still fast asleep and Peter's room neat, tidy and empty.

'Oh, he made his bed!' she sat down and sobbed a storm of tears, reading the letter over and over.

'What's happened?' asked Miriam, appearing at the door dishevelled and sleepy.

'Oh, Miriam. Look. The stupid, stupid people have taken him away, to their stupid, silly war.'

Now Agnes Ebrington found herself doing the same mundane things that she would normally do on a Tuesday morning. But she had arrived at Cumming's Haberdashery and General Stores without remembering anything at all of her walk. The ring of the doorbell above her head as she entered the shop was shrill and alarming.

'Good morning there, Mrs Ebrington, how are we today?'

Agnes Ebrington tried to remember why she had come in to the shop and what, if anything, she needed.

'Ah, yes, these are trying times indeed,' continued Mr Cumming, rearranging goods on the counter and interpreting the woman's distracted face as a general state of worry following the outbreak of war. 'Let's hope it's all over soon and we can get back to normality. Of course, it was only a matter of time before someone decided to get rid of him. All these unspeakable things we've been hearing about, torture, corruption. About time, I say, for all our sakes. What can I do for you today, Mrs Ebrington?

We've had a delivery of some very attractive cotton. Would you like to see?'

Mrs Ebrington nodded without thinking and watched the dapper man as he reached behind him to the well-stocked wooden shelves.

'Of course, if it goes on then we might find supplies being disrupted, what with all these blockades. Hopefully it won't come to that.' The man placed three rolls of cotton on the polished mahogany counter and pulled several yards of fabric from each one. 'Best quality, woven in Lancashire.'

Mrs Ebrington thought vaguely that the pink cotton was not unattractive and agreed to take six yards.

'A nice dress for Miriam?' smiled the man, pushing up the metal sleeve garters on his arms.

He put away the spare rolls and then flipped the chosen pink fabric until it unwound with a *thud, thud, thud* on the counter. Counting six yards against the inlaid brass marker, he allowed an extra few inches as usual, then reached for some menacing fabric scissors. 'Just in case,' he smiled up at her and then cut confidently across the fabric with the crunching blades.

The fabric was folded neatly, wrapped in brown paper with a reel of pink thread on top, tied with string and placed carefully in Mrs Ebrington's basket.

'Give my regards to Peter and Miriam,' said Robert Cumming as he opened the door for his customer, 'I hope to see them soon.'

With another shrill ring, the door closed behind Mrs Ebrington and she found herself back on the busy street. A sea of horses, carts and people moved around her, but she saw none of it. She had been naive, she realised now. She had assumed that people's allegiance would be with the government and with a legally appointed president. She had no idea that people like Cumming might think otherwise. And why would he assume that she held the same views? From now on she and Miriam would need to lie. They would need to make up some story to explain why Peter was not around. No one could know that they had taken sides, or what that side was.

'It's all very well escaping the corvette, but what do we do now?' said Moraga, leaning over the charts. 'I need to land my men somewhere, and I can't walk them all across the Atacama.'

Davy had heard tales of the Atacama. Where it was so hot that people's blood boiled in their veins and the light of the sun was so piercing that it made you blind.

'We could land them in Antofagasta if we knew that the railway was still in government hands,' replied Davy, not really knowing whether this was a feasible option. He was a sailor and knew the coastline, her rocks and inlets, her devious currents and fickle shallows, but as for the routes inland he had no idea how a general was supposed to get his men across a landscape which looked from Davy's perspective like a vast swathe of nothingness.

Davy had felt obliged to ask Webb to join them, as William was still recovering. For what purpose, he wasn't sure in retrospect, as the man stood there quietly, away from the table, not sulking exactly but not engaged at all in the discussion and contributing little of any value. Davy was increasingly annoyed with himself for having spoken to the man harshly earlier on that day. A second's patience could have saved him a lot of ill feeling and awkwardness. *I really don't have time for this*, he thought. Then, desperate to make a decision and equally keen to get out of the claustrophobic room, David announced, 'Colonel Moraga, we'll land the troops in Antofagasta. But we shall land them under cover of darkness so that we have at least the advantage of anonymity if there is any doubt about the other vessels that are present. We think it is unlikely that the *Esmeralda* would be lying in wait?'

'It is impossible to say. We have had little recent intelligence. But if that is the best option, then we have speed and your excellent captaincy on our side.'

Davy reached for his cap and made for the door. Moraga was trying his best to be supportive, he thought, but in truth Davy was thinking about William.

'Get this brute off me, will you?' William turned towards Davy.

Davy arrived at William's cabin to find Tony the cook struggling to put fresh bandages around his patient's head.

'He's trussed me up like one of his Sunday beef joints. Will you stop that?'

'Oh, shut up you fool! Who'd want to eat you? If it were up to me I'd let you bleed to bloody death. Sodding, awkward, ungrateful …'

'So,' Davy interrupted, 'Officer Whiteway doesn't make such a compliant patient it seems?'

Tony leaned back and jabbed the air with his scissors, 'God in Heaven.'

Then he turned back to William and stuck a vicious-looking wire safety pin into the end of the bandage and snapped it shut.

'There! Now you can stop your complaining and I can go back to my proper job – where I'm appreciated!'

Tony gathered up his equipment, muttering profanities under his breath as he did so. He went through the door and turned to nod politely towards Davy. 'Captain.' Then he left.

William rolled his eyes, and for a second Davy wondered whether he was concussed.

'What is it with the two of you? How come he treats you like royalty and the rest of us like deck scrapings?'

Davy sat down in the chair next to William's bunk and looked at the young man closely.

'He knows a good captain when he sees one, that's what. Look at me, I think your eyes are a bit odd.'

'You're a doctor now, are you? But seriously, what is it with him?'

'I saved him from someone who was making his life hell, a long time ago. Shut your left eye.'

'Oh, for God's sake, there's nothing wrong with me. He's the most objectionable, cantankerous, vindictive …'

'Well, he speaks highly of you. Now close your right eye.'

William paused but then screwed up his face in disgust and carried on.

'Oh, don't be ridiculous. And I keep telling you, there's nothing wrong with me!'

Davy leaned back in his chair and considered William. He was as pale as a sheet but he would be all right. At least he hoped so. Of all the officers he had ever worked with, he admired William the most. He was intelligent, well read, thoughtful, efficient, smart, often witty, always honest. It occurred to Davy that he could not have dealt with the events of the last two months without him.

'William …' he began, and it was only then that he really noticed the dark red blotches of blood on the other man's shirt.

'I know, I know! Don't say anything. I need to change my shirt. It wasn't too bad before that butcher got his tools out.'

'You're not going anywhere,' said Davy, getting to his feet and projecting his voice in the way he would speak to anyone else in the crew. 'I'll get Sep to bring you a clean one. I want you to stay here and rest. I'm not happy with you coming back on deck just yet. That's an order.'

William relaxed back on to the bunk and Davy was pleased with the tone of authority in his own voice. Over the years he trained himself to sound like someone who shouldn't be argued with, even at times when he wasn't actually sure. Indecision, even the slightest suggestion of indecision, was the death of any captain.

But then he smiled. 'I'm glad you're all right. I'll call on you later.'

Uspallata Pass, Argentina

'His name is *El Ministro*,' declared the chief muleteer, stepping back proudly with hands on hips as if he was admiring some rare mythical creature that had just descended from the skies. The mule looked at Hervey and Hervey looked back at the mule. It was probably the tallest specimen Hervey had ever seen, and without doubt the most gaunt-looking.

'He's the best *macho* I've got and used to be one of the quietest. But ever since he carried *Señor* Godoy, the Chilean minister for *Londres*, well …'

'Which is why he's called *El Ministro*,' interjected the second muleteer.

'He's become proud and plays tricks occasionally.'

The mule's gaze was disconcertingly self-possessed and Hervey, unable to break his own reciprocating stare, wondered whether perhaps this was some kind of mule challenge.

'I dare say he will go quietly enough with your Excellency, but be careful of his heels just at first when you mount him.'

The mule tilted his head and appeared to shrug nonchalantly. But the muleteer was right about the heels. As soon as *El Ministro* felt the weight of Hervey's foot in the stirrup the animal lashed out like a thing possessed, turning and kicking in all directions. Hervey hopped frantically around the creature, desperately trying to keep up with his foot, which was now firmly wedged in the stirrup. Eventually, Hervey managed to detach himself and was catapulted into an awkward heap on the dusty ground. The mule turned to face *El Corresponsal*, snorted once more then looked down at the journalist with endearingly innocent brown eyes as if nothing had happened.

'You murderous brute,' muttered Hervey, dusting himself down and ignoring snorts of laughter from the muleteers.

'We're not going anywhere until you've learned who is master.'

And before the mule had time to blink his languid eyelashes at his new travelling companion, Hervey was up on the stirrup and planted firmly in the saddle. The entire mountain range seemed to echo with the mule's horrendous screeches. It bucked and shook itself violently, turning this way and that in a confusion of ears, hooves and tail. And when it looked like the mule might get the better of its rider, Hervey remembered his secret weapon and plunged his spurs into the creature's lean ribs until every one of the mule's sinews stood to attention, stunned by the rider's sudden violence.

'Ah, you see! *El Corresponsal* is not so easily dismissed!' shouted Hervey above the animal's indignant squeals. The rider's spurs were clearly an effective and potent deterrent, and before long the mule had reduced his antics to harmless and docile shuffling.

'*Ah, ¡Señor! ¡Lo ha vencido!* You have beaten him!' the chief muleteer shouted.

'He is *El Ministro* no more. We will christen him again in your honour! *¡El Corresponsal!*'

11 March, Antofagasta

The *Imperial*, making its second attempt to land the troops and artillery it had collected in Valparaiso, cruised into the harbour at Antofagasta under cover of darkness. A dense covering of cloud hid the moon and all the stars from view with little prospect of them being revealed soon. There was not a breath of wind. Antofagasta was a wide open harbour and Davy was more than familiar with its rocks and landmarks. He leant on the rail, peering through the darkness for anything unexpected.

It was nearing two o'clock in the morning and all was quiet along the harbourside. Usually there would be a forest of masts lying in wait for their next consignment of nitrates, but the war was making merchants nervous and many were staying away. The engines of the *Imperial* were subdued as she slid past the deserted decks and the bare masts of the wooden barques. How the world is moving on, thought Davy, glad that he didn't have to sleep in a swaying hammock any more. He had been awake since five the previous morning and his eyes and limbs were numb with exhaustion. Moraga had been at his most demanding all day, needing desperately to get the troops ashore but wary of landing them in Antofagasta.

'I fear it is very exposed, Captain Davies,' he had muttered. 'How do we know that she won't be waiting for us? I fear the *Esmeralda* more than any other rebel ship.'

Davy could give no assurances. All he could say was that the *Imperial*, although fortunate to still have a good stock of coal on board, did not have an infinite supply with which to circle the Pacific in an eternal search for a safe harbour.

'It's a risk worth taking,' Davy had replied, thinking uncomfortably how strange it was that he should be saying this – it was not even his war. By rights, he was the one who should be urging caution. As it was, they seemed to be anchored safely out of harm's way for the evening.

Yet, they did not want to draw attention to themselves, and instructions were given with low voices and calm efficiency. Moraga had sent some of his officers ashore on the launch to reconnoitre. They were taking their time returning. Everything seemed quiet and unremarkable.

Moraga came towards him. 'Captain Davies, you should turn in now.

All seems well. We will let the troops disembark at first light. I will send for you if there is anything unusual.'

It still jarred with Davy to be instructed by another leader on his own ship. Moraga was politeness itself so he could not fault him for his manner. This is a strange captaincy, he thought, so tired now that he barely cared. As his head hit the pillow, just before the oblivion of sleep obscured everything, he caught himself thinking of the trajectories of flying fish and whether he needed to make a calculation as to their speed and angle as they hit the decks.

12 March, Antofagasta
'Davy! Davy!'

In his dream, Davy is sitting in the second row of the Royal Opera House. Adelina Patti is singing an aria from *Aida*, the music reaching its glorious yet tragic crescendo. Suddenly, he recognises the woman in front of him. It's Estella. A section of hair has come loose from its pins. He wants to replace the strand for her. All the other women are immaculate in their silks and gems and feathers. But Estella's dress is plain. He does not want her to feel out of place, so he leans forward to touch her hair.

Davy! Wake up! The Esmeralda! She's here!

Only a little further, Davy thinks as he leans, I can pin that curl and no one will notice. He feels the person next to him in the audience leaning into him.

Let me be. Go away.

'Davy!'

His eyes opened. William was at his bedside, wearing what appeared to be a turban.

'We're off to India?' gasped Davy, still half asleep and wondering what his chief officer was doing in the opera house.

'They think they can see the *Esmeralda*.'

'Who?'

'Not 'who', 'what'!' hissed William.

Exasperated, William thrust a jacket into Davy's lap and led the way to the upper deck. Speaking quietly and with his head still bandaged from the cut to his scalp, William explained that as it was getting light one of the lookouts had seen a ship's hull tucked in at the bottom of the harbour. They thought it was her. So far, it was still dark enough not to be seen, but not for much longer.

Moraga arrived on deck, followed closely by Evans who was the first to whisper, 'Sir, we have enough coal to get away, but as soon as she sees us we're done for.'

'Are we sure it's her?' asked Davy, putting on his cap.

Moraga did not reply but murmured gravely, '¡*Maldita sea!* We should have disembarked the soldiers last night.'

But there was no time for recriminations or analysis. There was urgency in the crew's tasks, but no shouting or indiscriminate clattering on deck. Davy took out his spyglass and peered at the mystery ship. Was it her? Through the soles of his feet he could feel the engines beginning to turn. The steel around him trembled. Evans would want to build up a good head of steam before moving out. How long could they wait before being spotted or heard? The troops were on their feet with their rifles at their sides. If it came to it, they would fix bayonets, but not yet. *Dear God*, thought Davy; it had not really occurred to him that they could be boarded, that he might see hand-to-hand fighting on board the *Imperial*. Then he thought of the *Esmeralda*'s torpedoes: it would not come to bayonets.

The *Imperial* began to make her way out of the harbour. The sky was getting lighter and the dark cloud that had shrouded the sky the night before was separating, revealing areas of inky blue sky. Davy caught sight of a distant lone star. *A clear sky, that's all we need.* In the tally of advantages and disadvantages, the *Imperial* would need to score highly to stand any chance of getting away. *If it is her?*

They were underway, and all the crew were at their stations. As they pulled further out into open water, away from the camouflage of ship masts, everyone held their breath. Those with spyglasses peered silently and those without leaned over the rails and strained their eyes to see what they could.

Davy could feel blood pounding in his ear. *Is it her? Is it her?* Condensation formed on the lens. He drew back to let it clear then blinked hard and looked again. He focused, and as he did so two figures rushed into view on the ship's deck. The figures froze and stared at the *Imperial*: one of them had a spyglass. There was a brief exchange and one ran back along the deck. It was the *Esmeralda*. And they had been seen.

'¡*Más Vapor!* ¡*Más vapor!*' Now there were shouts all around. Davy found himself bellowing one order after another until his throat burned.

Within seconds the *Imperial*'s speed had increased, all need for stealth redundant now. The deck was alive with activity and thick dark smoke surrounded them. Once again Davy prayed that Evans would work his magic and get them away. In the harbour the *Esmeralda* was still stationary. *Advantage to us*, thought Davy. There was a great deal of commotion on the enemy ship's deck, and steam began to rise from her funnel.

'She's in a tight spot,' William said lightly, coming to stand next to Davy.

Not half tight enough, thought Davy. William could always be relied on to find something positive to say even when the odds were stacked against them. Davy glanced either side to check that no one was near, then turned to his chief officer and said, under his breath, 'We're not going to make it, William. She has fourteen hours of daylight to give chase. We would need a miracle.'

William was called away by one of the crew before he could respond. For a moment, Davy stayed at the rail watching the shadow of the *Esmeralda* turn in the dark waters of the harbour. She was readying herself like a great white shark, lining herself up, making her calculations, sizing up her kill. Dawn would come soon; they would see their opponent all too clearly. The sky cleared briefly overhead. A star shone out between the clouds, and as Davy's gaze returned to the pursuing warship he thought he saw her bare her teeth.

'We will be within range of her guns by midday,' said Davy, who had been pondering the charts. By the time the *Esmeralda* had manoeuvred awkwardly in the harbour, the *Imperial* had put six miles between them. Even so, the *Esmeralda* was gaining on them now, and the missiles that she had been hurling at them in a fury of dramatic effect would soon become real and serious threats. It would be no game of cat and mouse this time. She was no underpowered corvette, and the men's rifles and bayonets would be of little use.

Moraga leaned back in his chair and drew slowly on his cigar. The room was filled with smoke even though William had opened a porthole.

Davy had made his calculations several times. He had worked out the best- and the worst-case scenarios, all variations on a theme, depending on whether the *Esmeralda* could reach her top speed and whether Evans could keep going without having to clean out the furnaces. But whichever way he calculated, they were not going to get away. It was just a matter of time. Moraga blew a long puff of smoke in the air and, as if he had heard Davy's thoughts, looked up at him. 'I cannot surrender the ship.'

Davy had expected these words sooner or later. He had prepared himself for them, so that when the time came he would not betray his feelings. Even so, he suddenly felt very tired. He was not yet defeated, but he was caught between an enemy he did not hate and an ally that had a different vision of success.

'Colonel Moraga, sir,' said William, 'surely they will not want to sink the ship? It would be a useful vessel for them to commandeer themselves? What benefit would it be to them to sink her?'

Moraga smiled and leaned forward to flick ash into a small dish. 'You are right, of course. In the practical world, what purpose could it possibly serve? But in war we are not merely in the practical world. We are appealing to men's hearts, which, as you know, cannot be won with metal and machinery alone. *El Capitán* has raised the status of the *Imperial.* Before the war she was a fine mailboat, a fast mailboat to be sure – perhaps the fastest of all, but no more than that. Your conquests, Captain Davies, your dashing raids through the lines of blockade, have elevated her to the status of a worthy adversary. Everyone knows the *Imperial* has been supplying guns and troops to the government all along the coast. When Balmaceda had no other ships to speak of, the *Imperial* gave us a chance. The *adversarios* will not be interested in surrender.'

In the background the men could hear the distant firing of the warship's guns and the nearer thud of missiles as they landed in the sea.

'But seven hundred Chilean troops? Surely?' urged William.

'Seven hundred *enemy* troops, Officer Whiteway.' Moraga shrugged and leant back again.

Moraga turned to Davy. 'Captain Davies, did you hear about Minister Rivero?'

Davy shook his head. He had not really been listening, but rather was wondering whether they should consider unloading ballast or ditching supplies to lighten their load and gain more speed.

'He was – or rather is, as he is still alive, they tell me – a very popular man. He was Balmaceda's second-in-command until the war began. He has, perhaps unwittingly, played some dubious role, given information to the wrong people.'

Moraga looked down and flicked more ash from his trouser leg. 'He has been tortured, they say.' He drew deeply from the cigar and concentrated his gaze on Davy. 'They dislocated his arms and crushed his hands. He cannot speak. He is destroyed. That is what they say.'

Moraga leant forward again to the desk and ground the remains of the cigar into the ashtray's base. 'I say "they" when I mean "we". We have done these things. I say this merely to underline the fact that, unfortunately for us, we have not shown mercy to the *Opositores*. I don't expect we shall see much in return. If we get within range, I fully expect them to sink the

Imperial regardless of who is on board. In truth, Captain, if they seem keen to preserve the ship and board us, I would rather we scuttle the ship ourselves. Balmaceda cannot win the war without the *Imperial*. At least, not until the *Lynch* and *Condell* arrive from England.'

The room descended into silence. Moraga was right of course. There would be no surrender, and they would go down. *But not yet.*

'Officer Whiteway,' said Davy, 'I want you to look at ways of lightening our load. If we can throw off anything that will damage the *Esmeralda*, then so much the better. I want every member of the crew to take turns moving the coal. I want it all close at hand so that Mr Evans can give us the greatest possible speed.'

William left to carry out instructions, and just as he reached the door himself Davy turned to Moraga, 'Do the lads know any good fighting songs, Commander? I think we could do with some encouragement now, don't you?'

Davy followed William out of the room, but instead of heading for the deck he descended the iron steps towards the engine room. It became hotter and dustier as he went until he reached the engine room itself.

Evans appeared at the doorway, wiping coal dust from his hands with a grubby rag. His shirt was smudged with soot and his face was running with sweat. Evans held the cloth to his temples and added another dark smudge to his face.

'All right, Captain?'

For some reason Evans' face always reminded Davy of a vicious bulldog that had chased him down the street in Trieste. Davy had run for his life from the vile thing, all frothing at the mouth. But Davy felt only respect for Evans – jealous respect for his priceless engineering skills. And also for his voice and the way his brutish face was transformed by music whenever he relented and agreed to sing for the crew.

'Glan,' he began. *Glanmor*. He rarely used people's Christian names, apart from William's and that out of earshot.

'The *Esmeralda*'s on to us, as you know.'

Evans looked at him gravely and nodded.

'She has seventeen knots on a good day.'

Again Evans nodded. Davy knew that he wasn't telling Evans anything he didn't already know.

'She won't catch us if I've got anything to do with it, Captain, you can be sure of that. Me and the lads will make her move like she's never gone before. I still have a few tricks up my sleeve.'

Davy frowned. Before the war, he had heard Evans tell stories of dangerous things that could be done with quantities of paraffin and other volatile substances.

'Don't take any risks for the moment. I've asked the chief officer to give you all the help you need.'

The sweat glistened on Evans' forehead and a drop gathered and ran to his eyebrow.

'Glan, I must ask you – no, order you.' Davy thought again on the best sequence of words and started again. 'When it comes to it, they will sink us. No surrender.' Evans stood back and ran the dirty rag over his hands. 'There are not enough boats. And even if there were …'

Evans nodded. 'Yes, sir, I see. Right you are, Captain.' he nodded again.

'So, what I'm saying is this: that there may still be a chance for us, the crew, as we were commandeered. Do you see? They may be lenient as we are not technically on the side of the government. We had no choice.'

Evans didn't nod this time and Davy knew exactly what he was thinking. Stewart had a choice. He made the right choice. We made the wrong choice. And, anyway, their torpedoes won't be sorting us out as we sink.

'Sir, fear not, we'll do our best. The Chilean lads are saying the *Esmeralda*'s bottom hasn't been cleaned in years. Hell, we're as clean as a whistle! It all adds up, Captain, mark my words.'

Evans wiped his forehead with the rag, leaving fresh black streaks of dirt.

'Thank you, Evans. But remember, when the order comes, I want you on deck.'

'Aye, aye, sir. If it comes to it.'

Davy raised his hand and clapped Evans firmly on his shoulder.

Davy headed back up to the deck, feeling the ship shudder and scud all around him. *My God, Evans' shoulder was made of iron itself*, he thought. He could still climb to a topsail if he needed to. *Could I?* Davy wondered, bringing his hand up to his own shoulder. And then it occurred to him that Evans hadn't started as a seaman at all. He had come from the mines. He remembered their first conversation.

'I figured, if I knew how to work the pithead engine, I'd know how to work a ship. And there's not much difference when it boils down to it, you see, Captain,' and Evans had laughed at his own pun. 'Lord, and this way I get to do the same work and see the world in the bargain!'

And not have to deal with the pithead manager either, Evans had added, years later when they knew each other better. The closest Evans would ever get to a real compliment. Davy wondered whether Evans regretted leaving the Valleys now, chased by a foreign man-of-war, stuffed to the gunnels with deadly ammunition. Not even his own enemy.

Davy climbed the stairs, registering the hundreds of rivets on the metal steps, thinking how they were like so many numberless soldiers, advancing towards war. And if they were going down, he didn't want Evans and his lads drowning in the engine room with their faces flat to the cold iron ceiling gasping for air. There's drowning and drowning, thought Davy.

Davy and William were on the *Imperial*'s bridge.
'As much as we can spare thrown over?' asked Davy
'Yes,' William nodded, 'we even threw over the barrels of Marsala.'
Davy winced at the thought. 'We thought Montt might have stopped to pick them up. He likes his wine, doesn't he?'

All morning the *Esmeralda* had been firing random shots at the *Imperial* to gauge their range. The shots had come ever closer, and now, as if they had been deaf to all the previous missiles, they heard the sudden descending tone of a whistle and a loud 'thud' that shook the cabin. Between them they had examined every avenue, they had racked their brains, thought of every story they had ever read about the Armada or Waterloo … anything that could bring inspiration. *There must be something, something we haven't thought of.*

'Captain Davies!' Moraga burst onto the bridge, his face purple with anxiety. '*¡Más vapor, Capitán!* We must have more speed!'

'Believe me, Commander,' Davy squared up to him now, 'Evans is getting every last ounce out of her. She is at her limits. We have looked at every option.' Then before he actually thought the words in his head, Davy found himself saying, 'All we can do now is pray.' Moraga opened his mouth, but no sound came out. 'There is nothing more to be done. She will sink us. It will be quite decisive. Our men will have minutes.'

Moraga shrugged hopelessly then added, as if he had seen it a million times before, 'Oh, they will be shot in the water. They won't go far.'

Moraga adjusted his collar and turned to make his way back along the corridor. Once he was gone, Davy turned to William.

'William, I have a dilemma. We may be able to give our lads a chance if we tell them to keep their company scarves at the ready, not to be worn until the very last minute. It may help to set them apart. It's not their war, after all.'

William nodded.

'Between ourselves,' whispered Davy, 'I don't think the *Esmeralda* will get close enough for it to make a blind bit of difference.'

'It's worth a try,' William agreed.

'But, and this is my dilemma, William, many of the crew are Chilean, as you know. They might not like the fact that we are trying to save our skins, regardless of sides. They might spill the beans to Moraga. We could find ourselves caught between two adversaries instead of one.'

William leaned forward and thought carefully.

'Is it better to give our lads some chance of escape by behaving dishonourably?' asked Davy, more to himself than to William. To deal differently with his men, it went against the grain. It was not the way to lead.

'We've been caught in something that is not of our making,' started William.

There was another whistle and an immense thud. This time they could even hear the displaced water landing near the ship.

'Tell the lads to keep their scarves ready,' said Davy, 'but not the Chileans. At least, not for now.'

As Davy approached the deck he could hear singing. It was the familiar 'Battle Hymn of the Republic'. Davy had heard it for the first time during the American Civil War when Laird Brothers Ships were evading the North's blockades so that the cotton mills of Lancashire still had something to weave. This time the words were Spanish. Davy's Chilean crew often chose to sing it on a Sunday. More soldiers joined in; even his own crew, Chilean or otherwise.

It was a beautiful afternoon for war. The *Imperial* was cutting an elegant channel of foam through the turquoise sea. Davy had never seen her move so fast. Everything around him vibrated. Another missile slammed into the waves. The air around them shook. The *Esmeralda* continued to gain. Soon Montt would try out the torpedoes.

The hymn reached its triumphant close and Moraga stepped out in front, shouting orders to one of the companies. Around twenty men came forward through the crush.

'*¡Abran paso!*' he shouted at the men to let the group through until they were all lined up and evenly spaced at the rail, facing the *Esmeralda*.

They readied their rifles. *What on earth are they playing at*, thought Davy. *They are never going to hit anything from here.* As if to prove a point, Moraga ordered the men to point their guns in the air. Moraga didn't plan to hit anything: it was all for show. The noise was immense and prolonged, and when they stopped a massive cheer rose all around them like a wave.

'¡*Vi-va, Vi-va Bal-ma-ceda!* ¡*Viva, Viva, Moraga!*' The soldiers waved their fists at the *Esmeralda* and shook their rifles.

'Sixteen knots, Captain,' came Evans' voice at his side. Davy turned to see Evans, his neck and hair black with soot and sweat.

'Phenomenal. Well done, Evans. We can ask no more.'

'Aye, sir, she's a fine ship. I came up for a breath of fresh air, Captain.' Evans looked surprisingly cheerful for the chief engineer of a doomed ship. 'Having a bit of a sing-song are they?' Evans didn't wait for a reply but headed into their midst with a grin which suggested he'd show them how.

There was another noisy volley of shots, followed by more cheering and stomping of feet. Then as the company dispersed there came a sound, rising above the engine, the chattering troops and the lapping waves – a beautiful lone voice.

'*I bob un sydd ffyddlon, dan Ei faner Ef.*'

Evans' tenor voice rose out of the noise and smoke like a challenge to the pursuing warship. Davy had sung the hymn a hundred times and knew the words like the shape of his own hands, but he had never thought of them in the light of a real war.

... the throngs of God and Satan meet now ... we go to meet our foe ... all with clean weapons ... hell is against us with its pick-axes of fire ... the conqueror of the world and of death is at our side ...

He had never understood why this, of all the hymns of his childhood, was guaranteed to bring a tear to his eye. Perhaps because it was full of fight, the perfect hymn of hope in the face of total adversity. Davy looked away from the men and across the waves at the *Esmeralda*. She was a striking ship, a fearsome killing machine. The end would be quick, he thought, looking at her smoking guns.

When he turned back to the men he realised that many more voices had now joined Evans. There were a handful of Welshmen on board but they often learned each others' songs no matter what their nationality. This was clearly a favourite with many, even the Chileans. They sang, and now in their separate parts, with the tenors weaving their way between the bass voices like a ribbon through fabric, here below and there above the melody. Davy opened his mouth to sing but his throat was locked. They came to the refrain again, each time louder and more passionately.

'*I bob un sydd ffyddlon, dan Ei faner Ef*

Mae gan Iesu goron fry yn nheyrnas nef'
'For all who are faithful, under His banner
Jesus has a crown in Heaven.'

Even Moraga seemed to have picked up the tune and was keeping time with his fist on the rail while he stared defiantly out to sea.

They repeated the final refrain four times, more often than they would have done even in a packed-out Easter service at Bethania chapel with the most fervent worshippers gathered together in the *côr mawr*. The hymn came to its final phrase and it was followed again by a loud cheer, *'¡Viva Balmaceda! ¡Viva Moraga!'* And then, unexpectedly, a deafening *'¡Viva El Capitán!'* The lads on deck looked in his direction and cheered, and again, and again. Davy tipped his hat to them all and laughed: his proudest moment on the threshold of total annihilation. There was a God after all – He was a perverse and cruel being.

Then in the midst of the laughter and shouting, the smoke and the pulsating air there was a shout, a request for a final song. The shouts and chatter died down in anticipation. What was it to be? Evans' pure crystal tenor voice rose again, like a soaring skylark high above them. For a few moments the war evaporated: there was only the song and the beautiful sky. Davy knew every word – *Y Deryn Pur*, The Pure Bird – but he couldn't remember ever learning them. *They must be in my bones.*

Gabriel sidled up to him through the crowd and whispered, 'Captain Davies, what is he singing about? Why is it so sad?'

'He is calling on a pure bird with blue wings to be a messenger. To take a letter to his loved one because he misses her and wants to see her. She is so beautiful and kind that he thinks she must truly be an angel.'

'But why can't he take the message himself?'

The first words that came to his head were 'banished' and 'exiled'. Then 'shipwrecked'. But they were not the words of the song.

'He's a very long way from home,' Davy smiled.

Gabriel nodded earnestly and gazed at Evans with awe.

Only some of those on deck would have understood the words. Davy looked at the solemn faces of the young soldiers and the familiar faces of his crew. He realised that, despite his conversation with William earlier, he could not bring himself to set themselves apart from the Chilean crew. They would go down as they had sailed. As one.

When the song came to an end there was silence. For a second, there was no war, no *Esmeralda*, just a sleek ship on a turquoise sea and a crew in quiet contemplation. But their thoughts were dashed by yet another piercing whistle and an immense thud. *Too close now.*

'Gabriel, when Officer Whiteway returns, tell him that I have gone to fetch the logbook. There's a good lad.'

Gabriel nodded.

CHAPTER 17

The strangeness of the welcome struck Estella immediately. Myrtle Villa's smart front door had opened to reveal not only Miriam but also Mrs Ebrington deliberately filling the doorway.

'Are you all well?' asked Estella, stepping back on to the path when it became clear that neither of them was going to invite her inside.

'Yes, thank you,' answered Mrs Ebrington sternly while Miriam nodded too eagerly.

'And Peter?'

'He's unwell,' 'He's ill,' the women answered simultaneously.

Estella looked from one to the other.

'Unwell? Why didn't you send for me?'

Agnes and Miriam had agreed the previous afternoon that they would tell everyone that Peter was ill so that there would be no suspicion as to his whereabouts. They had agreed on chickenpox, which was not deadly but contagious enough to put people off visiting him. The only person who could expose the flaw in their story was standing right in front of them.

'I should be happy to look at him.' Estella stepped forward, but neither of the women moved. It occurred to Estella that this was not the first time she had arrived at Mrs Ebrington's house to a dubious welcome.

'In case of complications?' Estella added.

It was the tiny movement in Mrs Ebrington's lower lip that gave them away.

'What's wrong?' Estella whispered.

Agnes Ebrington seemed to turn in on herself like a deflating sail, and within moments Estella was ushered into the parlour. They sat, Miriam with her arm around Mrs Ebrington in a gesture of fondness that Estella could not have imagined beforehand.

'Mrs Taylor, you must promise not to tell anyone. It's so awful. Peter has joined the army. He left with them yesterday morning. We knew nothing. He said nothing to Miriam or myself.'

'But how did you find out?'

'Captain Davies, bless him, sent a boy with a message all the way from the ship.'

'From the *Imperial*?'

'Yes. She's been taken by the government to carry troops.' Agnes dissolved into tears once more and reached into her pocket to take out a handkerchief and a battered piece of paper. 'I spoke to Mr Cumming yesterday. It seems that everyone supports the rebels.'

'Not everyone.'

'And I'm afraid that if they find out about Peter … please don't tell anyone, I beg you!'

Mrs Ebrington handed the letter over. Estella had never seen Davy's handwriting before. It was a confident, elegant hand although the note had clearly been written in haste.

Dearest Mrs Ebrington,

It is my duty to tell you that Peter has embarked with the troops this morning and has admitted to me that you knew nothing of his decision. I know it will not be welcome news, but for the time being at least he is safely on board.

Captain D. Davies, Imperial

'He is the captain now?'

'Yes, but a forced command. Captain Stewart brought the news before he left for Liverpool. He said that if they were spotted by the *Esmeralda* they would be as good as dead.'

Miriam laid her head against Mrs Ebrington's shoulder and Estella tried to imagine all that must have happened on board the *Imperial* since she last saw Davy. She tried to imagine him on a man-of-war, evading enemy ships.

'He's so clumsy. He can't even carry the ash bucket without making a complete mess. How will he ever shoot anyone?'

'Who, David?'

Agnes Ebrington looked up at Estella with a look of helpless confusion.

Realising her mistake, Estella looked around the room and found what she was looking for on top of a bow-fronted chest of drawers.

'A glass of sherry. To calm the nerves.'

Estella poured all three of them a sherry: a small measure for Miriam, which she sipped meekly, a generous glass for Mrs Ebrington and a middling one for herself. They sat in silence and Estella began to construct a series of events that would convince everyone around them that Peter was at home, indisposed and unavailable for visits.

12 March, South Pacific

When Davy leaned across to open the drawer of his desk the drawer-runner, which had never played up before, caught on something and the drawer refused to open. Davy tugged carefully at first, unwilling to damage the desk, until he realised that soon he, the desk and the logbook would, in all probability, be spiralling their way through the deep dark waters of the

Southern Pacific towards a silent seabed.

With a sharper tug and a cracking sound the drawer gave way. He took out the leather-bound logbook and placed it in front of him. What to write? At the very end?

Stick to the facts. That's what Stewart would say. *Don't ramble on.*

So he wrote: the date, the time, their last co-ordinates, current speed in knots. *Sixteen. Amazing. How had Evans achieved that? The engineers at Laird had only ever claimed fourteen, maybe fifteen. On a good day. With a clean bottom.*

Pursued by the *Esmeralda*: estimated speed, a fraction over 16 knots (capable of 17). Troops on board the *Imperial*: 400. Crew on board: 50.

Cargo: guns, rifles, ammunition, horses.

God. The poor horses. Perhaps the enemy would take pity on them and hoist them on board. Or shoot them too before they swam around in ever more frantic circles.

Another thud. Another brutal shudder of the ship.

Engagement imminent.

Quickly David opened the second drawer in his desk. In it there was a piece of folded oilskin. This was his best hope of keeping the logbook dry. If anyone found his body on a distant shore and took pity on him, perhaps even wanted to give him a decent burial, they might find the book and hand it to the *Compañía*. He had heard of such things. He placed the book inside the oilskin, but before wrapping it he reached in one more time to the back of the second drawer and pulled out a closed envelope. On the front he had written, in his best handwriting, *Señora Estella Taylor, Villa D'Este, Avenue Lautaro Rosas, Valparaiso*. Shortly after completing the letter, he had returned to the drawer and crossed out the word *Señora* replacing it with *Doctor*. He smiled, and hoped by some miracle that she would receive it.

He placed the letter between the last pages of the logbook and wrapped it tightly in the oilskin, folding the corners carefully to keep out as much water as possible. Properly folded, it could be watertight for years. In the last few weeks Davy had asked Sepulveda to sew an extra large pocket inside his jacket, just the right size. He brought the corner of the package up to his lips for a moment then placed it carefully inside his jacket.

12 March, Houses of Parliament, London

'Order! Order! Order!' shouted the Speaker again above the bellowing Members of Parliament.

'Really, this is quite ridiculous,' groaned Fergusson, turning to the man next to him. 'We'll never get through all these questions at this rate.'

Fergusson wondered how it was that so many of these men – who had attended the best schools in the world, who were supposedly some of the country's brightest – could end up here in parliament's Chamber behaving more like cattle on a Scottish estate.

'Order! Order! Order,' the Speaker shouted again, his voice cracking with the strain.

'The Honourable Member for West Bromwich.'

The shouting and jeering abated a little, and Mr Edward Spencer rose to his feet armed with a daunting collection of papers.

'I beg to ask,' he began, but a private joke relating to the last few questions still rippled through the ranks and the shouting and jeering rose again and threatened to overwhelm the next Member's question.

'Ooooo-rder!' shouted the Speaker once again, looking increasingly exhausted.

'I beg to ask the Undersecretary of State for Foreign Affairs,' continued the Honourable Member for West Bromwich, 'whether he has any confirmatory news of the battle which the evening papers state to have been fought in Chile, on the 15th, 17th and 18th instant, and of the fact also stated that no foreign residents have been killed, and that much loss of life and damage to property was avoided by the presence of the English warships *Warspite*, *Espiègle*, and *Pheasant*, under the command of Admiral Hotham?'

Fergusson rose to his feet, by which time the Chamber had quietened considerably. He checked his notes and began his reply.

'The last official news received by Her Majesty's Government respecting Iquique is, I believe, up to the 20th instant, and is generally as regards affairs similar to those given in the paragraph which my honourable friend showed to me. In the telegram, which was from the naval commander-in-chief to the Admiralty, there was no mention of the British or other foreign residents, from which I think it may be presumed that they have been unmolested. There has been also today a telegram from Her Majesty's minister at Santiago, dated the 24th. The commander-in-chief will remain on the coast in the meantime for the protection of British interests.'

Sounds of patriotic approval could be heard around the Chamber. Then it was the turn of the Member for Greenock, Mr Thomas Sutherland, to ask a question. Fergusson watched him keenly. The man was rumoured to be soon in line for a knighthood. His business interests were wide and varied and included shipping.

'I beg to ask the Undersecretary of State for Foreign Affairs if he is aware that British vessels have been prevented by the Chilean government from leaving Valparaiso for another port in Chile, for the purpose of loading a nitrate cargo; and if Her Majesty's Government will cause inquiries to be made in reference to this matter, with a view to preventing British vessels from being subjected to unwarrantable interference in pursuit of their trade?'

The Chamber was almost completely silent now. Even those irritating Members who coughed as if they suffered from a perpetual chest infection were silent. Proof perfect, thought Fergusson, that even the most ill-bred people could be silent when something related to them and their financial interests. Fergusson was pleased that he had prepared his answers particularly thoroughly that day. He rose to his feet and aimed his reply to the furthest parts of the Chamber.

'A telegram was received two days ago from Her Majesty's minister at Santiago, stating that the Chilean government now refuses clearances to vessels for ports north of Chañaral. Her Majesty's Government do not consider that they can interfere with the discretion of the Chilean authorities in regard to this matter. They have not heard of any attempt to prevent vessels by force from leaving Valparaiso for other ports in Chile, and they cannot doubt that such action, if known to Her Majesty's Legation, or to the British Admiral, would have been reported.'

Fergusson sat down and the Chamber, apparently satisfied with the replies, moved on to the session's next questions. Thereafter the afternoon was relatively subdued, although Fergusson was irritated that he hadn't left the Chamber before the discussion regarding the non-payment of tithes. It appeared that schoolchildren from some remote and unpronounceable part of west Wales had been allowed a day off school in order to engage in riotous and unlawful behaviour to protest against the levy of tithe arrears.

'I mean, really, gentlemen, is that the kind of topic which we should be debating in parliament? Who are these people?' grumbled Fergusson as he left the Chamber at the end of the session.

His colleagues muttered agreement and complained of how little time there had been for other, more important topics – trade with British Colonies, the plight of Crimean veterans and the failure of the potato crop in Ireland, to name just a few.

'Not to mention the situation in Russia,' said one.

'What situation?' asked Fergusson, coming to an abrupt halt in the corridor.

The rest of the group also paused and looked from one to the other as if everyone was expected to know of the situation in Russia.

'The Russian press is reporting a plan to send 60,000 destitute Jews to the United Kingdom in the next few months. From Libau and Riga.'

Fergusson waved his hand dismissively and walked on ahead of the group. 'We'll never allow it. We already have too many foreign paupers. Where do they think we'd put them all? The Isle of Man?' Without looking back, Fergusson disappeared swiftly through the panelled doors and out into the tiled lobby.

The remaining Members of Parliament followed on slowly.

'It's no use, you won't get much sense out of him at the moment.'

'Why is that?'

'Oh, our James is courting again, I believe.'

'After poor old Olive?'

'There's life in the old dog yet.'

'Isabella Twysden, they say.'

'You don't say?'

'Who would have thought?'

'Good luck to him, I say!'

'Absolutely.'

'He's had a rough old time of it.'

'That's true.'

'A rough old time indeed.'

When Davy returned to the deck of the *Imperial*, he sensed that something had changed. The soldiers were quieter than before. All eyes were fixed on the pursuer. Another missile landed seemingly just as close, but this time, instead of rowdy jeering, there were whoops of excitement.

'What's going on, Will?' Davy asked.

William was looking through his telescope and, without taking his eye away from it, said, 'I'm not quite sure yet, but it does appear that she's stopped gaining. Perhaps even falling back. She's certainly not reaching her top speeds.'

There's not enough blue water between us just yet, thought Davy, and he looked around for Gabriel.

'Gabriel, take a message to Mr Evans. Tell him we're holding our own. Say well done.'

But there were still far too many hours left in the day. And anything could happen.

The *Esmeralda* chased them all day. At times she had been silent and menacing, saving her ammunition for what seemed to be an almost certain confrontation at close quarters. At other times her crew had driven her like some crazed mechanical dragon, spitting flames and smoke over the waves, willing each missile to travel further than the last, trying to scare her quarry into submission. And all the while the *Imperial*'s crew stayed faithfully at their stations. No one took to his bunk after a watch, and William could be seen pacing the deck with his right eye circled by a red band where he had kept his eyeglass pressed too tight, praying for a widening gap between the two ships.

Then it came at last: dusk, then dark, then black. Thank God there was no moon. Davy gave strict orders that they should sail in complete darkness, with the saloon windows heavily curtained and every deck light extinguished. They watched and watched as the *Esmeralda*, still pursuing, faded into darkness. They strained to see her and caught occasional glimpses of her flashlights. Then nothing. They sailed in darkness through the moonless night.

'When I give the order, I want you to ask the stewards to open the curtains briefly, as if someone has tampered with the blackout,' said Davy as William passed.

'Yes, Captain,' William replied. Despite his compliance, Davy knew that his chief officer would be wondering why on earth they had gone to all the trouble to cover up their lights only to reveal them deliberately.

Moments later, on Davy's signal, they saw the lights of the saloon reflect on the water briefly, then all was darkness again.

'Now, let's steer a course northwards. And I will personally thrash anyone on board who so much as lights a match in the next few hours,' said Davy to the remaining officers.

They strained to see anything. The *Esmeralda*, also blacked out, could be anywhere. *One flare would reveal all, but she is scared of becoming the quarry and that we will round on her. We must use her fear and evade her in the darkness.*

'The night is come, but not too soon,' murmured William. 'Longfellow,' he added smugly, leaning his elbows on the rails. Together, at the ship's stern, they watched the white foam recede into inky black night.

'If we hit her in the dark, we will all go down,' said William.

'Oh yes, at this speed. Without a trace.'

Over the ship's hum they could hear little else around them in the water. They scanned their surroundings, trying to take into account their change of course, but nothing visible suggested the outline of a ship or her blacked out windows.

'How goes the rest of it?' whispered Davy.

William thought for a moment then recited:

'There is no light in earth or heaven
But the cold light of stars;
And the first watch of night is given
To the red planet Mars.

Is it the tender star of love?
The star of love and dreams?
Oh no! from that blue tent above
A hero's armour gleams.'

William looked up and scanned the stars, finding Mars instinctively. 'I forget the rest.'

Davy marvelled at William's ability to remember long passages of poetry in the same way that, as a child, he had marvelled at the preacher's ability to extract long sections of the Bible for the purposes of illuminating some moral argument. Davy wondered at the consoling nature of words and their ability to provide strength like fuel in times of doubt. He wished he could draw on a reservoir of words like William seemed able to do.

Just then, from somewhere in the darkness to port, came a prolonged explosion of air. The noise made the men jump backwards from the rail and a fine spray of water came towards them on the breeze. It was no enemy but rather the unexpected waterspout of a curious whale close by in the darkness.

'I'll lend you my volume,' William added, laughing with relief.

13 March, Santiago

Maurice Hervey awoke from a deep sleep to find himself nestled in the freshly laundered sheets of the Gran Hotel de Francia, Santiago. He suspected that, for the entire six hours that he had been asleep, he had not moved a single muscle. The final leg of the journey over the Andes had been exhausting, even though his mule had quickly learned the value of docility and had not given Hervey any further cause to fear for his life. They had made it safely to Santa Rosa de Los Andes, and from there by train to Santiago arriving around 11 o'clock the previous evening. But his joy at waking in a clean and luxurious bed was quickly overtaken by irritation when he remembered the words of the despatch that had been waiting for him at the hotel desk. In the vain hope that he might have imagined it, he sat up and leaned across to the bedside cabinet. There it was, just as he remembered it, and the words had not rearranged themselves during the night.

'Report facts only. Editor.'

He had been too tired to be incensed the previous evening. But what on earth did the editor mean? Report facts only? As if Hervey had been reporting anything else but facts all along! He hadn't travelled 12,000 miles and risked his neck half a dozen times just to echo what the Congressionalists were saying! Hervey washed and dressed and made his way downstairs to the lobby to find a sizeable gathering of patriots, who had heard of his arrival, eager to divulge all they knew for the benefit of *The Times*' enlightened readership.

Crowding around, the men insisted at length that the president was a 'tyrant', a 'ruffian' and a 'murderer'.

'Gentlemen, with respect, I cannot write about these things without evidence. Where is the evidence of his tyranny, his ruffianism and his murders?'

'You can see for yourself the abundant evidence of Balmaceda's tyranny all around you!' replied one of the businessmen.

'Where?' asked Hervey, notebook and pencil at the ready.

'Well, in the first place, Santiago has been declared in a state of siege.'

Hervey looked at the faces surrounding him and it occurred to him that he was also in a state of siege *sans petit déjeuner.*

'From what I could see on arriving here last night, gentlemen, this state of siege does not press too heavily on the citizens of Santiago. A deaf man might live here a long time without finding it out, I imagine.'

'Why, in the suite of rooms opposite to yours a leading member of our party is confined to the hotel on parole, and a special gaol has been fitted out for political prisoners where upwards of forty prominent men are at the present moment under lock and key. One of the very chiefs of the revolutionary movement, Carlos Walker Martinez, has been driven to hide himself at the British Embassy to avoid arrest. Is not all this tyranny?'

Hervey was still poised, pencil at the ready over his notebook.

'Unquestionably,' said Hervey, 'but you must admit, gentlemen, that this is not very sensational. Detention in a first-class hotel? The conversion of a British Embassy into an asylum for a person who, on your own admission, is a rebel leader? I must have more than this. A great deal more.'

The visitors promised to bring him ample evidence the following day, and so, making a hasty escape, Hervey left the hotel to further his research elsewhere. After an entire afternoon of interviews he took a detour to the rock of Santa Lucia that overlooked Santiago. Here Valdivia the *Conquistador* had built a stronghold to guard the area from Indian attack. Subsequent rulers and mayors had made their own mark, and by now it was a marvel of twisting pathways, gazebos, gardens, glassy palms and icy fountains.

Sitting on a low wall overlooking the town, Hervey took out his notebook and reviewed the notes he had collected during the afternoon. The editor's words came back to him ominously: 'report facts only'. When war was declared the British press, no doubt thinking that the conflict would be over within weeks, had been almost totally ambivalent. Very few reports came out of Chile, and those that did were vague and contradictory. Then, as the war progressed and it appeared that the Congressionalists were gaining more of a foothold than expected – or perhaps, thought Hervey cynically, because Balmaceda was not overthrown so easily – the British press had turned increasingly against the president. Stories of his tyranny and despotism were found everywhere, though much of the reporting Hervey thought was of the lowest order, relying on repetition of secondary evidence, hearsay and supposition. Even reputable publications had carried articles that began with words such as 'Rumours from Chile suggest …' No names, no sources.

And something else bothered him too. Something the businessman had said that morning. That Carlos Martinez had sought, and found, asylum in the British Embassy. It was rather difficult to pretend any more that Britain was still taking a neutral stance to the conflict. Hervey really needed to meet with the president to find out for himself what kind of ogre he was. He snapped the notebook shut, shoved it back in his pocket and began making his way back down to the centre of Santiago.

After her miraculous escape from the *Esmeralda*, the *Imperial* made it safely to Coquimbo to disembark the troops. Davy watched as Peter shuffled his way down the gangway packed in tightly with the other troops. When the boy reached the harbour he sought out Davy's face on deck and gave an apologetic half-hearted wave. Davy smiled and replied with his own wave but once Peter's back was turned, Davy's arm fell heavily by his side; he felt a crushing sense of dread.

When the *Imperial* returned again to Valparaiso it seemed as if a good percentage of the city's population had turned out to welcome her home.

The *Esmeralda* was the navy's fastest gunboat, and news of her inability to catch up with and sink the marginally slower and less well-equipped *Imperial* was interpreted as a sign that perhaps, after all, the president's cause was just and that it was only a matter of time before his troops regained the towns along the coast. The crew, buoyed up by their apparent success, asked Davy for shore leave.

'Lads, I can't. You know I can't. It looks innocent enough here at the moment, but you know it wouldn't be safe. The rebels have spies and agents everywhere. I can't afford to lose you.'

One of the able seamen took out his penknife and flicked it open. 'I'd soon sort them out if they tried it on, I would, *Capitano*.'

Some of the other lads laughed at his bravado.

'Of course you would, Bruno. But you know, you wouldn't see them coming. Particularly where you'd be heading for!'

'Ha! Too right,' laughed the lads again.

'Three pints and a visit to Madame Florries and you couldn't defend yourself from a gnat.'

After that the crew's conversation degenerated into a muddle of half-hearted insults and feigned offence, culminating in an irritated, 'Oh, fuck off, Bruno, and put your sword away!'

Davy felt enormous sympathy for them. They had worked like Trojans, but he couldn't reward them with the usual well-deserved freedoms.

'Look, lads, we picked up crates of Portugese beer in Coquimbo. Get Sep to crack them open. Make sure they're shared around.'

The crew's mood lightened immediately, and they left in search of the steward with Davy shouting after them that they should go easy in case they received fresh instructions. But, in truth, there wasn't enough beer to have too much of a detrimental effect on their hardened livers.

As the sun set over Valparaiso harbour that evening, some of the crew perched themselves on the railings of the upper decks and whistled at passing girls. The Italian crew were always the most successful in attracting admiring glances. They shouted their compliments with such easy conviction. And when they ran out of Italian words, for they never bothered with translations into Spanish, they would sing. Even girls with the hardest of hearts would have to return a wry smile.

'*Tiamo! Sposami!*' the lads declared with their arms outstretched.

For a brief moment Davy wondered whether it would be possible for him to leave the ship unnoticed, slip across the harbour and climb the steep pavements of the Cerro Alegre to Estella's house without being caught.

When the ship had arrived at Valparaiso he had scoured the faces in the crowds hoping that she would be there. But she wasn't. He watched the sun until it melted below the horizon, then made for his cabin. The lads had tired of their catcalls and all the decent girls had left for home.

CHAPTER 18

*F*og. Davy hadn't seen fog like it for years. It hid the town from the ship and distorted all distances and sounds around them. Soldiers' orders echoed off the ship's funnels, but no soldiers could be seen. Invisible horses neighed from the harbour waters, but no horses were drowned. There were glimpses of artillery wheels turning eerily in thin air.

'They'll never find us in this,' laughed William, appearing spectre-like from the milky gloom, 'or else they'll mistake us for a ghost ship.'

'Where do they find them all?' asked Davy, watching yet more lines of infantry moving steadily up the gangway. 'Surely they'll run out soon?'

William replied that the army numbered over forty thousand in all.

'But we're not transporting many injured back home, are we? If you think about it, they all seem to be taking a one-way trip.' Davy thought of Peter and Mrs Ebrington and prayed that the war would end before the lad saw a single day's fighting.

'Has Moraga said anything about Peter's regiment?' asked William as if he had heard Davy's thoughts.

Davy shook his head. 'I haven't asked.'

William pulled his jacket close and declared that he was going to get them some mugs of hot tea. 'That's if Cook's not too grumpy,' he said, disappearing once more into the fog.

Standing still on deck, the cold seemed to penetrate his bones. Davy was about to follow William below when, between the troops coming up the gangway, he thought he saw a woman's head.

Davy pushed his way forward through the crowd until he could see her clearly. 'What on earth are you doing here?'

'Oh. I knew you would react like this. Please pretend you haven't seen me.' Estella turned away from him and motioned to the young lads who were carrying her trunk and bags to come up the gangway.

'Where do you think you're going?' Davy was at Estella's shoulder now.

'Please don't cause a fuss. I'm going to nurse the casualties. My help will be needed.'

Estella pushed her way through the men on deck to get away from him, but he followed, soldiers standing aside more quickly for him than they did for her. He leaned down and whispered closely at her shoulder, touching her arm as he did so.

'Please get off this ship. I won't take you to … wherever you're going.

It's too dangerous.'

'It is not within your power to put me ashore.'

'I can assure you, as captain it is well within my capability to put you ashore.' Davy grabbed her arm as discreetly as he could.

'I won't go.'

'You will go!'

Estella pulled her arm violently from his grasp. 'Let me go!' She raised her voice above the chatter on board and suddenly there was silence all around them.

Everyone on deck seemed to be looking at them.

'Captain Davies,' Moraga's voice came from behind him. 'Is there an issue with Mrs Taylor joining us?'

Estella looked past Davy's shoulder and was clearly relieved to find support.

'My apologies, Captain Davies. I should have told you that Mrs Taylor has offered us her kind assistance, which I have accepted. I trust there is no problem with her joining us as far as Taltal? We intend to set up a field hospital there.'

Davy turned to Moraga and apologised for any misunderstanding. Any medical staff supporting the war effort would be most welcome on board. As Davy turned to leave, he glanced back at Estella, half-expecting a look of triumph. But there was none. He moved through the soldiers on deck and climbed the iron steps to the bridge. As he did so, he passed a smirking sailor.

Davy stopped abruptly and turned to the unsuspecting man. 'What exactly are you doing up here, Rivas?'

'Sir?'

'Sneaking about on the upper deck when there's work to do. There's a war on, for God's sake! Do you think you have time to saunter about listening to people's conversations? Do you?'

'*Capitán*, I didn't …'

Davy walked up to the man until there was barely a hairs-breadth between them. 'You smirk at me like that again and your arse won't touch the ground again until it gets to Panama. Do you hear me?'

Davy spat the words and colour drained from the man's face.

When Davy reached the bridge, the officers stepped back and made way for him, saying nothing. The fog was beginning to lift, and as he looked out over the harbour at the long lines of troops ready to embark he could see guns, carts, wooden boxes of ammunition and horses.

'Christ. More horses.'

'Sir?'

'We're turning into a bloody ark.'

'Sir?'

Davy turned to the nearest officer and gave him a string of directions regarding the stowing of the carts, the appropriate places for the soldiers to gather on deck, where to stay clear of, where to secure the horses so the damn things didn't panic and run amok on board. The man disappeared quickly with his orders, leaving two others. Davy looked at them both askance, making an assessment of which of them could be relied upon to be the more discreet, then took one aside.

'Karlsen. Please find Mrs Taylor and bring her to …' Davy wondered where he could possibly find privacy on a ship that was overrun with troops.

'Sir, there's nowhere. There are soldiers everywhere.'

'Well, then. My cabin. Bring Mrs Taylor to my cabin.' He looked out again at the dockside chaos. In an hour or so they would be ready to leave.

'Quick as you can now. And Karlsen, you have my permission to insist.'

No emotion whatsoever passed across the young man's face; he merely nodded and left. *I will be promoting that lad as soon as I can*, thought Davy, in between the whirlwind of thoughts crowding in on him.

He left the bridge and descended to his cabin. He sat. Then he stood and paced to the porthole. He opened the window. He paced to the door. He strode back to the window and closed it. He paced to the desk. He picked up his logbook, opened it at the right page then closed it again.

Sooner than expected a knock came on the door. Karlsen opened it and Estella stepped inside. She smiled nervously at the officer as he left and closed the door politely behind him.

'So,' she turned to Davy, 'I've been summoned.'

'Estella. Please. You must leave.'

'They need me. There are so few nurses and doctors. I've promised Moraga I would go.'

'It's no place for a woman.'

Estella gasped with incredulity. 'Do you think that I haven't seen blood before? Do you think I will swoon at the sight of the first casualty with his innards hanging out? Do you?'

Davy turned away and thought of the soldiers who had been carried aboard after the battle of Iquique with makeshift rags tied around stumps of limbs, bulging bandages hastily applied in a futile effort to save blood and flesh.

'David. Do you know what it is to die slowly of pointlessness? To lie awake at night watching the hands move around the clock, to know that you've been placed on this earth only to live some fleeting, empty existence and then disappear? Not having made an ounce of difference to any one or anything? Just like some pathetic china ornament? Look at me, I'm not even decorative!' She laughed.

As she spun around, waving her arms, he thought she was the most beautiful woman he'd ever seen.

'Then think of your father,' said Davy.

'Next you will be telling me to think of Laurence and how he would feel coming home to an injured cripple. That would be hell indeed, wouldn't it? Imagine. To be forced to tend to an inconvenient wife, who can't even do you the service of dying properly so that you can run away with your whore!'

Davy looked down at his feet. He had not seen this side of her before. She was on some kind of wild trajectory that he could not understand or stop, but he suspected that whatever he said would only make her anger worse.

'Then think of me.'

Estella paused, fixing him with such a steady look of concentration that Davy thought, for a moment, perhaps his words were having some effect. But she lowered her voice to a whisper and continued. 'I am such a lucky woman. So, now I have three men to consider. Three to tell me what to do. Isn't it strange that men can waltz through life doing as they please, wherever they please, with whomever they please, and no one dares express an opinion on their activities, no matter how questionable? Whereas I, what do I get in return for my servitude? Not even a wage. Even the woman who cleans the chamber pots at the Hotel Franc is saving up for a passage to Australia. But not I! Oh, no. I have to stay in purgatory and consider everyone else first. For what gain, Davy, tell me? What benefit to me?'

Estella's voice had grown louder as she spoke and they were both aware that somewhere on deck their conversation could probably be heard. She began again, calmly now but just as deliberately. 'I am going to help the troops. It makes no difference if I die of cholera or starve. Perhaps it will be a blessing.'

Davy, who was leaning forward with his elbows on his knees, heard Estella move towards the door. This was his last chance to say what had been on his mind for weeks. He had taken for granted that there would be more time, other opportunities. But time had slipped through his fingers like a mainsail rope. 'It won't be a blessing to me, Estella. Do you understand?' He looked up at her. 'Don't you care what I want?' Davy thought he saw the shadow of sympathy come over her.

'Davy. You're not in any position to want anything. You said it yourself. If. If you were …'

She didn't say the words but they both knew what she meant. *So that was it*, Davy thought. This is why she was so angry. Now instead of being on a barren, trackless sea, there was a horizon. But no horizon she could reach. *To drown within sight of land.* The worst fate. A distant shore but no engine and no sails.

If they had been listening to the ship, they would have heard the footsteps coming towards them in the corridor. Davy might even have recognised the walk, the weight of his feet. But at that moment they were both listening to their own thoughts, rewinding the conversation, hearing again what had been said. Trying to interpret. So when the feet came to a stop outside the door and the knock came and the door swung open, neither of them had been paying attention and Davy was already committed to the words.

'You make a difference to me.'

Davy looked up to see William, frozen in the open doorway. Looking mortified, he retreated. But Estella slipped past him so quickly through the door that he almost trod on her, and then she was gone.

'Captain, my apologies, I had no idea …'

Davy remained motionless, leaning forward, staring at the floor with his hands clasped. No doubt William had come to tell him that the troops were on board, that they were ready to sail once again, that Moraga was waiting, that they needed him on the bridge. But Davy was not sure he could make it to the door, let alone through a blockade.

'All's set, captain.' William was trying to sound as if nothing extraordinary had just happened.

'Well, then,' Davy smiled as he stood up, 'we had better go to war.'

Davy put on his captain's hat and walked past William without saying anything more. Somewhere along the corridor, or perhaps on his way up the steps to the bridge, he would transform himself again into the hero-captain he needed to be, ready to command his ship through the impending teeth of war.

Maurice Hervey, special correspondent to *The Times*, was ushered swiftly into the president's room. The man who appeared before him was impressive, at least six feet tall, of spare and wiry build. Balmaceda stepped forward and shook Hervey's hand.

'You arrive at a disastrous chapter in Chilean history, *Señor Corresponsal*, and I fear you will carry away with you but a poor opinion of our common sense, or of our patriotism.'

Hervey, who suspected that his response to the president's statement would determine whether the interview continued beyond the first crushing handshake, took his time to reply. Two brocade-covered chairs appeared to have been placed in the window for the purposes of the conversation. Maurice Hervey chose his words carefully. 'No country has yet ever worked out its political salvation without such differences of opinion as at present exist between yourself and Congress.'

Balmaceda searched Hervey's face with keen, penetrating eyes.

'Nor can Chile expect to be an exception to the universal law.'

Balmaceda looked away, pondering this final statement. It gave Hervey a moment to contemplate the man's appearance. He had a head that a phrenologist would have found fault with – the broad forehead a little too sloping, the chin a trifle weak, the mouth *un tant soit peu* sensual. But the good-humoured gleam in his eyes and the smile, half-playful, half-cynical, gave no indication of the Nero-like qualities attributed to him by his opponents.

'What you say, *Señor*, is historically correct,' began Balmaceda, in pure Castillian, 'especially of England. Your records indicate a continuous struggle between a dominant aristocracy and a liberty-seeking people. And over time you have contrived to reconcile the pretentions of both.'

Balmaceda guided Hervey slowly towards the chairs in the window.

'But your ways are not the ways of the rest of the world, and most certainly they are not our ways. Your hereditary throne, your hereditary House of Lords and your popular elective House of Commons appear to harmonise with the character of the English nation. But they do not meet the views of younger nationalities which invariably adopt a republican form of government.'

The men reached the chairs but did not sit.

'Now, here comes the great difference,' said Balmaceda, becoming more animated, 'with you, but one of the three powers which form your constitutional system is elective. In a republic all three are elective. Your two hereditary powers are, more or less, automata. That is, neither crown nor Lords dare oppose a strong expression of the national will. We have no such automata. Least of all is a Chilean president an automaton, being invested by the Chilean constitution with powers greater even than those of Congress. That his powers are excessive is quite possible, but that they exist is certain.'

Balmaceda turned and pointed to the original Chilean constitution, framed in gold, which adorned the wall behind them.

'Do you follow me?' Balmaceda asked.

'Perfectly, your Excellency,' replied Hervey, pleased that his rusty Spanish still seemed up to the job. 'However,' he added cautiously, 'your opponents would assert that custom and precedent had modified this constitution to an extent you refused to recognise.'

The president's eyes narrowed.

'No, ¡*No es cierto, Señor!*' he replied, 'that is not the case. I did nothing that has not been done over and over again by my predecessors. But I am the first representative of the Liberal party who has ever held office. Ever since 1833 the aristocracy has had a monopoly of the presidency, and up to my election the presidential powers were never called into question. Moreover, when I was sworn in I took an oath to uphold and maintain the constitution *as it stands* without reference to alleged precedents or philosophical theories. Congress, by the express terms of that constitution, has no more right to dictate to me what ministers I shall choose than it has to ordain what food I shall eat or what clothes I shall wear. If I have in any way exceeded my powers, then let Congress impeach me when my term of office expires. I did not frame the constitution nor am I responsible for its provisions. But I am responsible before God and man to observe my oath, and this, *por Dios, Señor*, I shall do while breath remains in my body.'

There was no doubting Balmaceda's conviction or his immense personal presence. Hervey was finding it difficult not to be impressed by the man, but it was the journalist's role to challenge.

'It would seem then, your Excellency, that the simplest solution to this conflict would be to revise and remodel the constitution?'

'Unquestionably. And this has always been a prominent feature of the Liberal programme. But the way to effect constitutional reforms is neither to render government impossible, nor to seduce the fleet, nor to play into the hands of foreign capitalists, nor to incite a civil war.'

Despite his assertiveness, these last words were said with a tinge of sadness, and their discussion moved on to the practicalities of war.

'Does your Excellency believe that the struggle will last long?'

For the first time during their conversation the president appeared weary. 'As you know, my hands are tied for want of ships to transport troops to the north. We have the fine ship *Imperial*, and if only we had three or four such vessels the rebellion would be crushed in a fortnight. Our new warships, the *Pinto* and the *Errázuriz*, are still being fitted out in France. The torpedo catchers, the *Lynch* and *Condell*, are still on their way to Valparaiso. Too many mistakes have been made in battle. Some of my generals should have displayed more prudence and less impetuosity.'

Just then there was a knock on the door and Balmaceda's secretary entered with a note. The president scanned the contents then nodded decisively to the man, who left again swiftly. The interview is over, thought Hervey, and sure enough when Balmaceda turned his attention back to the journalist it was with a hand outstretched, thanking him for his visit and with the hope that the president's cause would be fairly represented in the British press.

Hervey took his leave and was escorted to the grand entrance hallway. As he passed through the outer doors and into the wide boulevards of Santiago, he realised with a smile that the whole interview had been conducted on their feet and that, despite Balmaceda's welcoming demeanour, neither of them had in fact sat down in those inviting brocade chairs. He could not help being impressed by the man. Hervey had not taken a single note, but he could remember every word.

The *Imperial* was approaching Taltal. The dense fog that had enveloped them at Valparaiso had dispersed only to give way to strong winds and a rough sea. Many of the new recruits spent the voyage leaning over the rails trying to pin their gaze on what they could see of a solid horizon. But, as the winds worsened and the horizon disappeared behind rolling banks of water, some found it was better to retreat to the corners, however cold, shut their eyes and stay as still as possible. Most of the soldiers looked a little green: some of them had no colour at all.

Since the outbreak of war Davy usually approached their planned destinations with a welcome sense of relief. Relief that their engines needed no major repairs, relief that their coal supplies were still good, and mostly relief that they had not encountered the *Esmeralda* again.

'We've got a bloody lucky captain!' he had heard some of the lads shouting at Valparaiso harbour just before they left. Sailors from a German merchant ship had asked them how it was they were still afloat with at least forty enemy ships searching the coastline, looking to sink them at the first opportunity.

'And he's got this!' added the boatswain, who didn't like Germans much, jabbing his own forehead with an insistent finger. 'Don't want them thinking it's all down to bloody luck,' he'd muttered.

But this time was different. Davy approached Taltal with dread. The familiar landmarks of the harbour crystallised slowly on the coastline. Within the hour they would be busy unloading another consignment of troops and Estella would be gone.

'All clear!' the lookout shouted, and Davy's heart sank. He realised that he had been hoping for another menacing corvette to chase them back out to sea, a crack enemy warship that would fire at them all the way to the cold waters of the Antarctic. He made his way through the soldiers and crew who acknowledged him with grateful smiles. Their captain had evaded the enemy ships once again and brought them safely to their destination.

When Davy arrived at the bridge, William and two of the other officers were already there. 'William, you've lost your turban,' said Davy, looking closely at the gash on his head. 'Healing nicely, I see. Tony did a good job after all.'

William was not so easily impressed. 'Estella took the bandages off, actually. She was much less cantankerous.'

Davy turned to William again and asked, more quietly this time, 'William, could you see whether we have any spare whistles on board?'

'Yes, Captain,' answered William, only the briefest of questioning looks passing across his face.

'One. That's all I need. And a length of chain. Or ribbon. Even better.'

Davy turned away without explaining further, and once William had left he and his officers watched in silence as the harbour approached, their silence broken only by Davy's direction to adjust speed or course. *We are raising Taltal.* How odd it was, thought Davy, that sailors saw land as being raised or lowered by their own actions. They felt the turbulent open sea give way to calmer waters as they approached. On the harbour soldiers and carts gathered, awaiting the arrival of reinforcements and new supplies.

'Officer Webb. You have the bridge,' said Davy, turning to leave, and when Webb faced him with a look of panic Davy was calm and matter-of-fact.

'You've watched me bring her in countless times, Webb. No time like the present.'

'Sir,' replied Webb, looking around at the other officers.

William was on the way up the steps when Davy came to meet him.

'Cook gave me this. And cleaned it,' said William, taking a shiny brass whistle from his pocket. 'I'm afraid this was the only ribbon we could find.'

Davy took the whistle and turned it over in his hand, letting the pale blue ribbon run through his fingers. 'Perfect,' he said, descending the stairs past William. 'Tell Cook he's a marvel, but not now. I've left Webb in charge of the bridge.'

William stopped momentarily with surprise then carried on towards the bridge. 'This should be interesting,' he muttered, and both men went their separate ways.

Davy walked the length of the main deck but could not see any sign of Estella. Since their encounter he had tried his best not to see her. He had caught only brief glimpses of her, reading in a corner or tending to some of the soldiers' minor ailments.

The harbour came ever closer.

'Dry land at last, eh?' said Davy to a young soldier who had spent most of the voyage clinging desperately to one of the rails.

'*¡Gracias a Dios!* My God, I would rather walk home across the Atacama than do that again, Captain. With respect.'

Davy patted him on the shoulder and wished him luck. These were the small human tasks of a captain. Lewis Davies had taught him how important they were all those years ago.

Davy walked on through the gathering soldiers.

'Make way for the captain!' came the occasional shout and people would stand aside, separating like the seas for Moses.

'Good luck, lads.' Davy responded automatically as another group parted. Did he really mean 'good luck', he wondered? Did he actually really care who won as long as he and his crew and Peter and Estella found their way home safely at the end? Was there any difference between the Congressionalists and the Balmacedaists? Weren't they all as crazy as each other? Everyone looking for glory and the last word? Perhaps what he really meant was 'try to stay alive'. *For the sake of your mothers and fathers, your wives and children, just try to stay alive.*

And then, Estella was there, with her back towards him, looking out over the bow, silent and still as the day he had seen her on the harbour. She was deep in her own thoughts, and Davy was relieved when the troops closed in around him again so that she did not see him.

We'll miss our mark completely at his rate, thought Davy, realising that the speed and angle of their approach was all wrong. The urge to return to the bridge was almost irresistible, but his officers had to learn. And he knew from his own experience that they could not learn if they had the captain breathing expletives down the back of their necks.

'Bloody hell! Where are we going?' shouted one of the crew.

The deck erupted into a chorus of bad-tempered jeering.

'Captain Davies, are we not landing at the harbour as agreed?' Moraga bellowed, head and shoulders above the other soldiers.

'Yes, Colonel. We are training one of the junior officers today. We are slightly off course.'

'Sir, this is not a good day to be playing games, I must say. I don't find this at all amusing.'

'Colonel, with all due respect, we have made good time from Valparaiso. We are here hours earlier than expected. We have not been attacked or commandeered, and if I get shot tomorrow you will need someone else who can take charge of the helm. We are merely taking sensible precautions.'

Moraga adjusted his collar roughly, the way he did when he had run out of expletives and could not bring himself to admit that perhaps someone else was right. Just then, there was a dramatic change in the sound of the engines. The ship slowed and turned sharply towards the harbour again. Gentler waters lapped past the bow. William's at the helm, thought Davy. *Just in time*.

The soldiers on the harbourside let out a wild cheer when they saw the *Imperial* turn towards them, and their cheers were echoed by the soldiers on board who now jabbed their rifles excitedly in the air. Moraga shook his head in disgust and walked off towards the gangway.

Anyone watching Davy at that moment would have thought him a picture of calm but when he looked down at his hands, the knuckles on his clenched fists were a little too taut, the white sinews clear through the weathered skin of his hands. He shook his hands loose, and felt the whistle's weight in his pocket.

Soldiers were moving towards the gangway. In all directions there were people shouting instructions, gathering, carrying. The deck was alive. Everyone had their part to play and Davy paused to take in the ordinariness of extraordinary circumstances. The boy who bent to tie his laces was carrying a rifle on his back. The stevedores were unloading crates, but the cargo was lethal dynamite. The man leaning against the taffrail was not sharpening his knife for innocent whittling. And for all their bravado, their ready smiles and frowns, they were hiding something that none of them was man enough to name aloud. *Myself too*, Davy thought.

Suddenly, a man's cry rose above the others, then another, and another, punctuated suddenly by the terrified whinny of a horse. Over the soldiers' heads, Davy saw it rearing. He pushed his way through the scattering crowds, eventually reaching a clearing where the horse was loose. An injured man was lying in a pool of blood on the floor and another was kneeling on the ground, cradling his arm. The crowd around had been forced backwards on to the rails, open-mouthed and helpless.

'Where are the other handlers?' shouted Davy, scanning the men's faces. No one answered and the horse turned in frantic circles, snorting aggressively. It reared again. This was no spindly racehorse. It was a creature built for dragging artillery and loaded carts. Yet it was beautiful and its anguish was terrifying to see. The man lying on the ground was dragged backwards to safety, leaving a path of fresh dark blood. Davy took off his jacket and thrust it into the nearest pair of hands. 'Get back! All of you!' he shouted. *'¡Apártense!'* He searched the sea of faces. Where were the other handlers? The men's agitation was making everything worse. 'Be quiet! All of you!'

Froth appeared at the horse's mouth. Soon it would lose all sense and not even an army of handlers would calm it down. It would most likely see a sudden gap and leap over the rails to dash its brains out on the harbour below rather than endure any more of this nightmare corral.

Again, Davy motioned for the crowd to get back. The horse wheeled around and although its head was turned away, Davy knew it had sensed his presence. '*Dere, 'nawr.*' Davy said, quietly, not moving. *Come now.* The chatter around him died down. The horse stood still, although Davy could tell by its wide black eyes and the way its veins stood proud on its muzzle that it was barely containing its fear.

'*Dere, 'nawr.*' The fractious crowd was bemused, he realised, and it was only then that it occurred to him that he had spoken to the horse in Welsh. '*Dere, paid a meddwl amdanyn nhw. Edrych di arna i.*' The horse turned and fixed its eyes on Davy. *Come on, don't worry about them. You look to me.* Davy let out a long calming breath and as if in response the horse gave a prolonged exhaling snort, its nostrils vibrating with released energy. '*Dere 'nawr. Dere.*'

He needed a rhyme. The rhythm would be soothing. He had done it before. He approached the horse calmly. And he was back in the stables with Gruffudd, tending to Lady and Flower at the start of the day, mucking out, laying clean straw. Taking a brush and singing in time to each stroke, he laid his head on Lady's mane. It was a love song.

*Mi sydd fachgen ifanc ffôl
Yn byw yn ôl fy ffansi
Myfi'n bugeilio'r gwenith gwyn
Ac arall yn ei fedi.*

He could smell her skin. It smelt of wood chips and straw and the sweat of ploughing. He hummed the song in her ear and kept stroking. But when he drew back, he was no longer in the stables but outside the crumbling barn. Lady's mane began to smell of smoke. The stable walls had turned to flames. He buried his face in her neck and sang louder to block out the scene. But no matter how hard he brushed or how loudly he sang, the flames kept rising.

'We'll take her now, *Capitano*,' said a voice and when Davy opened his eyes, he realised that he was clinging to the mane of an unfamiliar horse. It was calm now. Had he been singing to it? He glanced around. The crowd was still there as if frozen in time.

'She'll be all right with me now, sir.'

Davy stepped backwards and passed the reins to the handler, who led the animal towards the gangway. This is how that creature felt, thought Davy, looking around at the circle of silent, mesmerised faces. Each one trying to read my thoughts.

The task of leaving the empty space was a mammoth one. His feet seemed weighted with lead. He propelled himself forward and as he reached the first soldiers they stood aside, making a pathway along the deck. Davy walked the length of the ship before coming to an unsteady halt by the stern. He reached for the rail, just in time to stop his legs buckling, then cursed himself over and over.

'Davy?' Estella's voice.

No doubt she had seen his performance and come to gloat or worse. He sensed her step towards him but he felt like the corralled horse and let go of the rail. There was no way back to the bridge except past her. She had not responded to him earlier so there was nothing more to say. But turning and drawing level with her, something in him gave way.

'You are unkind, beyond words,' he whispered. His arm brushed her shoulder but he was not looking at her now. 'You join my ship, to go, God knows where, in such a manner that it is impossible for me to stop you. And you do this, knowing my feelings. I have not hidden them from you. And all to spite a man you hate. Do you hate him so much? Do you love me so little?'

Estella drew breath as if to reply, but in the space where she would have spoken Davy turned towards her. His face brushed against her forehead. He could smell a faint trace of Castile soap on her skin and feel the warmth of his own breath rebounding.

The decks had cleared and there was a shout from the gangway.

'It's time to go,' said Estella.

Davy took half a step back. Only half a step but he thought his heart would break with it. 'I have something for you. Something small. It may come in useful. You never know … if you need help, sometimes above the noise and chaos, you can hear it when you might not hear a voice.'

Davy stretched out his palm and offered her the whistle. 'I used to make them years ago out of willow, you know … they are just as good, in terms of sound, that is … but brass is obviously stronger … it doesn't …'

Burn. His hand shook and he couldn't look at her.

'Cook put a ribbon on it.'

'A blue ribbon.'

Yes.

Estella took the whistle from his hand. For a moment he thought she was about to say something. But she must have reconsidered because instead she leaned towards him and kissed him silently on his cheek. Davy closed his eyes. He knew that if he watched her walking down the gangway he would need to run after her and beg her to come back on board. He waited and waited until, when he did look up, he could see her, a long way up the harbour, about to turn the corner by the Custom House, following the ammunition carts and disappearing into a sea of troops.

CHAPTER 19

15 April, Santiago

Balmaceda had not seen his family in days. He had taken to sleeping on a temporary bed that Vásquez had arranged at the offices, partly to be close to things and partly to spare his family the constant disruptions of being woken during the night with telegrams and urgent requests. But that afternoon Balmaceda decided, late in the day, that he wanted to spend the evening with his wife and children. Not that some of his sons and daughters could be called children any more, ranging in age as they did from twenty-one down to six.

The presidential home was only a short way from Congress and guards had accompanied him back there with their usual efficiency. As Balmaceda entered the house, he heard the soldiers exchanging friendly banter with those who were permanently posted at the house.

A housemaid came to take his coat, looking unusually flustered. 'Oh, your Excellency, we didn't expect you. *La Señora* is on the terrace with …'

'No matter! It will be a surprise.'

Balmaceda walked through the house, wondering why the place was so quiet. The lamps were not yet lit and it was a typically mild autumn evening. When he stepped on to the terrace he realised that his entire family, his wife Emilia and their seven children, were all present, each one turned with varying degrees of concern and horror towards their eldest daughter. His wife was the first to notice his arrival and rushed towards him.

'Oh, *mi amor!* Something horrible has happened, José Manuel! Something awful and evil!'

Balmaceda's daughter Sofia fell back, sobbing, into the wicker chair behind her. In her lap she held a crumpled newspaper.

'They have been telling lies in *El Mercurio*. How could they?' said Emilia.

Balmaceda walked across to Sofia and took the paper from her hands.

'Oh, father! It's not true!' sobbed the girl.

Balmaceda read the headings quickly and found the one he was looking for.

President's Daughter Distraught

The revolution in Chile has driven the eldest daughter of the President Balmaceda out of her mind. Occasionally she has sane intervals when she implores her father to resign and not to plunge the country into further bloodshed.

'*Sane intervals?* Father, how can they write such lies? Surely there are laws? How can they just make things up when they don't know the truth?' Sofia turned to her father and pulled at his arm. 'Father, I haven't spoken to anyone. Believe me! How would they know what I think?'

Balmaceda drew up a chair close to his daughter's. He folded the newspaper and placed it at his feet on the floor then took Sofia's hand. 'Sofia, my darling girl. We all know they are lies.'

'But how can they?'

'They can write what they like. I see it all the time. If there is no news, they make it up. If they don't like the stories they have, they make up some new ones. These people, they are not interested in the truth. They are interested in selling newspapers.'

Sofia leant her head against her father's shoulder. 'But even if we know they are lies, other people will still believe them. How will Emilio's family know that they are not true?'

Balmaceda looked across at his wife. They had not had the heart to tell their daughter that her fiancé's family had already come out in support of the Congressionalists.

'He won't want to marry me if he thinks I'm insane!'

Sofia's shoulders shook with sobs. Balmaceda held his daughter close and stroked her hair. Over her head he looked at his other children, from one to the next, their dark eyes full of confusion, fear and loss. Balmaceda thought of his meeting with Hervey a few days earlier and wondered how that report would appear. At the time he had thought it was strange that the man had not taken any notes. Perhaps he has a good memory? Perhaps he had already written his story and merely wanted an excuse to meet the tyrant himself. Was there anywhere on God's earth such a thing as an honest journalist?

After leaving Davy behind on the deck of the *Imperial*, Estella had calmly followed the men from the first regiment as they made their way from the harbour. She had walked mechanically, trying not to think of what lay ahead, mesmerised by the sound of the soldiers' hobnailed boots and the rhythmic squeaking and jangling of the field artillery. As the soldiers in front of her reached the Custom House and began to make their way in to the narrow streets, a thought came to her that, beyond this corner, the ship would no longer be visible.

She slowed down and came to a halt. Her thoughts, which had been so ordered and logical, erupted like a flock of angry crows. Why had she been so unkind? Why had she not at least been able to show some understanding?

He had declared himself openly and honestly and she had run away. Literally.

The footsteps of the regiment ahead of her were fading now and she would need to run to catch up. But, instead, she gathered her skirt about her and turned to look again at the ship. She could still make out Davy's silhouette, standing motionless and alone on the deck with his back turned to the harbour. The crows in her head were screaming now *Run back! Run Back! Run Back!* She could tell him the truth. Every sinew in her body was poised, but the way forward and the way back seemed equally terrifying.

'Careful, *Señora*, or you will be run over!'

The second regiment of soldiers was approaching fast, a sea of men interspersed with mule carts and artillery.

'It's not too late to change your mind!' laughed one of the soldiers, more to his comrades than to her.

And that's when the fear gripped her, like a strange and invisible human form, it surrounded her with its clammy embrace and squeezed the breath from her lungs. The 'brave' step of joining the war now seemed idiotic and selfish.

'Move along there, lady,' came a bad-tempered shout.

Estella stood back and strained to see the ship through the oncoming crowd, but the view had been obliterated. Soldiers marched past her, hardly moving out of her way. Someone's bulky knapsack caught her shoulder and she heard a muttered apology. She stepped from the path of a cart and went headlong into another soldier. Strange, solemn faces came towards her like breakers in a rising storm. Her knees trembled. *It is too late.*

Estella turned away from the sea and fell in with the men again, as they turned the corner past the Custom House and headed inland.

16 April, Caldera

For what seemed like minutes the boy was suspended in mid-air. When he did eventually hit the ground, the sky itself seemed to have swallowed the earth and was now regurgitating it all on his head. Lumps of earth and gravel filled his mouth and there was the metallic taste of blood. Grit and warm liquid seeped into his eyes. He needed to see what was going on around him, but to open his eyes he needed to clear them of dirt and he couldn't do that without moving his arm. Someone would surely see that he was still alive. The urge to weep and give up was almost overpowering. More earth and debris fell on his head, blocking out the light.

Slowly he moved his right arm towards his face. There was a sudden movement behind him. Repeating shots rang out and something fell near his feet. Something touched his ankle and twitched briefly. In quick succession came the urge to vomit, to cry out, to flee in any direction like a chicken being chased by an axe. His hand was at his eyes scrabbling awkwardly, making things worse. More missiles landed further away. The enemy would be looking in another direction, so the boy slid his hand underneath himself and hauled at his shirt. He tugged and pulled it all the way to his chest and curled his face towards it so that he could wipe the grit and blood from his eyes. He felt no pain. But there was blood everywhere. *Not my blood.* To his right there was a soldier's boot, larger than his own. It lay empty and on its side. It lay on a severed hand that still had colour in it. Blood trickled slowly from its cavities. The repeating fire of the Hotchkiss guns rang out without pause. For every shot he could fire, they could fire ten. They didn't stand a chance.

RUN. Don't think. Just run. Don't look. Jump over the body. Through the puddles of blood and ... RUN. Don't trip on the helmets, the bayonet sticking up from the ground. Shots all around. Don't look. Go AROUND ... the cart. Make your legs work. Make them go. MAKE them run. Don't stop. Don't stop. Don't stop. Don't stop. Don't stop.

Offices of *The Times* newspaper, London
Sir James Fergusson didn't feel inclined to wait around to be announced and so had already sat down at the editor's desk by the time the secretary alerted George Earle Buckle to his visitor's arrival.

Without a word of greeting, Fergusson tossed an open copy of *The Times* across the desk towards the editor. Buckle, who was evidently casting his eye over an article written by a junior journalist, carried on reading.

'I thought you were going to do something about this man, what's his name?' said Fergusson.

Buckle read on and made some small, precise marks in the margins. 'Good morning, Fergusson. To what do I owe this pleasure?'

'He can't be allowed to carry on. It's all utter nonsense!'

'Hervey.'

'Pardon?'

'The journalist's name. Maurice Hervey.' Buckle looked up at Fergusson over his half-moon glasses and frowned. 'Are you sickening for something? You're looking quite unwell.'

'I thought you said you were going to recall him, or re-distribute him, or whatever you do with journalists when they start making things up.'

Buckle slowly peeled off his wire glasses and called an assistant's name. Within seconds a young man entered and went straight to Buckle's desk.

Buckle, speaking quickly and quietly, pointed out the changes and gave him instructions to get the copy to the printers post haste.

'His reports contradict everything that's coming out of Buenos Aires.'

The door closed behind the departing assistant and Buckle placed his glasses carefully on the desk. 'Buenos Aires?' he smiled, 'Buenos Aires is a fair distance from Valparaiso and Santiago. Not to mention the small matter of it being in a different country.'

'I'm telling you, Hervey's been bribed by the government. Balmaceda has got to him!'

Buckle leaned forward languidly and opened a box of cigars. 'You really must take a holiday, you know. The Swiss Alps are excellent at this time of year. I find the air extraordinarily good for …' he opened the box towards Fergusson, 'One's temperament.'

Fergusson declined the cigar with a shrug and leaned back in his chair. He watched Buckle as he rose to his feet and took a taper from a canister on the mantlepiece. Buckle leant down towards the fire, lit the taper then used it to light the end of his cigar. He pursed his lips and inhaled twice; then, inspecting the end of the cigar to see whether it was properly lit, he blew out the taper and replaced it in the canister. The sweet smell of cigar smoke wafted across the room.

Fergusson looked down to see the knuckles on his right hand tapping irritatingly against the chair arm. Just the effect Buckle was looking for, no doubt. Fergusson stilled his hand and inhaled very slowly.

'As you know, James, *The Times* prides itself on its impartiality.'

'Oh, please …' Fergusson looked away in disgust.

'Hervey's one of my best men. He's not some common hack. He's written books and papers on trade policy and imperial federation. He understands politics. He's interested. It's not something he's fallen into by virtue of birth.'

Fergusson pinned his sights on the gnarled branches of the pollarded lime trees outside the high window. He knew full well that Buckle was attempting a sideways swipe at him but he was determined not to be ruffled.

Buckle persevered. 'Hervey has something on the way to print at the moment – with Sonnenschein, I think. There's no question of him making things up, as you put it. He's been meeting people on the ground. He's using reliable sources, on both sides.'

Buckle puffed on his cigar then took out his pocket watch and checked the time.

'Bring him back,' said Fergusson.

Buckle coughed. 'I'm not entirely sure we know where he is at the moment. The last we heard he was trying to secure a berth on one of the president's warships.'

'That's a surprise! I bet you they haven't put him in steerage.'

Buckle sighed and sat down at his desk again. 'Who's putting pressure on you, James?'

'"Sir James" to you.'

'Colonel North? Balfour?'

'Don't be ridiculous.'

'The news is the news, James. We can't rewrite it to suit whatever agenda you happen to have going on at the moment.'

Fergusson got up slowly from his chair and walked towards the door. When he reached it, placing his hand on the door handle, he hardly bothered turning to face Buckle at all.

'Really, Buckle? Are you sure? Are you absolutely sure of that?'

Fergusson left and closed the door behind him. As he passed through the offices on his way out, he thought there was something rather seedy about the place. All the young men seemed to work in grubby shirtsleeves, their arms crumpled with garish sleeve garters.

A flustered-looking young man rushed towards him with his coat and hat and as Fergusson put them on, he thought of Buckle and hoped that the man's cigar had taken on a rather bitter taste.

16 April, *The Imperial*, Valparaiso

'*¡Ah, El Corresponsal!*' declared Moraga and stepped forward to shake hands with the expensively dressed, rather portly man who had laboured up the gangway on to the *Imperial*'s deck. Tales of *The Times*' special correspondent had preceded him, and Davy's first thought on meeting the journalist was for the poor mule that had transported him over the Andes. *A journalist's life is clearly not one of dietary hardship*, mused Davy.

'And this,' said Moraga, turning to Davy, 'is Captain Davies, who, as you know, was our saviour in the first few weeks of the war. If it had not been for his ability to steer the *Imperial* safely through the rebel blockades, and get supplies to our troops in the north, then Iquique would have fallen at the start of the war.'

The journalist shook Davy's hand warmly. 'What part of England are you from, Mr Davies?'

'Wales, Mr Hervey.'

'Ah, that part!' the journalist laughed and turned to Moraga. 'Wales is a stunning country, Colonel, with scenes to rival anywhere in the world. And a rich and ancient literature too, The Mabinogion, Dafydd ap Gwilym, Taliesin …' Hervey turned back to Davy. 'I mean no offence, Captain. You see, I am from that part of England they call Ireland.'

Hervey went on to tell them that before boarding the *Imperial* he had visited the British *Warspite* and the American Cruiser *Baltimore*, both now moored at Valparaiso harbour. There was no doubting where their allegiances lay. When questioned, Rear-Admiral Hotham of the British Navy had declared that his sympathies were very strongly with the revolutionists, although he happily admitted to knowing very little about the merits of the political questions beyond what he had been told by the insurgents. The Americans wholeheartedly supported the government, and were convinced that the whole affair had been worked up by agitators on behalf of European nitrate syndicates.

'However,' the journalist continued, 'the British and the Americans were at least unanimous in one respect. If I should be caught on board the *Imperial*, my nationality would not protect me. I would most likely be tortured and hanged along with the rest of you. The whole bally shoot!' Hervey laughed.

Davy looked across at Moraga and remembered the conversation they'd had when the ship was first commandeered. At the time, the colonel had promised the crew some kind of amnesty.

'There is no need to worry about torture or hanging, Mr Hervey,' said Moraga. 'This ship will not be taken because if we lose this ship, we lose the war. It's as simple as that. Come! Let the steward show you to your quarters. Then we shall sample the delights of our Chinese cook. He makes the best *carapulcra* I've ever tasted.'

Davy watched as the two men strolled along the deck then turned and disappeared through one of the saloon doors. Moraga had discussed Hervey's arrival a few days earlier and was clearly keen to ensure that this journalist wired favourable reports back to London.

'And, if they are not favourable,' Moraga had grumbled, 'then let's hope they are at least accurate.'

17 April, Taltal
'Stop!' Estella looked up from the dying man to see a boy, face drenched in blood and dirt, running like a crazed animal back through the lines of relief soldiers.

'¡*Alto!*' the soldier bellowed again and, stepping into the battle-blind boy's path, felled him to his knees with a single swipe of his rifle.

'*¡Cobarde!* How dare you flee from the battle like some pathetic girl?'

'I lost … my gun, sir.'

'Bastard!' the soldier grabbed the boy by the tattered jacket and hauled him to his feet with a jolt. 'This is what we do with deserters!'

The soldier paced backwards and took aim at the swaying boy. Then, just as he was about to pull the trigger, the woman stepped between them.

'No! I know this boy. He shouldn't be here. He's too young.'

'Get out of my way. He's old enough to carry a gun. He's old enough to die as a traitor.'

Estella raised her arms to shield Peter. 'No. You will have to shoot me. He's only a child. He lied.'

For a second the soldier's gun wavered, but he raised it again and took aim properly this time. 'Stand aside!'

Estella closed her eyes and heard Peter sob in terror behind her.

'You idiot! Put the gun down!'

A man covered in blood came pacing forward from the rows of injured soldiers and wrenched the gun from the soldier's hands. 'Hundreds of men are dying over here and you're going to shoot the only doctor we have? You're a bloody lunatic. Which side are you on?' the man shoved the soldier's shoulder so forcefully that he sprawled backwards on to the ground.

'This child,' said the man, walking around behind Estella and grabbing Peter roughly by the arm, 'Is Mrs Ebrington's boy. The most dangerous thing he's done in his life so far is fill up a coal scuttle or run an errand. We're not trying to win a war so that you can turn us all into barbarians!' The man dragged the boy away and Estella followed. Suspicious eyes watched them and Estella knew that Peter was by no means safe. 'Make yourself useful, lad,' hissed the man as he walked off back to his injured comrades.

Great waves of terror still shook the boy. 'Look at me, Peter,' said Estella firmly and the boy turned to her immediately with huge haunted eyes. 'You must help me now. Do you understand? I need your help.'

'Yes, Mrs Taylor,' Peter answered mechanically, his voice breaking as he said her name. Estella took his arm and held him in an iron grip. 'I can't do this on my own. Do you understand?'

Peter's face softened a little and he nodded. Estella gave him a cloth to wipe his face and hands and together they set to work on the men's wounds, Estella making sure that Peter's hands were never empty and that he was holding the scissors or the end of a bandage or ready to pass the needle and thread at the right time. From the corner of her eye Estella could tell that the soldier's eyes were on them still, waiting for the moment when Peter's resolve would evaporate, when he would pick up his legs and run again as fast as he could, the deserter, across the barren ground, only to be shot in the back as he fled.

CHAPTER 20

18 April, 1891, Valparaiso

At long last the brand new government vessels, the *Almirante Lynch* and the *Almirante Condell*, had made it over from Laird Brothers in Birkenhead. They and the *Imperial* now steamed in company out of Valparaiso harbour destined for Iquique. Colonel Moraga was now commander-in-chief of all three vessels and sailing on the *Condell*. Captain Fuentes commanded the *Lynch* and Captain Garin, replacing Moraga, was now in charge of the *Imperial*. As old soldiers Fuentes and Moraga were deemed to be better suited to the work of the armoured torpedo catchers than Garin who, as one of the few members of the Chilean navy who had remained faithful to the government, was a sailor first and a soldier second. The ships did not sail immediately to Iquique but rather paused at Quintero Bay for a couple of days' torpedo practice.

At 8 o'clock in the morning on the third day the convoy sailed north towards Caldera Bay, the *Lynch* and *Condell* hugging the coastline while the *Imperial* stood out to sea some five miles. The plan was for the two torpedo catchers to venture as close to Caldera harbour as possible in an attempt to sink the *Aconcagua*, while the *Imperial* stood ready to support the ships with coal and supplies if necessary.

'But what will I see at this distance?' complained Hervey when their plans became clear. 'I will see no more of the action than a man in Fleet Street at this rate!'

'We have our orders, direct from the president himself,' replied Garin, 'that on no account should the *Corresponsal* be placed in any mortal danger. Neither the *Corresponsal* nor the *Imperial*.'

Hervey thrust out his finely trimmed beard and breathed deeply. This was not what he had in mind when he left London.

That night, as darkness closed in around them, the *Imperial* lost sight of the torpedo catchers, and men on the night watch swore they could hear guns in the distance.

The following morning Hervey was going through his papers. He had been impressed with the *Imperial* from the first. Every possible arrangement had been made for his comfort: two spacious cabins had been arranged *en-suite* so that he had a bedroom and a sitting room suitable for writing; he had been assigned the 'seat of honour' beside Commander Garin, and everyone on board had treated him with the utmost courtesy and kindness. During the first few days Hervey had tried, rather unsuccessfully, to keep a daily diary, but what with the constant pounding of the torpedoes, the big guns including a large Armstrong bow-chaser, quick-firing guns, Gatlings and rifles, concentrating on anything at all was virtually impossible. He had even resorted to the relatively unchallenging task of describing the ship. She was comfortable and endowed with all modern luxuries including costly furniture, a handsome music saloon complete with piano and harmonium. She had generous, well-fitted cabins and a spar deck running the full length of the ship, which made an excellent promenade. Even though they were in a state of war, Hervey also had to concede that the cuisine was not bad at all and the wines more than tolerable.

Hervey read his notes: 'We carry about seventy riflemen, a crew of nearly one hundred and about thirty officers of various grades. I notice five out of seven quarter-masters are British as are also the captain and chief engineer.'

Without warning, a monumental barrage of firing broke across his thoughts.

'God damn it! Not again. This is intolerable!' Hervey leapt up from his chair and made his way down the corridor and up the stairs to the deck. 'Surely they don't need any more bloody gun practice', he muttered, emerging into the daylight. He was about to shout over the din to ask Garin whether they would have any ammunition left at all for actual battle when Garin gave the signal to stop. A ship had been sighted and the firing was Garin's attempt to get her to heave-to.

The ship turned out to be the *Diana*, a German steamship bound for southern ports. A contraband search party was sent across, and in due course the boat returned and the signal was given 'all clear'. But instead of steaming ahead the *Diana* lingered and passed close to the *Imperial*'s stern, eventually signalling for another boat to be sent across.

'What's up?' asked Hervey,

'Ach! I don't trust them,' muttered the bosun in reply.

'By them, I take it you mean the Germans?' enquired Hervey.

'I do, sir,' replied the bosun, more than a little irritated that the journalist didn't appear to agree with him.

The boat returned almost immediately with one of the officers waving a sheet of paper and yelling at the top of his voice. 'Caldera! *Blanco!*' he shouted, and made a sharp gesture downwards with his forefinger. What? Everyone held their breath to listen. The men in the boat were pulling like fiends and the man shouted again. 'The *Blanco*'s been sunk in Caldera Bay!'

The *Imperial*'s deck erupted into a chorus of shouting and cheering. ¡*Viva!* ¡*Viva!* The men shouted, embracing each other. What a pity, Hervey thought, that there are no nice Chilean girls on board to share in the general enthusiasm. It appeared that the *Diana* had not wanted to pass on the good news until they were sure of the ship's identity, and this explained why she had circled them after being given the 'all clear'. The boat came alongside and the paper was passed up to Commander Garin, who read its contents aloud.

'The valiant Captain Moraga has just returned to Valparaiso in the *Condell* with news of which all loyal Chileans may well be proud. At 3am on the 23rd instant he, with the gallant aid of Captain Fuentes of the *Lynch*, attacked and sunk by the application of torpedoes the flagship of the revolutionary fleet, the *Blanco Encalada*. Another ship, believed to be the *Huáscar*, was attacked and it is believed, also sunk.' There were more hysterical shouts and cheers and Garin had to wait for everyone to calm down again.

'Then ... then the *Lynch* engaged in a desperate action with the transport *Aconcagua*, but unfortunately sustained damage to her machinery, as did also the *Condell*. The *Aconcagua* escaped hotly pursued by the *Imperial*.'

This last sentence sent everyone into fits of laughter. It was an excellent example of the government's own *bolas*, thought Hervey. Garin looked concerned. How were they to believe the rest of the report when the last sentence was so patently untrue? But the troops and crew were undeterred. It made perfect sense. They had lost the *Lynch* and the *Condell* in the darkness. They had heard guns during the night and there had been no further sightings of the enemy ships for a very good reason – they were probably now at the bottom of Caldera harbour providing homes for whelks.

'I don't like it,' said Garin, frowning, 'the *Lynch* and the *Condell* depend on our supplies. How can we return to Valparaiso without being sure that they are safe?'

The prospect of cruising the coast waiting to rendezvous with the torpedo catchers, or worse, being spotted by the *Esmeralda*, did not fill Hervey with glee. He thought back to the efforts he had made and the very real dangers he had faced in order to reach Chile in the first place. The terrifying ride on a cow-catcher and traversing death-defying Andean ravines on that infernal mule. And now it seemed that the major naval engagement of the war had taken place and all the while he was on the wrong ship!

'Ah, this is too bad,' Hervey muttered, making his way to his cabin, and wondering whether that nice Chinese cook would make him a sandwich or two to tide him over until dinner.

4 May, South Pacific
For the next few days they waited for the torpedo catchers. It was a tedious business and Hervey was thoroughly bored. He caught himself wondering yet again whether journalism really was the best course of action for him. But the truth was, he reminded himself, that his options were getting rather limited.

Things had begun promisingly enough for him as a youngster. Education at a public school, albeit minor; law at Cambridge. He had impressed his tutors with his eloquence and he could stand his ground in any verbal bun fight, even if he was not quite sure of his facts. Somehow he always managed to sound convincing and fared pretty well at the hustings.

The fatal mistake was probably the move to London. His father had wanted him to fulfil the promise of his expensive education and do something reliable at the Inns of Court. But there had been so many distractions. The races, the newest fashions on Jermyn Street, the ladies at the Gaiety Theatre! Was it so wrong to want a life of broad horizons? Of adventure! Glowering at the musty reference books of the law library one day, Hervey had been sent a chilling vision of his life dwindling away to a pitiful, yet beautifully formed, pyramid of dust.

His debts had been mushrooming and the potential disclosure of a scandalous interlude with a baronet's wife was looming. Yet, the final straw had come in the shape of a summons to appear before Bow Street magistrates for the non-payment of the trifling debt of one pound and three shillings. If only they knew! Hervey had gasped, wide-eyed, at the report in *The Morning Post*. The complainant, a taxi driver, had been engaged by Hervey at the Gaiety Theatre, at four-thirty in the afternoon. From there they had gone to Moore's hotel in Jermyn Street, then to several other places in the neighbourhood before going on to an address in Brixton Road. Hervey had then asked the driver to take several of his friends to Waterloo Road before returning to him in Brixton Road and then on Jermyn Street. There, the driver had been asked to wait for several hours, finally being discharged at two in the morning. Unfortunately, it was only then that Hervey realised he did not have enough money to pay the whole fare. Worse still, he had been compelled to borrow two shillings from the unfortunate man. Hervey realised in retrospect that this had been rather louche of him to say the least, but he had fully intended to repay the loan the following day along with his outstanding fare. It couldn't be helped that he had been called away so early.

Of course, the embarrassing newspaper report had been like a red rag to his dyspeptic father who had sent him a succinct telegram within minutes it seemed. The words 'disreputable' and 'disinherit' had virtually leapt off the page, clobbering Hervey around the ears. It had all got out of hand, he reflected.

Then, an old school chum had suggested a teaching role in Illawarra, Woollongong, about as far away as Hervey could get from his debtors. So he had absconded again. His next embodiment had been, at least initially, rather more successful. The populace of Illawarra seemed pleased to receive him. People tipped their hats to him in the street, the pupil numbers grew and the teaching itself was surprisingly rewarding. In his spare time, he gave lectures and wrote papers about trade policies on behalf of the Imperial Federation League. Everything was going swimmingly, and for three years Hervey thought that he might have found his true vocation at last.

It was his colleague, the principal, who put a spanner in the works that time with a rather nasty incident involving a young girl of eight. Within weeks the man had been tried, found guilty and sentenced to two years of well-deserved hard labour. All of which could have been a blessing for Hervey's career, promoted as he now was to principal himself. But once he was in possession of the college's ledger books he found them to be in complete disarray. Fees had evaporated like spring water in the dusty outback.

Once again, Hervey's instinct had been to invent his own feat of evaporation. He left his lodgings in the dead of night, heading for Sydney and the first steamship out of Australia. On the last leg of his return journey to Southampton, having called in a series of favours that brought him in one long connecting chain all the way back to England, Hervey had noticed an advertisement in *The Times*: 'Special Correspondents required in all foreign parts including Paris, Vienna, St Petersburg, Constantinople, the Cape, the United States, Persia, China, Japan &c.' How thrilling was that 'etcetera', perched as it was at the end of a long list of fabulous locations! At last, he thought, he had found a profession that perfectly suited his enquiring temperament. What could be better than to be paid for writing and travelling the world? And surely, a Gaiety lady would much rather spend her precious evenings with an audacious author who could entertain her with tales of plucky escapades than with some tedious chap who would bore her rigid with the mysteries of jurisprudence.

But now he was not so sure about this latest incarnation. He had assumed that facts and figures were the foundation of all reputable journalism. *Il faut appeler un chat un chat*, as it were. Writing about politics was his interest, but he had not realised that the act of writing about events could, in itself, be such a political act. This was the only explanation he could find for the editor's baffling response. The facts he had been wiring back to London were clearly not the 'facts' that Buckle wanted to hear. And here he was, risking life and limb or death by boredom to gather information that would probably never see the light of day. It really was too bad.

Dear God, he could murder a decent glass of champagne. Earlier on that day, someone had told him that the remaining bottles were now being reserved for anyone with a fever. Two of the officers had already developed some suspicious ailment. Hervey placed the palm of his hand on his forehead and wondered whether he could detect any noticeable increase in temperature or a vague touch of clamminess about the temples. He sighed. The only other thing to think about was food, and that was at least another two hours away.

Hervey got up from his chair and decided to take a turn about the deck. When he reached the main deck Captain Davies and Officer Whiteway were staring at a point on the horizon.

'What news?' Hervey asked expectantly.

'Give the order. Full steam ahead!' said the captain, and then, turning to Hervey, 'We have spotted a mailboat. A British ship, we believe. Perhaps she has some news that can help us.'

The telescope was passed to Hervey, who scoured the horizon searching for the tiny point.

'How can you tell it isn't an enemy ship at this distance?'

'In all honesty, sir, we can't be sure. But all things considered, her usual route, her speed, what we know of other ships in the area, it is probably the *Puno*. We may have to turn tail pretty quickly if it isn't.'

'At least we'll see some action that way,' laughed Hervey, returning the glasses.

'You'll see plenty of that, Mr Hervey, don't you worry.'

And it wasn't long before Garin lost patience with the ship ahead of them and decided to send a couple of cannonballs in her direction.

'We haven't got all day!' Garin shouted. 'Surely she's got the message by now, unless she thinks she can outrun us?'

'If that's the *Puno*, Commander, I'd like to see her try,' the captain replied.

And he was right. It was the *Puno*, a British mailboat on her way back to Liverpool, and as soon as the shots were fired she very quickly hove-to.

The usual boarding party went across and Hervey decided to go with them for variety's sake.

As Hervey loitered on the main deck waiting for the officers to conduct their searches, the *Puno*'s chief officer turned to him and asked, 'You're English, aren't you?'

'Yes, I am *The Times* correspondent,' replied Hervey.

The chief officer's eyes narrowed as he looked across the choppy stretch of water towards the *Imperial*. 'Sir, perhaps you can tell me what right that armed steamer has to stop a British vessel on the high seas?'

Hervey thought for a moment then smiled. 'I regret to say I cannot,' he replied, 'unless it be that long gun you see projecting over her bows.'

The young chief officer's cheeks flushed a little. 'It's a good thing for her that there's no British man-of-war in sight, and what's more it will be a very bad thing for you if she chances to be caught by one of the revolutionary cruisers.'

'Quite possibly, my friend, but then you see she is not going to be captured. It is quite an arranged matter that she will be blown up first. Now tell me the truth of this Caldera business.'

Despite his tetchiness, the officer was helpful and brought Hervey copies of the latest newspapers, which he then took back with him to the *Imperial*. If the reports were accurate, only the *Blanco Encalada* had been sunk. But what losses for the opposition! A well-aimed torpedo, dispatched at close range, had sunk the famous *Blanco* in a mere three minutes. The entire crew, captain, officers and troops were all drowned. The *Lynch* and the *Condell*, both damaged by the engagement, had limped back to Valparaiso to an ecstatic reception.

Davy, William, Commander Garin and some of the other officers gathered around to hear Hervey read the reports.

'That's it! The tide has turned in our favour!' exclaimed Garin, 'Captain Davies, at last we can make our way back to Valparaiso!'

The *Imperial* steamed southwards, keeping well away from the coast. Garin and the troops were jubilant. Despite a series of early military blunders, the war was turning their way. Soon the *Errázuriz* and the *Pinto* would arrive from Le Havre and they would have two new warships to add to their growing arsenal. Once the president had ships enough to move his 40,000 troops around the coast, the uprising would soon be crushed. It was only a matter of time.

7 May, Valparaiso

The *Imperial* returned to Valparaiso to yet another rousing welcome. Enormous crowds had gathered along the wharves and on the adjacent high ground to witness her return. At least half a dozen bands played the national anthem and every flag and length of bunting in Valparaiso had been put to good use.

Davy and William watched from the bridge as the ship arrived. According to men who shouted across from the tugs, stories had circulated claiming that the *Imperial* had been sunk by the *Esmeralda*.

'We've returned from the dead!' laughed William as they watched the jubilant crowds.

'And they still insist on saying that no one supports the president!' said Hervey as he joined the men briefly on the bridge. 'I am going to telegraph the editor as soon as I get ashore. He can hardly argue with this reception, can he?'

And before they knew it Hervey could be seen crossing the gangway and making his surprisingly sprightly way up the harbour to the telegraph office.

Three days later the *Imperial* and the *Condell* sailed north again to Coquimbo, leaving the *Lynch* behind in Valparaiso for further repairs. Nearly 1,300 soldiers were embarked on the two ships, many of them accompanied by their wives, children and dogs.

'These don't look like hardened soldiers to me,' muttered Davy, as he and William inspected the spar deck one evening, picking their way carefully between the sleeping bodies. It was touching to see how many of the men had given up their coats and ponchos to cover their female comrades and niños. 'It's no place for women and children.'

William stopped and looked around him. Even on the spar deck alone there must have been nearly five hundred people.

'No. But perhaps,' replied William quietly, 'with all its dangers, it is better to be in the midst of conflict rather than far away, feeling helpless and impotent. Better to die with the people you love than be left behind?'

Davy looked around him. Everywhere he looked there were people leaning on knapsacks; women sleeping on their husbands' shoulders, children sleeping in their mothers' arms, dogs curled up in soldiers' laps. It seemed such an inexplicable thing that a few months earlier these same people would have lived and worked and played alongside the people they were now so intent on killing.

When they arrived at Coquimbo the following day they noticed that the Union Jack was very much in evidence. The Royal Navy's *Warspite* and *Champion* were both moored at the harbour. It was a dismal town but it was still under Balmaceda's control, so once the soldiers disembarked the *Imperial*'s crew were allowed a degree of shore leave.

'There's a rotten bar and a stinking bar!' someone shouted. 'Where shall we head for, lads?'

Davy watched the crew as they spilled out of the ship and away from the harbour. They ran like men who feared that they could be recalled at any moment.

'Hey, there!' a voice came across the water from the direction of the *Warspite*.

'Fancy a beef sandwich?' the shout came again.

Davy's initial thought was that this was some strange kind of coded insult and that some of the Royal Navy sailors were being rude about Balmaceda's army. He was deciding whether to respond to the jibe or turn aside and head for a tumbler of whisky in the *Imperial*'s saloon when the voice came again, 'Or an apple?'

Davy turned and looked carefully. There was something puzzling about the voice. The *Warspite* was less than fifty yards from the *Imperial*, and the only man facing him on deck was slim and handsome with slightly rosy cheeks.

The man took off his officer's cap and laughed. 'I haven't changed that much, have I?'

In an instant, the years fell away and Davy was faced with Frederick, the shy, chubby boy who had climbed the mast with him in Cardigan harbour; the boy who had offered him half his lunch the day he had nothing to eat.

'Well, look at you!' Frederick laughed, 'Captain now!'

'Well, God dammit! What about you, then? Impressive and distinguished, I should bloody say so!'

The two men laughed with delight across the harbour.

'You must join us for supper, Frederick, my friend. I have a hell of a lot to thank you for.'

And so, within the hour a formal invitation had been sent, permissions were granted and Frederick Sambrook joined the officers of the *Imperial* for dinner. Tony excelled himself in the kitchen and joined them at dinner. The galley boys waited at table under Gabriel's fastidious directions.

'You know, I never thought you were going to make it over the futtocks that afternoon,' said Davy, raising his glass to Frederick.

'Neither did I. I was terrified. You were the only lad who spoke to me that day. The others thought I was so well-to-do and didn't bother.'

Davy thought back and tried desperately to remember anything in particular about the other boys or their reaction. But the truth was he couldn't remember.

'And you didn't make fun of me when I talked about navigation!' exclaimed Frederick.

Tony, Evans, Sepulveda and William looked on in admiration.

'A toast!' Evans sprang to his feet, looking a little worse for wear. 'To beef sandwiches and navigation!'

Several more toasts followed, each one more bizarre than the last, and for the entire evening all talk of war was avoided. Eventually, Davy and William escorted Frederick back to the harbourside.

'You know, Frederick, I would never have made it to captain if you hadn't told me about Sarah Jane Rees' navigation classes. I owe it all to you.'

'And I would never have made it over the futtocks if you hadn't eaten half my lunch!'

They embraced, promising to see each other again soon and wished each other good night.

Davy and William were about to return to the *Imperial* when they noticed Hervey weaving his way across the harbour, skilfully avoiding a series of large but invisible obstacles.

'Ah, gentlemen!' he slurred, recognising Davy and William in the darkness. 'You should have joined me for a damned excellent supper at the garrison. As good as anything dished up at the Royale, I should say. Although I must admit to being a little fuzzled.' Hervey swerved, narrowly avoiding another imaginary obstacle as he approached the men. 'Coquimbo, however, is a different matter altogether. Generally speaking, after a regimental dinner one usually sees things *couleur de rose*, as it were. But I must confess, Coquimbo strikes me as being a particularly unappealing town.'

And with a dramatic sweep of his arms Hervey turned about as if to underline his assertion, spinning far too quickly on his heels and falling flat on his back.

The *Imperial* was 60 miles west off the coast of Iquique, keeping well away from land and the danger of being seen by enemy warships. For the best part of the day they had been transferring coal to the *Condell*, which, even in the calmest of conditions, was a tricky job. The crew were exhausted.

'Evans is arranging some poker,' William announced cheerily, leaning his head around Davy's cabin door. But Davy was putting on his coat and looked as if he was heading for the deck.

'Wish him luck. But tell him not to lose the lot otherwise he won't have anything left for shore. I'm hoping Garin will let the crew loose again when we get to Taltal.'

Davy fussed with something in his pocket and began doing up his coat buttons. Ever since the encounter with Estella he had found it difficult to look at William properly. He felt somehow diminished in his officer's eyes. Davy waited, thinking that William would go back out into the corridor. But William was still there, looking at him with concern.

'Right. To the deck,' Davy announced.

But rather than following his cue and stepping out of the cabin, William entered the room and closed the door behind him.

'Davy, as a friend …'

'Oh?'

'I know you are worried about Estella …'

'Oh!'

'And you are in an impossible position …'

'Oh?'

'You know you can't always choose who you love.'

These last words felled him like a sapling under a skilful axe. Davy sat down at his desk still not wanting to meet William's gaze. He felt utterly exposed, in the way Stewart had been able to expose him as a young chief officer. But this was different.

'I know she isn't a Miss Hetherington.'

Davy laughed and looked up at William. 'How did you know about her?'

'Oh, your famous exploits.'

'Infamous …'

Davy looked down again and felt a tight ball of emotion rise in his chest.

'You know, William,' he began, knowing that some dam had been breached and wondering whether he could safely control the flow of his thoughts before being drowned. 'When I was a lad, my sister …' He stopped to breathe slowly and deliberately before going on. 'My sister died in a fire. She was seven. She was playing in the barn. We don't know what happened exactly. She tipped some paraffin, perhaps …' Davy shrugged his shoulders. 'I wasn't there. They tried to save her but she was trapped and the horses were beside themselves. Hysterical. They couldn't pull a thing. By the time I got home, it was too late. We couldn't get the door down in time and the barn collapsed. Perhaps it was a blessing.' Davy struggled to breathe and the weight of remembered sadness swelled up like a living creature inside his throat. 'When it happened, they, my mother, said it was my fault. If I had been there, I could have helped the horses. There would have been more hands. Elen wouldn't have died.'

'It was an accident,' said William.

'She wanted to be a sailor!' Davy looked up at William. He felt such a surge of pride and amazement that he couldn't help laughing. For a moment Elen seemed as real to him as his own hands: Elen at her maths lessons, studying navigation, dressed as a boy, giving the other sailors a hard time, standing her ground, becoming the world's first female merchant captain. Davy raised his arms in the air and brought his hands to rest on the back of his head. The world seemed changed for a moment. But joy never came alone. He should know that by now. It trailed weight in its wake and the familiar stab.

'The last thing I said to her was that she should go play with her doll.' Davy drew in as much breath as he could but something large and heavy seemed to have settled on his chest. 'So, my father got me a berth on the *Royal Dane*, and for the next year and a half I barely saw land. We took emigrants to Australia. I tried not to think about home. I sent the occasional letter and sometimes got a reply. I studied my books …'

'Navigation …' William smiled.

'Yes, and just worked hard.' Davy paused again and tried to order his thoughts. 'I remember being on the top sail yards on the *Dane* one day and having a conversation with myself. I thought how simple it would be just to let go and fall through the air. Hit the deck. To shorten the struggle, because in the end what did it matter whether I lived or died? Who cared? What difference a murderer?'

'No …' whispered William.

'And then it occurred to me that on that particular day, on that particular rope, that it was just as easy to hold on as it was to let go. And because I knew that I had a choice but that I didn't have to make the choice that day, it came as a huge relief. And that's how I went on after that. From day to day only hanging on because it was just as easy as letting go. Changing ships, learning the ropes, passing exams, becoming a captain.'

'But when I met Estella, I felt things change. Before I realised it, the choice had become important. And when war broke out, I thought, perhaps now there is a reason to get through. Perhaps, for the first time, there is someone to make the choice for.' Davy leaned back and dragged the palms of his hand down over his face. 'But now it seems so silly, William, because she is on the battlefield and I have no choice at all! I never had a choice.'

'Only a field hospital. She will be relatively safe.'

For a while they sat in silence, listening to the hum of the ship's engines and the wind whistling at the porthole.

'Yet,' began William, 'you can't save someone unless they want to be saved.'

'Save people, William? Look where I've got us. Scudding along on enemy shores. What was I thinking? All these sons and fathers, brothers, lovers … the odds are so stacked against us, it makes me laugh! For a bag of money I have risked my ship, my crew and the lives of everyone they love. To fight someone else's war! The sea is littered with enemy ships. We're not going to make it, William. We can't survive. It is an impossibility. We will be sunk or blown to smithereens or worse, captured, tortured, executed. All for some bags of gold! I can't save anyone.'

Davy stood and pulled his coat around him. He wanted to get out on to the deck but William was barring the way. Davy could have pushed past but there was something about William's demeanour that held him in check.

'You have no idea, do you? Only yesterday, Evans was telling us a story …'

'Oh, that!' Davy waved his arm dismissively and made a determined move towards the door.

'No! Wait,' said William. 'They all have stories! We all have stories. You may not think they are significant. They may not be significant to you. But they are to them. They are to us. Tony, Sep, Evans all the way down to the errand boy. They talk of the many kindnesses, times when you stepped ahead of them to face down trouble, loose ropes caught in time because you were paying attention, words that made a difference. Faith. Respect!'

'I pay them …'

'No! That's not it. They had a choice …'

'I'm not sure they did …'

'They have legs. When the fancy takes them, they can choose with their feet. How many vessels are stranded in Valparaiso every week, half the crew has jumped ship because the captain's a pig? Oh, I know they find men in the end, but what then? Two weeks later they're in Panama, stuck again. Or else the crew has run the risk of a gibbet and mutinied all together, dumped the captain on some godforsaken island or pushed him over the side in a freakish storm.'

Davy scratched his chin as if William was talking nonsense.

'The men follow you for a reason. Perhaps things will be bad but they'll take their chances because if anyone can get them out of a scrape then you will.'

Davy shoved his hands in his pockets.

'And although Estella's on the battlefield, you may be saving her already, but that you don't realise.'

Davy gave up trying to get past William. He sat and put his head in his hands. 'Will, what have I done?' Tears escaped and ran down his cheeks. He covered his face with his palms.

For a while, the room was quiet. Beneath them, there was a subtle change in the engine, a different gear, rougher waters ahead, perhaps? Gulls cried out and in his mind, Davy could see them skimming the waves, diving for scraps and peelings. There came a memory, like a shaft of sunlight catching a white sail.

He was calm again and when he looked up he could see William opening the door.

'Not everything is of your own making, Davy. Try to remember your navigation lessons when there's a storm on the horizon – all you can do is find the best way.'

William closed the door gently behind him and left Davy pondering the sounds of the creaking ship and the approaching gale.

19 May, Taltal
Because he was the only crew member to die that day, they kept Gabriel's body until last. The *Imperial* had sailed into Taltal, not expecting the place to be fortified, when someone opened fire on them from the beach. While the bullets ricocheted all around, bouncing at unexpected angles off every metal surface, the soldiers on board had piled, almost ecstatically, into the boats and made for shore. Moraga's men opened fire from the ship too, first with the Gatling guns and then with the bow-chaser once they'd manoeuvred the ship into position. The opposition hadn't held their ground for much longer after that, and it was only then, when the government troops had gained control of the beach, that they noticed Gabriel face down on the deck. He had emerged from the galley, errand in hand, just as they opened fire.

Fifteen of Moraga's soldiers had been killed. The repeating guns had cut them down even before they left the boats at the water's edge. Their comrades had hauled their bodies back to the ship, thinking that burials at sea would be quicker and less dangerous. Even so, Moraga had been apologetic when he said his few words.

'Our brothers belong in Chile's earth,' he said, looking across the decks at the receding coastline, 'and we pray their spirits find their way home.' He read the names as their bodies slipped over the side and under the waves.

When Gabriel's body was brought forward, Moraga stepped aside for the captain. Davy had scribbled some thoughts on paper. He wanted to explain to the crew how Tony had taken Gabriel under his wing when he found him, starving and half-dead in some godforsaken Portuguese harbour. He wanted to explain to everyone that, despite his blaspheming and shouting, Tony was Gabriel's family and the boy would no sooner have sailed on a different ship than cut his own legs off.

But when he came to it, the words seemed superfluous. Davy looked blankly at the scrap of paper then folded it back into his pocket. The words that actually came to him were the words of the superintendent on the *Royal Dane* all those years before and which he knew by heart. They seemed to reach him across all seas and all nations, all men and women that he had ever known and lost.

'The wind blows to the south and goes around to the north; around and around goes the wind, and on its circuits the wind returns. All streams run to the sea, but the sea is not full; to the place where the streams flow, there they flow again.'

Gabriel's body was smaller and slighter than the soldiers'. Someone had found a *Compañía* flag and wrapped it tightly around him.

'Captain,' said Tony, stepping forward quickly, 'I nearly forgot.' Tony drew a cook's white hat from his pocket and tucked it neatly under the flag around Gabriel's feet. 'He never could remember his bloody hat.' His face was contorted with emotion, and as he stepped backwards, William extended his hand and supported the man's arm.

The rest of the words came as automatically to Davy as any naval instructions. They were words that he had heard a hundred times at sea and he said them quickly.

'We therefore commit his body to the deep, looking for the general Resurrection in the last day, and the life of the world to come, through our Lord Jesus Christ.'

And so it was that Gabriel slipped as easily as melting snow from a ledge, over the edge and into the dark sea.

11 June, Cardigan, West Wales
Ten-year-old Benjamin Lewis Davies fairly belted out of the *Teifi Emporium*

into the eager arms of his friends. Lately the *Emporium* had begun to stock a range of more expensive magazines and periodicals. Everyone in town had said it would never last. But Ben was glad because Mr Morgan, the local preacher, had said that he was pretty sure there was an article about his uncle in this week's *Graphic*. The shopkeeper, on seeing Ben's grubby hands, had refused to let him look inside the magazine until he'd parted with his hard-earned savings. *Tight bastard*, Ben had thought, but hadn't said anything, of course. He'd left the shop with a polite '*diolch yn fawr*' as usual.

'Don't touch it or I'll kill you!' he shouted at the boys as soon as he was outside.

The others stood well back, but their enthusiasm was undaunted.

'Let's see, let's see!'

Ben told them that the best thing would be for them to run up to one of the benches in the newly opened Victoria Gardens so that they could read it properly. That way there was less danger of it getting damaged or destroyed in the scrimmage.

When they got to the park, four of them huddled on to a bench near the bandstand with another two standing behind Ben looking over his shoulders. The boys stared at the cover in awe. It featured a painting by someone called F. Brangwyn. The title was 'Home from the West'ard'. It showed a majestic sailing ship being towed in to harbour by a squat little tug.

'Come on. Is it in there?' the boys urged Ben to turn the pages.

The only time Ben ever spoke or read English was at school and that was only in front of the teacher. So scanning the pages for Captain Davies' name or the name of the *Imperial* was no easy task. And there was so much writing! And it was so tiny! In any case, it was the portrait that caught his attention first and the other boys saw it in the same instant.

'There he is! That's him! Bloody hell! Your uncle's really in *The Graphic!* What does it say, Ben?'

There were four pictures in all. The first was of his uncle, in full *Compañía* uniform. To his right there was a portrait of the steamship *Imperial* with three masts and two funnels with seven or eight small boats and launches at her side. Below there was a picture of the dining saloon with its panelled ceiling, framed pictures, blinds, curtains, arrangements of flowers on the tables, carpets and chandeliers. Ben had never see anything so grand!

'*Dduw Mawr!*' gasped one of the lads, 'It doesn't look like a ship. It looks more like a palace!'

'Come on, Ben, read it out.'

Ben brought the paper closer and read each word out carefully. 'The

Civil War in Chile: the *S.S. Imperial* which ran the … blockade … of the … insurgent fleet.'

Ben let out a long sigh of admiration.

'Who's he?' asked one of the lads, noticing a second portrait at the bottom of the page. Ben read again, 'W.K.Whiteway, Chief Officer.'

'Bloody hell,' one of the lads gasped again.

Ben looked carefully at the young man's face. He looked fair and young and slighter than his uncle. He looked less weather-beaten and nothing like the rough sailors that stumbled around Cardigan town after dark. He desperately wanted to be like Officer Whiteway, but the one and only boat trip he'd ever taken around Cardigan Island had left him feeling as sick as a dog and praying to be back on land.

'Look, there's more!' one of the lads pointed to a reference at the bottom of the page, which said that more of the story could be found further on. They turned the pages, past articles on exotic-sounding countries like Mosambique and reports of the Royal Naval Exhibition at Chelsea. There were advertisments for summer holidays to the fjords of Norway and theatre performances of 'The Corsican Brothers' at the Lyceum.

'There it is!'

'The Chilean blockade-runner *Imperial*.'

The best part of the entire page was taken up with the continuing story. Ben's friends gasped with excitement and admiration and pummelled his shoulders unhelpfully as he began reading. 'The *Imperial* is a steel built vessel of about 2,700 tons register and 3,000 horse power, and was built by Messrs Laird Brothers of Birkenhead in 1889 for the Compañía Sud Americana de Vapores, and has for the last two years been engaged in the above Company's mail service between Valparaiso and Panama.'

With growing confidence Ben read out the entire article, which detailed the *Imperial*'s exploits and came to the final sentence, 'The *Imperial* is at present reported as missing. A late rumour of her having been blown up is said to be without foundation.'

The lads were quieter now and the words 'blown up' echoed in the air around them. Ben turned back to the portraits and looked again at the face of his uncle in his *Compañía* uniform, the badge with the cross which Ben knew was red on white, and the shiny black leather strap across the front of his cap.

'Ah, heck! He'll be all right, your uncle. He's escaped them all so far, hasn't he? Right Scarlet Pimpernel he is.' And Ben was pummelled again on his shoulder until he winced.

Before long the others had put aside thoughts of fame and glory in the Chilean Civil War, and were concocting plans for breaking into the lifeboat house near the estuary and setting off a few of the old flares just for a laugh.

'We'll do it in honour of your uncle and the great *Imperial*. What do you say, Ben? Come on!' they shouted as they left through the iron gates. Ben was only half listening and carried on turning the pages of the magazine, which seemed to him like a mesmerising window on an alien world. In one small corner there was a section for *Subscribers who will please note the following terms on which The Graphic will be posted to any part of the world for 12 months. Africa, Argentine Republic, Brazil …* the list went on and on.

For one and a half pence copies could be sent to China or Japan, although subscribers were invited *to order the THICK paper edition as that printed on THIN paper is greatly damaged by transit and the appearance of the illustrations very inferior.*

'China!' he gasped. People all over the world as far as China would be able to read this very same story about his uncle? He rolled up the newspaper carefully and put it safely inside his coat pocket.

'Come on!' he heard the boys' chorus again from a distance.

'Jesus! China!' Ben sprang to his feet, and ran from the park with its neat flowerbeds and iron benches and raced down the street towards the centre of Cardigan town.

CHAPTER 21

12 June, Chañaral Harbour

Early that morning the *Imperial* and the *Condell* steamed into Chañaral harbour. As they did so a train could be seen steaming away from the town. Guessing that it was carrying retreating troops, Moraga gave the order for the *Imperial*'s Armstrong bow-chaser to be discharged. The escaping steam train went over like a ninepin and exploded into violent flames.

There were no major fortifications at the town, and as soon as the all clear was given boats were sent across. The *Imperial*'s orders were to take on supplies, but it soon became clear that Chañaral was in a desperate situation. Cut off from regular communications by the rebel blockades, no ships ever called and no supplies were sent. The Congressionalist leaders had seized all the able-bodied men, impressing them into the army at Iquique, and had abandoned the aged, the women and children to starvation. Moraga promised safe passage for some, but soon found 800 famine-stricken wretches clamouring to get on board.

'Captain, we cannot take more than three hundred!' shouted Moraga from one of the departing boats. 'Decent women cannot be expected to huddle together like troops and camp followers.'

Davy watched as boat after boat was dispatched to collect the desperate refugees, who descended on them like ants on fallen fruit. Once at the *Imperial*'s side, those lucky enough to have found space in a boat clambered up the side of the ship, weak and clumsy from lack of food. A baby, swaddled tightly in a rough grey blanket, was handed up from hand to hand until it reached the deck.

'Here,' one of the crew passed it to Tony, who had only just emerged on deck.

'What on earth is going on?' asked Tony, looking down at the baby as if he had just been handed a dangerous missile.

'We're transporting these people to Valparaiso,' replied Davy.

'But I thought we were taking on supplies?'

'There don't appear to be any supplies,' replied Davy, helping an elderly woman to a sheltered corner.

Just then, two skeletal children stepped over the rail and, seeing the baby, came forward to take the child from Tony. A young woman, frail and anxious, followed them and she placed her hand gratefully on Tony's arm.

'*Gracias, Señores*, you have saved our lives. We have not eaten properly for over two weeks. And the food we had stored was taken by the troops.'

The woman would once have been beautiful, but her features were hard and bony. Her eyes were too prominent and her collarbone protruded like scaffolding through translucent skin. She looked down at the baby, mystified that it was still alive. 'He seems to sleep through it all.'

Cook looked down at the surprisingly bonny child partially hidden in the folds of dark wool, then back at the woman. 'I think we need to feed you first, don't we? How many are there, Captain?'

'Over three hundred, at least.'

Tony, who was usually so quick to curse the most trivial inconvenience, just nodded. They watched as more passengers came on deck, exhausted and wolf-like, their clothes hanging from bony shoulders and skimming over protruding joints. His crew were spare and wiry, but Davy had never seen people look so gaunt.

'No one came,' the woman murmured, following Tony towards the ship's galley.

The bad news didn't end there. When Moraga returned to the ship he brought news from Santiago. A British transport had landed at Iquique carrying five thousand rifles and two million rounds of ammunition destined for the rebels. Rebel troops were amassing at Pisagua. Yet more of Balmaceda's men had deserted under fire and joined the *Opositores*. The new warships were still delayed.

'Once we have taken these passengers to Valparaiso, I have been given orders to return to bombard Pisagua and Iquique. We have no choice,' said Moraga defiantly.

The *Imperial* was returning to Valparaiso with the refugees when Davy climbed the iron steps on to the upper deck, and heard Webb's high-pitched shout being carried by the wind. Webb was talking so quickly and sounded so angry that Davy only caught the last word.

'… gibberish!'

Webb was still on the tips of his toes with his arms in the air when Davy came round the corner.

'What's going on, Webb?'

Half a dozen of the Chilean crew were trying to lash a small boat to the railings. The boat was heavy and the fixings were inadequate. They were bathed in sweat and looked exhausted.

'Moraga asked us to move it.'

The men looked up apologetically at Davy. They were good workers. Not the kind of men to be creating problems.

'And so …?'

'It's just that when I give them orders they turn away and start talking all this gibberish. They understand English perfectly well.'

'I think you'll find it's Spanish, not gibberish.'

Webb drew breath as if to respond, but thought better of it.

Davy turned to the men and told them, in Spanish, to rest a minute. 'Webb, take a walk with me for a moment.'

As they reached the stern out of earshot, Webb fidgeted and looked uncomfortable. 'Sir, I'm sorry, sir, but they insist on speaking Spanish when they know I have no idea what they're saying. It's incredibly annoying. And not to mention rude.'

Davy sighed and watched the waters churning in the ship's wake. *Fourteen knots. A West wind and a lively cross current coming from the coast.*

'Webb, they don't "insist" on talking Spanish. They just do. It's what they speak. They don't think about it. It's the most natural thing for them. They're not doing it just to annoy you. Besides, they work much better when they're allowed to get on with things in their own language.'

'But they could be saying anything.'

'I think you'll find they're probably talking about their work. Believe me, those lads are perfectly capable of telling you to your face if they think you're a fool.'

Davy looked out at the waves and watched as a flock of gulls flew across their wake and settled on the foam. 'Do they follow your orders?'

Webb thought for a moment. 'Yes.'

'Are they disrespectful, apart from speaking gibberish, as you call it?'

Webb paused again. 'No, not that I'm aware. But that's the point, isn't it, sir? I don't know. They speak English perfectly well when it suits them, so why not when I'm around? They're not exactly going to get on in the world, are they?'

Webb stopped himself again and turned to examine something on the distant horizon. *He can't look me in the face*, thought Davy, and wondered why Webb was so worked up about it. The crew, like all the crews of the *Compañía* line, were from all parts of the world. There were Finns, Italians, Germans, Chinese – and all of them spoke at least one other language. Any one of the sailors on board would have a smattering of half a dozen languages, depending on their background. The common language was often English, but Davy frequently turned to Spanish or Italian when he needed to, to thank someone personally for an act of bravery or to dampen tempers in the midst of a fight. When lads who had left home for the first time cowered in corners terrified of their first storm, a word in their own language calmed them and brought them back to the task in hand.

Davy turned and walked back along the deck. The men looked forlorn, as if they were expecting to be punished.

'*Amigos* ...' began Davy, and continued in Spanish.

Every now and again Webb heard an English phrase or the names, 'Imperial' and '*Señor* Webb', '*la guerra*', which he knew meant war and '*gracias*', thank you. The men looked across and smiled at Webb then turned back to Davy and nodded. Whatever it was that Davy was saying to them, they were impressed.

'What did you say to them?' asked Webb once Davy had finished.

'I told them that you were frustrated because you are trying to learn their language and that you can't pick it up because they speak so quickly. I asked them to be a bit more thoughtful and to speak a little more slowly so that you can follow what they are saying. I asked them to help you with the occasional phrase when they can.'

'But ...' began Webb, aware that the men were watching him closely.

'They are impressed. They think you're a good officer. Just a little hot-headed at times.'

Webb's neck grew flushed around the collar and he smiled awkwardly.

'Give them a bit of slack, Webb, they'll thank you for it,' said Davy, turning away. 'After all, we are in Chile.'

When Davy reached the stern again and leaned against the rail, he noticed that his hands were trembling. I'm angry, he thought, and I've learned to hide it so well I'm barely aware of it. But he wasn't angry with Webb. He was angry because the incident reminded him of something else, some thirty years before.

He and Sam had been late for school, and running in through the gate they were still chattering to each other in Welsh when they crossed the threshold.

'What is this infernal gibberish?' Sgwlyn thundered, striking his cane on the wooden desk with his one good arm. 'Haven't I made it perfectly clear that English is the language of advancement? What use all this schooling if all you're going to do with it is speak W-Welsh!' Sgwlyn had a slight stammer that was always worse when he was angry. 'What use is all this W-Welsh? Eh? Eh?'

Sgwlyn brought the cane down on the edge of the desk again. Davy knew that their chances of avoiding a thrashing that day were slim, and sure enough, before they left he and Sam had to endure the dreaded weapon across their backs. On the way home from school Davy had rehearsed half a dozen things to say to the man if the subject ever raised its head again, one of them being, 'You could always go back to your own bloody country if you don't like it.'

And now, thirty years later, as he stood at the stern watching the Chilean waves churn and froth in the *Imperial*'s wake, he realised that he had finally managed to say to Webb what he would have liked to say to his teacher all those years ago. He thought of Balmaceda's 'Chile for the Chileans', and wondered whether those that were left of the Mapuche roamed the desert fringes, wishing that the 'bloody' Spaniards would go home.

15 June, Valparaiso
On his return to Valparaiso Hervey found a telegram waiting for him from *The Times*. He was to leave for London immediately and bring certain items of documentary evidence along with him. The message was curt and to the point, and Hervey wasn't surprised.

He, of all the British journalists, now stood alone in his support of the Chilean government. A review of other journals and newspapers published while he had been at sea showed clearly that more weight had been given to the fabricated intelligence received from Iquique and Buenos Aires than to the bare facts transmitted by him from Santiago. Despite the Balmacedist sympathies of its special correspondent, it appeared that *The Times* still supported the revolutionaries. Even the Chilean *Times*, owned by a German, had maintained its stance of 'holding a candle to the devil'. Hervey was in a hopeless minority of one. As far as European opinion was concerned, the entire mission had been a 'coup manqué'.

Hervey reserved a cabin on the *Liguria*, the Pacific Steam Navigation Company's mail steamer bound for Liverpool on the twenty-fifth of June. But once the word was out that the special correspondent had been recalled to London, he received rushed invitations to dinner from all the senior ministers, and finally one from the president himself, to dine *en famille*.

'You are leaving Chile because your judgement has led you to lean towards my side in this civil war, and doubtless the black shadow which has been cast upon my reputation will also dim your own.'

'Possibly, your Excellency,' Hervey replied, 'but that troubles me very little. I have followed my own judgement, based upon what I read and heard and saw. What do I care for the opinions of persons who either know nothing of the questions at issue or who have personal interests to serve?'

Hervey passed a very pleasant evening with Balmaceda's family, and for the most part all talk of the war was avoided. Only as he came to leave did Hervey venture some of his impressions of the conflict.

'Your Excellency, I am no soldier, but I have seen enough of soldiers' work. Do not underestimate the power of the new repeating rifles. Although the *Opositores*' men are not soldiers by profession, their weapons are vastly superior. One such regiment will be worth three of yours, carrying as your men do their *fusils Gras* or Martini-Henri. Given their arms, you will need odds of five to two against them to win. At anything like even numbers, your men will be shot down like rabbits.'

Balmaceda smiled and shook his head. '*Amigo mío*, you mean well, but in these matters I am in the hands of my generals, and their views do not correspond with yours. Politics I understand because I am a lawyer. Warfare I leave to them, because they are soldiers.'

Hervey left the president's house with genuine reluctance and a deep sense of foreboding. The following morning he caught the train from Santiago and looked back sadly from the carriage window until the city disappeared from view. He could not help feeling that it had been his last interview with the 'bogie-man' of English journalism.

And what now? Hervey wondered whether Buckle would keep him on. Would there ever be a next assignment? He very much doubted it. He had gathered a trunk full of material that would never see the light of day. Surely, someone would like to know how it had really been? A death-defying journey across precipitous peaks, torpedoes and explosions … could he not put it all in a book complete with maps and photographic plates? And given a sombre title, would it not sell? The journalist imagined it handsomely bound, 'Maurice H. Hervey' writ large in golden lettering along the spine. I shall call it *Dark Days in Chile*, he decided.

CHAPTER 22

12 July, Valparaiso

The weather in Valparaiso harbour was unseasonably changeable, and as the *Lynch*, the *Condell* and the *Imperial* steamed once more into open sea an unusual cross current came across the *Imperial*'s bow, throwing swathes of turquoise water over the deck.

Davy had just left William in charge of the bridge and descended the steps to the lower deck when half a dozen soldiers erupted on to the deck from the direction of the engine rooms. They were armed and agitated, and as they stumbled towards Davy two of them jabbed the points of their rifles into the young man in the centre of the group. Evans emerged from the doorway to reason with the soldiers, only to be forced violently backwards. In the same moment the young man was hit across the shoulders with a rifle butt until he fell to his knees.

'What the hell is going on?' Davy approached them and saw to his horror that the young man was Sepulveda. 'How dare you attack a member of my crew?'

Davy moved forward to help Sepulveda to his feet, but rifles were automatically turned towards him. Instinctively Davy raised his hands.

'You will want to shoot him, *Capitán*, when you know what he's done. *¡El cabrón!*'

The soldier jabbed Sepulveda viciously until he fell forward on his face and Davy saw that his hands were bound and bloody behind his back.

'Sep? What's going on?'

Two more soldiers emerged from below deck. They were carrying sacks of flour awkwardly as if they were trying not to handle them too much, as if the sacks themselves were full of deadly snakes.

Just as the men placed the sacks in front of the soldiers, Moraga appeared.

'So, these are the kinds of men you employ on your ship, *Capitán*?' he spat as he moved through his men towards Davy. Sepulveda still lay on the floor, but Davy could see the man's wrists straining against the rope. Moraga paced forward so quickly that Davy thought he was going to kick the man on the floor, but instead he drew a short knife from under his uniform.

'Here?' Moraga turned to the men and they nodded.

The knife was razor sharp and the hessian sack bulged its contents out with ease on to the deck like a disembowelled man. First there was only flour, but then in lumps came dusty sticks of dynamite.

'What has this got to do with my steward?' asked Davy, feeling his blood and strength draining to his toes.

'Get him up!' growled Moraga as he replaced the knife into its sheath.

For the first time Davy saw that Sepulveda had been beaten even before emerging on deck. His lower lip was bleeding and he had a purple gash on his forehead where he had been hit.

'How much did Cumming pay you?' Moraga asked, politely enough, but when the answer was not forthcoming one of the soldiers stepped forward and hit Sepulveda viciously across his backbone with the rifle.

Davy was forming the words in his head: there must be some mistake, some misunderstanding. The name Cumming was familiar to him. He was a merchant in Valparaiso, English by birth. Davy knew him well. He was not the kind of man …

'A hundred thousand pesos,' answered Sepulveda clearly.

The soldier nearest Sepulveda spat on the floor with contempt and a few of the others whistled with mock admiration.

'Ah. *¡Dios Mío!* That's a lot of money indeed. I can see that. For a humble steward.'

Sepulveda could not bring his eyes up to meet Davy's. He stared resolutely at the sack of flour and dynamite, the bruises on his face looking ever more garish as he became paler.

'What do you think of that, *Capitán?*' continued Moraga. 'A hundred thousand pesos for the life of your entire crew, your ship, and the honour of the country that has provided him with a home and a profession for all these years? Do you think that is a fair exchange?'

'Sep, is this true?' Davy lowered his hands slowly, praying that there was some misunderstanding, but the man nodded without hesitation.

'You have my vigilant soldiers to thank, *Capitán*. If it wasn't for their diligence we would have rivalled the Derby Day fireworks.'

Moraga's face darkened. '*Capitán*. Stop the ship immediately. We must search the *Lynch* and the *Condell*.'

Davy noticed Sepulveda's shoulders hunch slightly, and it was clear to him that Moraga's suspicions were well placed.

Within minutes, the *Imperial*'s engines came to a standstill. The *Lynch* and the *Condell* were signalled. Word came back that explosives were discovered on both ships. They knew that Cumming had bribed Sepulveda and another man, Nicholas Politeo, an Austrian, to lay explosives. Politeo and Sepulveda were to escape overboard in the nick of time and swim to a boat concealed near the shore, where Cumming was waiting for them.

Moraga said that his soldiers had been vigilant, but in reality the three had been betrayed by a member of the *Imperial*'s own crew whose identity Moraga would not divulge.

As Sepulveda was led away roughly by the soldiers Moraga turned to Davy. 'How do we know that others of your crew won't try something similar, *Capitán*? What guarantee can you give me that they will be more reliable than this traitor?'

'The same guarantee that you give the president that all his troops remain true to him.'

The irony was not lost on Moraga. They all knew how Balmaceda's troops had reacted when faced with the Congressionalists' Gatling guns at Pisagua, that they had turned on their own officers and deserted in droves.

'What will you do with him?' asked Davy as Moraga turned to leave.

Moraga paused, amused by the question. 'He will get a fair trial. We're not savages, Captain Davies.' Moraga adjusted his helmet and laughed. 'But I would be interested to know what the British army would do with such a man? Tell me honestly, Captain. A man who not only deserts but tries to kill everyone in his wake and admits it? How many are we? On each ship, two hundred? Three hundred? Nearly a thousand men in all? Ha! What a coup! I would like to see the British army showing mercy to such a man. Indeed I would. That would be a sight.'

Moraga followed the soldiers along the deck, laughing to himself.

13 July, National Congress, Santiago

Balmaceda was walking at speed from his private office in the Assembly buildings towards the public assembly rooms followed by his secretary, Vásquez.

'How dare they!' bellowed Balmaceda. His secretary paused momentarily, then hurried quickly to catch up again.

'Sir, if I may suggest, it may be wise to show some clemency. Cumming is a British citizen.'

'Was!' shouted Balmaceda, not breaking his stride. 'He was a British citizen by birth who has been fed, watered, nurtured and made wealthy by his adoptive country. He has assumed Chilean identity.' Balmaceda stopped abruptly, rounding on his secretary. 'He is a Chilean!'

The president turned and carried on marching towards the assembly room, where the British consul was waiting for a private meeting to discuss Cumming's fate.

'Next you will be telling me that I am not a Chilean. That I am in fact a Basque! That no one in Chile is a Chilean apart from perhaps the Mapuche. God help us! How far back must we trace our lineage? Why are we even talking about this? Does it matter what he is? He has tried to destroy three of my ships, hundreds of my troops and my best officers. I don't care if he's from the moon! He's in my country! On my soil! Trying to destroy my ships!'

As Balmaceda walked on he could hear the secretary muttering something about 'diplomatic incident' and 'world opinion'.

Balmaceda threw his arms in the air and stopped again.

'Vásquez, listen to me. Whatever his nationality, this man Cumming has been bribed. He has been bribed by British money. He has admitted as much, even though he will not give us any names. Tell me, do you think that the *Opositores* have money enough to buy Gatling guns and thousands of Enfield rifles? Even I don't have the money to buy such armaments and I still have my hands on the country's silver. Though for how long, God only knows. It's simple. Don't you see? These people are happy enough to come here, to exploit our mines, to set up their shops. But they don't do it for the love of Chile, do they?'

He turned towards Vásquez, pummelling his jacket pockets dramatically. 'Strangely enough, the moment we want to use the nation's wealth for the benefit of our own people, do you see what happens? Where does this ammunition come from? Where are these guns made? From whose pockets do these vast bribes emerge?'

Balmaceda turned away in disgust and carried on down the corridor. '*¡Malditos británicos!*' They already lord it over half the globe and it's still not enough!'

They had virtually reached the door of the meeting room. After all these years, Balmaceda knew exactly what Vásquez' body language was saying. *I know you're the president and you know I have the greatest respect for your opinions, but please try to lower your voice. You need to at least attempt to appear considerate and lenient, and all those other things that are the hallmark of a noble statesman.*

Balmaceda sighed and straightened the collar of his jacket obediently. '*Gracias, a mi amigo.*'

19 July, Houses of Parliament, London
The Right Honourable James Fergusson had just taken a seat in the lounge of the Houses of Parliament when he noticed a gaunt-looking Tom O'Connor, MP for Liverpool, crossing the room towards him at speed. Fergusson raised his glass of port to hide his mouth and turned to his colleague, Sir John

Eldon, with a groan.

'God help us … not again …'

The man pulled up a chair next to Fergusson and merely nodded a greeting to his companion. 'Fergusson, we need to do something about Cumming. We're running out of time.'

Fergusson thought O'Connor looked agitated at the best of times. He always seemed to be fretting about something or other. 'We? I thought you said the consul was going to speak to the president?'

'He did. But Balmaceda won't budge. I've just received a telegram.'

Fergusson pressed his head back against the dark green velvet armchair and his eyes wandered vaguely around the room.

'I'm sorry if this is inconvenient, Fergusson, but he's going to be executed!'

Eldon raised his eyebrows and shuffled uncomfortably in his seat. The chatter in the room died down, and although specific eyes weren't turned towards them yet, people were listening.

'We have a serious situation here,' continued O'Connor with vehemence. 'A British citizen is about to be shot or hanged or God knows what for supporting our foreign policy, and all you can do is sit here nursing your glass of port. It's a diplomatic disgrace!'

Suddenly, Fergusson was focusing intently and placed his glass down with care on the small side table. He leant forward so closely towards O'Connor that the man was forced to move backwards.

'Now listen here, O'Connor. Cumming was born British but has assumed Chilean nationality. Even if that were not the case, he has taken it upon himself to get involved in the country's scrappy little civil war, which has nothing whatsoever to do with us. Let me be absolutely clear on this, the British government is not taking sides in this matter.'

O'Connor rose to his feet in anger. 'That's a preposterous lie! The British government is funding all sorts of interference in Chile and you know it! Shiploads of weapons have been leaving Liverpool for weeks now. I know it for a fact. I've seen it with my own eyes! For Heaven's sake, man, Cumming has a wife and children. Have you no compassion?'

Fergusson stayed resolutely in his chair. 'Do you have names? Has Cumming said who bribed him? Don't tell me they haven't tortured him to find out? They've tortured him, and by God we know what these people are capable of, and still they have no names? They have no names because there are no names! He has funded his own pathetic attempt at sabotage, it has all gone horribly wrong and now he's trying to shift the blame somewhere else so that the British government gets him off the hook. Don't you see?'

'Unbelievable lies!' gasped O'Connor, holding on to the chair back by his side. 'You know North is involved!'

Fergusson rolled his eyes and lowered his voice. 'For God's sake, man,' he hissed with disgust, 'You can't go around making accusations like that without evidence. You know very well that the British government can't come to the aid of every Tom, Dick and Harry who purports to be carrying out stupid acts of aggression in our name. What nationalities were the other two?'

O'Connor looked coldly back at him. 'Italian and Austrian.'

Fergusson snorted dismissively. 'I think that tells you all you need to know, doesn't it?'

When the stewards approached O'Connor to lead him out by the elbow, O'Connor rounded on them saying that if they laid so much as a finger on him he would take great pleasure in flattening them both. But for all his talk he went quietly after that, and the usual chatter gradually resumed in the busy room.

The two men in the green armchairs remained silent for a while until Fergusson's companion lit a cigar, and, leaning forward for the ashtray, whispered discreetly. 'Of course, the Americans make no bones about supporting Balmaceda, do they?'

Fergusson considered his port. 'No, you're right. But we all know that the Americans will support every nation's underdogs apart from their own.'

'Is Balmaceda really the underdog now? Surely, he's still the country's legally appointed ruler? Who are these insurgents? Would they be any better for us?'

Fergusson swilled the port around in his glass, then emptied it swiftly in one gulp. 'I don't know. But haven't you heard the old saying, my friend? *In matters of government, when nothing better turns up, clubs are trumps.*'

21 July, Valparaiso
The three men, with their hands bound tightly behind their backs, were thrust one after another into the courtyard. The hearing had been short. Each one had admitted his guilt so the outcome was fairly straightforward. The only debate had concerned the nature of their punishment. One of the generals had insisted that the proper fate should be one of hanging. The other officials more or less agreed, but at the last moment, when it came down to it, they realised that there was no provision for a gallows and that actually some shots to the head would be so much easier given the lack

of time. A priest was called, but the men's requests to see their wives and children were ignored.

'We can't wait around here forever for them to say their goodbyes!' muttered an official. 'The rebel troops are gathering at Huasco. Mark my words, there will be an attack on Coquimbo in the next day or so. We have no time to be dealing with this! Moraga should have shot them on board the *Imperial* and thrown them overboard there and then instead of wasting our time.'

Flour sacks had been placed over the men's heads, so when they were shoved against the wall and the sacks removed each one looked a ghostly white, hardly able to see for the dust in their eyes.

'Untie our hands,' asked one of the prisoners, but the soldiers only laughed as they prepared their rifles.

'Ready!' shouted the commander.

'You always overcharged me, you bastard, Cumming,' muttered a soldier.

'Take aim!'

Cumming looked up at the soldier's face, blinking through the flour.

'I don't know you.'

'Fire!'

The bodies fell to the floor. There were tiny movements, then nothing.

Rhiannon Lewis

CHAPTER 23

15 August, Valparaiso

Rumours had been circulating that troops were amassing near Viña del Mar. Agnes Ebrington had hardly left the house for days, but the postman would bring snippets of information from time to time. He supported the *Opositores* and would always play up their successes. Even so, things did not appear to be going well for the government and Agnes tried her best not to sound disappointed when he mentioned their significant losses and inferior fire power.

At night she would bolt the doors and retreat upstairs as far as the attic rooms. Miriam slept better knowing she was near and so Agnes slept in Peter's room, listening out for suspicious noises and wishing that Albert was still alive. His shotgun was still locked in the storeroom, and throughout the war she had rejected all thoughts of retrieving it. But those thoughts came more frequently now. She had located the key to the gun case and kept it around her neck, hidden under her collar on a length of chain.

That morning, just as she and Miriam cleared the dishes away after breakfast, they could hear shouting in the street.

'*¡Viva la revolución!*'

Miriam and Agnes opened the door into the parlour and looked out through the lace curtains on to the street. A crowd of rough-looking men carrying rifles ran past, their boots clattering on the stone cobbles.

'*¡Muerte a Balmaceda!*' shouted the stragglers viciously.

Agnes stood back from the window and felt for the chain under her collar.

'That's it, Albert. I can't wait any longer. I have to do something.'

'What is it, Mrs Ebrington?'

'We must defend ourselves, Miriam. Have you ever seen anyone using a gun?'

Miriam shook her head vigorously and made a face like the one she would make when she was a little girl and didn't want to eat all her porridge.

'Miriam. How old are you now?'

'Mrs Ebrington! You know how old I am! I am nearly fifteen.'

'Do you remember anything of the orphanage? Before I took you in?'

Miriam frowned and shook her head. 'I don't want to remember.'

'Were you afraid when you came here?'

'Yes,' Miriam smiled.

'Was I very stern?'

'Yes.'

Agnes took the chain from around her neck and felt its shiny warmth.

'Miriam, I don't want you to call me Mrs Ebrington any more. I want you to call me Agnes.'

There were more shouts outside in the street. Agitated young men marched quickly downhill towards the harbour, shouting challenges and threats. Miriam looked concerned, but not about the shouting.

'It would be strange to call you that, after all these years.'

Miriam looked sad and Agnes felt a sudden stab of loss. She had come to think of Miriam and Peter as her children but hadn't realised it until now. She had not intended it, but it had crept up on her. For so long she had thought it would not be appropriate to adopt these foreign children. And Agnes was about to concede that it really didn't matter about the name and that whatever Miriam wanted was fine when the young girl added, 'I would rather call you Mother, if that was all right with you?'

For the first time in her life, Agnes Ebrington was speechless. She smiled and nodded and held Miriam's hands for a while.

'Shall we see about this gun? I fancy Albert gave it a good clean before he died and I'm sure there are plenty of cartridges. But it's a while since I looked at it.'

Agnes Ebrington put her hand on the girl's shoulder and they made their way towards the storeroom. 'Miriam, my dear, I hope you're a natural. We may not get a chance to practise.'

The *Imperial*, the *Lynch* and the *Condell* were moored at Los Vilos. As it was getting light, a launch was spotted heading for the *Imperial*. A man from the Custom House had brought urgent telegrams, and within minutes they were delivered on board. Davy and William watched as Garin shuffled the sheets of paper, looking increasingly perplexed with each separate reading.

'It makes no sense,' muttered Garin. 'Signal for Fuentes and Moraga,' he ordered, and soon two more launches set off from the torpedo chasers towards the *Imperial*.

The government commanders gathered in the *Imperial*'s saloon, accompanied by the ship's respective captains and officers.

'*Señores*,' began Moraga solemnly, 'we are told that rebel forces are amassing at Huasco. There are no numbers. Another force has landed at Quintero: eight thousand infantry, six hundred cavalry, eight hundred men of the naval brigade, three batteries of field artillery and a battery of Gatling guns.'

Fuentes made a whistling sound through his teeth. 'Surely, there must be some mistake? Where could they have found that many men?'

'Miners, children, deserters?' suggested Garin.

Moraga sighed heavily. 'We have one of the longest coastlines in the world and an interior which is virtually impassable. We have perhaps four serviceable vessels to move our troops around and it seems that our men, most of the forty thousand, are now in the wrong place.'

'Things will be different when the warships arrive,' said Fuentes.

'No!' shouted Moraga, suddenly angry, 'We have waited too long! The rebels know that their position is weakened once those ships arrive. They are making their move now.'

'On Valparaiso?' laughed Fuentes in disbelief.

'Yes, on Valparaiso. And Santiago. While we have been cruising the coast our friends have been hard at work, bribing soldiers, stockpiling foreign arms, and refining their strategies. They made their base in Iquique, and like fools we went after them and allowed them to dictate the terms of war. Now they are bringing the war to us, to our very doorsteps. And we are undefended.' Moraga screwed up the papers tightly in his fist.

It was clear, even to Fuentes, that their options were limited. The commanders agreed that the best course of action was for the *Imperial*, the fastest of the three ships, to make haste to Quintero, to prevent the landing of more troops and to bombard the coastline there if necessary. The *Lynch* and the *Condell* would follow on as quickly as their engines would allow, perhaps collecting troops on the way.

As the men dispersed Davy and William made their way to the bridge. The orders came instinctively, one after another without much obvious thought but all the while they made assessments regarding speed, wind and currents. Soon they were out in open waters again, and when the ship was safely on its planned course William took a sheet of newspaper from his pocket and handed it to Davy.

'We found some news of Sep.'

Davy found the small entry in the centre of the page.

'Ricardo Cumming, accused of complicity in a plot to destroy the three government vessels, the *Imperial*, the *Almirante Lynch* and the *Almirante Condell*, has been executed. Cumming, a British subject and owner of considerable business interests in Valparaiso, leaves a wife and three young children. Two other men were also executed: an Austrian named Nicholas Politeo and Pio Sepulveda, an Italian and erstwhile steward of the steamship *Imperial*.'

Davy folded the newspaper. Flocks of South American terns, more agile and graceful than common gulls, circled the ship.

'Could you have imagined it of Sep?' asked Davy.

'No,' replied William, without hesitation.

Davy wondered whether war was like some strange chemical that, once poured into a person's veins, transformed him forever into good or bad. Or was it just that the good became better, the bad became worse? He thought back to the day of the races when William, new to the *Imperial* and throwing his weight around, had ordered Sep about as if he was some young cabin boy. Once William was out of earshot he and Sep had laughed at the whole ballyhoo, agreeing that the new chief officer would soon calm down and learn his place.

'Or else!' laughed Sep, frantically sewing a seam in the seat of Davy's trousers while he, the captain, sat waiting patiently in his underpants.

That conversation seemed a world away from the last one he'd had with Sep. Davy had begged Moraga for five minutes in the steward's company.

'I need to understand why he did this,' Davy had pleaded. And despite Moraga's noisy objections and profanities, he had eventually relented.

'Only out of respect for you, Captain, not for that barbarous traitor. You understand me?'

Davy descended into the hold where Sepulveda had been chained to some crates of ammunition. When Davy asked him why, Sep looked past him with hard unseeing eyes. 'It was a shortcut, *Capitano*, to a better life. I could have returned to Salento, bought a small farm, some animals. I could look after my parents again before it was too late.'

'But the crew? Your friends?'

Sep bowed his head and Davy thought for a moment that he might be ashamed.

'I would do the same again,' Sep murmured, without lifting his face.

Davy wanted to feel revulsion and anger but he could not believe what he was hearing. 'I think you're too proud to admit it, Sep. You made a mistake.'

Sep turned away and as he did so the chains around him jangled on the iron floor. 'You can believe that if it makes you feel better.'

Davy gazed at what he could see of the man's face. His dark, curly hair fell forward over his eyes and hid them from view.

'How will your parents feel now?' asked Davy. It was a cruel shot. Sepulveda made no response. It was the slightest twitch at the corner of his mouth that gave him away and Davy knew that, no matter what he pretended, the man in front of him was already in hell. There was no need for Davy to bawl or parade his indignation and sense of betrayal like some cheap theatre actor. Sep would know as well as anyone what was going through his captain's head. Saying anything more would be like goading a dying animal caught in its own trap.

Davy turned to leave.

'*¿Capitano?*'

'Yes.'

'Would you see that my things are sent home?' The man's voice was utterly composed.

'Yes, Sep. Of course.'

And that was it, the last conversation between Davy and the man who had served him as steward for nearly three years.

'If I hadn't accepted the commission, William, none of this would have happened,' said Davy, handing the paper back to William.

As they made their way out to sea, the terns were joined by shearwaters. Soon there would be the occasional albatross, Salvin or Black Browed or, if they were in luck, a magnificent Royal Albatross.

'We should tell the crew,' said Davy.

'Some of them already know.'

'Do we know who betrayed the plot?'

'No.'

Suddenly a flash of white crossed the sun above the bridge. And there it was. The breathtaking Royal Albatross on its great wide ark of flight, flexing its massive wings in the wind.

'Hello, old friend. We haven't seen you for a while,' said Davy. 'Let's hope you've come to tell us that the war will soon be over, eh?'

William and Davy watched the bird wheel effortlessly around the ship.

The sound of footsteps interrupted the men's thoughts and one of the junior officers stepped on to the bridge.

'Captain, sir. It's Webb, sir.'

'What about him?' asked Davy, wondering why the lad looked so pale and hesitant.

'Sir. He's hanged himself, sir.'

Estella stood up, placed her hands behind her and stretched her back. All morning she had been tending to the injuries of a long line of soldiers. She had tried to categorise them into three groups: those that were serious but could be helped, those whose injuries were too grave for anything other than morphine, and those who could wait. It was a callous strategy, but it was the best way to save as many lives as possible. Even with Peter's help many in the first category would die before she could reach them. Not all of them were on the government's side, and some of the opposition's captured soldiers had found themselves in her care.

'Why are you helping them?' a soldier spat at her. 'We've spent months trying to kill them!'

'We're not on the battlefield now,' replied Estella calmly.

She was the only person there with any proper medical training. They were in no position to argue.

As the days went by the physiology of pain was as much of an enigma to her as ever. Some men could bear the gravest injuries with fortitude and stoicism, even a smile and a word of gratitude for the smallest attention, while others would moan and judder as if in agony when there was hardly anything more than a superficial wound. An attitude of mind affected so many things, it seemed. *Men. Boys.* Some were hardly older than children.

She had reached the last of the urgent cases. In the distance she could still hear the pounding of artillery. With a bit of luck she would get through 'those that can wait' before a fresh batch of injured arrived back on carts. She was about to kneel down again to tend to the next patient when she heard a stream of shouting rising to a hysterical crescendo. Estella turned to see a soldier mercilessly beating an iron-grey mule with a whip. It was the tallest mule Estella had ever seen.

'You stubborn, stupid, useless piece of shit!'

The mule was so exhausted that it could barely stand and did nothing to avoid the man's wrath apart from turn his head aside. Estella heard a shout beside her and before she could intervene, Peter had run forward towards the man.

'Don't do that! He won't work for you if you hit him like that!'

'What do you know? I should have left him in Santiago where I found him, him and his fancy name, full of airs and graces. The only thing he's good for is a bloody stew!'

And the man dropped his whip and drew out a pistol from his trouser pocket.

'No! I'll buy him from you! I have money. How much do you want? Tell me!'

The man paused, incredulous. 'Are you kidding? He's not worth shit. God would strike me down this instant if I took honest money from you. If I ever lay hands on that cheating bastard of a muleteer ...'

The man took aim at the mule's head but Peter jumped between him and the animal. 'A hundred pesos!' he shouted.

A hundred pesos! Estella thought. Did Peter have any idea how much money that was? Sure enough, the man paused and looked suspiciously at the lad in front of him.

'You don't look like the kind of person who carries a hundred pesos.'

'He doesn't,' said Estella, stepping forward, 'but I do.'

The man was confused now. Why were two people so intent on buying this useless creature? He turned to look at the mule again. Was there something about this animal that he didn't know? Did he have strange, magical abilities that he was unaware of? A hundred pesos, although it seemed like a lot of money, might not be nearly enough if this creature was so desirable.

Estella saw all these thoughts pass across the man's face, and although she carried money with her she was not sure whether she wanted to part with it just yet.

'Here,' she said, twisting a ring from her finger, 'it's the finest Burmese ruby you'll ever see, worth a hundred mules.'

The man squirmed as if they were trying to make a laughing stock of him. 'It could be glass for all I know!'

'My husband is Laurence Taylor,' Estella spoke quietly so that no one else would hear. 'I can assure you, it isn't glass.'

The man took the ring and turned it around in his fingers. Even to an untrained eye, the workmanship and the stone's brilliance were impressive.

'He's all yours,' said the man, placing the ring in his pocket quickly. 'You can keep the whip for free. You'll be needing it.'

Peter and Estella watched as the man disappeared into the crowds of soldiers.

'Did you have a hundred pesos?' asked Estella as she moved towards the mule and stroked his white nose until his ears relaxed.

'No,' answered Peter, picking up the whip and throwing it aside. 'How much was the ring worth?' he asked, sheepishly.

'Well, let's just say this is probably the most valuable mule in the whole of South America.' Estella smiled to think that she had given the ring away so easily. It was worth every peso to see Peter looking like a boy again.

18 August, Valparaiso
All day there had been riots in town. Now and again they came closer, and when they did Agnes and Miriam made their way upstairs, with the shotgun

and a small revolver. In various parts of the upstairs rooms they had hidden away jugs of water and dried food, thinking that if someone broke in and stole what they had in the kitchens they could still feed themselves until help came.

Help. Who would help, wondered Agnes Ebrington. She prayed that the government would win. They had not been perfect, but at least she had felt safe. These ruffians roaming the street, what kind of government would they create? The government of vengeance and retribution? Sometimes she and Miriam heard shouts that the troops were coming. But whose troops she didn't know. And all the time she thought about Peter and prayed that he was still alive.

'I have failed you both,' said Agnes as they sat at the top of the stairs one morning, holding on tightly to their weapons and trying to work out whether to venture downstairs or not. 'I should have taken more care.'

Miriam dismissed the comment.

'Just think how funny we must look, sitting here,' smiled Miriam, looking across at Agnes.

'Speak for yourself, young lady. I'll have you know that I shot a fair few rabbits in my time.'

'I would have liked to see that!'

They could hear feet running along the street, but the shadows that passed didn't linger.

'Eight months ago, we could not have imagined this, could we? You and me, sitting here at the top of the stairs with our guns.'

Agnes smiled. Shots rang out in the distance.

'What would Mr Ebrington have thought?' whispered Miriam.

Agnes paused for a moment and thought of her husband. 'Dear Albert, he would have been very surprised.'

23 August, Quintero
They buried Webb at sea, *en route* to Quintero Bay. The service was a hasty affair, squeezed, out of necessity, between a change of watch and more shooting practice by Moraga's soldiers. By chance, the man had discovered Sepulveda's plan, and rather than speaking directly to Davy, had divulged all to Moraga. Webb had bargained on leniency, but once the plot's full extent became known, the well-oiled wheels of revenge had been set in motion. Webb's parting note spoke of being caught in an impossible web. He could no more live with the guilt of betrayal than he could the poison of regret.

One way or another, he had betrayed them all. The world would be an infinitely better place without him. Some of the crew muttered words like 'coward' and 'selfish'. Davy remembered the thoughts of a lad as he clung to the ropes of the *Royal Dane*, and judged differently.

When the *Imperial* arrived at Quintero the bay was deserted. Apart from a few stray fishing boats there was no sign at all of enemy transports, and nothing to be seen through the telescopes that suggested the build-up of troops. A messenger was sent ashore, and soon the news came back that eight rebel ships had already sailed south in convoy. The ships had, it seemed, disembarked over 9,000 Congressionalist troops and, if the report could be believed, 4,000 Mannlicher rifles, 5,000 Gras rifles, 600 Comblain rifles, six large Krupp guns and ten mountain guns.

'The ships are bombarding Valparaiso. The city is burning. Parts of the harbour and the Almendral are already in ruins,' said Moraga.

'But there are no guns in the Almendral!' gasped William in disbelief.

'Only people. These are the terrifying tactics of a desperate army. They know that our warships are finally on their way.'

'But they will be too late,' said Davy.

'Yes,' agreed Moraga, 'they will be too late.' Almost as an afterthought he added, 'Placilla has fallen. Rebel troops are approaching Valparaiso and Santiago.'

'Do we know these reports are genuine?' asked Davy.

Moraga smiled. 'One thing has been consistent throughout this war, Captain Davies. That is, the good news has always been open to question. The bad news has always been unfailingly accurate.'

They waited for further orders by telegram. But no orders came. Eventually, late in the afternoon, a message arrived to say that the president had left the government buildings. No one knew where he was.

'It's all over, William,' said Davy, watching the launch approach the ship a final time before darkness descended.

'Valparaiso has fallen. Santiago has fallen!' came the shouts from the boat.

The National Congress, Santiago
'Your Excellency, the rebels have landed at Quintero,' began Vásquez, then he paused as if considering how he could present the news as painlessly as possible.

'And?' said Balmaceda impatiently, sensing his secretary's hesitation.

'They are marching towards Concon.'

'How many?'

'Eight thousand.'

'And? Come on, man! Out with it!'

Balmaceda snatched the paper from his secretary's hand and read the details.

'General Alzerreca's regiment has fallen,' said Vásquez.

Balmaceda looked puzzled and shook the paper. 'Where does it say that here? Where?'

'It doesn't. We have just heard. Three thousand dead and wounded.'

Balmaceda read the figures over and over but all he could hear was the word 'fallen'.

'Sir, we should think about getting you to safety.'

'What?'

'Their troops are getting closer.'

'They're not even in Valparaiso yet. What are you talking about? We can head them off at Viña del Mar. We'll send troops from Santiago and Concepcións!'

'The rebels have already abandoned their attack on Viña del Mar. They have turned towards Placilla.'

'Placilla?'

It made no sense. None of his generals had ever talked of Placilla as being of any strategic importance. Balmaceda tried to visualise the rebels' movements as if it was some hideous game of chess.

'They have completely abandoned their lines of communication?'

'Yes, it seems.'

A bold move. A confident move. The move of an army that knows it is winning.

'Your Excellency, I must insist. We must make arrangements. It is later than you realise.'

Balmaceda pondered his secretary's words. Is this how it ends? He wondered. A handful of grubby telegrams and a cowardly slither to a secret place of safety?

28 August, 1891, the *Imperial*, South Pacific

To escape by sea from Valparaiso, Chile to Callao, Peru: 1436 nautical miles. Davy, the captain, stood back and looked at the charts. Even at 15 knots top speed with no stops for fresh water or coal, it would take them four days. With one stop, possibly two, to pick up what coal there was left along the coast, after eight months of civil war, decent anthracite not 'this foreign shit', as his engineer called it, five days? Maybe six. With his left hand, Davy reached upwards and removed his captain's cap, then raised his right hand and scraped his fingers back slowly through his hair. *Jesus*. He couldn't fail now. He needed all the navigational skills he had ever learned to come together into one perfect final plan. He needed it to appear to him, clear as a divine instruction sheet. He needed it to appear soon.

Somewhere out there on the Pacific the enemy's warships were, at that very moment, scouring the horizon for signs of their smoking funnels, as many as forty ships, each with its own vengeful captain and crew, searching for the *Imperial*.

Escape: to flee, to fly, to bolt, to circumvent.

Davy placed the cap back on his head and stared at the unnerving expanse of trackless blue ink between the two ports on the map. One final time, they would need to be the fastest, the sharpest, the most devious, the least visible. Like a sleek eel passing through the dark shadows of a river current, against the flow. *If I am to succeed at anything, then let me succeed at this. Not for my own sake any more, but for theirs. Let me get them to Callao.*

CHAPTER 24

29 August, the *Imperial*, near Taltal

He knew it was illogical, but nevertheless Davy had plotted a course northwards which brought them far too close to land at Taltal.

'Is this wise, Captain?' Garin had queried, even though Davy had pretended his reason was to attempt the possible evacuation of stranded government troops. In truth he had scoured the horizon hoping to see signs of Estella's regiment, a single red flare or frantic white flag. It was a ludicrous and desperate idea and Davy knew it. All the other lookouts had their orders to keep their eyes glued to seaward. Davy was the only one who looked to land.

'What do you see?' asked William quietly as he joined Davy on deck.

When Davy didn't answer William took off his cap and leaned with his back against the rail, letting the wind blow through his hair.

'Absolutely nothing,' replied Davy eventually, collapsing the telescope in one swift stroke and placing it in his pocket. 'I see nothing at all.' But still he could not take his eyes from the coast.

Evans was, yet again, getting every ounce of power from the ship's engines and the wind brought pulses of salty spray across their faces.

'What will happen once we get to Callao?' asked William.

'Moraga's plan is for us to hand the ship over to the Chilean minister at Lima. He will plead for his soldiers' lives and I will plead for my crew.'

William's hair, which had grown long in the last few months of the war, was blowing across his forehead and into his eyes. 'Should we be concerned?' he asked.

Davy didn't answer but took out his telescope again, extending it quickly and bringing the lens up to his right eye.

'Look at it, William. You wouldn't credit it, would you? From here it looks as if nothing ever happened. No dents, no holes, no scars. We think we make a mark on the earth, we fight and have wars, build and destroy, but the sea and the mountains are immune. They couldn't care less. They hardly know we exist.'

William swept his hair back again, and, turning to Davy, placed his cap firmly back on his head. 'I suspect that can only be a good thing.' William smiled but his smile was short-lived. Tears were running freely down Davy's face and he was making no attempt to conceal them.

'Captain, sir,' one of the junior officers appeared from nowhere and interrupted, 'Moraga's saying we should stand out to sea now that we're past

Taltal.' The young officer looked expectantly at William and then at Davy whose back was still turned towards him. 'In case we're seen, sir?'

'Absolutely,' replied William, 'I have the captain's orders. Now get back to your post and tell the crew to keep their eyes peeled. A case of wine for the first man who spots a pursuer.'

'Aye, sir.'

The young officer dashed back along the deck and William turned to leave.

'William?'

'Yes?'

'The crew will be all right. The *Compañía* will make sure that no harm comes to us; their business depends on it. He may be spiteful, but Walker won't lay waste his greatest asset. Unless he's incredibly stupid.'

William left and made his way to the bridge as Davy collapsed the telescope and placed it once more in his pocket. *Or unbelievably vengeful.* Davy thought back over his own words to William. For the first time since the beginning of the war, it occurred to Davy that the circumstances of their being commandeered could only be properly verified by one independent person: Walker. If permitted, Moraga would undoubtedly go into exile: he would not be available to plead the crew's case in any court of law. Stewart had refused to captain the ship. Davy had been bribed. But what evidence did Davy have for that?

The cold realisation came over Davy that, even if they could successfully evade capture on their way north to Peru, their fate was far from certain. Davy took one last look at the coast, swept his face with the palms of his hands and made his way to the bridge.

Hills above Taltal
When word reached the regiment that Valparaiso had fallen, what remained of Balmaceda's troops began to disperse in different directions. Some went south to Chañaral, thinking that their journey home would be shorter from there. Others, still concerned about what the winning side might do to them if caught, went north, back to Taltal, hoping to catch sight of a friendly vessel that might take them home. The injured had no choice, so Estella and Peter followed the carts north.

At dusk, three days later, they reached the hills above Taltal, but the fading light made the descent into town too hazardous. They set up camp, and one by one, brilliant campfires were lit along the ridge. Some cursed the folly of it, saying that it would be better for them not to broadcast their location to the world.

'*Amigo*, you can eat more cold salt beef if you want to, but I'm damned if I will!' shouted one bad-tempered soldier as he dismantled a collection of empty wooden rifle boxes with his axe.

Estella had climbed on to one of the carts to look again at one of the soldiers who was gravely ill. When they brought him in from the battlefield her first thought had been that he was a hopeless case. She had reached for her dwindling supply of chloroform thinking that the dose, however generous, would not work for long. But he was so determined.

'I'm not going to die, am I, *Señora?*' It was a question, but everything about his demeanour seemed to suggest only one possible answer.

'No. You will be all right.'

And Estella had hoped that for once her prognosis could be proved wrong. Now, as she crouched down next to him in the cart, he looked pale in the lamplight, a million tiny beads of perspiration gathered and glistened on his brow.

'What's your name?' Estella asked as she took a cloth to his forehead.

'Benito Rafael Herrera,' replied the young lad, and then he smiled as if laughing at himself. 'You know, I am the enemy?'

Estella looked down at his clothing and failed to see anything that would have set him apart from the other men.

'The war is over. There are no enemies now.'

For a moment the lad's smile transformed itself into a wince. Then the smile returned. 'We won!' he whispered and fixed her with a steady, unrepentant gaze.

Estella took her cloth away. In the growing firelight his face looked older, the wavering flames casting strange moving shadows around his eyes.

'Could I see the fires, *Señora?*'

Estella moved around behind him and eased him up so that he leaned against her. He was light and bony as if the flesh was already making way for something else.

'Oh!' He gasped in awe at the long line of bonfires stretching along the ridge and into the distance, then added, in barely more than a whisper, '*Victoria.*'

Together they watched as dark figures approached the fires, throwing planks and boxes on the flames until they crackled and roared. Pungent woodsmoke filled the air. It was a still, clear night and the sparks seemed to dance unhindered on an infinite path into the starry sky. Just then Estella felt the lad catch his breath as if in surprise and she turned to Peter to ask for some water. But even as she did so she felt his body give way, and the hand that had been resting on his lap slid to the floor. She stretched her fingers up to the vein in his neck as her father had taught her to do, but in reality she knew he was gone.

'It's all right, Peter. Don't worry.'

Estella stayed still and watched the sparks rise. She looked at the glittering stars beyond and thought that perhaps they were not stars at all, but rather brilliant pin pricks of light in a dark canopy. Behind the canopy might be an incredible, undiscovered world. She turned and knew that to her right, in the darkness somewhere, lay the great Pacific. If Davy was out there, she wondered whether he could see their fires burning.

'He's gone?' Peter interrupted her thoughts.

'Yes.' Estella slid backwards and allowed Benito Rafael Herrera's body to slip gently on to the cart floor. She drew the hair back from his eyes and brought the corner of his blanket up over his face. He was still smiling.

5 September, Callao, Peru

It had never occurred to Davy that relief could weigh so heavily. He had imagined that his lads would shout and cheer and demand to be given immediate shore leave as soon as the ship reached Callao, or run around like winter calves let out for the first time in spring. But as soon as the *Imperial* let go her anchor, even the toughest and most hardened of his crew looked worn out, like rag dolls that had been played with for too long. Some of them sank to the floor near the bulkheads, closed their eyes and said thanks to their private gods. Others lined up to embrace the soldiers as they left.

'Good luck, *mis amigos*,' they muttered, embracing each other roughly and turning their heads aside so that no one would see their flushed faces.

'Captain, we must make our way to Lima,' said Moraga. Garin and Moraga stood facing Davy on the deck like two disobedient pupils who had been summoned to report to their headmaster. 'We have sent the minister a telegraph. He will be expecting us.'

During the train journey to Lima, an hour or so inland from Callao, the war did not feature in the men's conversations. How long had it been since they talked of everyday things such as families, children, homes, horses and dogs? By now these things seemed almost fantastical, as distant and magical as elements of a fairy tale. It was difficult to believe that a real world could exist again at all after such destruction.

The train burst through a ravine and the ground fell away on one side. Davy looked out of the window and saw the front of the train, five or six carriages ahead, curving around an almost sheer cliff face on an impossibly narrow rail.

'You see, Captain Davies, the skills of our brilliant engineers,' said Moraga. 'How they have placed rails where the llamas walked.'

'Polish engineers,' added Garin, thoughtfully.

Moraga looked at Garin in wonderment as if the man had revealed the meaning of the universe. Then his face fell. Davy remembered Peter's words about Balmaceda's proposed engineering school, and for the rest of the journey the three men sat in silence contemplating the many implications of their naval and military failures.

Colonel Moraga, Commander Garin and Captain David Davies entered the Chilean ambassador's office at the secretary's request. The ambassador had already come around the desk to greet them and shook hands warmly with each in turn.

'Gentlemen. The time for recrimination is past. We must look to the future, whatever our political leanings. We must return to the work of building a strong and successful nation and put the past behind us.'

The ambassador was smiling and his words seemed to be totally genuine. *It can't be as easy as this*, thought Davy, noticing the outline of one other person sitting at the ambassador's impressive desk, and another at the window with his back turned.

'I don't believe you have met the United States envoy?' said the ambassador, introducing the man at the desk, who then stood up and shook hands with them.

'But I believe you are familiar with the general manager of the *Compañía?*'

The ambassador gave a short cough and the man at the window turned to face them. It was Walker. He eyed the three men carefully then raised his hand to his mouth and exhaled a long, languid cloud of cigar smoke. For a brief moment the men in the room hesitated, waiting for Walker to step forward to greet the visitors as the envoy had done. But Walker returned to the desk and resumed his seat, leaving the men standing. He leaned far back in his chair so that he viewed the men over the tip of his nose.

The ambassador gestured to the three chairs that had been placed some four or five yards back from the desk, then returned with another short cough to his own seat.

'So, gentlemen, we have agreed to deal with military matters first,' he began, explaining that the United States were offering Moraga, Garin and their families political asylum. It was even possible that the authorities in Peru might find openings for them in the Peruvian army. The ambassador talked of the long history of cooperation between the two countries. He was a little more vague about the fate of the soldiers. There seemed to be some confusion about who would transport them back to Chile and under whose flag. The envoy insisted that everything possible would be done to ensure the soldiers' safe passage.

With a sharp intake of breath, Walker drew the cigar back from his mouth and interrupted the ambassador. 'Yes, I rather doubt you would want them to suffer the same fate as your comrades on the *Lynch*.'

Walker lowered his chin, not to look at the men but rather to flick specific flakes of ash from his trousers as if he was targeting individual adversaries.

'What of our comrades on the *Lynch?*' asked Moraga, slowly.

The ambassador looked down at his papers. 'Mr Walker is referring to the event at Valparaiso harbour.'

Moraga looked at Garin. They all knew that the *Lynch* had returned to Valparaiso for repairs. They assumed that she would soon have been seaworthy and would not have remained there for long.

'There was an incident,' the ambassador began, 'when the ship was stormed.'

'Stormed?' said Moraga, raising himself up in his chair.

'Yes. Their repairs were delayed, it seemed. In any case, Valparaiso fell and the mob took over. The crew tried to defend themselves, but the big gun backfired ... some issue with the gunpowder being impure ... contaminated perhaps ... who knows, sabotage? In any case, they couldn't defend themselves. They were overrun.'

The ambassador coughed again and brought his closed fist to his mouth. There was a pause where clearly he did not intend to go into further detail.

'It was quite a massacre,' said Walker, looking coolly at Davy.

Davy found the urge to jump forward over the desk and embed his fists in the man's skull to be almost unbearable. He looked down at his feet, trying to erase the vision of the *Lynch*'s crew being torn to pieces.

Walker smiled and leaned back again. 'Fuentes made a dash for it, though, didn't he, Mr Ambassador? Saved his skin just in the nick of time.'

Davy looked across at Moraga, whose shoulders were now hunched with shame.

The ambassador tried his best to move things on in a positive way. The war was over now, he said, and there was little to be gained from recriminations or analysis. Moraga and Garin were to accompany the American envoy back to Callao. There they would be joined by one of the American warships. Their families would join them in due course and the soldiers could be taken back to Valparaiso on a German merchant ship. The ambassador offered two of his own guards to accompany Moraga and Garin as far as Lima.

'I suggest you go without delay. In all honesty, I can't guarantee your safety until you reach that ship.'

The envoy rose to his feet and the ambassador, who was resting his hands on the paperwork in front of him and who seemed to be beating out the rhythm of some song that only he could hear, looked expectantly at Moraga and Garin.

But although Garin shifted in his seat, neither man got to his feet.

'If it's all the same to you, Mr Ambassador, we would like to remain here until Captain Davies' safety is assured,' said Moraga.

Davy glanced gratefully at the colonel.

'And that of my crew,' added Davy, turning back to the ambassador.

The envoy resumed his seat.

'We owe Captain Davies and his crew a considerable debt of gratitude,' added Moraga, directing his comment towards Walker.

Walker leaned forward in his chair to stub out his cigar, looking as if a disgusting smell had pervaded the room. 'How touching,' he murmured, without the glimmer of a smile, then sat back again. He raised his hand to his collar and loosened it by sliding his fingers backwards and forward slowly between his throat and the fabric. Then his face twisted into a wry smile. 'Mr Davies, the *Compañía* expects you to bring the *Imperial* back to Valparaiso, immediately. Now that the war is over, business needs to return to normal as soon as possible. We can't have ships floating around in harbour with nothing to do, can we?'

The ambassador coughed and looked up at Davy. 'Of course, it would not be wise to return just yet. As Mr Walker has very kindly pointed out, the fate of the *Lynch* was not entirely, how shall we say, helpful?'

Walker's smile remained on his face but his eyes grew cold. 'With all due respect, Mr Ambassador, I am running a business, not a nursery.'

The ambassador spread his hands out over his papers then held them there. There was no cough and for some moments he remained absolutely motionless. Then without looking up at all at his neighbour, he replied quietly and carefully, 'Mr Walker, please understand me. I am not about to release Captain Davies or his crew to you until I am ready. If needs be, I will lock them all up in the jail at Callao until it is safe for them to return to Valparaiso.'

Walker's colour was rising. 'You will provide the *Compañía* with compensation then? For lost earnings, Ambassador? The shareholders would expect nothing less.'

The ambassador laughed. 'I imagine the *Compañía*'s shareholders would prefer you not to endanger one of their most expensive and prestigious ships, don't you? The *Imperial* is still a new ship, is she not? So Captain Stewart tells me. I fancy its destruction by a mob would cause a rather noticeable hole in your balance sheet, would it not, Mr Walker? Compensation or no compensation.'

Walker's face twisted slowly to one side as if a sharp knife had been eased between his ribs.

It was an odd moment to be overwhelmed by relief. But, for the first time since the end of the war, it seemed clear to Davy that their future was secure. He and most of his crew had survived and there would be no reprisals. They would not leave Callao until it was safe to do so. Walker would have to return to Valparaiso by some other means.

The meeting was brought to a close. As Garin, Moraga and Davy took their leave, shaking hands with the ambassador and the American envoy, thanking them warmly for their support, Davy noticed that Walker's chair was already empty. Walker had circumvented the gathering and had left the room unnoticed. He was striding down the corridor with his chin in the air, like a schoolyard bully who'd had a taste of his own medicine.

'What a revolting chap,' whispered the ambassador, following Davy's gaze.

'Gone home to cry to *mamá*, no doubt,' added Moraga dismissively.

Davy watched Walker turn the corner at the end of the long corridor.

'The unmistakable bile of yesterday's man,' added Garin, thoughtfully, following Davy's gaze.

Taltal

What had seemed, until then, to be a calm and ordered retreat from the battlefields descended, the following morning at Taltal harbour, into utter chaos. There were not enough ships.

'Only the injured!' shouted a well-dressed officer from the deck of an American warship. 'No carts. No artillery. And definitely no mules!' shouted the man, seeing Peter leading the animal towards the end of the gangway.

Peter and Estella stood aside for the stretchers and walking wounded, then retreated back through the crowd to where the harbour was clearer.

'Peter, there's no other way. We will have to separate. I need to stay with the injured, and you must find a ship that will take your friend.' Estella half-expected the boy to cling to her and beg her not to leave him. But he nodded calmly and stroked the animal's neck.

'I will be all right,' Peter smiled, '*El Capitán* will look after me.'

Estella scanned the harbour. Apart from the one American warship, which had offered to transport the injured back to Valparaiso, all the other ships in Taltal harbour were privately run merchant ships. Each tethered ship looked as unwelcoming as the last. No one would be keen to take on a mule without some conspicuous financial reward.

'Here,' Estella reached into her skirt pocket and drew out a square of cotton tied at the top with string. 'I set aside some sovereigns for you,' she whispered. 'When you see a ship that looks possible, ask to speak to the captain and only the captain, do you hear? Show him the sovereigns and offer them to him. If he agrees to take you, give him one when you board but keep the others until you reach Valparaiso. That way you'll be sure to get there.'

Peter placed the money in his pocket and looked back at her with concern. Risking the young man's embarrassment, Estella threw her arms around him. 'I will see you in Valparaiso, very soon. Give my love to Mrs Ebrington, and tell her I am looking forward to a very large piece of her excellent cake. Now go, so that you can find yourselves a place.'

They parted and for a few moments Estella watched them both as they made their way through the crowds with their heads bowed. They moved serenely through the chaos, the boy and the mule. Soldiers and hangers-on moved out of their way instinctively, barely registering them. Guns and loaded carts yielded without argument.

Estella headed back for the American warship, and made her way up the gangway between long queues of stretchers. At the top, two officers seated at tiny folding tables were laboriously taking down names and details of those being embarked.

'*Jesús*, can't you write a bit faster,' grumbled the stretcher-bearer in front of Estella, 'this one's going to die before we get to the deck.'

Estella raised herself on to her toes to look over the man's shoulders.

His reclining companion looked thin and grubby but nowhere near death's door.

'Now then, Missie, you can't be coming up here. Afraid you'll have to find another ship,' said one of the officers, addressing Estella but hardly taking his eyes off the paperwork before him.

'I am the doctor who has been tending to troops on the battlefield, appointed by Colonel Moraga himself,' replied Estella. The officer's gaze slid lethargically off the end of his clipboard, landed somewhere around Estella's knees and made its way eventually up to her face.

'And I, Madam, am the pope,' replied the officer coolly, raising his pen in the air and jabbing it decisively in the direction of the gangway. Estella was about to argue that any ship's doctor, even an eminent one on board a First Class American man-of-war, would appreciate her help dressing wounds when she caught sight of the man on the stretcher smirking. Suddenly, the challenge of going against yet another flow, the effort of helping people where they did not want to be helped or making a difference where no difference was really longed for, was overwhelming.

She turned to make her way back down the gangway but as she did so, she raised her voice and declared, 'If the man on that first stretcher has any injury worth talking about and isn't actually just trying to get a free passage back to Valparaiso then I'm the Virgin Mary.' And as she passed them, on her way down the gangway, some of the soldiers giggled or those that she recognised smiled kindly. A few could have vouched for her if she had asked them, but her resolve had evaporated entirely. *Enough.*

Her first thought on reaching the end of the gangway was to search for Peter. But as she stepped off the wooden planks, her knees very nearly gave way. Further along the harbour, away from the crush of soldiers, there was a row of flat-topped moorings. Estella made her way towards them, and placed her doctor's bag on the floor where it flopped sadly to one side. It was no longer bursting with equipment. Much of what she'd brought with her had been used or lost. She sat on a mooring, glad to be away from the crowds. Sure enough, the three chancers, the two stretcher-bearers and their thin, grubby companion had been ousted from the ship amid shouts and jeers. Once they reached the end of the gangway, they tossed the stretcher aside, and the three of them made their ill-tempered way towards the nearest tavern.

'They're a rag-tag lot and no mistake,' said a man's voice behind her. 'No wonder they lost the war.'

Estella turned and saw that the man addressing her wore the

unmistakably dusty uniform of a nitrate ship's captain. He was carrying sheets of crew agreements and must have just come from the Customs House.

'Are you looking for a ship south?' he asked quietly. Perhaps it was the man's kindly tone of voice or the fact that it was so long since anyone had asked her what she wanted for herself but Estella's real urge was to weep freely on the man's shoulder and ask him to take her anywhere but there.

'I had an assistant,' Estella said, searching the harbour. 'They wouldn't let him board because he had a mule.'

'A young lad? With the tallest, thinnest-looking mule you ever saw?' asked the captain with a wry smile. Estella nodded.

'He's in luck. I saw him boarding a whaler and creating quite a stir.'

A whaler? Estella sighed. She had heard awful stories about whaling ships, the harsh conditions and the rough, brutal natures of the crews.

'Oh, you needn't worry about your lad. He'll be as right as rain with that lot. I know them well. But tell me, did you give your boy any money?'

'Yes,' replied Estella, feeling foolish, 'rather a lot, in fact.'

The captain laughed out loud. 'Ah, the old bugger. I thought the captain had a superior looking glow about him as I passed.'

Just then they heard the prolonged horn of a steamship. Estella turned to see billows of black smoke rising from the far end of the harbour. A battered-looking whaler was indeed underway. She hoped Peter had kept back some of his money and not handed it all over in his excitement to get home.

'Come along then,' said the man, stooping to pick up Estella's bag, 'let's give them a run for their money in a proper ship.'

The captain was already making his way to the waiting launch and beyond him, far out in the bay, lay a four-masted steel bark, tall and imposing with not a funnel in sight.

'Oh, she's …' Estella broke off not knowing how to finish the sentence without causing offence.

'My lovely *Pendragon Castle*. Newly launched this year. Built by Richard Williamson of Workington. We stop at Valparaiso for supplies,' said the captain, and then tapping the end of his nose, whispered, 'with a little unscheduled stop-off at La Serena on the way.'

Estella surveyed the distant ship with dismay. Lovely though she was, Estella would have much preferred to find a route home with a sturdy, even-keeled steamship. She didn't want to admit it but she had never ventured on to a sailing ship before.

'You know, she is quite comfortable,' said the captain, with some degree of sympathy, as he stepped into the launch and raised a hand to help her down. The lads guarding the boat, who had clearly been dozing, rubbed the sleep from their eyes and looked up in amazement at Estella as if she was some rare treasure retrieved from an Inca hoard.

'Look sharp now, you two. Mrs …'

'Taylor.'

'… will be accompanying us as far as Valparaiso. You will be a civilizing influence on these savages, Mrs Taylor.'

The young sailors took no offence and smiled shyly as they made a space for Estella. As they shoved off, rowing with confident easy strokes towards the *Pendragon Castle*, Estella thought how odd it was that after all her determined plans, she was now about to embark on a ship that she knew nothing about, with a captain she had met only minutes before. She thought of the disastrous decisions she had made in her life, some of which had seemed at the time to be so logical and well thought through. So many had come to nothing. Perhaps it was now time to take a different tack, follow her nose, as this captain seemed to do.

'Forgive me, Mrs Taylor, I am Captain Wood,' said the man, extending his hand. He did have a kindly face, and one that inspired confidence. As Estella shook his hand she could feel the leathery skin and calloused hands. Despite his advancing years, there was still strength and determination in his grip.

The captain sat back and admired the approaching ship. 'Taylor you say, like the famous Copper mines?'

It was a wholly innocent remark but Estella was not about to elaborate. 'Indeed,' she replied.

Mention of the name brought back the old familiar dismay. The *Pendragon Castle* loomed ahead. And for a brief moment she gauged the finely balanced scales of the returning dread within, against the approaching dread without.

'Does your family know that you are safe?' he asked, seeing her look of concern.

A thought struck her. 'Captain Wood, do you know if there is a telegraph office at La Serena?'

'Oh, yes. It's a little shambolic, but they are helpful enough.'

Estella smiled at the captain and she felt a sudden, unexpected surge of euphoria. 'Then, that will be my next port of call.'

The crew of the *Pendragon Castle*, on seeing their captain approaching, were preparing to weigh anchor. Men climbed the ropes like industrious ants, dark against the clearing sky. Out in open water a sudden gust of freshening wind caught Estella's bonnet. The ribbon came undone and, for an instant, the bonnet hung on by a solitary hatpin alone until a second flurry took hold of it, wrenching it from Estella's head, hurling it on to the green waves and foam.

The captain was horrified. 'Turn around, lads! Go back before it goes under!'

The oars came out of the water and icy splashes blew towards them in the breeze.

'No!' cried Estella, smiling and leaning forward to place a reassuring hand on the man's arm. 'There's no need at all. Please, let's go on. I don't want to go back.'

Another squall caught Estella's hair and this time the pins came away until every strand was streaming loose. She felt for the pins in her hair and laughed at the futility of trying to untangle it all.

'You can mend it on board!' laughed the captain through the sound of the wind. But Estella's thoughts were already somewhere else. She was walking across the harbour at La Serena and up to the telegraph office doors, bearing messages for Valparaiso.

Three days later, Valparaiso
Agnes Ebrington had just nodded off to sleep, fully clothed in her armchair, when she heard a noise from the back of the house. She stretched out her hand instinctively in the dark and found the barrel of the shotgun where she had left it, propped up against the mahogany sideboard.

'Miriam! Wake up!' she whispered. Miriam, sleeping on the chaise longue, woke instantly and Agnes could see her faint outline moving in the darkness. There must be a moon, thought Agnes. She knew the streetlights had been smashed some days before. Agnes explained that she had heard a noise and they both moved carefully through the silent house, feeling their way through the hallway. The garden could be seen clearly. A pendulous white moon hung serenely in the night's sky illuminating the high walls and wooden gate.

The gate rattled, then rattled again. Thank goodness I put a padlock on it, thought Agnes, thinking that it was one of the last useful things that Mr Cumming had sold her before the war.

'Perhaps they have gone?' whispered Miriam when they heard nothing more.

They listened in the darkness. The only sound was the languid 'tic, toc' of the grandfather clock on the mezzanine. They were about to turn away from the window when a dark shape appeared at the top of the wall.

'Oh my God! They're climbing the wall!'

The shadow paused at the top momentarily as if gauging the distance to the ground then sprang like a sinister devil into the garden.

'¡Dios Mío! It's so difficult to see. Shall I shoot?' asked Miriam, holding her quaking gun to the open window.

'No, Miriam, wait!'

Out of the moon's rays it was impossible to see. But there was something disconcerting about the shadow. It picked itself off the ground and returned to the gate, trying desperately to open the lock.

'I see him now,' said Miriam.

'No. Wait! Let's see what he does.'

'He will murder us and steal everything!'

The women watched as the shadow took something from his pocket and wrenched the metalwork away from the door. The lock fell to the floor with a thud and the gate opened wide. The garden was flooded with moonlight.

A second, towering shadow stood patiently in the gateway and the devil urged it quickly into the garden. Agnes realised why the first silhouette was disconcerting.

'It's Peter.'

Agnes and Miriam stepped in to the garden to see Peter closing the gate carefully behind him. His companion was an enormous mule. The three stood in surprised silence around the docile creature, whose eyes glistened and whose ears twitched in the moonlight.

CHAPTER 25

6.45am, 19 September 1891, The Argentine Legation, Santiago

José Manuel Balmaceda sat down at the head of the beautifully polished table facing the long windows. Inside the Argentine legation the corridors were quiet. Outside, the neatly cut grass lo oked fresh and well-watered, and in the distance two ancient monkey-puzzle trees stood dark and striking against the azure blue sky. Nearer the window, pale fronds of pampas grass swayed in the breeze. All was neat and serene in the garden. Balmaceda gazed at the sun streaming through the glass, the shutters drawn back behind the velvet gold curtains. He watched as the morning sunlight caught the specks of dust here and there: they slowly settled and disappeared. From the mantle, to his left, came the sound of the clock and its slow, resonant tick.

He brought his hands up to rest on the edge of the table and looked down at the neat sheets of writing paper before him. He had asked for good-quality paper, unlined, and plenty of ink. As usual, Vásquez had fulfilled the request efficiently, without fuss. He felt a sudden pang of gratitude, and despite his calmness tears pricked his eyes. How strange, he thought. He rarely thought of Vásquez. It seemed he had always been there, just getting on with things. Making everything easier. Loyal, but in the shadows. When he considered it, he hardly knew the man. Did Balmaceda even know whether he had a family? Did he have children? Who were his friends? He had paid him a pittance, he thought.

Balmaceda straightened up and filled his lungs deliberately. Breathing out, the calm returned. The clock ticked and the pampas swayed in the early morning sun. The weight in his pocket would distract his writing, so he reached in and took out the polished revolver, placing it gently on the table to his right. He had cleaned it carefully the night before – his father's revolver, given to him by a wealthy American landowner from Pulacayo, a Colt Single Action revolver. Last night he had read the inscription properly: 'To my esteemed friend Enrique Balmaceda with gratitude from Walter Beck,' and thought how much more adept his father had been at gaining and keeping influential friends. Perhaps it was that thought which had started his journey to this table? All his father's hopes and aspirations for the Balmaceda family had come to this.

This is the time when you should weep, he thought. *You should weep bitter tears for bringing your family name to ruin.* He imagined what his father would say now. He would say gravely, 'I am so disappointed.' His father wouldn't even bother adding the words, 'in you'. It was as if the whole world had become one enormous disappointment, through his son. There would be no commiseration or sympathy or persuasion, 'Son, I am proud of you – whatever you have done. Your effort alone has made me proud. That you exist: this makes me proud. Son, don't do this.'

Balmaceda bowed his head and smiled. How many more times would he have this conversation with himself? *To the last,* he thought resentfully, my father is there to the last, eminent in his disaffection, endlessly and permanently selfish. I have become an old man. I have loved and married and had children of my own, led one of the greatest countries on the face of the earth and still my father sits on his imperious cloud ready with his infinite store of put-downs and abundant disappointment. How fitting then, he thought, looking at the gun's shiny barrel.

Enough now. He leant forward and opened the ink bottle, carefully placing the lid to one side. Then he reached in to his left pocket and took out his gold pen, Emilia's gold pen. He took off the top, placing it to his left.

His last letter as president. All night he had rehearsed the words, so there was no need for great thought and further consideration. He paused, but only very briefly, his pen poised, then began writing.

Dear Sir and Friend,

I ought not to prolong further the asylum which you have so generously offered me, and which I recommend to my family as an instance of one of the greatest services I have received in my life.

Balmaceda continued writing, saying that he had scorned a vulgar escape while fearing that he would not receive a fair hearing.

May God have mercy upon a man thrown down by the blows of misfortune.

By now the sun was higher in the sky and had moved around the building. Only the window was in sunshine and the room felt colder. The sky that had been free of clouds was now streaked with thin veils of white far in the distance. He felt relieved. He had remembered all that he had set out to say. He hoped that one day someone would read it and think again on his actions. And judge him less harshly, perhaps – or if not less harshly, at least with some understanding of how he had done the best that he could, under the circumstances. He could do no more, and he was glad that Uriburu and his family had provided him with sanctuary so that he could write his version of events. His enemies would not have afforded him the luxury. He knew that well. It was done, and he was glad.

He placed his pen to the side for a moment and arranged his presidential letter neatly in front of him. Vásquez had remembered the wax and seal, but Balmaceda had no intention of sealing this letter. This was his last public statement as a politician, there for all to read. His last letter as president. But not his last letter as a man. In front of him there were a few sheets left.

He wrote first to his mother. He knew she would be appalled by stories of his tyranny.

My heart throughout was with Chile. I sought to rescue the country from foreign domination, and strove to make it the first republic in America. My enemies say that I was cruel, but circumstances compelled me to sanction certain acts. Many bad deeds attributed to my orders were never known to me until they had been committed.

He lined up the papers and took up his pen a final time. This time, his heart surged. This was the letter he could not rehearse, for which few words were needed because in between them there was a lifetime of love and understanding.

My dearest Emilia,

I set about the final act of my career with a calm mind. My death may alleviate the rage of my enemies against you, my dearest, and those who have supported me. Watch over our children.

The distance from this world to the other is less than we imagine. We shall see one another again, when we shall be without the grief and bitterness which now surround us.

Your loving and devoted husband,

JMB

He folded the letter and wrote on the outside,

Emilia de Toro Herrera Balmaceda

He smiled. He had loved her name. When they were young he would tease her when she was angry or irritable and say that it was the '*toro*' in her that made her so high spirited and difficult. It would not be lost on her that he had written her name in full, and hopefully, in the midst of all the pain, she might find it in her to smile at his final act of playfulness. My little '*toro*'. There was no other way, he was sure of it. His dying by his own hand might save his family. A grand Roman act of attrition. Surely not even Montt could be so bloodthirsty as to want the death of an innocent wife and her children? Their children.

Now his face was awash with tears. They streamed down his face without interruption. There was nothing more to do or say. It had all been in vain. A miserable failure. He was a miserable failure. He put the top back on Emilia's pen and placed it inside his left breast pocket. Then he reached inside his right pocket and took out two bullets. Two. Why two? In case he missed the first time, of course. How many bullets does a failure need to shoot himself? He is certain to miss the first time, don't you think? He could see the newspaper reports now *Breaking news – Balmaceda's failed suicide attempt – dictator is seriously maimed – fails to achieve his aim – Congressionalists agree – wholly typical behaviour.*

He loaded the revolver and rested it on his lap for a moment. With his left hand he wiped the tears from his face and composed himself again. Then, with irritation, it occurred to him that if he shot himself here, at the desk, then he would most likely fall over when it was done, on to the floor. It seemed such an ungainly, untidy thing to do at the very end. He turned to the bed and thought how much better then to die there where he could not sprawl. He walked to the bed and pondered whether to remove his shoes. But he wanted to appear as he would in parliament, smartly dressed, perfectly presented. He felt sorry that Uriburu's staff would have to deal with the blood. Perhaps there would not be too much.

The corridor of the Argentine legation was quiet and still. The clock ticked on ponderously. It seemed louder now. And outside, the high white clouds were moving more quickly across the sky. The pampas grass was being combed by the freshening breeze. Different weather was moving in. The world was moving on. A flurry of blossom from a neighbouring tree came across the window like tiny white feathers. He raised his right hand. The polished wooden grip felt warm in his palm. He turned left a little and felt the cool steel barrel touch his temple.

He can see the clock. The clock ticks. It is one minute to eight in the morning. There is a tiny chip on the clock's gilding. Time to move on. His finger moves, and keeps moving. There is surprise. Then brief gratitude for a small success. A thought of Emilia. Then nothing.

Callao Harbour, Peru
William burst in to the captain's cabin, grabbed Davy's jacket from the hook behind the door and threw it into his lap.

'For God's sake, let's get out of here,' said William, who was already out of the door and striding down the corridor in his best suit.

'What's going on?' Davy looked up from his logbook, exasperated that he had spent most of the previous hour thinking about Estella and staring at a blank page. 'What's wrong?'

William stopped in his tracks and made a growling noise under his breath. 'In case you haven't noticed, we've just survived an entire civil war. I think that calls for a bit of shore leave, don't you?'

Davy looked down to see an irritatingly large blot of ink blooming nicely in the centre of the page, obliterating part of his meagre entry. 'Damn it all.'

When Davy had returned to the *Imperial* that afternoon after his meeting with the ambassador, the lads had finally been allowed the luxury of full-scale celebration. With Balmaceda's bribe money jangling in their pockets, they had spilled out of the ship, clean faced and freshly razored, through the tall gates of the harbour and up through the wide streets of Callao, not expecting to be back at the ship until early morning. Davy, who needed to bring the logbook up to date, had descended immediately to his cabin without thinking of anything more.

'If the events of the last few days haven't been memorable enough for you to be able to recall them tomorrow morning, then I think you should be concerned about your faculties.'

William could always be relied on for a rather spiky turn of phrase, thought Davy, looking down at the ruined page.

'Besides,' shouted William as he came to the end of the corridor, 'I have something else to celebrate.'

Davy opened his mouth to respond but William had already disappeared. Two more blots had appeared from somewhere, so Davy directed the pen back into the well with less than helpful force. 'Damn and blast to hell.'

He took hold of his jacket and left his cabin, slamming the door behind him.

'This will do,' said William, eyeing up the flamboyant tiles at the entrance to the Silver Cannon Tavern and diving through its doors. It was 3 o'clock in the afternoon and the place was quiet. The lunchtime drinkers had gone and the evening drinkers hadn't arrived. Clearly it was too smart and expensive for the crew as they were nowhere to be seen.

'A bottle of your finest champagne, sir,' said William to the bar tender, slapping a handful of pesos on the counter. 'And three glasses.'

'Three?' asked Davy, perching on a stool at the bar.

'One for Mary.'

'Who's Mary?'

Davy looked carefully at William and wondered whether it was possible to suffer delayed reactions to wartime injuries. The barman popped open the bottle and, as instructed, poured three glasses. William gave one to Davy then held the other two in the air.

'I'm going to get married!' William chinked both glasses against Davy's and took an enormous gulp from the first glass.

'What?'

'You heard,' said William, taking another gulp from the second glass. 'To Mary!'

The bartender was clearly amused and lingered nearby, bottle in hand, ready to refill their glasses. Davy thought of the Almendral and wondered whether William had managed to conceal some complex private life until now.

'Is there some kind of … trouble?' asked Davy, quietly.

'For goodness' sake!' said William, now alternating the glasses quickly and taking gulps from each. Davy looked down at his own untouched vessel twinkling enticingly. William was right. If this wasn't a time to celebrate, they were a hopeless pair. Davy downed the entire contents of his glass then gazed at it in shock. William, who had already emptied both his glasses, placed them down on the counter to be replenished.

'I decided,' began William as he watched the effervescence subside, 'that if I survived the war, I would make amends.'

'For what?'

William had both glasses in hand again. 'Here's to me! And here's to Mary!'

Davy put his empty glass on the bar and reached out towards William. 'William. Put those down! You need to explain properly, otherwise I'll have to tell the crew that you've lost your marbles completely and should be locked in the hold all the way back to Valparaiso.'

'Liverpool. I'm going to Liverpool. That's where Mary is. Sir, another bottle if you please!'

It was difficult for Davy to keep up with William. Not only was the champagne disappearing too quickly down his friend's gullet, but Davy found that he couldn't drink his own glass because he spent so much of the conversation with his mouth open.

William explained between gulps that he had been in school with Mary's brother, Mary Bird Tucker to be precise. He and Mary had met at a ball when they were both seventeen. She had fallen instantly and, to William's mind at the time, catastrophically in love. William had been crushed by embarrassment and taunted mercilessly by his friends. Mary had written him a stream of scented notes that William had relished catapulting into the parlour fire. The more she tried, the less impressed he became.

When war broke out in Chile she had written again, for the first time in years. She was concerned about his welfare and the dramatic turn of events on the *Imperial*. She was single, living alone and working as chief clerk for the Liverpool Steamship Company. She was still, it seemed, utterly devoted.

'You can't marry someone out of pity!' gasped Davy.

William, who had seemed until then to be melting slowly like candle wax on to the bar, was now upright and indignant.

'There are many reasons why someone might marry: companionship and friendship and …' William paused to think for a moment.

'You're not the marrying kind!'

'Neither are you! Estella had the sense to know that and ran a mile, right into the veritable teeth of war!' said William, raising his glass to the barman.

No blow had ever landed so painfully. Davy put down his glass and, pressing the palms of his hands on his knees, dropped his head like a winded man. They were the unkindest words that he had heard in a long time. The barman drew back and swilled the champagne bottle absently to gauge how much was left.

'Oh, Davy,' began William, looking now like a man who knew he had drunk too much, far too quickly, 'I'm a fool.'

Davy was virtually motionless, still gazing at the bar room floor. The barman, who understood enough English to recognise a potentially explosive situation, smiled nervously at William.

'Please, have the rest on us,' William slid off the bar stool and took out a collection of smaller coins from his pocket and placed them on the counter.

'*Gracias, amigos,*' said the bartender jovially.

Once outside the Silver Cannon, the men walked in silence. Callao seemed even more cosmopolitan than Valparaiso, if such a thing was possible. The saltpetre mines had brought foreign wealth, and it was as easy to get a cup of English breakfast tea as it was to get a French baguette or a German bratwurst.

Davy was annoyed with himself. He knew that William hadn't meant to be hurtful, but still the words haunted him. *Ran a mile.* He needed a distraction, and when they reached the smart shops of Calle Arzenal he realised that he had found it.

'Come on,' said Davy, 'let's do something memorable.'

The bell over the wooden door jangled delicately as they came in and suddenly they were in a different world. Every vertical surface seemed to be draped with red velvet. Ornate, gilded frames peeped out between curtains to display images of clients. There were illustrious businessmen, sophisticated women and impossibly clean children in starched white collars. Their reflections were caught in a dazzling mirror, emblazoned with the words: 'Señor Castillo's Elite Photographic Salon'.

They didn't see him at first as he was on his hands and knees, putting the finishing touches to his window display. When he stood up, Señor Castillo appeared slight and elegant with a luxuriously dark, finely trimmed beard.

'Ah, *Señores*. English?'

'*Sí, Señor*,' replied William with a sudden air of authority.

The champagne fumes must have hit the man immediately because he gave a knowing smile.

'*Señor*,' began Davy, 'I am Captain Davies of the *Imperial* and this is my chief officer, William Keen Whiteway. We have just emerged from the civil war in Chile, and although we have survived we have come to the sad realisation that no one will remember us in years to come. Our exploits will be …'

'As dust?'

'*Sí, Señor*, exactly that.'

The photographer clapped his hands together. They had come to the right place. He would set up the plates immediately. They were lucky, as he had only a few moments earlier finished his appointments for the day and they had caught him just in time, before he closed up. Mr Castillo left them briefly to prepare the studio. Davy sat on the chaise longue while William walked around the room looking closely at the photographs, muttering comments under his breath.

'He looks like a hippopotamus,' said William seriously and Davy couldn't suppress a laugh. 'He does! Look here! He has tusks. And a tail.'

The effects of the champagne had clearly not worn off.

'That's *Señor* Patrick Bryce,' announced the photographer, who seemed to have the magical ability of appearing and disappearing at will. 'A world authority on Panamanian marsh fever. And one of my most esteemed clients.'

Davy got up quickly from the chaise longue.

'It has been a strenuous time,' Davy said apologetically, following the photographer quickly into his studio.

Eventually, after a great deal of fussing over combed hair and brushed jackets, William and Davy faced the camera between a theatrical, romanesque chair and an aspidistra stand. Davy stood on the left with William to his right. Powerful lamps had been placed at strategic points around them.

'So that we don't have any unflattering shadows, *Señores*,' said the man, his voice muffled by black fabric as he vanished behind the camera.

Davy, who sensed that William was about to dissolve into another fit of unseemly laughter, jabbed him viciously in the side with his elbow. But rather than take the photograph, the man emerged again from under the black hood, shaking his head.

'Alas. This is not a very interesting arrangement.'

Castillo walked forward and stood in front of William and Davy like a dissatisfied mother examining her badly turned-out children. '*Señores*, a good photograph must capture your very essence, your *joie de vivre!* It must be compelling. It must draw you in! Your descendants, if you ever have any, will want to learn a lot from the photograph I am about to take. You will not be able to talk to them or tell them your story. By then, they may not even know who you are. They will ask, "Who are these strange men? What did they think of each other? What experiences did they have?"'

Davy turned to look at William. What the photographer said was true: a viewer would not be able to tell much from the way they stood at the moment with their arms hanging limply by their sides.

'You have survived a war, have you not? With its many dangers and challenges. You have lost comrades, no? Friends, perhaps? You have seen horrors and hardships that most of us will, thankfully, never see. You have been changed forever. But throughout it all you have remained friends. This is the magnificent story we must convey in one dramatic image.'

Castillo, who looked as if he had been directing the final scene of a grand opera, had returned behind the camera. He raised his arms as if calling for the final curtain. 'Now *Señores*, tell me your story!'

Davy half-expected William to collapse with laughter again, but instead he felt William straighten up and draw closer towards him, extending his arm behind Davy's shoulder until his hand came to rest there.

'I'm sorry for what I said, Davy. You know it isn't true,' said William quietly. The photographer raised the black fabric and disappeared.

But Davy barely registered William's words because the dark corners of the studio, away from the harsh lamplight, seemed suddenly populated with faces. The descendants that Castillo spoke of were there in the room, looking out at him from the shadows, waiting silently for him to respond.

Davy raised his fist and brought it to rest defiantly at his waist. It was a stance that his crew would tease him for. 'Look sharp!' they would say, 'The skipper's not happy.' But as the photographer counted down from three to one, Davy's only thoughts were of blue silk, the colour of a cornflower, and how quickly they could get back to Valparaiso.

8am, 19 September 1891, The Argentine Legation, Santiago
Señora Leonora Uriburu, wife of the Argentine minister, Evaristo Uriburu, had been making the final adjustments to her hair and dress. The maid had just left the room when she heard a gunshot. Leonora listened again and wondered whether she had imagined it, but the door opened and the maid stepped back in nervously with eyes as dark as pools.

'Go to the children,' Leonora whispered, crossing the floor towards her husband's room.

Her husband's room adjoined hers, but before she could reach his door he appeared, face dripping, with a towel in his hand. His face was pale, and as he turned back into his room she knew instinctively that he had gone back for his pistol. She followed him as far as the doorway.

'Evaristo, I think it came from his room.'

Evaristo Uriburu paused at the desk with his hand resting on the open drawer. He stared downwards as if into a pit of snakes. *It came from his room. On the second floor.* He picked up the pistol slowly. He was not a man used to handling a gun.

By the time they reached Balmaceda's room at the bottom of the corridor, Vásquez was already at the door trying desperately to force the handle. He stood back and shouldered the door violently but to no effect. He was a slight man and the mahogany doors were stubborn and built to last. Vásquez stood back and Leonora noticed that his eyes were reddening and his breath came in deep, hoarse gasps.

Uriburu came forward and leaned his face close to the door.

'José Manuel?' he spoke gently like a parent who had been overly harsh with a reprimand and was now trying to make amends. They stood in silence as they strained to hear a response. Vásquez held his breath. But there was no answer.

'I must get Karl,' said Uriburu. He turned to pass the gun to Vásquez, but on observing him reconsidered and turned to his wife instead. 'Guard this room with your life. Let no one in.'

Uriburu ran along the corridor and disappeared down the stairs. Leonora raised the gun in both hands and pointed it in the same direction. Her hands looked like someone else's and they shook visibly. As she braced herself against the wall she thought how her father had taught her to shoot vermin and vultures with a shotgun. Not people with pistols.

Last night she and her husband had talked about how dangerous it was for them to be harbouring Balmaceda. How it was only a matter of time before the people realised where he was. How the mob might take revenge on them also depending on their mood. And what they should do if they did.

Leonora looked down the length of her arm at the shivering gun and prayed that no revolutionaries would hear of the president's death before he was safely removed. Behind her she could hear Balmaceda's secretary murmuring, '*Oh, Madre de Dios, Jesucristo,*' over and over again.

Evaristo Uriburu returned within minutes accompanied by Carl Walker Martines. Behind them both were two stocky men and Leonora recognised them as Martines' stable hands. One of them carried a crowbar. Uriburu took the gun gently from his wife's hand while the men set to work on the door, the beautiful wood cracking and splintering as they forced the crowbar between the door and the frame. The frame parted from the wall and lumps of dry plaster covered the floor. The two men cursed impatiently until at last there was a sharp crack and the weight of one, skilfully placed, forced the door open. They spilled awkwardly into the room and came to a sober halt. José Manuel Balmaceda lay on the bed, dressed in his smartest suit as if for a day in government. The white pillow behind him resembled a bed of poppies blooming slowly as the drips of blood traced down his neck and shoulders. One neat bullet hole gaped red and precise on his forehead, and his gently resting head was turned towards them on to his still upright shoulder. His right hand, flung away from them towards the window, held the pistol. There was the faintest smell of a gunshot.

Vásquez was the first to move. He walked forward under buckling legs to the side of the bed where he fell, reaching out to Balmaceda's hand, gently, gently, as if trying not to wake him. Then he rested his head on the side of the bed and wept slow, painful sobs as the others looked on.

Valparaiso

The two men rounded the corner carrying repeating rifles.

'Don't do anything stupid, *amigo*,' said one.

'Look around you,' said the other, 'It's still chaos. How will they know? That bastard gave them the ship. The war would have finished in a week if it hadn't been for him. And our brothers would still be here.'

The men, scarves wrapped tightly around their heads, had fought for the Congressionalist army. When the official fighting stopped there had been a good deal of confusion about the gathering in of arms and ammunition. They figured two rifles wouldn't be missed. Large parts of Valparaiso were flattened and charred. Most of the shops in the city's main streets had lost their windows to looters. Glass and debris still littered the streets.

The men arrived at the doors of the *Compañía*'s offices and, guns at the ready, kicked the doors open. A man wearing a grey suit emerged from a tiny room in front of them and put his hands in the air.

'We have no argument with you, old man. Where is he?'

The terrified man motioned towards the end of the corridor.

'Go home now, *Señor*. Take a holiday. You look as if you need it.'

Without pausing, the men strode down the corridor in their hobnailed boots and kicked open the door at the far end. There were low voices, then a third indignant retort, a shout, then shots. A chair fell heavily and more shots rang out, echoing around the empty building. The two men emerged again slamming the door behind them.

'Try throwing your weight around now, *bastardo!*'

They pushed their way through the outer doors and disappeared into the early morning sun.

CHAPTER 26

1 November, Valparaiso

As soon as the door to Myrtle Villa opened Davy could tell by Agnes Ebrington's face that all was not as it should be. The *Imperial* had barely brushed the harbourside, the deckhands still tying her up at her berth, when Davy leapt from the end of the gangway and half-walked, half-ran through the streets of Valparaiso towards Estella's house. The *Imperial* had been forced to remain at Callao until the end of October, the ambassador unwilling to guarantee the crew's safety until the new government was trusted and established.

Earlier that morning Davy had reached Estella's house only to find the elegant windows boarded up and the gates padlocked. A menacing-looking dog stood to attention near the grand doorway. Davy doubled over to catch his breath, but when he moved up to the gates and raised his hands to the iron bars the dog twitched, then sprang forward in a froth of spit and barking, thrusting its pearly jaws towards Davy's legs. The gaps in the gate were too narrow for the dog's head so the best it could do was make a dribbling and ineffective growling near Davy's feet.

Next, Davy had gone in search of Dr Edwards' house, but although he found it without too much difficulty there was no sign of its inhabitants. Everywhere he looked, he saw evidence of looting and violence, bullet holes scattered across plastered walls.

So, finally, he went to Mrs Ebrington's house, knowing that she would have news and fearing what it would be. It was not good. He could tell by her face as she opened the door.

They came in to the parlour where Miriam and Peter were already sitting.

'Oh, Captain Davies. We did not know how best to tell you.'

Peter, who was no longer a child and who seemed to have grown into a young man, sat opposite him on the chaise longue, with Mrs Ebrington and Miriam either side of him. Miriam held on to Peter's arm as he spoke.

'They told us it was all over. So the troops were making their way to the harbour. They promised us amnesty so no one was worried. Some people were actually cheering, I think they were so glad it was over, and they were still alive. Mrs Taylor and I had just loaded our equipment, the medical things on to a mule.'

'You were not fighting?'

'No. Mrs Taylor saved my life. I had …'

'Oh, Captain Davies, it's too upsetting …' interrupted Mrs Ebrington.

Peter laid his hand on Mrs Ebrington's arm and whispered, 'It's all right, Mother. Captain Davies wants to know.' The lad looked up. 'I had lost my gun. I was so frightened. I just ran. I couldn't see, I couldn't hear. Then I was stopped. I thought I was going to be shot. Mrs Taylor saved me. She came out of nowhere and stood in front of me and said they would have to shoot her first. Then afterwards she made me help her so that they wouldn't shoot me as a deserter.'

Peter held Mrs Ebrington's hand tightly.

'Until then, there had been no trouble. But when we reached the harbour, we realised that there were not enough ships to take us home. People were pushing and shoving, fights were breaking out all over the place. Mrs Taylor and I tried to get on an American warship. But they took one look at the mule and …'

'Mule?'

'Yes, I've named him *El Capitán!*' Peter's face lit up briefly but then Mrs Ebrington must have squeezed his hand to remind him of the task in hand because his face soon darkened and he took up the story again. 'Mrs Taylor and I had to go our separate ways. She gave me some money and I found a whaler for myself and *El Capitán*.'

'And Estella?'

Peter hesitated.

'Mrs Taylor returned to the American warship … I thought she was coming back with the injured …'

'Only we received this,' added Mrs Ebrington, unfolding a telegram. She handed it to Peter who rose to his feet and passed it to Davy.

PETER RETURNING BY WHALER STOP MYSELF REFUSED BOARDING ON U.S.S. BALTIMORE STOP MAKING PASSAGE ON PENDRAGON CASTLE STOP DUE VALPARAISO FRIDAY M.T.

'Refused …' Davy frowned then re-read the telegram, taking in the dates, the ships, the possible routes. Estella should have arrived back in Valparaiso weeks ago.

'On the last night, above Taltal, the soldiers had lit bonfires,' Peter began, smiling now. 'We were talking about the future and what we would do. She said I should train to be a doctor because I was careful and didn't rush things. She said I was brave and conscientious. Me!' Peter laughed. 'I asked her what she wanted to do and she said that she was going to be brave too. She had decided to go to California. "There's a medical school there," she said. "I have a friend who might come with me, she said, although I haven't asked him yet." That was her intention.'

'Him?' whispered Davy.

'I could come too, if I wanted. I think she was joking!' Peter laughed again, but Agnes Ebrington frowned and glanced up at Davy.

Peter was taking them on a deliberate tangent. He was remembering a different place and delaying the end of the story. He was looking out of the window of Agnes Ebrington's house in Valparaiso but his eyes were seeing scenes that were far away, the battlefield guns, the corpses strewn around and the stars above him on the first night of peace. Davy prepared himself for the next words. He knew that if he concentrated on them very carefully they might come out the way he wanted them to, not run away from him in some awful unexpected direction.

'She was so kind.'

Was. The word hit Davy like the vicious burning plank from his past.

Peter hesitated and Mrs Ebrington took over the story. She said that the *Pendragon Castle* had never made it to Valparasio. It appeared that the nitrate cargo had combusted spontaneously. Such things were possible, it seemed, even though the captain was an old hand, well respected. She had made enquiries. Perhaps a smaller cargo of flax had caught fire first. In any case, there had been an almighty explosion, seen and heard from the coast. No time for lifeboats. Rescuers saw floating debris, a few bodies, nothing more. *The ship was lost, all hands. None survived.*

For a moment, Davy felt absolutely nothing. How many times had he read those words in the shipping columns and felt barely a glancing blow? In the distance, he could hear the steady 'tick, tock' of the grandfather clock, high on the hallway mezzanine. And for a brief second he was transported back, all the way back to the lit hearth of his childhood home, listening to his father's tales, and to the sound of another long case clock. Now the clocks were as one, and he realised that the seconds pacing by had always been there, though he had turned aside for so long and had not heard them. Estella's seconds had dwindled to none. His own paced on.

Then, slowly, as if he was chained to an anchor in a rising tide, an icy cold body of water rose around him from his feet slowly upwards, reaching his chest, squeezing the air from his lungs, creeping upwards in waves towards his neck and chin.

Peter reached into his pocket.

'On the night of the bonfires, she lent me this. The soldiers were messing around singing songs, blowing trumpets, playing any instrument they could find. She said you had given it to her. That it would be useful in times of trouble. "Better for it to be used in a time of joy." That's what she said.'

Peter stood and crossed the room, holding out the brass whistle. Davy took it. It seemed to glow with Estella's warmth. He turned it over and over, running his fingers along its rounded edges until it glimmered more brightly. He laid the ribbon on the palm of his hand and smoothed its blue satin. Beyond the silent room, the clock ticked on.

'I must go,' he said, placing the whistle in his pocket and rising unsteadily to his feet. He registered some talk of food and surely he could stay to eat and if not, would he be all right as his room would always be there for him at Myrtle Villa, whenever he wanted.

'I must get back to the ship,' Davy repeated, feeling that any moment now the cold water at his neck would rise a final time and overwhelm him.

Once at the doorway Mrs Ebrington touched his arm. 'Peter didn't realise,' she whispered.

Davy could barely focus. The steps to the garden gate seemed giant-sized and entirely out of proportion with the rest of the world.

'I never liked that Laurence Taylor,' she added, as if to explain her thoughts.

Davy moved to the edge of the flight of steps and swayed as if he was faced with an abyss. 'Where is he now?'

Agnes Ebrington gave a quiet snort of disgust. 'It's rumoured,' she whispered, 'that he has gone to Australia with some German diplomat's wife from Santiago. Would you believe it?'

Davy stared at the steps. It seemed to him that all the ships' bells he had ever heard in his entire life were ringing frantically inside his head.

'Will you be all right?' Mrs Ebrington asked as Davy moved away from her and propelled himself forwards.

But Davy had passed through the garden gates and was gone.

Davy had placed the bag of Balmaceda's gold coins on the bar at the True Blue Saloon with the intention of drinking until the contents were gone, or until he passed out, which was the more likely outcome of the two.

But the barman, who knew Davy well and who could tell that something dreadful had happened, was not so unprincipled that he would have taken money from a man who had lost all sense. He eyed Davy critically.

'*Capitán*. Things are not so good, eh?'

Davy, who was still considering the bag on the bar, did not reply.

'How about one on the house, eh, *Capitán?*'

What the barman really meant was, 'One on the house and then get back to your ship because I don't want to be answerable for you in your current state.'

So Davy nodded in agreement, and for the next half hour he nursed a glass of cheap Marsala wine, still staring at the bag of coins.

While the war was going on he had thought of the bag of coins as something good that, if he could only survive the conflict, would open up all kinds of possibilities. There was enough there to buy some land and perhaps some animals, some shares in a ship if he felt adventurous. But now that Estella was dead, the coins seemed cursed. The same powers that had commandeered him and his ship had contributed to her death. He stared at the bag and slowly a plan emerged.

Davy slipped off the bar stool and he made to leave.

'Back to the ship now, eh?' the barman asked, hopefully.

'No, *Señor*, I'm going to make amends.'

Davy had only ever visited the Almendral twice in his life. Both times when he was a young sailor, long before he was ever an officer. The first time he had lost his friends in the labyrinth of narrow streets and was glad to get out in one piece before being set upon by a gang of thugs. That time he had not seen a single woman. The second time was slightly more successful although the woman who took him in was probably old enough to be his mother. She had ruffled his hair playfully as he left and had given him back half his money. He hadn't let on to the lads about that.

Now he was looking for someone. He had no idea where she lived or what she looked like. He had no idea whether she was still alive. Before reaching the Almendral he stopped in the shadows of a street corner and took out a few coins from the bag then put them in his pocket. *Bribery money*. He placed the bag in the inside pocket of his jacket and walked on. The first few people he stopped were too cautious to answer. It was still too soon after the war to go answering questions being asked by an unfamiliar man who didn't look as if he belonged in their part of town. Some of the streets had been reduced to piles of rubble and splinters by the bombardment.

'I'm looking for Taylor's mistress,' Davy said, finally, to a woman standing in a doorway whose young child looked at him suspiciously from behind her mother's grubby skirts.

'Who's asking?'

'A friend.'

The woman turned away in disgust. 'Donatella doesn't have any friends, 'least not like you.'

So that was her name.

'Wait! There could be something in it for you.'

The woman paused before retreating into the shadows. '*Cariño*, you don't have anything I need.'

A man's gruff voice shouted from within and she raised her eyebrows as if to say 'see what I mean?'

Davy took out a gold piece from his pocket and showed it to her briefly. 'Take me to her.'

The woman considered the coin then disappeared into the house, shoving the child in front of her. From inside the building there was a brief bad-tempered exchange in a language that Davy didn't understand, and the woman emerged again, shawl around her shoulders, slamming the door behind her.

'The coin first,' she said, extending her hand towards him.

It was the closest Davy had come to finding Taylor's mistress. He placed the coin on the woman's palm and prayed that they were talking about the same person.

The woman who replied to the knock on the door was just as Davy had imagined her, and when he saw the two skinny children in the room behind he knew for sure that this was her. She must have been as old as Davy but still retained the beauty that would have attracted Laurence Taylor.

'Are you one of Laurence's friends?' she asked coldly, with her arms folded.

Davy wondered which answer would be the most likely to make her let him in and then remembered the rule he had always lived by on board ship.

'No.'

The woman smiled wryly. 'Good. I hope he rots in hell.' She turned back into the house and was about to slam the door. Davy sprang forward and wedged himself between the door and the frame.

'I am his wife's friend. Please, let me talk to you.'

Whether the woman let him in out of inquisitiveness or pity he would never know, but she did. The house, which was little better than a wooden shack, was shabby but clean. There were some incongruous items: an expensive wicker chair where she indicated he should sit, and ill-fitting taffeta curtains that looked as if they had come from another house.

The woman sat opposite him on a stool with the two children standing behind her. They were both paler than their mother and the boy looked strikingly like his father.

'Do you want them to go?' she asked.

'No, it concerns them too,' he said, bringing out the bag of gold coins and placing it on his knee.

Then he told her everything he knew. How Estella had found out about her. How she couldn't bring herself to confront Laurence but decided instead to help the children without telling them who she was. At first the woman listened in disbelief, challenging him at times, then arguing that no woman in her right mind would support the children of a mistress.

'She must have been crazy!' she gasped, looking around at the children for support. But the children looked sad.

'She's dead, isn't she?' the girl asked, and it was only then that Davy realised that they couldn't possibly have known.

'Yes.'

The girl came around from behind her mother and leaned heavily against her. Tears began to run down her cheeks. The boy sat down on the floor at his mother's feet and averted his face.

'I have this money,' Davy began, 'which I don't want to keep. It would please me very much if you would take it from me. Estella can't help you now.'

The woman looked in horror at the bag. 'It's her money?'

Davy explained that it was his own money, bribery for commanding the *Imperial* during the war.

'But I don't understand? Why don't you keep it? Why should you care about us? It is blood money, isn't it? Someone will come looking for it!'

Davy smiled. 'No. No one will want it back. No one else knows about you.'

For the first time the woman looked as if she might believe him.

'It's what Estella would have wanted.'

Davy picked up the bag and passed it to the woman.

Feeling its weight in her hands, she looked up at him, almost terrified. She eased open the drawstring and when she saw what was inside, crossed herself. The woman felt a coin between her fingers and passed it to the girl first, then the boy. Eventually she looked up at Davy with a lifetime of sadness in her eyes.

'You loved this woman?' she asked, searching Davy's face for agreement. Her face broke into a tearful smile full of sympathy.

'Such things still exist, *Señor?*'

Soon afterwards Davy left the house, passing through the narrow streets of the Almendral and clambering over piles of rubble where the bombs had landed. Where the streets opened out to the harbour he stumbled and fell near the shattered boards of a cart. Fragments of white cotton were strewn all around. There were splatters of blood in the folds. He pulled himself up and sat on what looked like the remains of a collapsed doorway. The sensation of slow drowning which had abated while he was at the woman's house had returned.

I will go before thee and make the crooked places straight. I will break in pieces the gates of brass, and cut in sunder the bars of iron. This is what he should have said to Estella. *I will go before thee.* Could there be a greater love? To make the way straight, not according to his wishes, but to her design. These were the words he should have said. Then, she would have understood.

He was drowning in memories. Estella walking towards him in the sunlight on Derby Day, Estella and her tiny ruby earring quivering as she read near his sickbed, Estella looking up at him from the harbourside, the back of Estella's head, disappearing through the troops. He wanted so much to be back on the topsail yards of the *Royal Dane* where he could feel his own equilibrium hold for a moment, then give way. He thought of Gabriel and Sep, of tiny white bundles disappearing under waves. He thought of the sea of faces that marched down the gangway and never returned. He thought of a burning plank. He thought of Elen. He felt Estella's brow against his face. *All is lost.* Davy opened the palms of his hands in front of him. The ropes that bound him to the world were still there. Could he not just let them go?

In the distance he could make out the *Imperial*'s funnels in the setting sun, but it was too soon to return. He had a better thought. He stood and turned inland again, up the steep hill towards the heart of Valparaiso.

Davy looked up to see William crossing the square at Plaza Victoria, his jacket flying, looking like a man who had searched every corner of Valparaiso. William's pace slowed and, as ever, he knew when it was time to say nothing. With a long, faltering sigh, he took off his jacket and sat next to Davy at the fountain's edge, leaning his elbows on his knees.

After seeing Laurence's mistress Davy had bought some Dewar's whisky from a shop near Cerro Concepción and headed for the only place where he thought he might find a trace of Estella's spirit lingering – the Neptune Fountain. Davy considered the label in front of him, its promise of rich and honeyed oblivion, then passed the bottle to William. It was very nearly empty.

'What do you know, my friend? A man may drink and not be drunk.'

William raised the bottle to his lips and took a long swig. Wiping his mouth with the back of his hand, he passed it back to Davy. But Davy had a second bottle, and it was already open.

The last of the sunset's glow was receding over Valparaiso, and gradually crowds of people passed by, dressed in their finery and carrying lanterns. The war had come and gone, but to these people the fixed points of the year still remained: the saints days and the holy days, the feast days and the days of effigies and parades. This was All Saints Day, Davy realised, taking another long gulp of whisky and passing the full new bottle to William.

Together they watched the crowds. There were people wearing traditional and colourful chamantos, European couples in their latest Parisian finery, dark-eyed Chilenas with their black lace headdresses. The people laughed and joked together, and Davy thought back to the chapel that he'd known as a boy, how dour and unforgiving it seemed to him now.

'I think I prefer their God,' said Davy, taking another long swig. The faces of the people as they passed in the lamplight seemed like an elaborate piece of theatre. They were flawed and imperfect, and like all nations on earth had fallen too easily into the trap of hating each other. But they had grace and beauty too and they did not fear their own passions. Davy loved them for that.

Suddenly, a dazzling white track of light shot up into the sky. A ship in trouble sending up a flare, thought Davy instinctively. They and the crowds raised their faces to watch as it climbed high above their heads. It climbed until their faces were flat to the sky, then, just as they thought it was about to disappear, it wavered for a brief second and burst with a bang into a million brightly coloured stars. The crowd in the square dissolved into cheering and laughter, and soon after more missiles sprang and bloomed in the night's sky. Not a ship in trouble after all, thought Davy, and he looked down again at the bottle.

I am that ship in peril. Drowning is inevitable.

And with that thought, all the whisky in the world could not hold back the dark waves of sorrow and loss that engulfed him. If the crowd did notice anything at all at the fountain's edge, they would have seen this: a man weeping, and a friend with his arm around him trying to save him from the flood.

Rhiannon Lewis

CHAPTER 27

Company Office, *Compañía Sud Americana de Vapores*, Valparaiso, 1906

Imperial	November 1891 to June 1892
Loa	June 1892 to March 1894
Imperial	April 1894 to May 1897
Lautaro	May 1897 to January 1902
Truxillo	February 1902 to August 1904
Imperial	August 1904 to -------

Sitting down for a moment to catch his breath outside the *Compañía* offices in Valparaiso, Davy took out a pencil and filled in the final date in his service record: 1906. By now the marble patterned cover was very worn; it was the same book his father had given him all those years ago.

Davy thought back to his father's death. By a stroke of luck he had been in Liverpool and on shore leave when word reached him. He and William had caught the first train, working their way down through Wales to the rain-swept cemetery on a high hill above a stormy sea. They had stood by a pile of sticky clay earth straining to hear the preacher's words above the wind. At that moment Wales had seemed a more alien country than any he had seen in an entire life at sea. Strange people he did not recognise stepped forward and shook his hand, exchanging words of condolence. Davy watched his brother Gruffudd as he moved with ease amongst them, and felt strangely excluded. Davy still spoke the same language, but somewhere during all those years away the meaning had somehow evolved. It seemed to him that he now missed tiny cues that marked him out as a stranger. The words of the sermon meant nothing to him: he thought instead of conversations by the fire, his father's advice and his gift of faith.

Davy had turned to William as the mourners dispersed, the gravediggers already getting on with the job in hand. 'I feel like a stranger.'

'Thirty years at sea, you are a stranger,' William replied, honest as ever.

Davy looked through the pages of his book. Life had carried on in increments as it had done before the war. Another entry in the captain's log, another embarkation of passengers, another loading of cargo. Davy was allocated to different ships, sometimes newer and faster, sometimes older, slower and full of history. Walker's replacement had no axe to grind and Davy's career was secure. William stayed with him. Over the years he became an agreed condition of Davy's service. Where I go, so goes my chief officer. Evans and Tony too, where they could. They all grew older and less agile together.

Every day he thought of Estella and where he would be if one nameless, faceless officer had not refused her space on his ship or a single piece of cargo had been stowed differently. He thought of his parallel life: what the other Davy would be doing now, where he would be living, of Estella's touch and how his children's hair would smell as he held them close. He yearned for these things as if he had lived them and lost them.

Even as he felt these things other women, of a certain kind, seemed drawn to his loss. Some bizarre mechanics of the heart meant that to some he seemed like a puzzle to be solved, a wound to be healed, a greater prize to be won. But Davy found their attentions irritating. He longed for the day when he could join his other self.

Then, when the unravelling came, it was decisive. On board the *Imperial* en route to Callao, the lookouts had shouted in unison that there was something on the horizon.

'"Something"!' Davy had muttered in disgust, 'Who the hell's on the lookout?'

'Jenkins and Solis, sir.' William replied. *Eyes like hawks.*

But within seconds a Chilean sailor who had seen the phenomenon before burst through the doors. 'Captain, sir! There has been an earthquake under the sea! Please believe me. We will all be drowned!'

Davy rushed outside and extended his telescope. At first he could see nothing unusual. He scanned left to right, then back again. There was nothing. Nothing. He looked again. He thought his eyes blurred. He took his eyes from the glass, focused on the deck for a moment and blinked deliberately a few times. Then he peered again. There was something. What was it? A mist? Where the sea had been crystal and azure, there was a haze. Something indistinct. The horizon blurred again. Damn his eyes. Then he realised, before he saw. He realised with his intellect before his eyes could see. The horizon was slipping. Or rather splitting, one below the other, and the nearer, under the mist, was moving towards them.

'Wave!' came a shout from starboard.

Then almost immediately from the other lookout, 'Wave!'

The sea, which a few moments earlier had been a flat calm, appeared to be boiling. Under the surface it was moving in inexplicable circular currents, like the surface of a pan of water about to come to the boil.

'William, get the passengers below deck!'

Davy gave the order to increase speed and turn her bow directly towards the wave. The double horizon was now clear to see, even shrouded in mist. *Turn, damn it*, thought Davy. They weren't coming around fast enough. If the wave caught the ship starboard on, they would be swamped with no chance for lifeboats. They would plummet to the bottom like a stone. The ship shuddered.

'Thirteen knots, sir,' someone spoke beside him.

'It's not enough.'

And they were enveloped by smoke. There were no points of reference any more. The air was black. Where was the horizon? Which way were they headed? He could feel the ship turning more sharply now. Did they have the speed?

'Fourteen knots, Captain.'

Good ship. But she was struggling. She was struggling like Flower ploughing the steep barley field all those years ago, Gruffudd willing her to reach the top of *Cefn Bach* one more time. That's my girl. My beautiful *Imperial*. One more time. You can make it. Then, the ship rose up. She rose up out of her own smoke and kept rising. The view cleared, and in front of them, no more than half a mile away, a gigantic wall of water was bearing down on them, moving at an immense speed.

They were perfectly placed, head on to the wave.

'Hold your course! Full steam ahead!' The chaos and shouting stopped. There was a strengthening breeze and the distant sound of the very crest of the wave rippling with white spray. But no roar. Just the stealthy menace of unstoppable nature, and all the while the ship was rising, rising to unimaginable heights towards the wall. It seemed impossible that the wave should not break over them, but they continued to rise and almost reached the crest. Now there was nothing ahead, only sky. In a few short moments the wave passed beneath them. The ship tipped forward, and there, below, was a valley so deep it took Davy's breath away.

'Full steam ahead!'

There was a spate of shouting and screaming. The prow tipped forwards headlong into the valley of water. Davy heard the screws lift clear of the water behind them and screech horribly with the sudden shock of being free as the ship passed over the ridge. Facing them was another wall of water, this time beneath them, the dark locker of childhood nightmares. They descended, gaining momentum, and as they did so the sun disappeared behind the wave. They were being hurled into shadow and the sea grew darker and colder. Davy was powerless. He had placed his ship in the best position: her speed was perfect. There was nothing more to be done. He loosened his grip on the rail and closed his eyes. He thought of Estella and wondered if the moment of realignment had come.

But the *Imperial* survived and the journey south was heartbreaking. The wreckage and floating bodies reached them long before they sighted Valparaiso. When they arrived at the harbour there was so much debris along the shoreline that it was hard to see where the water ended and the land began. The city was unrecognisable.

'Let those with families go first!' William shouted as the crew clambered frantically into the boats.

Everyone went ashore to help. Once Davy had done all he could, he made his way over rubble and bodies to where Cerro Alegre had been. The small house he had built for his retirement, perfectly placed overlooking Valparaiso Bay, was no longer there. He looked around, thinking that in the devastation he had walked up the wrong avenue. Looters scattered as they saw him approach. Then his heart sank as he recognised his own front door jutting out from a heap of rubble. He climbed over it and saw his old sea chest in pieces, the contents scattered or stolen. There was nothing left. Fifteen years' work and preparation had been reduced to dust.

Davy remembered these things as he sat for a moment on the low wall outside the *Compañia* offices. He put the logbook in his pocket and examined the small leather case he had been given less than half an hour earlier by the company trustees. Inside was a gold pocket watch with a freshly inscribed dedication on the back.

'*To Captain David Davies, in honour of 30 years' faithful service. Compañia Sud Americana de Vapores, 1906.*'

Davy turned the watch over in his hands and felt its golden smoothness.

'*Capitán*, I wasn't even born when you started with us. What do you say to that?' said the jolly young man who presented it.

Davy had smiled graciously and accepted the gift without passing any further comment. It was difficult to know what to say. Davy suspected that they would have liked him to sum up an entire life in a few short sentences, mixing the appropriate amount of levity with a respectable dose of gratitude and humility. But this final challenge had proved beyond him.

Davy put the case in his pocket and rose to his feet, turning to face the sea. Between the crumpled rooflines he could see teams of builders and carpenters hard at work, reconstructing their shattered city. She would rise again, he was sure of it. And so, for the final time, Davy made his way down through the narrow winding streets, descending towards the azure sea until the vista widened. It was a clear day, and on Cerro Alegre he paused for a moment to gaze across the bay towards Viña del Mar. From there the mountains rose, one after another in lilac-coloured waves, each one higher than the last. And behind them all the brilliant snow-capped peaks of the majestic Andes.

EPILOGUE

April 1914

Benjamin Lewis Davies climbed the hill, past the derelict mill, and up towards his uncle's house. It had not been a good morning. Stupidly, he had shared his marriage plans with his elder brother, who'd then told all his other brothers and sisters. All twelve of them. Why had he done this, he wondered? Surely he knew better by now? He was thirty-three years old, not some stupid child. But every now and again he forgot, perhaps deliberately, that his siblings were not all they should be. The truth was, they were vindictive, sly and selfish, and because they shared the same flesh and blood he could not escape their scheming smiles and falsehood.

As the lane became steeper he paused to look back along the road. In the distance he could see the blue-grey peaks of the Preseli hills, and in the valley between the estuary of the river Teifi, smooth as a mirror, leading out into the wide ark of Cardigan Bay. It was nearly midday and he should be ploughing the bottom fields. But the last snide remark of the morning, the very last in a long line of equally belittling comments, had finally hit home. Over thirty years of self-deception had fallen away in an instant. Now it was clear to him. In the past they had mollified him with their, 'We didn't mean it that way' or 'You misunderstood what we meant' or 'You're too sensitive.' With their arch eyebrows almost skimming their high foreheads, these were the things they had squealed, even as they turned their very knives in his back.

The veil had fallen, and without fuss he'd walked from the field, cap in hand, passing his siblings' gaping mouths and incredulous gasps.

'You've put me down for the last time,' he'd said, walking calmly across the yard and out of the farm entrance, not knowing where on earth he was going.

After an hour of aimless wandering it struck him that one person might understand his plight and, not wishing to visit empty-handed, he collected some milk from a neighbour, borrowed a pail and promised to return with some eggs the following day. At the very least his uncle couldn't make him feel any worse.

Davy heard the knock on the door as if it came from the next constellation. He had dreamed of entire worlds while he was asleep. These days his dreams seemed so much more vivid and colourful than the room into which he woke. He heard the knock again, close now, and as he raised his head, the blood flowed in rivers of needles back into his leaden arms.

'Uncle Davy? I'm sorry. Were you sleeping?'

Without saying anything more Benjamin took off his jacket and rolled up his sleeves. Silently, he went about sweeping up the fireplace. He took a wooden pail and went outside to collect water from the stream, and while he was outside Davy could hear him chopping blocks of wood into kindling. Benjamin returned and lit the fire, then hung the kettle carefully on the chain above. Davy went in search of tea and found some black leaves, fine as dust in the bottom of an old caddy. He washed two enamel mugs in the pail and saw that Benjamin had brought milk.

Eventually the two men sat by the fire, each with a mug of tea.

Davy watched the glowing flames with a sense of dread. People rarely came to see him now unless it was to tell him about the dangers of the demon drink or to remind him that he really should go to chapel, or if he must, church, but at least somewhere. To pray for his damnable soul, no doubt.

'I wish I was more like you, Uncle Davy,' said Benjamin.

Davy began laughing until the laugh turned into a rasping cough. And then, when he recovered from the cough, he laughed again with surprise but mostly relief.

'You made a life for yourself. You were brave and saw the world. You've seen people and places that I will only dream of. No one took you for a fool.'

Davy laughed again, but as he looked up from the fire he could see the bitterness in his nephew's face. The young man stared resolutely at the flames, his knuckles white as he grasped the tin mug with both hands.

'I think I want to become a sailor,' said Ben. Then, as if realising immediately how ludicrous an idea this was, he laughed, 'I hate being at sea!'

Davy saw the young man's hands loosen on the mug. He has a kind and gentle face, thought Davy. Such a face that he had not seen for a very long time.

'Shall I tell you what it was really like?' asked Davy.

Benjamin looked up and smiled as if someone had opened a sanctuary door. 'Yes.' Benjamin leant forward and poured more tea into their mugs.

And for the rest of the afternoon, until the yellow flames turned into golden embers, Davy told Benjamin all about his life. He told him about his first long voyage on the *Royal Dane* and long-dead Hoskins with fists the size of mallets. He told him about his brush with Neptune and about the ships that came afterwards, the rough *Kilvey*, the sleek *Britannia*, all the way up to the war. He told him of Stewart and Walker and Mrs Ebrington, and lucky

Peter who saved an oddly named mule from certain death in war. He spoke of journalists and presidents and irreplaceable friends.

'It's incredible,' said Benjamin.

'I was lucky. They called me the lucky captain. When we sailed to Peru to turn ourselves in at the end of the war, I asked Moraga what he would have done if we'd all refused to stay. He said, "I had to accept Stewart's resignation. I had foreseen it because he was well connected. But thereafter we would have had to start shooting, each according to his rank until someone agreed to sail the ship. There were no alternatives."'

Benjamin stared gravely into the fire but as Davy turned to look at him he was startled to see a flash of blue pass across the corner of the room. He looked again, and although there was nothing there he shook his head and smiled.

'All right, Uncle?'

'Yes, lad,' smiled Davy, 'You know, they were right. You never really get rid of this malaria. It sneaks up on you when you least expect it.'

Benjamin turned back to the fire, and although Davy knew it was illogical he scanned the corner of the room again quickly, feeling his heart beating.

'So you would never have come back here if it hadn't been for the earthquake?'

'No,' replied Davy remembering how, in the first few months after Estella's death, he could still feel her presence in certain places – at the races in Viña del Mar, amongst the crowds at the harbour side, at Neptune's fountain.

'What happened to the others?'

All the others. Davy could see them as if they were seated for a family photograph. A rowdy lot, all of them. No chance of getting them to sit still.

'Mrs Ebrington survived the earthquake.'

'I knew she would!' smiled Benjamin.

'Formidable as the house her husband built. Myrtle Villa was the only building in Cerro Alegre that wasn't damaged or destroyed. The Mapuche said that because she'd protected Miriam and Peter the spirits had protected her. "Poppycock," she said. She knew that Albert had paid for particularly deep foundations. "This house isn't going anywhere," she said afterwards. Good old Mrs Ebrington, still going strong at 86. She has six grandchildren, I believe.'

Davy laughed and wished he could see them.

'Tony retired and opened up a bar in Coquimbo. Miserable place, but the British navy has a base there so he's making himself a small fortune on the quiet. Evans came back to Wales. He bought a terraced house with a garden and spends every waking hour outdoors growing the biggest prize vegetables you've ever seen. So they tell me.'

'And William?'

Davy shook his head in disbelief.

'William married Mary Bird Tucker, just as he said he would.'

'She really did exist?'

'Yes! For years I thought he was making her up. They took long enough about it, though. Twenty years of courting before they tied the knot. Too late for children. He's now chief officer of the *Sagamore* sailing between Liverpool and Baltimore, one of the Warren Line's finest ships.'

Davy paused and his eyes filled with tears. 'Damn it all,' he said, laughing at himself and wiping his face with the back of his hand.

Benjamin leaned forward and placed another log on the fire.

'You're the first person I've told,' said Davy, 'No one else has shown the remotest interest. It all happened a long time ago on the other side of the world.'

Benjamin relaxed back into his chair again but looked sad. 'It makes my life seem very small and insignificant.'

Davy was about to say that no life was insignificant when he saw it again, a blue flash of silk caught in the firelight. He could almost hear the brush of fabric.

'Come on, Ben,' said Davy, 'let's get you home. Why don't I go with you halfway? I fancy a bit of a walk.'

Benjamin rose to his feet with as much enthusiasm as a condemned man, Davy noticed, and he felt sorry for him. 'Listen, come back again tomorrow. I need some help here. We can talk some more and you can tell me of your plans.'

Ben shrugged.

'I want to know,' said Davy, pointedly.

Benjamin smiled gratefully.

Then, just as Davy was about to lift the wooden latch on the front door and lead Ben outside, a thought occurred to him.

'Wait. I want you to have something.' Davy walked back to the dresser and opened the middle drawer. He took out a wicker frame and passed it to Benjamin.

'I know these pictures!' Benjamin laughed. 'They were in *The Graphic*, the year of the war. I spent half my savings buying a copy!'

Benjamin read the dedication aloud: '*The Civil War in Chile: The S.S. "Imperial" which ran the blockade of the insurgent fleet.*'

'I won't have descendants myself, but perhaps it will mean something to yours.' Davy ran his fingers along the edge of the frame. 'This and the photograph album were the only two things that survived the earthquake.'

Benjamin thanked his uncle, and the two men left the house and turned towards Pen Garn. The road climbed, and soon they were above the town, watching the red sun sinking into the bay. Now they spoke only of the future, of automobiles and how the Americans were going to start mass production; of the first scheduled airline flight; the first ship through the Panama Canal; of suffragettes and German expansion; of Charlie Chaplin.

'All this in my lifetime!' laughed Davy as they reached the crossroads. The men paused where the road split five ways, and as they turned to say goodbye two curlews flew over the treetops and towards the sea, their melancholy calls fading into the distance.

Ben said nothing when he entered his parents' farmhouse. He took the frame straight to his bedroom and propped it up with a Bible on top of the chest of drawers. That's going on the wall as soon as Mary Ann and I have a house, he thought, and every time they start their tricks I'll look at it and it will remind me not be cowed and brought down by their meanness.

Davy chose the long way back to the cottage in order to see the sunset. Great bands of crimson and gold wove jubilant patterns in the sky, and for the first time since he could not remember when, he made his sober way along the lanes. He was over the brow of the hill, and in a few steps the sea was revealed before him, sparkling like a bed of jewels. He paused to catch his breath and felt for the warmth of brass in his pocket. Before him the lane came to another junction, and this time he turned away from the sun, towards the rising moon and the salmon-pink flicker of the red planet Mars.

AUTHOR'S NOTE

My Beautiful Imperial is based on the actual events of the Chilean Civil War of 1891 and the experiences of my ancestor, Captain David Jefferson Davies. In the words of *The Graphic* magazine at the time, he and his ship, the *Imperial*, gained 'no little fame' for the part they played in the war. But Davy and his ship disappeared from the history books. A framed set of etchings and an old photograph album were almost all I had to go on when I began my research nearly twenty years ago. Once I started, I was hooked. At every turn, the story became more incredible. The discovery of each new piece of evidence became chapters in my own personal adventure. Uncovered, the story was a gift to any aspiring writer. I have tried to make the novel as historically accurate as possible, which was not difficult as the truth was invariably more astounding than anything I could have concocted myself. Ultimately, however, this is a novel, and a work of fiction.

I owe a debt to Maurice Hervey. Now a long-forgotten journalist, his contemporary impressions of Chile and reports of the war were utterly rejected by *The Times*. He published them, nonetheless, in his own book, *Dark Days in Chile*.

I owe an even greater debt to my parents, Owen and Menna Davies. We all stand on the shoulders of giants and I was lucky enough to be born into a family that placed enormous value on learning for its own sake. They also respected the achievements of those who had gone before, and kept their stories alive. When Davy's photograph album was about to be hurled on to a house clearance bonfire, my mother saved it from the flames because she felt it was important. *My Beautiful Imperial* was born that day.

ACKNOWLEDGEMENTS

The following people have shared parts of the journey with me:

Enid Lewis, Gwyn Jones, Liu Jie, Wendy Morgan, Clive James. Your support gave me confidence. *Diolch*.

My early readers: Nina Davies, Peter Cox, Tanya Gething. Thank you for your encouragement.

Jo Verity for your sound advice and words of wisdom born of experience.

Menna Elfyn, Jon Meirion Jones, Carol Byrne-Jones, Dafydd Wyn Jones. Proof that the influence of great teachers can last a lifetime.

David Hopkins, for convincing me that I don't need to ask anyone's permission to call myself a writer.

Aki Schilz, Karl French and Michael Langan at The (fantastic) Literary Consultancy, TLC. You are all stars. I think Rebecca Swift would be proud.

Mary Jones and Catherine Hanley, for your careful proofing of earlier drafts and for your continuing enthusiasm.

Minisha Wahi. Your hugs and coffee breaks kept me sane so many times. Thank you for being a rock.

The reader's scheme at Literature Wales has been discontinued, but the two reports I received by the same anonymous reader were incredibly valuable. Whoever you are, thank you. I hope the book has turned out as you hoped.

Liz and Giles Evans. Thank you for your eagle eyes, friendship and support.

Megan Hayes, a role model in so many ways. Thank you for being there, for taking such an interest and for leading the way. We're doing our best to keep up, but you're a hard act to follow. *Diolch*.

My siblings, Gareth, Delyth and Gwilym Peredur for not asking too many awkward questions when there were no easy answers. To Phil and Heidi too.

To the Anglo Chilean Society, including G. Claudio Duran, Secretary, and in particular, Robert Hart, Treasurer, for your invaluable advice on publishers.

Thank you to Juan Guillermo Callejas Q., Lieutenant Commander, the Chilean Navy's Mission in the UK for your help on Davy's itinerary.

To Catalina Herrera Acuña, Cultural Affairs and Press Attaché at the Embassy of Chile, for your help in arranging the London launch, and your enthusiasm for the book.

To Jack Williams at Jaxx Design for your careful design of the interior, and Charlesworth Press for the handsome finished article.

Diolch Steffan Glynn (with the help of Lottie Fry) for creating a perfect book cover. *Dau yn erbyn y byd.*

Consuelo, Sophie and Victorina Press – I'm so pleased I found you. Thank you for allowing Captain David Jefferson Davies to live again and *My Beautiful Imperial* to see the light of day. *Muchas, muchas gracias.*

Steffan, Rebecca, Darcie and Gareth. What can I say? I couldn't have done it without you.

ABOUT THE AUTHOR

Rhiannon Lewis was raised on a small farm near Cardigan on the West Wales coast. She studied Welsh, English and Drama at Aberystwyth University and spent five years as a teacher and lecturer. After gaining a master's degree in education, she went on to work in public relations, marketing and communications.

Rhiannon has won prizes for her short stories, including *Gabriel's Halo* (1st prize, Writers' Forum, November 2016) and *The Jugs Stay with the Dresser* (winner of Frome Festival Short Story Competition, July 2017).

My Beautiful Imperial is Rhiannon's first novel. It was inspired by the experiences of her great-great uncle, Captain David Jefferson Davies, who was also from Cardigan but spent most of his life sailing the coast of Chile.

Rhiannon is currently working on a collection of short stories and planning the sequel to *My Beautiful Imperial*.